DUDLEY POPE

Ramage's
Diamond

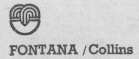

FONTANA /Collins

First published in 1976 by The Alison Press/Martin Secker and Warburg Ltd
First issued in Fontana Books 1977
Second Impression June 1978
Third Impression April 1979

Made and printed in Great Britain by
William Collins Sons & Co Ltd, Glasgow

For Susan and Nick

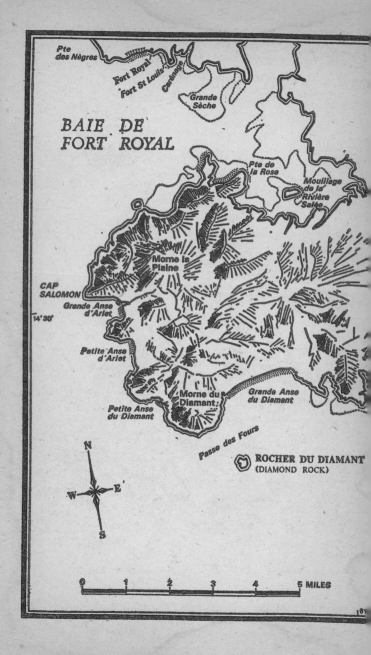

Pte
des Nègres

Fort Royal
Fort St Louis
Carénage
Grande
Sèche

BAIE DE
FORT ROYAL

Pte de
la Rose

Mouillage
de la
Rivière
Salée

Morne la
Plaine

CAP
SALOMON

14°30'

Grande Anse
d'Arlet

Petite Anse
d'Arlet

Petite Anse
du Diamant

Morne du
Diamant

Grande Anse
du Diamant

Passe des Fours

N
W   E'
S

ROCHER DU DIAMANT
(DIAMOND ROCK)

0   1   2   3   4   5 MILES

16°

ARTINIQUE

Bourg du
Marin

Shoaïs of one
fathom or less

Sand beaches

PTE DES
SALINES

David Charles

CHAPTER ONE

There was a faint smell of oil, turpentine and beeswax in the shop, and while an assistant scurried off to fetch the owner Ramage glanced first at the sporting guns in the racks round the walls and then at the pairs of pistols nestling in their mahogany cases which almost covered one end of the counter.

The guns accounted for the smell of oil. Then he noticed the polished floor of narrow wooden tiles, laid in a herringbone design to take advantage of the grain pattern. Turpentine and beeswax – the gun-maker used the same polish on his floor as he did on the stocks of his guns.

His father gestured round the shop with his cane. 'My first pistol came from here nearly fifty years ago. This fellow's father owned it then, and my father was one of his early customers.'

Ramage looked at the tall figure of the Admiral. His face was lined now and his hair was grey, yet he was erect, his brown eyes alert and looking out on the world with amused tolerance from under bushy eyebrows. He pictured his father as a shy young midshipman – a 'younker' nervously choosing a pistol, and no doubt anxious to be off to the sword cutler's to complete his martial purchases before joining his first ship.

The Admiral nodded at Ramage's right shoulder. 'Your epaulet is crooked. I know it's the first time you've worn it, but . . .'

Ramage tried to straighten it but the padding of the strap was new and stiff, unwilling to sit squarely on the shoulder bone, and he was unused to the tight spirals of bullion hanging down in a thick fringe round the edges. The light reflecting on them caught the corner of his right eye and made him feel lopsided. He would get used to it, he thought wryly, but probably not before he had three years' seniority and was entitled to wear an epaulet on the left shoulder as well.

Don't grumble, he told himself as he tugged at the strap; it's taken long enough to be made post and get this single epaulet. He was so used to being addressed as 'Lieutenant Ramage' that it was going to take a while to become accustomed to

'Captain Ramage'. Admittedly his name was right at the bottom of the list of 'The Captains of His Majesty's Fleet', but by next year many more lieutenants would have been 'made post', their names coming lower on the list, thus increasing his seniority and pushing him up the ladder of promotion.

Progress up the list of lieutenants had been slow: he had been less than a third of the way to the top when he had been unexpectedly made post three days ago. The jump from lieutenant to post captain was reckoned to be the hardest to make because in time of war it did not depend on seniority so much as on doing something that caught the Admiralty's eye – or having enough 'interest' in high places. There was a lot of satisfaction in having been promoted as a reward for things done: he had begun to think he was remaining a lieutenant because his father was still out of favour, still regarded as a scapegoat for the stupidity of politicians some twenty years ago.

Cross-eyed, he tried to jerk the epaulet but was interrupted as the plump gun-maker came through the door at the back of the shop, a delighted smile spreading across his face as he hurriedly removed his leather apron.

'My Lords!' the man exclaimed with a quick bow and, noticing Ramage's single epaulet, said with obvious pleasure: 'Congratulations, *Captain* the Lord Ramage. Well-deserved, if I might say so, judging by the *Gazettes* for the past few years! It seems only a few months ago that the Earl brought you here as a young midshipman just off to join your first ship.' He turned to the Admiral, his brow wrinkling in concentration. 'It must have been a dozen years ago ... yes, going off to join the *Benbow*.'

The Admiral nodded. 'You have a good memory, Mansfield. He was made post last Friday.'

The gun-maker's eyes twinkled as he put his oil-stained apron behind the counter. 'The bullion of the epaulet ...'

'It'll soon lose the new look,' Ramage said. 'It hasn't had a breath of sea air yet.'

The Admiral sniffed. 'The smoke and fog in this damnable city are enough to turn it green, even if it is gold.'

He pointed his cane at the sporting guns. 'Well, Mansfield, mustn't take up all your morning. I want a lighter gun for snipe – I'm getting a bit stiff in the joints and those blessed birds seem to jink more today than when I was younger. The Captain wants a pair of pistols. He lost that pair you made, and he's been making do with those confounded Sea Service models.'

As Mansfield moved towards the cases of pistols the Admiral said: 'You'd better attend to me first; the Marchesa is buying the pistols as a present, and she's raiding the shop next door. She'll join us in a few minutes, after she's bought a few cables of lace and ribbon.'

For the next twenty minutes, as carriages clattered along Bond Street and hucksters shouted the merits of their wares, the Admiral and the gun-maker discussed sporting guns. Once they had selected a suitable design, Mansfield insisted on checking the measurement for the length of the stock, and when the Admiral protested that he had had those measurements for years the gun-maker said respectfully, 'You keep a youthful figure, my Lord, but – ' he tapped the right shoulder, 'you have put on a little flesh here, just where it makes a difference.' He went behind the counter and consulted a heavy ledger, then came back again with a rule. 'If you'll just lean forward slightly – ah, yes, a difference of nearly an inch . . .'

The Admiral sighed. 'So that's it! I haven't been happy with any of my guns lately; they just don't sit right. I thought my muscles were getting stiff.'

The gun-maker nodded knowingly: 'It's not unusual, my Lord. Try the new gun when I've finished it, and if you find it comfortable I suggest you return your other guns and I'll shorten and reshape the stocks accordingly. It won't affect the balance – but 1 can guarantee it will affect your game bag. And – '

He broke off with an apology and hurried to the door as a small but strikingly beautiful woman in a pale blue cape swept into the shop. Over her shoulder Ramage saw Hanson walking away to their carriage with a large packet holding her latest purchases. The old man was always delighted to leave his domestic duties and go off on shopping expeditions with the Marchesa: her Italian accent and bizarre and impish sense of humour reduced any shop to an excited uproar in a matter of minutes. Ramage wondered idly whether the usually staid establishment they had visited in Albemarle Street an hour earlier had managed to get all the rolls of dress material back on the shelves. The Marchesa would still be there, asking to be shown yet more cloth, if the Admiral had not called a halt by protesting that they had seen enough material to make a suit of sails for a ship of the line, and declaring that her first three choices were by far the best, even though she had changed her mind a score of times since then.

The owner of the shop, surprised to find that Admiral the Earl of Blazey could not only stop the Marchesa but do it in a way that left her laughing and agreeing with him, hurriedly scribbled down the lengths she wanted and looked still more surprised when she nodded good-bye, turned to Ramage and said: 'Now let us go to Bond Street for the pistols.'

The gun-maker welcomed her, guessing that she was 'the Marchesa' the Admiral had mentioned, and Ramage winked at his father: the poor fellow was in for a shock. Although she was only five feet tall, with finely-chiselled features, high cheekbones and the imperious manner that befitted the ruler of the little kingdom of Volterra, her appearance gave no hint of her adventures in escaping from Bonaparte's troops when they invaded Italy. That episode had given her a surprising skill in the use of pistols and a knowledge of firearms more usual in an army officer. She could load, aim and fire a pistol with the casual elegance of a woman removing a necklace from a jewel box and placing it round her neck.

She nodded to the gun-maker and said to Ramage: 'I hope you haven't chosen yet?'

'We've been waiting for you. I saw Hanson staggering off with your last purchases! Did you find all the ribbon and lace you wanted?'

'The lace I want is still in Italy. They have a poor selection here. This 'Oniton they talk about – is that the town we pass through on the way to St Kew?'

' "This Honiton", young lady, happens to be the centre for the finest lace in this country,' said the Admiral with mock indignation.

'Perhaps,' she said coolly. 'But if the selection they have next door is a fair example of their work, then Volterra is the centre for the finest lace in the world.'

The Admiral flicked an imaginary speck of dust from the lace of his stock. 'My dear Gianna, poor Nicholas and I have to make do with this – smuggled from Bruges, no doubt.'

'No doubt,' Gianna said tartly, eyeing the lace edge of the stock with disdain. She turned to the gun-maker. 'Now, the Captain wants a matched pair of pistols. Not duelling pistols,' she added, 'because a hair trigger is dangerous on board a ship. Those might – '

She broke off as Ramage took her arm and led her to the far end of the counter. He knew from long experience that it was useless to tell her that even though she was paying for them and knew about pistols, it was wiser to leave the actual choice between the man who made them and the man who was going to use them. In any other woman it would have been intolerable but in Gianna it was partly her upbringing and partly a measure of her love for him. He needed a pair of pistols and she wanted to give them to him as a present to celebrate his promotion. She insisted on the best because, better than most people, she knew that his life might one day depend on how reliably and truly either or both guns shot.

Ramage pointed to the case at the end of the counter.

'The pair with hexagonal barrels,' he said. 'Mansfield will have to fit belt-hooks but – ' he lifted one of the guns from the case and turned it on its side, so the pan was downwards – 'yes, that is easy enough.'

'They're very *plain*,' Gianna said and pointed to the pair in the next case. 'Look, what about these? Look at the design on the barrels – and the wood: the carving is beautiful.'

'I want hexagonal barrels,' Ramage said firmly. 'The flat top surface makes an excellent sight when you have to shoot quickly, and I don't like a lot of fancy work on a gun.'

The gun-maker heard Ramage's comment. 'A pair of good plain guns with nine-inch barrels, my Lord?'

Ramage nodded. 'But I'll want belt-hooks fitted. Can you do that and have them ready in three days?'

'Of course, of course. Your Lordship has chosen exactly the pair I would have recommended.' He took the other gun from the case. 'The safety bolt is ready for the thumb, and I've made sure it doesn't protrude so much it might catch in clothing. The stock – will you grip it, please? Yes, it fits your hand nicely. Just watch one thing, my Lord: on this model I have made the trigger guard a little wider here – you see the flare on the forward side? You need to remember that. Or,' he added hurriedly, 'if you find it too wide I can change it to the normal width.'

Ramage ran his index finger along the guard and quickly crooked it round the trigger. 'No, don't change it: that is a good idea. What about belt-hooks?'

The gun-maker excused himself and went to the workshop, returning with a case which he put down on the counter and opened. He took out one of the two pistols inside and held it out to Ramage. 'The same pattern of gun, my Lord, with a belt-hook already fitted.'

Gianna sniffed. 'I don't like that wood so much, and anyway, I prefer gold-inlaid mounts.'

'I prefer silver,' Ramage said firmly, 'and this darker wood – cherry, isn't it? – is more serviceable. Remember the salt air, and they'll be getting only an occasional wipe with an oily rag. No one is going to spend hours polishing them.'

'Silver tarnishes,' Gianna reminded him, 'gold does not.'

'Quite so, my Lady,' the gun-maker said politely, 'but . . .'

'Gold inlay would not look right on this pistol,' Ramage said firmly, then added in a lighter tone: 'When I become an admiral you can have Mansfield make me a pair of duelling pistols with as much gold work as you like.'

'By the time you are an admiral,' she said crossly, 'I hope you won't be depending on pistols for your life. Well, you decide what you want, I'm going to see what the Admiral has chosen.' She looked at the fob watch hanging on a thin chain round her neck. 'Don't forget we still have to visit Mr Prater for your sword.'

When she had walked to the other end of the shop the gun-maker said: 'A complete refit, sir?'

Ramage smiled ruefully. 'I lost everything in the West Indies. Since then I've been using a Sea Service pistol and a cutlass, but the Marchesa decided to celebrate my promotion with . . .'

Mansfield grinned conspiratorially. 'Well, sir, I think you'll find these pistols are an improvement on the Sea Service! Clumsy brutes, they are.'

'They have to be: they get dropped on deck and tossed into arms chests, and a seaman's idea of using a pistol is jabbing the muzzle in the enemy's belly or fetching him a bang on the head with it.'

The master gun-maker shuddered and changed the subject: 'I saw Mr Prater the other day when I was down at Charing Cross. He has some lovely blades now. There's such a call for them these days that he can afford to carry a good stock.'

'Yes,' Ramage said gloomily, 'but I want a fighting sword; a solid blade slung in a shoulder belt. I have a feeling that the Marchesa will try to persuade Mr Prater that a post captain should always wear a dress sword suspended from slings on the waistband of the breeches.'

'A lot of naval gentlemen wear a broad belt over the right shoulders these days,' Mansfield said. 'Outside the waistcoat and under the coat. More practical, I suppose, sir, though I must admit it doesn't look so smart.'

'When you're boarding an enemy ship it's more important that the scabbard doesn't get between your legs,' Ramage said lightly. 'Now, these pistols . . .'

'Ah, well, you have all you need here, my Lord: two powder flasks – note the spring measures work easily, and be careful no one oils the springs: it is quite unnecessary, and a drop of oil in the powder . . .' he warned. 'Wad cutter, shot mould, box for flints – I'll fill that with a good selection; I have a new supply in from my flint knapper in Sussex – and oil bottle. Here you have the proof certificate from the Gunmakers' Company – the Proof House on Tower Wharf is a busy place these days, I can tell you! Two keys for the case . . . ' He picked up one of the pistols and deftly checked it over. 'Rammer – that is a choice piece of horn.' He tapped the pointed spiral of the metal at the other end: 'I've made this wormer a little stronger than most.' He cocked the gun and squeezed the trigger. 'I think you'll find that a nice compromise, my Lord; not a hair trigger, but it doesn't need a wrestler's grip.'

Ramage picked up the second gun, checked it over and looked at the belt-hook. It was wide and substantial, with just enough spring to slip inside a belt without sticking and yet not bind when drawn in a hurry. More important, the whole gun fitted comfortably in his hand, so that the barrel seemed an extension of his forearm.

'They'll do,' he said, putting the pistol back in the case, 'and you'd better give me two spare rammers. Hmm . . . yes, do you have a complete spare lock?'

The gun-maker nodded and, taking an oily rag from his pocket, carefully wiped the metal of both guns before putting them back again. 'Finger marks,' he said, 'they lead to rusting. Are you going to be away a long time, my Lord?'

'A long time, and I'm going a long way.'

'The West Indies again, my Lord?'

There was nothing secret about it, so Ramage nodded. 'Their Lordships like to keep me moving about!'

'You were in the Mediterranean at one time, were you not, sir?'

'Mediterranean, Atlantic, West Indies, back to the Atlantic . . . The Admiralty is changing the pattern by sending me to the West Indies this time, instead of the Mediterranean.'

'Rust,' the gun-maker said sorrowfully, 'that's my biggest enemy in the West Indies. Some of my gentlemen bring back

15

pistols from the West Indies that are just a useless mass of rust.

'Yet they only need wiping over with an oily rag every week, and avoid finger marks. Must be a very wet place . . .'

'Not so much wet but hot and damp,' Ramage said. 'The damp gets into everything – clothes mildew, metals rusts, wood rots and tempers fray, too!'

'It must have its compensations, I suppose; many of my gentlemen seem to like it out there.'

'Plenty of prizes to be taken,' Ramage said. 'We poor naval officers need the prize and head money to pay your prices, my dear Mansfield!'

The gun-maker grinned as he locked the case and gave Ramage the key. 'Since the Marchesa is buying these for you, my Lord, she'll probably want you to take them now?'

When Ramage nodded, he said: 'I will choose some more flints, and I'd like to give you a gross of lead balls which I cast myself. They're polished and packed in a special box so they don't get dented. You are staying at Palace Street, sir?'

'Yes, Blazey House. I leave for Portsmouth on Thursday.'

'My man will deliver them this afternoon, along with the spare rammers and lock.'

That night Ramage excused himself early and left the family to go to his room. There was much to do before he left for Portsmouth to take up his new command, and he knew that Gianna would be disappointed if he did not spend his last whole day in London in her company.

The table in the small room – he preferred one on the third floor because it was quieter – was covered with the day's purchases. There was a black japanned speaking trumpet with a braided silk lanyard, the case of pistols and the sword and belt. Prater had started off by taking Gianna's side in trying to force an ornate sword on him, a wretched affair more suitable for a subaltern in some fashionable regiment that never saw active service, but he had got his own way in the end. There were also two pairs of gold buckles for his shoes. He had always made a point of using pinchbeck while a lieutenant – some captains were touchy about young officers wearing gold – but gold buckles were an economy in the long run, since pinchbeck corroded so quickly.

He put the purchases on the floor. Items of clothing had

already been put away in drawers and would soon have to be stowed in a trunk and sent to Portsmouth, but this evening he wanted to catch up with some of his paper work: once he was on board there would be so much more awaiting him that he would soon be swamped.

He put the inkwell, pen and some paper in the middle of the table, retrieved the sand box from the dressing-table, and took his commission from the drawer. It was an imposing document and he delighted in its archaic language, but it had cost him two guineas. He had officially acknowledged receipt of it already, now he had to send the money.

His instructions had arrived that afternoon and they too needed acknowledgement, but most of the evening was going to be taken up with drafting his 'Captain's Orders'. He bitterly regretted not having salvaged his original set when the *Triton* brig was lost; he had copied those from another commanding officer, adding various items of his own, but now he had to start from scratch.

Drawing up the Captain's Orders was always a difficult business. They were really a set of standing orders showing how the captain wanted things done on board the ship while he was in command. Most captains had them already written down in a little book, which they handed to the first lieutenant soon after they stepped on board. Ramage knew from bitter experience as a midshipman that getting a sight of the book and copying out the details was a matter of urgency for all the ship's officers since every captain had his own way of doing things, his quirks and idiosyncracies . . .

Some captains made the mistake of putting too much in the Orders. Others put too little, afraid of committing themselves to some routine, that, in a million-to-one chance, might not meet a particular situation and so leave them open to blame. And some captains, he thought ruefully, sat at tables staring at blank sheets of paper.

He jotted down several headings which covered sail-handling and the day-to-day routine on board, and then he added half a dozen 'Do nots'. Then he started writing them out in full – knowing that his clerk could make a fair copy when he went on board – and beginning: 'Captain's Orders, His Majesty's frigate *Juno*, Nicholas Ramage, Captain.' He glanced at his list of headings, and wrote first: 'Slovenly evolutions: Any evolutions performed in a slovenly manner will be repeated until satisfactorily executed. There will be no unnecessary hailings from aloft or from the deck.'

He had added 'from the deck' to ensure that enthusiastic but noisy commission and warrant officers watched their tongues: you could always be certain that a ship was badly run if you heard a lot of orders being bellowed by all and sundry.

'Captain called: the Captain is to be called at daylight; when the course cannot be laid; if a strange sail is sighted; if the weather threatens, or the barometer falls or rises suddenly or excessively.' He could add that he should be called if land was sighted, or for a dozen other reasons, but the officer of the deck would be quick enough to call the captain in unusual circumstances. And that reminded him: 'Appearance of land: all appearances of land are to be reported and the Master called at once.'

He glanced at his list and then wrote: 'Trimming and shortening sails: the officer of the deck should trim, make or shorten sails as required, reporting to me after having done so.' That made lieutenants use their initiative and judgement; there was no point in an officer rushing to the captain for permission to carry out a routine task.

'Men's dress: officers of the deck are responsible for the watch being correctly dressed and in a manner suitable for the climate.'

He reached for the list of headings. He had completely forgotten the section dealing with going into action. And 'starting' – that was strictly regulated in any ship he commanded. If the bos'n's mates could not get the men moving fast enough without hitting them across the shoulders with rattans the fault was more likely to be with the bos'n's mates – or even the captain – for not having a properly trained and willing ship's company.

List of clothes: he had forgotten that, too, and he jotted down the items the seamen were expected to have – '3 jackets, 2 waistcoats or inside coats, 2 blue and 2 white pairs of trousers, 3 pairs of stockings, 2 pairs of shoes and 2 pairs of drawers.' He could remember that without any effort, having inspected the clothing of hundreds of seamen since he first went to sea.

Keys – damnation, he seemed to have forgotten everything that mattered. 'Keys of the magazine and storerooms are to be kept in the possession of the First Lieutenant. The magazine is never to be opened without the Captain's permission. Storerooms must never be opened without the knowledge of the First Lieutenant and the officer of the deck, and always with a midshipman present. The keys of the spirit, bread and fish rooms and the after hold are to be kept in the care of the Master, one of whose mates is to be the last man out of the hold or room to guard lights and lock the doors and generally take care there is no risk of fire.'

He was slowly getting through the first part. 'Every day after dinner, and before hammocks are piped down in the afternoon, the decks are to be swept . . . Whether at sea or in harbour, no lights are to be left unattended in any berth or cabin and only lanthorns are to be used in the tiers . . . There will be no smoking except in the established place, which is under the forecastle . . . Spirits are always to be drawn off on deck and never below, and never by candlelight because of the risk of fire . . . No boats are to be absent from the ship during mealtimes except upon a special service, in which case the Captain must first be informed . . . Every man on board shall be clean-shaven and freshly dressed by 10 o'clock every Sunday morning before being mustered by divisions . . . Likewise on Thursdays the ship's company is to be shaved and put on clean shirts and trousers . . . The ship's cook, immediately breakfast or dinner is ready, shall bring aft to the Captain (or First Lieutenant if the Captain is not on board) a sample of all provisions being served to the ship's company . . . Work done for an officer or warrant officer by any member of the ship's company must not be paid for with spirits or wine . . . Officers will draw the Captain's attention to deserving men so that their merits are not disregarded . . .'

He had been writing for half an hour and, pausing for a few minutes, found himself thinking how remote it all seemed; how distant from this comfortable room and quiet house. These orders were for the conduct of a ship of war, where at any hour of the day or night two hundred or more men could be fighting for their lives against a sudden storm or enemy ships. He was responsible for the ship, down to the last roundshot and length of marline, and for ten score men, from their seamanship to their health. Yet at this moment it seemed remote, and the case of pistols, the sword and scabbard on the floor beside him, seemed as out of place as a dog kennel in a church vestry.

He began wondering what officers the Admiralty would send him. So much depended on luck, even his own promotion to command a frigate. He would probably still be a lieutenant but for the fact that he had had to report personally to the First Lord after carrying out his last mission, which had been a complete success. Lord St Vincent had been so pleased that he had decided to make him post and give him a frigate. Not only that, but he had told him to name his own first lieutenant, something the old tyrant rarely did. It was just Ramage's bad luck that he had had no name to put, forward.

His wary mention that he would be grateful if he could have old Southwick as Master had struck some chord in His Lordship's memory and he had agreed and at the same time said jokingly that he assumed Ramage was also going to ask for that bunch of scalawag seamen he seemed to manage to drag from one ship to the next.

Ramage knew enough of the Service to realize that by not asking for a particular first lieutenant he had left a vacancy which would be filled by one of His Lordship's favourites, or a man long overdue for promotion, and that His Lordship was well aware of that when he agreed to let him have Southwick as Master. So Ramage had grinned and said that by chance there were a dozen of those scalawags at Portsmouth and with His Lordship's approval of course . . . Lord St Vincent had given one of his dry chuckles and told Ramage to leave a list of the men's names and their ships with the Board Secretary, Mr Nepean.

There had been a knowing look in the old Admiral's eye: he was a fine seaman and knew that a young captain who had never before commanded anything bigger than a brig needed an experienced master whom he knew and trusted – and who knew and trusted him. And a dozen prime topmen were far more useful than a smart first lieutenant. A good captain and an experienced master might make up for a slack first lieutenant, but however good the captain and first lieutenant, they could never make up for a bad master. One could sail through an anchored fleet and point to the ships with bad masters . . .

Lord St Vincent had allowed him to have Southwick and the dozen men – but then he had settled down to a little barg-ining of his own. By tradition the captain chose his own midshipmen, often relatives or sons of friends. With four allowed for every hundred men, Ramage was entitled to a maximum of eight. His Lordship had said, very casually: 'I suppose you have all the midshipmen you need?' knowing full well that Ramage had only learned ten minutes earlier that he was being given a frigate. He had only one candidate. A young nephew of Gianna's had recently arrived in England and been given permission to join the Royal Navy if he could find a captain to take him.

A newly-promoted captain would have a dozen applications in as many minutes after it was known outside the Admiralty that he had been given a ship, but so far the news had not travelled outside the First Lord's office, so Ramage mustered a pleasant smile and said: 'I have only one at the moment, sire – a nephew of the Marchesa's. Can I be of service to you?'

It so happened that he could, Lord St Vincent had said with obvious relief. The son of a cousin of Her Ladyship needed a berth – although it was entirely up to Ramage. Ramage nodded his agreement as he remembered Bowen, who had served with him in two ships: a brilliant surgeon who, ruined in London by drink, had joined the Navy but had now been cured. He was an amiable companion. If the First Lord's wife's cousin had a problem, now was the time for trading!

'I should consider it an honour, sir. If the young gentleman will present himself on board at Portsmouth?'

'Of course, of course; I'll see to it myself. Much obliged to ye, Ramage – and look'ee, Ramage, make sure you get a round turn on him right at the start.'

'Aye, aye, sir. By the way, may I make so bold as to request a particular surgeon? The man who was of especial service in the *Lady Arabella*, sir.'

'That was the Post Office packet you saved, wasn't it? Yes, I remember. Very well, then, give Nepean his name. I presume he is in England?'

'Yes, sir, he is on leave at the moment: he and his wife had dinner with us a few days ago.'

'Drink!' the First Lord suddenly exclaimed crossly. 'Doesn't he drink heavily?'

Knowing that next to officers who married too young, the First Lord most abhorred heavy drinkers, Ramage said hurriedly: 'He did, sir, before he first joined me.'

'Then what happened?'

'Well, Southwick – that's the master I requested – and I managed to cure him. He hasn't touched a drop for more than two years now.'

'By Jove!' the Admiral said. 'Curing the sawbones, eh? Now look'ee, I've just remembered a chaplain . . .'

He paused for a moment, watching Ramage closely. The captain of a frigate was not required to carry a chaplain unless one applied to join his ship. There were good and bad chaplains. A 32-gun frigate, with a ship's company of only 215 men, rarely provided a chaplain with enough work, even if he gave lessons to the midshipmen, so the captain and ship's company tended to be at the mercy of the man's quirks, foibles and prejudices. A High Church chaplain soon upset all the Low Church men on board; a Low Church chaplain inevitably ran foul of the Catholics. Ramage had long ago decided that the men's spiritual needs were quite adequately catered for every Sunday morning by a short service conducted by the captain. Some rousing hymns did the men the world of good, and were the captain's best weathercock as far as their spirits were concerned. A contented ship's company sang lustily; a disgruntled crew did little more than mumble, with the fiddler's scraping nearly drowning their voices.

Lord St Vincent gave a wintry smile before Ramage answered, and said: 'Very well, I'll place him somewhere else. Currying favour with senior officers is not one of your faults, my lad; most young officers just told they're being made post and given a frigate would willingly ship ten chaplains if they thought it'd please the First Lord.'

'I was thinking of my ship's company,' Ramage said, then realized that he could hardly have made a more tactless remark added: 'I mean, sir, that –'

'I know what you mean,' the Admiral said, obviously enjoying Ramage's embarrassment. 'I was a young frigate captain once. I doubt there are any tricks you'll contrive that I don't know about.'

He had gone on to tell Ramage that the *Juno* frigate was lying at Portsmouth; that Ramage was replacing a captain removed from his command by sentence of court martial; that the ship's company wanted licking into shape, and that all the officers and midshipmen were being transferred to give the new captain a chance.

'Discipline had become too slack,' the Admiral growled. 'I can't give you more than a few days to get a round turn on them because Admiral Davis needs a frigate in Barbados to carry out the instructions you will be taking with you.'

His Lordship was notoriously a man who disliked questions, but Ramage could not resist asking, 'May I take it, sir, that the instructions refer to some – er, some mission for me?'

'That depends on Admiral Davis. The *Juno* is to join his command. My instructions for him concern a particular service, but whether he chooses you or one of his own captains is up to him.' His eyes twinkled. 'Nothing to stop him sending off one of his own frigates, and using you and the *Juno* for convoy work. Plenty of that, you know; very essential work, too, up and down the Windward and Leeward Islands. Just the thing for keeping a ship's company taut: plenty of sail handling, anchoring and weighing . . .'

His Lordship had finally sat back in his chair and said: 'Your father keeps well?'

When Ramage said that he did, the First Lord commented: 'He will be pleased at your promotion. It hasn't gone unnoticed here that the Earl had never tried to use his interest on your behalf: he left you to earn your promotion. Now you've got it, take care you always deserve it.' His face became stern again. 'I've said this to you before, and so has my predecessor in this office, and I say it again: you've done some good work and you've been devilish lucky. But if you are going to rise in the Service, you've got to stop disobeying or stretching orders. You got away with it half a dozen times or more as a lieutenant, but now you have been made post all that's changed. You are supposed to be a mature and responsible man, and that's how you'll be held to account. Discipline, Ramage; that's what holds this great Service together.'

He had stood up and held out his hand. As Ramage shook it the old man said: 'I'm no believer in rapid promotion. At each step fewer men are chosen, and it is part of my job to make sure they are the best. This is going to be a long war, and if we are to win it, our captains must be the finest in the world.'

Ramage had left the Admiralty walking a foot above the ground. A post captain with a frigate! But he had not crossed the cobbled courtyard to pass through the gateway into Whitehall before the exhilaration subsided, and he pictured himself doing convoy work in the Caribbean, work only slightly less dreary than shepherding Atlantic convoys.

He picked up the pen and for the next hour wrote rapidly, rarely crossing out. Then he put the pen down and read through the Orders from start to finish. They were longer than he intended, but luckily they were still shorter – crisper, anyway – than many he had read in the past. He would let Southwick go through them before the clerk made a fair copy.

That put an end to paperwork for a day or two, though there would be a mountain waiting for him on board the

Juno. The stores and equipment had to be signed for, certifying that they were on board, quite apart from the papers needed for getting to sea. The whole damned Navy floated on a sea of paper . . .

He went over and picked up the case of pistols. They were not as ornate as Gianna would have liked – though only because she wanted a present that was beautiful as well as useful – but they were splendid examples of the gun-maker's art. Opening the lid he looked at the two guns nestling in their recesses. They were well made, and so were the accessories: the shot mould was sturdy, not something that would rust quickly after constant heating; the flasks were shaped so that they fitted the hand; the lever which was pressed down to let out the right measure of powder fitted the thumb perfectly. He closed the box. He ought to start checking through his clothes; Hanson would have to pack the trunk tomorrow, and he had only the morning to buy anything he lacked.

A quiet knock on the door interrupted his thoughts and Gianna came into the room, pausing for a moment in shadow. In that moment Ramage went a thousand miles in space and back three years to the time he had first seen her: she had suddenly flung back the hood of her cloak and stood there watching him: candlelight had glinted in hair shining blue-black like a raven's feathers and shown a beautiful face with high cheekbones and large, widely-spaced eyes, a mouth a little too wide and with lips too full and warm for classical perfection. A face that could be coldly imperious or warm and generous. He had thought of Ghiberti's carving of 'The Creation of Eve' on the east doors of the Baptistry in Florence, the naked Goddess with the bold slim body and small jutting breasts . . . But the Eve standing at the door was holding an envelope and even before she spoke he recognized the heavy Admiralty seal on the back.

'A messenger just brought this: your father signed the receipt,' she said without expression. 'I hope it doesn't . . .' she did not finish the sentence but Ramage knew what she meant. The letter might say he was not to have the *Juno* after all. Gianna would be sorry for his sake yet delighted if he went on half-pay for three months or so – she had seen little enough of him since she had reached England from the Mediterranean.

He broke the seal and opened the letter. It was from the Board Secretary, Evan Nepean, and began with the usual time-honoured phrase, 'I am directed by My Lords Commissioners of the Admiralty . . .' He read through to the end. It took five lines of flowing prose to say that he was to leave for Portsmouth in time to arrive on board the *Juno* by noon on Wednesday, take command according to the commission already in his possession, and be under way by Friday. Why the Admiralty should suddenly decide to order him on board two days earlier Ramage was not told.

'Stop making faces and shrugging your shoulders,' Gianna said impatiently. 'What does it say?'

'I must leave for Portsmouth first thing tomorrow—'

'But that is two days *early*!'

'Something must have happened.'

'Nonsense, it is just that some silly man in the Admiralty is impatient and thoughtless—why, you've had only a few days' rest after carrying out those last terrible orders. Lord St Vincent should be—'

'*Cara mia*,' he interrupted, 'there are hundreds of captains but only a few frigates. I am very lucky.'

He heard his father's heavy tread outside and the Admiral, a worried look on his face, came into the room. 'They haven't changed their minds, have they?'

Ramage gave him the letter and when he read it the Admiral shook his head. 'You have trouble down there, my boy. I don't think Admiral Mann was exaggerating when he told me that your predecessor's court martial was a messy affair and that most of the officers should have been tried at the same time. The fellow was only in command six months, but in that time he let the ship's company go to pieces. A bad business. And you have to be under way by Friday with new officers . . .'

Ramage nodded and Gianna knew that she was temporarily forgotten: already Nicholas's face was animated as he called for Hanson to help him pack. Father and son were alike. Looking at the Admiral, she could see how Nicholas would be in thirty years' time—if he wasn't killed in this damnable war. Both were slim—the Admiral was putting on a little weight but would never let himself get plump—and it made them seem taller than they were. Both had the deep-set brown eyes and aquiline nose of the Ramages—most of the men in those family portraits at St Kew stared down at her out of their frames with those same eyes and made her shiver: those forebears were all dead, and yet the painters somehow kept them alive, the great-grandfathers and great-great-grandfathers . . .

Nicholas was nervous; she saw he was rubbing the upper of the two scars over his right eyebrow. Each was the result of a wound; on two separate occasions he had been lucky not to have his skull split open by the enemy. For a moment, before she could crowd the picture from her imagination, she saw him lying in a pool of blood on the deck of a ship, dying from a third wound. She crossed herself: she had this terrible fear that if the picture kept appearing, then it would happen.

The Admiral took her arm and led her from the room. As they walked down the stairs he said gently: 'It is always worse for the people staying behind. Watching Nicholas beginning to pack makes me realize what my wife must have gone through so many times . . .'

'But it is so unfair,' she burst out. 'They give him such fantastic orders. That last affair – fancy sending him to France! How he escaped the guillotine I shall never know, and it goes on and on and on. This war will never end!'

'Nicholas chose the Navy, my dear,' the Admiral said quietly as they reached the drawing-room and his wife stood up and came towards Gianna, her arms outstretched. 'Nicholas now has to leave first thing tomorrow,' he explained. 'Naturally Gianna is upset.'

The older woman led Gianna to a chair. 'For years I was always saying goodbye to my husband, and now it is to my son,' she said simply. 'I find it helps to think that the sooner I say goodbye, the sooner I welcome him back!'

'But every time it is a miracle he *comes* back,' Gianna sobbed. 'Every time he is a little changed, a little more *preoccupato*!'

'That is not the Navy's fault,' the Admiral said crisply. 'Our experiences change us little by little. That's maturing.'

His wife glanced at him. 'I think you should go up and help Nicholas pack his trunk: he has not much time.'

Gianna jumped up, dabbing her eyes with a handkerchief. 'No, no, I will. I am sorry; it is just – well, the West Indies are so far away.'

The Admiral held her shoulders for a minute and said with deliberate harshness: 'Yes, nearly a quarter of the way round the world from London. But remember, the French coast is only twenty-one miles from Dover, yet that's where Bonaparte's men caught him and wanted to cut off his head . . .'

CHAPTER TWO

Vauxhall turnpike, Putney Heath, Esher . . . on to Godalming, Liphook, Petersfield and Horndean . . . Change horses here, change horses there, hurried meals, and then the Porstdown Hills, Cosham and finally, after more than seventy miles, Portsmouth. His new breeches were uncomfortably tight and his coat stiff; his shoes were hard and his feet throbbed. As a younker, posting to Portsmouth to join your ship had always been exciting; as a lieutenant it eventually became tedious; as a captain, Ramage found it seventy miles of unrelieved irritation. The 'chaise jogged and rattled too much for him to be able to write down the things he suddenly remembered, and each thought was crowded out by a succession of others before the 'chaise reached the next stop to change horses. An alteration to his Captain's Orders, something more to insert, an important note for the Surgeon, several items for the Master – all forgotten between changes of horses. His memory was like a bucket without a bottom.

He reported to the crusty old Port Admiral at his office in Portsmouth Dockyard, found that the *Juno* was anchored off the Spit Sand outside the harbour, and was told that the new Master had gone on board but that the new lieutenants had not yet reported. From the Port Admiral's attitude it was obvious that the *Juno* was not his favourite frigate, and his parting words were: 'We have so many court martials at the moment that captains don't have time to get their ships ready, so keep your troubles to yourself.'

It was a discouraging hint about the state of the discipline in the *Juno*, and an ambiguous warning that the Port Admiral would not welcome Ramage bringing any delinquent officer or man to trial. He was to get the ship ready 'and sail in execution of your orders'.

Early on Wednesday morning the little cutter carrying him from the Point steps out to the *Juno* at Spithead was close-reaching in a brisk south-westerly breeze, the boatman moving the tiller from time to time to ease her over the occasional large wave. Ramage's trunk was wrapped in a tarpaulin to keep off the spray, and he was thankful to be wearing his boat cloak.

The burly boatman and a lad who was probably his son had glanced at each other when he hired them and named the *Juno*. The shortcomings of her previous captain were obviously common knowledge. A spot of bother in one of the dozen of ships of war anchored at Spithead was always interesting gossip for the seafaring folk living at Portsmouth or Gosport.

'Took the new Master out last night, sir,' the boatman said conversationally, raising his voice against the wind and the slop of the waves.

Ramage nodded. 'There'll be more business for you today or tomorrow, if you keep a sharp lookout at the Steps; four lieutenants, some midshipmen, a surgeon, Marine officers . . .'

The boatman grinned his gratitude: knowledge that particular officers were expected helped with the tips: it flattered a young lieutenant to tell him that the captain had mentioned he was due. You could usually tell a lieutenant's seniority – the more junior the larger the tip.

He watched the young Captain out of the corner of his eye, wondering if he dare ask a question or two, but decided against it: those eyes looked as though they could give you a very cold stare. He contented himself with a grunt to the boy that he wanted the mainsheet easing as they bore away for the last few hundred yards to round another anchored ship before luffing up alongside the *Juno*.

Ramage had already begun his survey of the *Juno*. Her yards were not square and there were two boats lying alongside at the larboard gangway, instead of being streamed astern. The paintwork looked in fair condition though, which was fortunate since there was no time to do anything about it before sailing. The black hull and sweeping sheer were shown off nicely by the pale yellow strake just below the gunports. She was one of Sir John Willams's designs, and he had a reputation for building fast ships, though Ramage had heard some captains grumble that they were rather tender and apt to heel a lot in a strong breeze, making it hard work for the gunners.

As the cutter drew nearer he saw some marks on the black hull forward, which showed that the ship's company threw buckets of dirty water and rubbish over the side instead of going straight forward to the head and lowering the buckets well down before starting them. Within the hour he would have men over the side with scrubbing brushes.

The more he saw as the cutter closed the distance, the more furious he became; the ship was thoroughly neglected. Seamen were lounging about the deck as though they were on the Gosport Ferry, and he could see the hats of a group of officers gossiping on the quarterdeck. They are in for a shock in a minute, he thought grimly, as soon as the sentry challenges, in fact.

'What ship?' came a casual shout, and Ramage nodded to the boatman to make the time-honoured answer that would tell everyone on board the *Juno* frigate that her new Captain was in the boat. '*Juno!*' the boatman bellowed, as he glanced at Ramage and risked a wink.

For years the old boatman had been taking officers out to every kind of ship of war, from tiny sloops to 98-gun ships of the line. Better than many junior officers he could glance at masts, yards, sails and hull and tell a great deal about a ship's officers. He had looked at the *Juno* and had seen her through Ramage's eyes. And he had seen the taut look on the Captain's face.

Heads were now appearing over the *Juno*'s bulwarks and fifty men's faces from one end of the ship to the other were staring down at the little cutter. An officer appeared at the entry port, gesturing to someone behind him. A bos'n's call shrilled faintly, and then Ramage could not watch any more. The little cutter was coming alongside and he had to keep an eye open to make sure that the flapping mainsail did not scoop off his hat as it was lowered, or that a dollop of sea thrown up between the two hulls did not hit him in the face and make a farce of his arrival on board his new command.

Then the cutter was alongside, lines were thrown, and there were the gangway steps dancing up and down as the boat rose and fell in the swell waves. He pulled the flaps of his boat cloak clear, jammed his hat firmly on his head, swung back his sword scabbard and, as the boat reached the top of a wave, grabbed a manrope in each hand and began climbing up the wooden battens which passed for steps. The manropes were greasy and dirty, instead of being scrubbed white.

Then he was standing on deck with a confused set of impressions. Two sideboys were standing to attention, others were running from forward, and a lieutenant was saluting but without a telescope under his arm. Long untidy tails of ropes were snaking over the deck as though the ship was a chandler's shop on a busy afternoon, and there were many spots of grease on the deck, which had not been scrubbed for days.

Not a man on deck was properly dressed.

A tall, thin and pale-faced man lieutenant with bloodshot eyes stood in front of him at the salute. There was a moment of complete silence on board and he knew every man on deck was watching: in this instant they would form their initial impressions of the new Captain, impressions that often turned out to be lasting.

He eyed the lieutenant coldly but for the moment did not return the salute, so the man stood there, arm crooked. Then he slowly stared round the ship. First his eyes ran along the deck forward, across the fo'c'sle, noting that the ship's bell had not been polished for a week, then up the foremast where at least four topsail gaskets on the larboard side were too slack and two on the starboard side of the furled topgallant were almost undone.

Where was Southwick? Ramage returned the lieutenant's salute and nodded as the man repeated his name. He was the First Lieutenant. 'Muster the ship's company aft, if you please,' Ramage said, his voice deliberately neutral, 'and then report to me in the cabin. My trunk is in the boat . . .'

As he turned aft to go down to the Captain's cabin he saw he had made the impression he wanted: the men were looking apprehensive, like naughty boys caught raiding an orchard; the First Lieutenant looked crestfallen, and Ramage had guessed the fellow had followed Ramage's eyes and perhaps seen the ship's condition for the first time in many weeks. He was half drunk, Ramage was certain.

As he reached the companionway he saw Southwick hurrying up the ladder from the lower deck, his face shiny and freshly shaven. Southwick saluted, his round face showing his obvious pleasure, his flowing white mop of hair already beginning to escape from his hat as random eddies of wind tugged at it. 'Welcome on board, sir: I was shaving – the sentry . . .'

Ramage returned the salute and then shook the old Master's hand. A few seamen were watching curiously and Ramage gestured to Southwick to precede him down the companionway to the cabin. Unbuckling his cloak and throwing it on the settee, Ramage sat down and told Southwick to sit opposite. The low headroom made it uncomfortable to stand, and he suddenly felt tired after the journey from London and the hurrying round Portsmouth.

'Is it as bad as it looks?' he asked.

'Worse, if anything, sir. We'll never do anything with these lieutenants!'

'We don't have to try,' Ramage said grimly. They'll be off the ship first thing tomorrow. We're to have all new officers, although I know nothing about them. His Lordship kindly gave me the choice of First Lieutenant, but I traded it for you as Master.'

Now it was Southwick's turn to grin. He was a good sixty years of age but for all his red face, stout build and white hair – which once led someone to liken him to a martial bishop from a country diocese – he was a fine seaman, firm with the men but fair. 'I'm grateful, sir, but I'm afraid we have more than our share of scalawags in this ship.'

Ramage went to the door and closed it, and when he sat down again he said: 'Everyone I've met keeps dropping hints. All I know is the Captain was dismissed the Service. The Port Admiral is suitably mysterious, and the ship looks more like a fairground.'

'Drink,' Southwick said cryptically. 'The Captain was a drunkard. He was tried for "conduct unbecoming . . . " but in fact he used to lock himself up in his cabin with a bottle for days on end.'

Ramage remembered the First Lieutenant with the bloodshot eyes and slightly hesitant manner. 'The First Lieutenant drinks too: do you think he found the strain too much?'

Southwick shook his head vigorously. 'At least, sir, not in the way you mean: for him the only strain is keeping away from a bottle too.'

'And the other lieutenants?'

Southwick shrugged his shoulders. 'I haven't seen much of them, sir; but from the gossip I picked up in Portsmouth they are good men who had no backing from the First Lieutenant, so they gave up.'

'With the Captain and the First Lieutenant drinking, it's a mercy they didn't put the ship ashore.'

'The First Lieutenant nearly did, I gather, right here at Gilkicker Point. The other three managed to get her anchored, and the Port Admiral came out to see what was going on and found the Captain insensible here in the great cabin and the First Lieutenant standing with his back hard up against the capstan to avoid falling down.'

'I wonder why they didn't try the Captain for "negligently hazarding the ship"?' Ramage mused.

'Hard to prove, sir: you need the evidence of the First Lieutenant on a "negligently hazarding" charge, and here the two of them were at fault.'

There was a loud rapping on the door, and when Ramage answered the First Lieutenant came in, stood to attention as best he could with the low headroom, and reported the ship's company mustered aft.

He was drunk all right, and although he was not yet thirty years of age the muscles of his face were slack and the flesh puffy, the eyes shifty and his brow and cheeks covered with perspiration. He had been a heavy drinker for years.

'Very well. I notice there is no sentry at the door of this cabin.'

'No, sir, I er . . .'

'Is my trunk on board yet?'

'Well, yes, sir, but –'

'Come along, Southwick,' Ramage said, taking a small parchment scroll from a pocket in his cloak and picking up his hat.

On deck the sun was occasionally breaking through low cloud; there was enough breeze to knock up occasional white horses although the *Juno* was tide-rode. Ramage strode to the capstan and turned to face forward. The men were drawn up in a hollow square in front of him. To his left the Marines stood stiffly to attention, a diminutive drummer boy at the end of the file. In front of him and to his right were the seamen and behind him the officers.

The deck was even filthier than he had thought at first: cracked pitch in many seams showed they were long overdue for re-paying or running over with a hot iron. Many ropes' ends needed whippings, the wood of many blocks was bare and showing cracks for lack of oil. Even on deck the stink of the bilges was nauseating – when had they last been pumped? Curiously enough the 12-pounder guns were newly blacked, the carriages freshly painted and the tackles neatly coiled. Perhaps the gunner was the only conscientious man on board.

Ramage looked at the sea of faces. It would be days, if not weeks, before he could put names to them all. They were an untidy crowd but they were nervous; there was just enough movement of feet and hands to reveal that. Every one of those men knew what was about to happen: the Captain was going to 'read himself in' by reading aloud his commission.

Until it was done he had no authority on board, but after that he could order them into battle so that not a man lived; he could order them flogged – which was more than the King could do – and he could have them arrested and charged with crimes which put their necks in hazard. He could be judge and jury, father and confessor . . .

The drunken First Lieutenant shouted 'Caps off!' as Ramage removed his own hat and, tucking it under his left arm, unrolled the scroll, and began reading it aloud. He pitched his voice so that the furthest men had to strain their ears above the wind humming through the spars and rigging. From long experience he knew that was the best way of getting their attention.

'By the Commissioners for executing the Office of Lord High Admiral . . . to Captain the Lord Ramage . . . his Majesty's frigate *Juno* . . . willing and requiring you forthwith to go on board and take upon you the charge and command of captain . . . strictly charging and commanding all the officers and company of the said frigate to behave themselves jointly and severally in their respective appointments . . .'

It was a long document and from time to time he paused deliberately. He wanted to be sure they all absorbed the full significance of the last line, however many times they had heard it before. He glanced round and saw he had the men's attention all right. 'You will carry out the General Printed Instructions and any orders and instructions you may receive . . . hereof, nor you nor any of you may fail as you will answer to the contrary at your peril . . .'

He put on his hat, rolled up the commission, tucked it in his pocket, and then stood with his hand clasped behind his back. A ship's company always expected a new captain to make a short speech after 'reading himself in', something that set the keynote and gave the men a chance to have a good look at the person who now had more direct power over their lives than their King. More than most ships' companies, this one needed some indication of what they could expect from their new Captain. They were going to be warned that from now on things would change, radically and abruptly. They all knew why their previous captain had left the ship and they had seen that Southwick was the new Master. They did not yet know that the rest of the officers were being replaced.

He took a deep breath. The men saw the swell of his chest, and they interpreted it as Ramage intended: as a sign of exasperation.

'The *Juno* is supposed to be a King's ship,' he said loudly, his voice a complete contrast from the even tone he had used when reading the commission, 'but just look at her. The first thing I see even before I get on board are badly-furled sails, and the yards aren't squared. The first thing I touch on boarding are greasy manropes. The first thing I see on deck are untidy men lounging round and tripping over uncoiled ropes. I get the impression that this frigate has just been recaptured from a couple of score of bumboat women . . .'

He paused because he expected at best that the men would give nervous giggles, but instead he heard genuine if somewhat embarrassed laughter.

'Tomorrow everything changes. Tomorrow any sentry or lookout who has not reported a boat heading for the ship the moment he sights it will spend the next five hours at the masthead. Any man in dirty clothes – unless he is doing a dirty job – will find himself scrubbing the messdeck for a week. If any man thinks he will get away with that in future – ' Ramage half turned and gestured up to the badly-furled sails on the yards, 'he is an optimist. By noon tomorrow I don't expect to find a speck of dirt or grease on any deck or in any locker, nor any piece of brasswork without a shine . . .'

He had their attention all right but he was damned if he was going to end up on a conciliatory note: the former Captain had been at fault and the First Lieutenant had taken advantage of it. The remaining lieutenants might have done their best, but the previous Master had obviously let everything slide, regarding it as a holiday in disguise, and the petty officers had slacked off. Every commission, warrant and petty officer in the ship had taken advantage of the situation. They might just as well have spent the last six months on shore. So they were being warned, and from tomorrow morning onwards no man would have an excuse. He looked at the men again. They had stiffened themselves up already; here and there a man tugged his shirt straight.

'There is plenty of work for the bos'n's mates, but I warn each and every one of you: there is not so much that they will be too busy to sew a few red baize bags if they are needed.'

He looked slowly at the men and glanced round at the First Lieutenant and nodded, then turned and strode below.

As he made his way to his cabin he knew that the last sentence had struck home. It was useless talking to a ship's company and using abstract terms like discipline, loyalty, responsibility – they treated them as mere words. What had really made every man straighten his shoulders had been the new Captain's last remark: a red baize bag was something that every man recognized and feared.

Some of the old traditions were useful, and this was one of them. The sight of a bos'n's mate sitting on deck methodically making a cat-o'-nine-tails, carefully splicing the nine thin tails into the thick rope handle, and probably covering the splice with a Turk's head, had a fascination for the men, who always knew the man who was to be flogged. The sewing of the red baize round the handle was part of a ritual which was rounded off by the bos'n's mate stitching a small bag from the red baize just large enough to hold the coiled cat-o'-nine-tails. With his work completed the cat was put in the bag and the whole thing handed over to the master-at-arms. The expression 'letting the cat out of the bag' had a grimmer origin than landsmen realized.

Since a new cat-o'-nine-tails was used for each flogging, if the captain was a harsh one then indeed the bos'n's mates were kept busy. As Ramage reached his cabin and walked through the door – that damned fool of a First Lieutenant still had done nothing about a Marine sentry – he found he did not want to think any more about flogging.

It was frequent enough in many ships; setting up a grating vertically at the gangway and lashing a man spreadeagled to it, or putting a bar in the capstan and securing a man to it by roping his outspread arms . . . He was certain that it rarely served its purpose as a punishment. Captain Collingwood had once said that it spoiled a good man and made a bad man worse, and Ramage agreed. He had ordered only three floggings in his career so far, all three officially for drunkenness, though in fact two were for mutiny. The men should have been court-martialled, and if a court had found them guilty, as it certainly would have done, they would have been hanged, so they were grateful for the floggings. Ironically, Ramage reflected, by ordering the floggings and logging them for drunkenness instead of requesting a court martial for mutiny, he had laid himself open to be court-martialled . . .

There seemed to be irony all round. Ironic that the first time he entered the Captain's accommodation on the *Juno* he had been so furious at finding the First Lieutenant the worse for

35

drink that he had had no time to enjoy its spaciousness. Ironic, too, that as he approached in the cutter, instead of proudly surveying the ship, largest he had yet commanded, and as a frigate one of the most coveted commands, he had been eyeing her critically, noting badly-furled sails, lounging men, dirty topsides, gossiping officers . . .

For all that, his accommodation was excellent. The great cabin right aft, the full width of the ship, was bright and airy, lit by the stern lights, with a settee, a large table athwartships and half a dozen chairs. A mahogany sideboard had been built in to the bulkhead on the forward side with a lead-lined wine cooler to one side covered in matching mahogany. The cabin sole was covered with canvas which had been painted in black and white squares, a chessboard pattern, yet the whole cabin was long overdue for more work with a paintbrush. But by the standards of the ships Ramage had previously commanded, it was a spacious great cabin. Of course it was all comparative; calling it the 'great cabin' would strike most landsmen as sarcasm, but the name referred to its function rather than its size, and even when in it no one could forget that the *Juno* was a ship of war. There was a 12-pounder gun on each side, the barrel and breach gleaming black and the carriage and trucks painted deep red. The train tackles of each gun were neatly coiled; both were secured for sea. Out of curiosity Ramage went over and ran a hand over the breeching and tackles, and then glanced down at the painted canvas beneath the wide trucks. Obviously the gun had not been run out, in practice or in action, for many months; the wide trucks had not been rolled over that paintwork . . . He glanced across at the gun on the other side. That too had its ropes neatly coiled, but had not been moved for months.

The two remaining cabins were half the size of the great cabin, although each held another 12-pounder. A section of the ship the width of the great cabin and forward of it had been bulkheaded off and then divided in half along the centre-line, making the bed place, or sleeping cabin, to starboard and the coach – some captains referred to it as their state room – to larboard.

He walked through to the bed place to inspect the cot, and was thankful that it was well scrubbed; simply a long, shallow wooden box suspended from the deckhead by ropes at each end so that it could swing as the ship rolled. A mattress spread in the box and some sheets and blankets completed the bed . . . he felt sleepy at the thought of it.

He could hear men padding about overhead, for the quarter-deck was above, while one deck below and forward of him was the ward room, with cabins on each side for the four lieutenants, Master, Surgeon and perhaps the Marine officer. Forward of that but outside the ward room were the even smaller cabins, boxes, really, with bulkheads made of canvas stretched over frames made of battens, of the purser, gunner, carpenter, bos'n, and captain's clerk. And, larger, the midshipmen's berth.

Forward of that the Marines were berthed, and even farther forward the ship's company lived. They ate their meals at tables slung from the deckhead, each table belonging to six or eight men and called a mess, with a number. The mess system often provided a thoughtful captain with an indication as to whether or not he had a happy ship's company. Once a month a seaman could make an official request to change his mess, which was usually a signal that he had quarrelled with his shipmates. Half a dozen requests a month were acceptable; more than that should warn a captain that there was too much quarrelling and bickering on the mess deck.

At night the tables and forms were stowed and hammocks were slung: hammocks which spent the day stowed in nettings along the top of the bulwarks and covered with long strips of canvas, out of the way and, in action, providing some protection against musketry fire.

Only the captain lived in solitary glory on the main deck, along with twenty-six of the *Juno*'s 12-pounder guns and a Marine sentry. Ramage wondered if it was the loneliness that had driven the previous captain to drink. Loneliness and responsibility, two things faced with confidence by a competent captain but which became corrosive acids to destroy an uncertain man.

A competent captain: for a moment Ramage mulled over the phrase and then felt a spasm, if not of fear, of something deuced close. Alone in the great cabin wondering what had destroyed his predecessor suddenly brought home to him that he now commanded a frigate. Not that captain walking down the Admiralty steps, nor the one hailing a passing boat, but Nicholas Ramage, who had never previously commanded anything larger than a brig.

He had dreamed of it for years and now he had achieved it, but thanks to a drunken predecessor the excitement was not there. The *Juno*, a 32-gun frigate, carrying twenty-six 12-pounders on the main deck, four 6-pounders on the quarterdeck, two more on the fo'c'sle. A typical frigate, in fact. She was 126 feet long on the gun deck and had a beam of thirty-five feet.

Ramage recalled some other details he had looked up hurriedly before leaving London: when fully provisioned her draught was sixteen feet seven inches. She had a complement of 215 men, and her hull had cost about £13,000, her masts and yard more than £800. By the time she had been rigged, sails put on board and boats hoisted, the total had risen to £14,250. The Progress Book at the Admiralty had ended up with a total that included a halfpenny.

He sat back in the chair and stared out through the stern lights. Prices, weights, lengths . . . They were a ship on paper, yet the *Juno* frigate was so much more. You began with six hundred tons of timber, carefully selected and shaped; you needed some forty tons of iron fittings, bolts and nuts, and a dozen tons of copper bolts. Her bottom was sheathed with more than two thousand sheets of copper, to keep out teredo and deter the barnacles and weeds. Eighteen thousand treenails locked futtocks and planks, beams and breasthooks, stem and stern-post . . . Four tons of oakum had been driven into hull and deck seams by skilled and patient caulkers, and there were twenty barrels of pitch and twice that number of tar used in her construction. Two hundred and fifty gallons of linseed oil – much of that rubbed into masts and yards. Three coats of paint for the whole ship weighed two and a half tons, yet that was nothing when you realized that masts, yards and bowsprit weighed more than forty tons. Fifteen tons for the standing rigging, twelve for the running; six tons of blocks and nine of spare yards and booms. Six tons of sails (the main course alone needed 620 yards of canvas), thirty-five of anchor cables. Weight, weight, weight – and water, provisions, men and their chests, stores for the gunner, carpenter and bos'n, let alone guns, powder, shot . . . She's all yours now, he told himself, until the Admiralty say otherwise, or you put her on a reef or sink her in a storm of wind. Like all ships, the *Juno* would be a demanding mistress but an exciting one.

She was a great deal bigger than his first command, the cutter *Kathleen*, which he had lost at the Battle of Cape St Vincent; she was a lot bigger than the *Triton* brig, his next command lost after a hurricane in the West Indies. Yet the most important thing – what he found daunting at the moment – was that the complement was 215 men, which was twice that of the *Triton* and four times as many as the *Kathleen*.

Captain the Lord Ramage was now, by virtue of the commission still in his pocket, the commanding officer of the *Juno* frigate.

The responsibility for the ship and her men was his from now on, to wear like an extra skin. All he had to show for it so far was an epaulet on his right shoulder, but the printer of the Navy List would eventually lift the type and move his name from the list of lieutenants and put it at the bottom of the list of captains . . .

As he stood up to put his commission away in a drawer he heard a noise outside the door and found that the First Lieutenant had at last provided him with a Marine sentry. Ramage told him to pass the word for the Master and Southwick arrived so promptly that Ramage guessed the old man had been standing by the capstan, waiting for the call.

The Master sat down in a chair at Ramage's invitation, his hat on his knees, and when he saw Ramage's eyebrows raised questioningly he nodded: 'Your talk worked, sir; I can see a difference in the men already. I think it was the red baize bag: I saw a lot of 'em straighten themselves up when you mentioned that!'

'They've probably noted me down as a wild man with a cat-o'-nine-tails,' Ramage said ruefully. 'Damnation, you can remember the only times I've had men flogged.'

'Don't you fret, sir; one man came up to me not five minutes ago – one of the Kathleens who served with us in the Mediterranean. He was all excited that you'd joined the ship and by now is probably talking up a gale o' wind on the messdeck!'

Ramage nodded, and then waved at the sideboard. 'There's nothing to drink yet. My trunk is on board – I hope – and some purchases I made in Portsmouth should be out later in the day. In the meantime I shall have to eat by courtesy of the ward room. Now, to bring you up to date.'

Quickly Ramage explained that the *Juno* was under orders for the West Indies and was to sail as soon as possible. All four lieutenants on board would be leaving the ship in the morning – their orders from the Admiralty were on the sideboard – and four new ones would be arriving during the day. Southwick's old chess opponent, Bowen, was due on board during the day, and so was a Marine officer.

By the time Ramage finished the Master had a contented grin on his face: he had looked glum at the prospect of four new lieutenants – all strangers to each other as well as the ship, he grumbled – but brightened at the mention of Bowen's name. The Surgeon was a fine chess player and had spent many hours teaching the Master. And between the two men there was a bond that included their Captain: Ramage and Southwick had spent most of their time in the *Triton* brig during a voyage from England to the West Indies – Bowen's first in one of the King's ships – curing the Surgeon's alcoholism. They had nursed him through the horrors of delirium tremens, and kept his mind occupied in the critical weeks after that, which was when Southwick had been under Ramage's orders to cultivate an interest in chess.

'Midshipmen,' Southwick said suddenly. 'The four on board with the previous captain have all transferred. I hope we aren't sailing without any . . .'

'You might end up wishing we were,' Ramage said. 'We'll have at least two. The Marchesa – '

'Excuse me, sir,' Southwick interrupted hurriedly, 'how is she?'

'Very well, and she wishes to be remembered to you. She has a young nephew who arrived in London recently. Apparently he was in Sicily when we rescued the Marchesa, and stayed there until he could get to Malta. He came back in a frigate and, according to the Marchesa, learned a little on the way and now talks of nothing but ships and the sea. We shall be having him with us. He's fourteen years old and speaks good English. A lively lad. I had no others, so when Lord St Vincent heard there were vacancies . . .'

Southwick nodded understandingly. 'I hope his choices are good but – '

'I think he is only providing one, but don't complain,' Ramage said with mock earnestness. 'His Lordship intended to nominate a chaplain.'

Southwick's face fell. 'I hope that – '

'I bargained very gently. I did not ask for a particular first lieutenant – but I mentioned you for Master. His Lordship was delighted. I did not ask for a particular second lieutenant – but I said I would like a particular surgeon. His Lordship was still delighted. When His Lordship said he had a chaplain who wanted a berth, I mentioned casually that I was not asking for particular third of fourth lieutenants either – nor a Marine officer.'

'His Lordship did well out of it,' Southwick commented. 'In giving you your Master and Surgeon, he has four lieutenants, three midshipmen and a Marine officer for himself.'

'I forgot to mention that he allowed me a dozen men for you . . .'

'For me, sir?'

'Yes – Jackson, Stafford, Rossi, Maxwell and a whole lot more former Tritons.'

'By Jove, sir,' Southwick exclaimed delightedly, 'how did you manage to trace where they were?'

'Well, of course, Jackson, Rossi and Stafford were with me in France, so I could trace them, and Maxwell and the rest were all in the *Victory* here at Portsmouth, and one of them wrote to me on behalf of the rest a month ago, asking if I was ever given a ship . . .'

'They're lucky fellows,' Southwick said. 'Anyway, I must admit I'm glad to be getting them. From the look of some of the men we have at the moment, we'll be able to promote some of the lads. By the way, sir, the ship's already provisioned for four months; that's the only pleasant surprise I had when I came on board!'

For the next half-hour the two men discussed how they would get the *Juno* into a condition where she could join the squadron of the most eagle-eyed of admirals, a discussion which ended when Ramage remembered that his trunk had not been brought below, and was sufficiently angry to send for the First Lieutenant, telling Southwick to wait in the coach.

The man stood just inside the door of the great cabin, swaying slightly and with a befuddled grin on his face. He was drunk not from a few incautious tots earlier, but because he had long ago reached the stage where he needed a tot an hour to get through the day, just as a ship could only get to windward by tacking. Apart from Bowen, he was the first officer ever to be drunk on duty in any ship Ramage commanded, and his eyes had the cunning look of a ferret. He was making no attempt to hide his condition and Ramage suddenly guessed the reason. An officer found drunk on duty would normally be sent to his cabin, if not put under an arrest. This wretched fellow, finding that the new Captain had done nothing about it, had concluded that Ramage was nervous and unsure of himself and, like the previous Captain, would let him stay happily drunk.

He did not know that Ramage had orders from the

Admiralty to send the man off the ship and that it was unlikely he would ever be employed again. The letter transferring him out of the *Juno* was there on the sideboard and for a moment Ramage considered giving it to him. Then he decided to wait until next morning: the man ought to be punished, however lightly and briefly, for his part in reducing the *Juno* to its sorry state.

'My trunk?' Ramage asked quietly. 'Why has it not been sent below?'

'You told me to have it hoisted on board – sir.'

'I forgot to order you to have it sent below?'

'Yes.' The man was grinning.

'Very well. I hardly expect the First Lieutenant of a ship I command to need orders for such a routine matter. However, you are drunk; you were drunk when I came on board and now you are under arrest. Go to your cabin and stay there. If you have any liquor in your cabin you will leave it outside the door. If you touch a drop more I'll have you put in irons –'

'But you can't put me in irons!' the man exclaimed. 'I'm –'

By now Ramage was standing in front of him, his face expressionless. The First Lieutenant looked up and saw the narrowed eyes but he was too drunk to notice anything except that the Captain was not shouting: he was not the first man who failed to realize that the quieter Ramage's voice became, the more angry he was.

'Can't I?' Ramage asked, almost conversationally. 'If I thought it would sober you up I'd have you put in irons and stand you under the wash-deck pump for an hour.'

The man, suddenly alarmed, tried to stand to attention but banged his head on the beam overhead.

'Go to your cabin,' Ramage said. 'Report to me at seven tomorrow morning with your trunk packed. In the meantime you are relieved of all duties and are under close arrest.'

The man lurched from the cabin and Southwick came back, shaking his head. 'There's no saving a man like that, sir; he's drunk because he is bad, not bad because he's drunk. I'll rouse out the master-at-arms and arrange for a sentry. I'll have your trunk sent down in five minutes.'

Ramage nodded. 'Well, we've made a start, but it's going to be a long job . . .'

Next morning Southwick grumbled to Ramage that the *Juno* was more like Vauxhall Turnpike when the Portsmouth stage came in than a ship of war. The former Tritons were arriving with sea bags, the officers leaving the frigate were cursing and swearing as sea chests were accidentally dropped, and each of the new lieutenants was wandering round the ship with the lost look of a Johnny-Come-Lately. Ramage gave up long before the sun had any warmth in it. He met the dozen former Tritons and welcomed them on board with bantering warnings that their recent holiday on board the *Victory* was over; he watched stony-faced as the former First Lieutenant left the ship, sober for the first time in many months and perhaps even ashamed of himself.

Bowen arrived just before noon and, with three leather bags of surgical instruments, looked more like the prosperous surgeon from Wimpole Street that he had once been than a surgeon of a frigate. He greeted Southwick with obvious pleasure and, waving at the sea chest being hoisted on board, told him he had brought him a present of a set of chessmen. This announcement provoked a loud groan from the Master, who protested that he had vowed to play only on the even-numbered days of the month.

The new First Lieutenant, John Aitken, arrived an hour after the Surgeon. He was a fresh-faced and diffident young Scot from Perthshire who, half an hour after climbing the gangway steps, had changed into his second-best uniform and set the men to work cleaning up the ship. Head pumps were soon squirting streams of water across the decks as seamen sprinkled sand and scrubbed with holystones; aloft topmen were refurling sails, tying and retying gaskets until the quiet Scots voice coming through the speaking trumpet announced that the First Lieutenant was satisfied.

The other three lieutenants had arrived together and Ramage, with memories of joining ships in similar circumstances, saw from the way they behaved towards each other that they had already compared the dates of their commissions. The vital dates established their seniority and sorted them into the Second, Third and Fourth Lieutenants, without the need for a decision by Captain Ramage, the Port Admiral or the Admiralty.

To Ramage, now in his late twenties, the three junior lieutenants looked very young. Each must be more than twenty, because that was the youngest age allowed; but he was himself getting older, and this was the first time for a couple of years that he had seen a group of young lieutenants. They seemed cheerful and competent fellows: Wagstaffe, the Second Lieutenant, was a Londoner, Baker, the Third, was a burly youngster from Bungay, in Suffolk, and Lacey, the new Fourth Lieutenant, spoke in the easy relaxed burr of Somerset, having been born at Nether Stowey.

As he walked round the ship, watching but not interfering, storing items in his memory, noting the way certain men were working and others were hanging back, Ramage kept an eye open for the midshipmen. Gianna's nephew was due today – Ramage had emphasized that if he did not get on board today he would be left behind. To be fair to the boy he was having to make his way from somewhere in Buckinghamshire to London, buy his kit, and then get down to Portsmouth. Ramage stopped walking for a moment, appalled at the prospect of Aunt Gianna taking the boy shopping; he would probably arrive with a large trunk full of expensive nonsense, instead of a small sea chest tightly packed with the items on the list that Ramage had left behind.

He was thankful that the shop in Portsmouth had sent out his own purchases: two chests of tea, cases of spirits and wine, boxes of freshly-baked biscuits they swore would last two months without going hard, and after that could be freshened by soaking in water for a couple of minutes and putting in a hot oven. He had a good selection of preserves: cucumber put down in vinegar, quince jam, mint sauce in bottles, and there were a small string of garlic and several large ones of onions, stone jars of lime juice, a box of apples packed in hay . . .

Promotion to the command of a frigate brought other changes, apart from the number of men and the size of the ship. The Captain of a frigate, with four lieutenants, Marine officer, midshipmen, Master and Surgeon, was expected to entertain; from time to time he would have to invite three or four of them to dinner, and spend an amiable hour being pleasant. It was up to the Captain to provide a palatable meal and make sure plenty was available: young midshipmen and junior lieutenants came to dinner with the Captain with awe and a hearty appetite.

By late afternoon Ramage was heartily sick of the ship. Every time he wanted to walk the deck to ease his tension he had to dodge groups of busy seamen. The ship stank of pitch because Aitken had the carpenter's mates and caulkers hardening down some of the deck seams with hot irons; there was brick dust blowing around as seamen tried to work up a polish on brasswork that had been left to corrode for weeks. New coils of rope were being unrolled as Southwick and the bos'n replaced running rigging that had aged and stretched to the point of being dangerous. Cursing seamen struggled with fids as they spliced in new thimbles, and the gunner and his mates were systematically picking up shot from the racks and passing them through gauges, metal rings of an exact diameter which would show if too much paint or hidden flakes of rust on a shot would make it jam in the bore of a gun. Only Aitken was entirely happy: Ramage seemed to hear his soft Scots voice coming from a dozen places at once as he encouraged, cajoled and bullied the men to get the work done.

Gianna's nephew arrived at four o'clock with the midshipman sent by Lord St Vincent. Each boy had two sea chests and Ramage watched Southwick glaring as they were hoisted on board. He decided not to say anything unless more midshipmen arrived: with these two and the master's mate, the berth would not be too crowded because the chests made up for the lack of chairs.

Ramage gave both boys half an hour to settle in and then sent for them. Paolo Luigi Orsini was a typical young Italian: olive-skinned with black hair, large and warm brown eyes, and an open friendly manner. At the moment he was very nervous, overwhelmed at being in uniform and serving in one of the King's ships. Ramage suspected too that warnings from Gianna were still ringing in his ears about what would happen to him if he did anything to incur the Captain's displeasure. The high-spirited boy who had romped through the house in Palace Street, teasing *Zia* Gianna had vanished; in his place was a lad who gave the impression that he feared that at the slightest lapse he would vanish in a puff of smoke.

The second midshipman, Ramage was relieved to find, had been to sea before: Edward Benson, son of a cousin of Lord St Vincent's wife, had spent a year in a 74-gun ship of the line and was two years older than Paolo. Red haired and freckle faced, he was obviously high-spirited and Ramage recalled the First Lord's remark. Ramage had already met Edwards, the young master's mate who would be the senior in the midshipmen's berth, and he seemed more than capable of keeping an eye on both boys.

At five in the afternoon Aitken reported that the *Juno*'s cutter had returned from the Dockyard after taking all the mail on shore, and Ramage guessed that the canvas bag had contained a bizarre collection of papers. He had written to Gianna and his parents, Bowen had written to his wife, the newly-joined lieutenants had scribbled letters to relatives and the seamen had sent four or five score letters telling wives and sweethearts that they were about to sail on a long voyage.

Ramage had spent much of the previous evening and most of this morning working with his clerk, trying to get all the lists, affidavits, musters, invoices, pay tickets, surveys and inventories checked and signed where necessary. Together they accounted to the Admiralty, Navy Board, Sick and Hurt Board and the Port Admiral for just about everything on board the *Juno*, from her men to spare sail canvas, powder and shot to stationery, spare beer cask staves to caulkers' mauls. Fortunately the clerk had had everything ready up to the time the previous Captain went off to face the court martial, but there was no chance of Ramage checking whether all the items he was signing as having been received since then were actually on board. He would have to make up any shortages later out of his own pocket but for the time being he had to sail as quickly as possible, and he could not leave until the paperwork was done.

The gunner, bos'n, carpenter and various others had prepared their inventories, but it would take another three days to go through the paperwork item by item – as he had every right to do – and by that time the voice of the Port Admiral would be shrill and signals from the Admiralty would be arriving on board like broadsides. That was one of the disadvantages of the new semaphore telegraph set up between Portsmouth and the Admiralty building in London. In an emergency signals could be passed in a matter of minutes, but it also meant that the First Lord could sit in his office in London and ask questions and get answers back within half an hour . . .

The sentry announced the First Lieutenant again. Aitken reported that all the ship's boats had now returned and had been hoisted in and secured. The ship was trimmed correctly, and the replacement stun-sail booms had arrived from the dockyard. The guns were secured – Aitken paused a moment, thought and went on – the tiller had been checked and was moving freely, sails were ready for loosing.

It was always a good thing for the Captain to be able to remember something that the First Lieutenant had forgotten: it kept him on his toes. Ramage searched his memory: 'The sheet anchor?'

'Stowed, sir; I forgot to mention it.'

Ramage nodded. 'We are ready to man the capstan?'

'Aye, aye, sir.'

It wanted an hour to high water and by some miracle the ship was ready a day early. Ramage picked up his hat and led the way on deck. Apart from some clouds sitting over the hills to the north, the sky was clear; the wind was from the north-west. When the *Juno* left Spithead – which she would do within the next fifteen minutes – she would leave behind the brief memory of a captain court-martialled for drunkenness, and another story to add to those told about Lord St Vincent's ruthlessness: that he had cleared all the commission officers out of the *Juno* frigate because the captain liked to tipple. Like most such stories it would be only partly true but it might serve as a warning.

Ramage stared for a moment at the rest of the ships at anchor nearby, and gave a shiver. The story of the *Juno*'s drunken captain could in fact be the story of the captain of any ship: everything depended on him. Every failure on the part of a captain showed immediately in the ship. His lack of seamanship was revealed in the way the ship was handled; his lack of leadership in the way the officers and ship's company behaved. His courage of lack of it would be shown the moment the ship went into action. The captain was not the tip of a pyramid, as most people thought; in fact it was just the reverse: he was the spindle on which everything else balanced.

He looked up at the waiting Aitken. 'Is the fiddler on the quarterdeck? Ah, I see him. Very well, man the capstan!'

CHAPTER THREE

Ramage wiped his pen and put it away in the drawer as he waited for the ink to dry on the page of his Journal. The figures he had written in under the 'Latitude In' and 'Longitude Made' columns showed that the *Juno* had almost reached 'The Corner', the invisible turning point just short of the Tropic of Cancer where she would pick up the North-east Trade winds to sweep her for 3000 miles across the Atlantic in a gentle curve to the south-east that would bring her to Barbados.

The 'Journal of the Proceedings of his Majesty's ship *Juno*, Captain Nicholas Ramage, Commander', told the story of the voyage so far in terms of winds, courses steered, miles run from noon one day to noon the next, and apart from the column headed 'Remarkable Observations and Accidents', mercifully almost blank, told the Admiralty all it wanted to know.

As he flicked over the earlier pages, Ramage thought that the journal told very little of the story. His Log and the Master's faithfully recorded the time when the Lizard sank below the horizon astern, the last sight of England for many months – the last sight ever for some of the men on board. It mentioned the westerly gale that caught them off Brest and drove them into the Bay of Biscay, noted the three occasions when they sighted other frigates and made or answered the challenge, recorded the time that the tip of the island of Madeira was sighted and its bearing . . . But it made no mention of the afternoon, with the Lizard still just in sight, when he had finally lost his temper with the whole ship's company, mustered them aft, and given them a warning.

For the first few hours after weighing from Spithead it had seemed that the men were trying, that they realized they had grown slack under the previous captain and were anxious to make amends. But as the *Juno* beat her way out to the Chops of the Channel they had eased off and became sullen. A topsail had been let fall with a reef point still tied so that the canvas ripped; evolutions that should have taken five minutes had taken twenty. In fact it seemed that all the work was being done by the dozen former Tritons.

Aitken and Southwick had done their best and he could not fault the other three lieutenants. The new Marine Lieutenant, Rennick, had a firm grip on his men, who were always smartly turned out. Yet there was an insidious sullen air on the mess deck, and that afternoon Ramage had vowed to get rid of it. With the glass falling and the *Juno* thrashing her way westward out of the Channel, he mustered them aft and, using a speaking trumpet to make his voice heard above the howl of the wind, he had given them a solemn warning.

The day after they reached 'The Corner' he would inspect the ship from breasthook to archboard; he would exercise them aloft and at the guns with a watch in his hand. If at the end of the day he was satisfied, then the rest of the voyage to Barbados would be a routine cruise; but if he found so much as a speck of dirt in even one of the coppers, if furling a topsail took thirty seconds longer than it should, if there was any hesitation or delay over emergency procedures (and here he was warning the officers more than the seamen), then he promised them 3000 miles of misery, when they would beg for a flogging to get some relief.

Only Southwick and the former Tritons had known he was not ruthless enough to carry out such a threat, but he could rely on them not only to warn the Junos that he was capable of doing so, but to embroider the threat that even the toughest of them would turn uneasily in their hammocks every night as the *Juno* made her way south-westwards to 'The Corner'.

Now 'The Corner' was less than thirty miles to the south, and unless this present calm patch lasted the *Juno* should pass the magic spot, twenty-five degrees north, twenty-five degrees west, during the night. Tomorrow would be the day the ship's company were dreading. Yet he was certain the threat had worked; for many days now Aitken and Southwick had been licking them into shape. They had reefed and furled in all weathers, sent sails down on the deck in half a gale and hoisted them up again, sent down yards for imaginary repairs and swayed them up again as black squalls drove down on them. The men had loaded guns, run them out, fired them and loaded them again until they were ready to drop. They had been roused in the middle of the night for fire drill, hoisting up the fire engine and rigging head pumps to fill the cistern, then roused again to repel imaginary boarders, man the chain pump or find imaginary leaks. They had been startled by orders to round up and pick up a man (a dummy the sailmaker had made out of a hammock) who had fallen over the side. That, Ramage reflected, had been a disaster; the seaman ordered to keep an eye on the 'body' had confused it with a large patch of floating seaweed, and the sailmaker had to make another 'body' which even now was waiting for the moment Ramage chose to repeat the manoeuvre.

Eventually Aitken had begun reporting much better times for sail handling, and the sullen atmosphere had gone. Perhaps the sunshine helped; they were now almost in the Tropics and the cold and damp of the Channel were but memories. Tomorrow he would know. Never before had he been forced to treat a ship's company like this – but never before had he inherited a ship from a drunken captain and first lieutenant, when the normal methods of training and leadership had proved useless.

It was ironic that this present calm patch was prolonging the agony: from what both Aitken and Southwick reported, the men viewed it with all the apprehension of a flogging through the fleet. Well, the *Juno* still had not reached 'The Corner' and found the Trades, although it looked as though she was going to be lucky this time. There was always an element of luck in it. Sometimes the North-east Trades arrived on time but many ships had to carry on south, down as far as the Cape Verde Islands, before picking them up. This time the wind was fitful and still mostly north, but for the past two days it had often veered north-east for an hour or two and, just as Ramage, Aitken and Southwick were congratulating each other that the Trades had arrived, it would suddenly back north and there would be a flurry of sail trimming. But they were nearly in the Tropics: the imaginary line in the heavens marking the Tropic of Cancer was almost overhead.

The sea was a fresh, deep blue, and the spray was warm. All the men new to the Tropics were keeping an eye open for their first sight of flying fish. The canvas awning was now rigged over the quarterdeck, and by ten o'clock in the morning the deck was getting hot. In a few days, another four or five degrees farther south, the deck would be uncomfortably hot by nine in the morning and no man, whether barefoot or wearing boots or shoes would want to stand still unless he was in shade. Paint would flake more quickly, the pitch in the deck seams that at Spithead had been brittle and cracking would be sticky, and long thin cracks, or shakes, would appear in the masts as the sun dried the wood out, and no amount of oiling would prevent it. Furled sails would have to be kept aired, otherwise they mildewed overnight; cold-weather clothing that had not been carefully washed before being stowed in seabags would sprout rich, remarkably coloured mildew, which seemed to flourish on food stains.

Already Bowen was treating half a dozen men for bad sunburn, men with very sensitive skin who had been affected before Ramage forbade anyone to be on deck without shirts for three hours either side of noon. Despite these problems caused by the hot sun, it was good to have the ship well-aired with scuttles, skylights and ports wide open; the sun, almost overhead at noon, penetrated parts of the *Juno* that had not seen sunlight since the ship was last in the Tropics.

As he dried his razor and put it away in its leather case, Ramage reflected that one of the few advantages of commanding a ship the size of a frigate was that the Captain could usually have hot water for shaving. Today was an exception, and his own fault, since he chose to get up a couple of hours before the galley fire was lit.

The *Juno* was bowling along in the darkness – groaning along, some might say, since her timbers creaked as she pitched in a sedate seesaw motion. The Trade wind had settled steadily from the north-east and with luck they would now carry it all the way to Barbados. With the following wind came the following seas and the pitching and rolling, so that water slopped out of a basin filled more than a third full and fiddles had to be fitted to the tables – narrow battens which were the only way of preventing plates and cutlery sliding off.

He could hear the rudder grumbling as the men at the wheel kept the frigate on course, and ropes creaked as they rendered through blocks. The pitching was just enough to make the lanthorn flicker as the flames tried to stay vertical – and enough to make him sit down as he prepared to pull his stockings on.

Monday morning and the first full day after passing 'The Corner'. Well, the ship's company knew what it meant. The silk of the first stocking was cold; they would have to be a few hundred miles farther south before clothes always felt warm at this time of the day. He smoothed out the wrinkles and reached for the second one. No, there would be few men on board who were looking forward to the approaching dawn. He had not been entirely fair to the men in those early days: he had discovered, by way of his coxswain, Jackson, that the drunken captain had not been the only cause of the *Juno*'s condition. The one before him had been slack, had rarely made more than a cursory inspection of the ship, and his seamanship had been lamentable. Orders to reef or furl as a squall came up were usually given too late, so that men were injured and sails were ripped. As far as Ramage could make out, the men had spent most of their time repairing sails. And discipline had been almost non-existent.

This had inevitably thrown all the responsibility on to the other officers. Had they been good men they might have been able to manage, but they were poor specimens who played the game of favourites, hoping that by toadying to a few chosen seamen and petty officers they would have a nucleus who could be relied on. As a result, the rest of the men became the scapegoats for everything that went wrong. Naturally enough, the ship's company had split into two groups, one large and one small, the victimized and the favoured, and they had hated each other. Then that Captain had been replaced by the drunkard who had cared nothing for the way the ship was run and who had brought his own drunken First Lieutenant with him. Apparently this had finally proved too much for the other officers, who had begun drinking from sheer frustration.

Because they were frequently drunk, or ill-tempered next morning from the effects of it, the victimization had become worse. The majority of the ship's company had been reduced to sullen hulks of men who did not give a damn whether a single reef point was left tied so that a sail ripped when it was let fall, and the officers did not give a damn either, knowing that the Captain would not back them up if they tried to punish delinquents.

Ramage wriggled into his breeches, pulled on a shirt, tucked it in and buttoned up the flap. By the time Captain Ramage came on board and read himself in, the men had no faith in captains, no faith in officers and precious little faith in petty officers either, because many of them had taken advantage of the situation to indulge in bullying and they too had played favourites. It was easy enough for a bos'n's mate to 'start' a seaman he did not like, giving him a slash across the back with the rattan cane that was his badge of office. A 'starting' took only a second but the pain lasted for hours, and the bruise for several days.

By the time Ramage had learned all this he had been more than thankful that Lord St Vincent had let him have Southwick and the dozen Tritons and sent him Aitken. Perhaps the First Lord had known more about the situation in the *Juno* than Ramage realized. The Admiral was reputed to be able to see through a three-inch plank, apart from being a stern disciplinarian – *very* stern. As a captain he had become famous in the Navy for the fact that his ship invariably had the smallest sick list of any; he was ruthless in his determination that the ship should be kept well-aired below, that the men's bedding should always be clean and dry, that they should have fresh vegetables whenever possible (it was said that he paid for them out of his own pocket at times).

As Ramage tied his stock he wondered if His Lordship had deliberately chosen him for the *Juno*, with all her problems. There were several 32-gun frigates in Spithead and Plymouth and any one of them would have been suitable for the West Indies. But it hardly mattered now what had been in His Lordship's mind; the fact was that Captain Ramage now commanded the *Juno* and even if he had inherited two years of problems created by previous captains, the Admiralty would not give a damn: he was the commanding officer and the ship's efficiency was his concern and his alone. If he could not knock the ship's company into shape there were dozens of other captains at present unemployed who would leap at the opportunity. Captains with distinguished records, brave men and fine seamen, men who were relegated to half pay simply because there were not enough ships to go round. For every dozen captains ready and willing to go to sea, there was probably only one ship.

He picked up his coat and flicked the spirals of bullion on the epaulet. A ship's company judged its captain on performance: he was judged a fair man if he enforced discipline fairly. Contrary to what many people on shore thought, a ship's company did not like an easy-going captain – he left them at the mercy of bullying officers and petty officers. They liked a captain who ran a taut ship and enforced a consistent discipline. In other words, if a seaman hoarded his tots of rum for a few days, contrary to regulations, got drunk and was caught, then the punishment was a dozen lashes. But it had to be a dozen for *any* man who got drunk, not a dozen for one man and two dozen for the next.

Taut and consistent discipline: that was vital. Lack of consistency, from all accounts, had cost Captain Wallis his life in the Caribbean a year or so ago. He had been a strange man who apparently delighted in having men flogged and was utterly arbitrary. He had ordered one man four dozen lashes for drunkenness and let another go unpunished on the same day. He had court martialled one man for attempted desertion and then freed another. It had gone on like that for months in the *Jocasta* frigate until the ship's company had become like wild animals trapped in the jungle, frightened and reduced to fighting for survival against an unpredictable captain. One moment he might smile at them, the next he would order them six dozen lashes (though the regulations permitted no more than two dozen).

The Navy was shocked when the news had eventually filtered through that a number of the ship's company had mutinied, murdered Wallis and his officers, leaving only the master and a midshipman, and sailed the ship down to the Spanish Main, handing her over to the Spaniards at La Guaria. Then a few men who had not taken part in the mutiny escaped and managed to get back to Barbados and Jamaica with the whole miserable story of Wallis's behaviour. Although captains had not dared speak their thoughts aloud – obviously mutiny could not be tolerated – few had sympathized with the dead Wallis. Fortunately many who might have eventually shared his fate learned a lesson in time.

Ramage picked up his hat, snuffed out the lantern and left the cabin, acknowledging the salute of the sentry at his door as he climbed up the companionway. On deck it was still a starlit night, the air fresh but not yet warm, the crests of the waves picked out as swirling lines of phosphorescence. The men would not expect the inspection and drills to start before half past eight and it would do no harm for those on watch to know that the Captain was on deck freshly shaven at half past three, even before they began to wash the decks.

Aloft the great sails showed as black squares blanking out the stars. On deck there was no movement except for the two men at the wheel, the dim light from the binnacle just showing their features. Near them was the quartermaster, and Ramage knew that lookouts were watching the whole horizon, one at either bow, one at the mainchains on each side, and one on each quarter. He walked aft and as his eyes became accustomed to the darkness he saw that Aitken was the officer of the deck.

The First Lieutenant was pacing up and down the larboard side, leaving the starboard side to Ramage, who decided to take a turn round the ship. He walked forward, careful not to trip over various eyebolts, tackles and coils of rope. That was one thing about a tropical night, it was rarely ever really dark. A figure moved as he reached the mainchains – that would be the lookout stationed there. As the *Juno* surged forward on the long swells her bow wave reached out diagonally in the darkness as far as he could see. Occasionally a flurry of phosphorescence showed a large fish swimming away, or darting after its prey. The lookout on the starboard bow recognized him in the darkness – it was Rossi, the Genoese seaman who had served with him for more than three years.

'Nothing in sight?' Ramage said conversationally.

'Two dolphins playing under the bow, sir. You can see them – look there!'

Through the half port Ramage saw two pale green shapes moving fast through the water, crossing back and forth across the bow, missing the stem by only a few feet.

This was a good opportunity to talk to Rossi about young Paolo. The boy was full of high spirits and anxious to learn seamanship, but there was no way of teaching him properly. The other midshipman, young Benson, had been at sea eighteen months or more and his knowledge of mathematics and navigation was advanced enough for him to work with the Fourth Lieutenant. Paolo still had much plain seamanship to learn before he buckled down to mathematics and navigation. Ramage was determined that the boy should first become a prime seaman, able to knot and splice, lay out on a yard in a gale of wind and furl a sail, serve a gun and handle a boat. In a ship the size of a frigate, there was only one way to give him that kind of training, and that was put to him in the charge of a good seaman.

Rossi was the right man for the job. He and Paolo could talk Italian together and Rossi had the shrewd and pleasant manner that would make it work, as well as being a prime seaman. More important, perhaps, was that to Rossi the Marchesa was almost a goddess. He was one of the dozen or so former Tritons about whom Ramage had to give news whenever he wrote to Gianna.

It took only two or three minutes to describe what he wanted done. With a man like Rossi there was no fear that he would take advantage of the job by seeking extra favours. He was proud to be chosen, he liked the boy, and was confident it would work. Choosing Rossi had yet another advantage: since both he and Paolo were Italian, it would not make the other Tritons jealous. Several of them shared the same feelings for the Marchesa and would have been proud to instruct her nephew.

With Paolo's immediate future settled, Ramage continued his walk round the ship. There was a slight dampness in the air, just enough to soak into the tiny particles of salt in his coat and make it smell musty, as though it had been in a wardrobe all winter. The ship surged under the press of sail, the long and low swell waves picking her up on the forward side of their crests so that she hissed along like a toboggan, then leaving her to pitch gently and subside as the crests passed under her, speeding on to the westward as though trying to catch up with the wind.

James Aitken walked up to the binnacle for the twentieth time during his watch and glanced at the compass. South-west by a quarter west, though he did not expect the men at the wheel to hold the ship to within a quarter point; indeed, nothing annoyed him – or the Captain – as much as men turning the wheel back and forth unnecessarily, since the rudder moving from side to side acted like the brake on the wheel of a cart. Now the ship was well balanced, with the sails trimmed to perfection, and although she wandered off course for a minute as a swell wave lifted her, she usually came back as the crest passed on. The quartermaster noticed his movements and glanced anxiously at the helmsman, and then up at the sails and out to the dogvane on the bulwark, where the corks and feathers on a line streamed from a small staff to give the wind direction.

Aitken would not be sorry when the Third Lieutenant relieved him: today was the famous day when the Captain had promised them an inspection and exercises the like of which they had never seen. Aitken's heart had sunk when he heard the Captain's announcement to the ship's company off the Lizard. He had estimated then that it would take a couple of months to knock the ship's company into shape. Now he thought that there was a fair chance they would get through today without too many disasters.

What had bothered Aitken was the men's attitude when he – and the other officers for that matter – joined the ship. The drunken sot who had previously commanded her had not only let the ship go to pieces – the devil knew what he did with the paint the dockyard supplied, for it certainly had not been applied to the ship, and it was not in the storeroom – but he had let the men go to pieces, too. It took a long time to train a ship's company, but they could go to ruin in a month if they were not kept up to scratch.

It was like a reputation: he remembered his old uncle Willie Aitken, a pillar of the Church in Perth if ever there was one. He had been a widower with a parcel of land, and his fences were always mended so his sheep did not stray: he was a great believer that good fences made for good neighbours. He had a reputation for driving a hard bargain but a fair one, and never a man in Perthshire could say he had ever been slow to pay his bills. But at the age of fifty Uncle Willie had taken up with a housemaid: not one of his own, but a neighbour's, and within a week Uncle Willie's reputation was not worth a handful of sheep's wool hanging on a briar. He had ended the affair within a week, but by the time he went to his grave twenty years later his reputation was only just cleared.

Perthshire seemed ten thousand miles away, and Dunkeld twice as far. As he walked away from the binnacle he thought

56

of his home in the lee of the ruined cathedral at Dunkeld, with the River Tay sparkling and gurgling nearby, bitterly cold and alive with trout. Many a trout he'd tickled as a boy and cooked over a bonfire, and never did fish taste so delicious, even though one side was usually burned to charcoal and the other side raw. It had been a hard life as a boy, since his father had been away at sea for one and two years at a time, and his mother had to rule her family of three boys and three girls with the sternness of a drill sergeant, and there was never enough money. Until he had first gone to sea he had not known what it was to wear clothes specially bought for him: as the youngest son he had always had the clothes which his older brothers had outgrown.

That was something Captain Ramage had never experienced – there was obviously plenty of money in his family – yet you would never think it from the way he behaved. He was not mean but he lived simply and had simple tastes. He always set a good table when he invited any of the officers to join him for dinner, but there was none of the ostentation that Aitken had so often seen in wealthy captains. The patronizing comment about a vintage wine, for instance, knowing that a poor damned lieutenant's only knowledge of wine was probably the 'Black Strap' issued instead of rum when the ship was in the Mediterranean.

Aitken had heard some stories about Captain Ramage's father, too, the Earl of Blazey. Men said that as a captain and as an admiral the nickname of 'Old Blazeaway' was used with pride and affection by everyone who served with him, from the cook's mate to the most senior captain, and that it was a nickname earned not only because of his behaviour in battle but because he commanded ship, squadron or fleet sternly and justly, and woe betide anyone, cook's mate or captain, who did not measure up to his standards.

The son had puzzled Aitken at first. The son of a man who held one of the oldest earldoms in the kingdom and who had been one of the country's most famous admirals could have expected very rapid promotion if he chose the Navy: captain's servant or midshipman in ships whose captains would ensure he had the finest training; appointment as a master's mate the moment he passed his examination for lieutenant and waited until he was twenty, the lowest age he could serve as a lieutenant. And the day after he was twenty he would receive an appointment as lieutenant, and probably in some flagship so that he was readily available the moment a vacancy occurred in one of the ships of the fleet for a more senior lieutenant. By the time he was twenty-three or so, he could reckon to be made post, after having spent a year or two commanding a smaller vessel. He might have the necessary knowledge of ships and men but, Aitken reflected bitterly, it was rare: 'interest' mattered more than seamanship.

That had not happened with Mr Ramage; so much was obvious. He had commanded several ships as a lieutenant but Aitken knew that if 'interest' had been at work he would have been made post at least a couple of years ago, whereas in fact he had been made post only a few days before taking command of the *Juno*.

When the word had reached him from the First Lord's office that he was to be the *Juno*'s new First Lieutenant, Aitken had been delighted: Lord St Vincent had certainly always kept his word that he would look after the son of the master of the first ship he had ever commanded. But as soon as he heard that the *Juno*'s new commanding officer was to be Captain Ramage he had grave doubts. He had heard enough stories to know that he was brave – foolhardy, some had said – and a good seaman, but Aitken had been worried by two things. The first was why he had never used his title, and the second was why he had not been made post earlier. Perhaps his reputation for being a fine seaman was simply talk.

It had taken only a few hours to get the answers: the *Juno* was hardly clear of the Wight before he realized that this young Captain – he guessed they were about the same age – was not only a fine seaman, but a fine *instinctive* seaman, which was quite a different thing. There were few men who really had the feel of a ship, who could make a vessel do what they wanted with the vessel's co-operation. That was the secret; handle the ship like a horse, so you guided it, not fought it. And know the weather. Mr Ramage often said quietly that he thought it was time to furl topsails, or reef, when clouds on the horizon would not have worried Aitken, and sure enough an innocent-looking patch of grey cloud would suddenly turn into a screaming squall that would have ripped the sails from the yards but for the Captain's instinct. Back in Dunkeld, Aitken thought, it would have been called the second sight.

The three lieutenants who had joined the ship at the same time agreed with what Aitken had told them off the Lizard. They had grumbled at the Captain's announcement, and said that what he wanted was impossible and that they needed more time. But Aitken had told them flatly that they were lucky to be serving in the same ship as this Captain – and this Master, for old Southwick had more seamanship in his little finger than most men had in their whole bodies.

Having satisfied himself about his new Captain's seamanship, Aitken had set out to discover, as discreetly as possible, why he was never known in the Service as Lord Ramage. Old Southwick, who had served with him for three or four years, soon gave him the answer: senior officers without titles sometimes became vindictive about junior officers with, and few hostesses knew where to seat titled juniors in relation to their untitled seniors.

Aitken saw now that Lord St Vincent really had been keeping his promise: he had deliberately chosen the *Juno* for him, knowing he would be under Mr Ramage. If the stories he had read in the *Gazette* were authentic, serving with Mr Ramage could bring you honour or it could get your head knocked off by a roundshot. It was not so much that he went looking for trouble but that he seemed to be given tasks that, even reading the dry-as-dust accounts in the *Gazette* afterwards, must have been almost impossible to achieve. He must get singled out for them. Well, whatever the reason, it meant that Mr Ramage was more than likely to have a detached command; orders which would mean that the *Juno* would carry out some special service in the Caribbean and not be attached to Rear-Admiral Davis's command at Barbados. For the whole of Aitken's life at sea so far he had served in ships attached to a particular command, usually working with a fleet in the Channel or Mediterranean ... Dull work, and irritating, too, because any slackness was sure to be spotted by the flagship, and even if whatever drew down the admiral's wrath was not slackness but one of those mishaps that are bound to happen – a rope snagging on a cleat, a seaman slipping on a wet deck, a rips sail ripping from luff to leach – no excuses or explanations were accepted. Indeed, it was a stupid or unsure captain or lieutenant who even bothered to offer one.

Aitken thought about the coming day and took off his hat to wipe his brow. Mr Ramage was walking round the deck now, and he tried to think of the manoeuvres the Captain was likely to order him to perform in that quiet voice of his. All the usual sail-handling he knew the men would perform well – better than he could have hoped even a week ago. But from the talk he had heard, from the stories that Southwick had told him of past operations, Mr Ramage had a reputation for doing the unexpected. Admittedly Southwick's stories had all been about doing unexpected things against the French and Spanish, but any captain wanting to test his ship's company was likely to order something unexpected too . . .

The truly remarkable thing, for which Aitken was thankful, was the change that was coming in the men's attitude. Efficient ships were always happy ships with firm but just captains; men like Captain Herbert Duff, with whom Aitken had once served. Captain Duff had insisted that all his officers had at least one pair of silk stockings – to be worn when going into action. When he heard that the Fourth Lieutenant could not afford a pair, Captain Duff had passed along a new pair as a gift. Silk stockings were not just some quirk on Captain Duff's part; the old Scot had explained in his dry Aberdeen accent that silk made it easier for the surgeon: a leg wound while wearing woollen stockings usually meant that scraps of wool were driven into the wound and often led to gangrene, while silk never did. Aitken shrugged his shoulders at the memory: poor old Captain Duff had been cut in half by a 24-pounder shot that went on to lodge in the mizenmast . . .

Suddenly he realized a figure was standing next to him and the familiar quiet voice said: 'There's a bad fire in the Master's cabin, Aitken . . . a good start to a Monday morning eh?'

It took the young Scot a few moments to switch his mind from Captain Duff's death to the realization that Captain Ramage's promised day had begun early. As he began shouting the sequence of orders that set the calls of the bos'n's mates shrilling he tried to remember everything written in the Captain's Orders under the heading of 'Fire'. They had practised it twice, off Ushant and again off Madeira, and Aitken's mind became a blank as men began running across the deck in the darkness, swarming up from below. But he knew another minute of this and there would be complete confusion unless he began giving specific orders – and there was Mr Ramage standing by the binnacle, the watch in his hand illuminated by the binnacle light.

Aitken snatched at the speaking trumpet beside the binnacle box and began shouting, his broad Scots accent emphasized by the excitement and the trumpet: 'Boarders, engine and firemen to the quarterdeck; look alive there!' He paused a moment and then ordered: 'Boarders to starboard; firemen with you, buckets to larboard!'

Ah, at last the Marines had woken up: there was the Marine officer – puffing and blowing, he was much too fat – and making for the poop, where they were to stand under arms. Now Baker, the Third Lieutenant, was waiting beside him, still in his nightshirt with breeches dragged on and his hat jammed askew on his head. And there's a thing, Aitken reflected crossly: the Captain's Orders said the First and Third Lieutenant were to go wherever the fire was and direct operations there, with the Captain taking the conn. But Captain Ramage was just standing by the binnacle and at that moment he turned, as if reading the First Lieutenant's thoughts, and said: 'Regard me as dead in the fire, Mr Aitken . . .'

Aitken turned to Baker: 'Find Mr Southwick and go with him to the seat of the fire. It's in his cabin so maybe he's there already. Tell him I'm staying here at the conn. Hurry, man!' He thought a moment and called hurriedly: 'Tell him the Captain died in the fire and I am in command!'

All the other officers and warrant officers should have gone to their proper stations – but had they studied and remembered the Captain's Orders? He weighed up the risk of giving too many orders against the danger of men wandering around having forgotten what they were supposed to be doing, and jammed the speaking trumpet to his mouth.

'Gunner to the magazine . . . Bos'n and carpenter to their store rooms . . . Master-at-arms to examine the tiers and then report to me here . . . Carpenter's mates with their mauls and axes to the larboard gangway . . .'

What had he forgotten? Where the devil was Wagstaffe, the Second Lieutenant? – he and the Fourth Lieutenant, Lacey, were in charge of the pumps and hoses. He saw the two midshipmen waiting behind him, ready to run errands. He thought for a moment and chose Orsini. 'Run and find Mr Wagstaffe. Ask him how soon the pumps will be ready and whether he has the hoses led down to the Master's cabin yet, and report back to me.'

The boy hurried off and Aitken saw the Captain bend slightly so he could see the face of his watch by the binnacle light. Or was he looking at the compass?

'How are you heading?' Aitken snapped at the quartermaster. As soon as he knew they were still on course he took a quick glance astern to make sure no squalls were sneaking up in their wake and gestured at the other midshipman.

'Benson, find the Surgeon and tell him to report to me here.'

Even before the boy had time to point the First Lieutenant heard Bowen behind him saying gently: 'I did report, Mr Aitken, but you probably did not hear me.'

'Very well,' Aitken said, and realized it was time he had a report from where the fire was supposed to be: he did not want some over-eager idiots chopping away at bulkheads. 'Benson, get down to the Master's cabin and ask the Third Lieutenant for an immediate report!'

The whole business was a disaster; that was the only thing that Aitken was sure about. A good ten minutes must have elapsed since Mr Ramage appeared alongside him in the darkness and a real fire in the Master's cabin would probably have reached the magazine by now, since it was just below, and blown the ship to pieces.

At least the engine was now in place; he could see that much. Head pumps were rigged over the side and hoses were being led across the deck like long twisting snakes. Kinks in them, no doubt; there always were. He glanced aft – there were the Marines lined up with the Lieutenant in front of them. Well, even if he was a fat fellow no one could fault his efficiency.

The head pumps! Damnation, they were rigged over the side: there was not a faint hope their hoses would suck at the speed the ship was going: they should have been led below to the cistern – and had the carpenter started to let water into the cistern ready for the head pumps to pump it up to the tank on the engine? Did Mr Ramage want him to flood the cistern or – he was about to walk over and ask him when he remembered the quiet 'Regard me as dead in the fire . . .'

He looked round hurriedly for a reliable messenger and saw Orsini scurrying towards him. The boy saluted and said excitedly: 'Mr Wagstaffe says the pumps are ready, sir, but Mr Southwick's compliments, sir, and he says the fire is out!'

Aitken managed to stifle a sigh of relief: obviously the Captain had given the Master instructions earlier. He saw the Captain looking at his watch and then waving for him to come to the binnacle. At that moment a horrified Aitken saw the two helmsmen spinning the wheel, bringing the ship round to starboard and up into the wind: already the fluttering of the sails was turning into thundering claps and as the First Lieutenant turned to shout at the two men, Ramage said, his voice loud to make himself heard and holding on to the binnacle box as the ship began to roll: 'The tiller ropes seem to have parted, Mr Aitken . . . I'll take the conn.'

By dawn Aitken and the rest of the ship's company were exhausted. One party had no sooner clapped emergency tackles to the tiller as topmen furled the topsail and the great mainsail and foresail were trimmed to get the strain off the rudder, allowing Aitken to report to the Captain that the ship was under control again, than Ramage had ordered the ship to be hove-to, using the tiller tackles, and a cutter hoisted out to starboard, rowed round the ship carrying ten Marines, and recovered on the larboard side.

When that had been done – with the decks still strewn with hoses and the engine sitting by the mainmast, well lashed down and its handles resting like a seesaw – Ramage had told the Second Lieutenant to take the conn. Aitken relaxed and was thankful that while they had been working on the tiller tackles he had remembered to make sure the lookouts were sent aloft just before dawn. He watched Ramage walking forward to the companionway and envied him: no doubt his steward would soon bring him a cup of hot tea.

But at the top of the companionway Ramage paused, looked ahead and turned suddenly to the Second Lieutenant. 'Mr Wagstaffe – I see breakers ahead. Your masts have gone by the board, so you'll have to anchor.' With that he disappeared down the companionway.

Wagstaffe stared helplessly at Aitken. Since they were in the middle of the Atlantic, more than a thousand miles from land in any direction, they were nowhere near ready: the anchors were secured with preventer stoppers, the cables were ranged below, bucklers closed off the hawse-holes so that seas did not sweep through them and flood into the ship.

Aitken paused a moment. It was obvious that the Captain intended that Wagstaffe should carry out the first moves to deal with this particular emergency. He shrugged his shoulders and said: 'You are the officer of the deck; we'll be on the rocks in a few minutes unless you do something!'

The moment Wagstaffe recovered from his surprise, like Aitken before him at the fire alarm, he seized a speaking trumpet and began bellowing orders. The First Lieutenant was about to take over – the normal procedure once the officer of the deck had discovered the emergency and given the preliminary orders – when Orsini came scurrying up from below. The Captain was to be informed, he told Aitken, the moment they were ready to anchor.

The next ten minutes, as far as Aitken was concerned, had been chaos or, at best, partly-controlled confusion: seamen working in almost complete darkness in the tier had wrestled with the cable, which was seventeen inches in circumference and 720 feet long, stiff and heavy – it weighed nearly four tons. The buckler closing the hawse had been removed so the end of the cable could be led out and round the bow and secured to an anchor and finally, hours later it seemed, Aitken was able to hurry below to report all was ready.

He found Ramage sitting at his desk, a pile of papers in front of him. The First Lieutenant recognized them – the routine reports that would have to be ready for the Admiral when the *Juno* arrived in Barbados: muster tables giving details of every man in the ship's company, slop book showing what each had bought from shirts to tobacco, sick book, returns from the bos'n, gunner and carpenter concerning their stores . . .

Ramage glanced at his watch as Aitken began his report and scribbled the time on a piece of paper, commenting sourly: 'I'm glad they weren't real breakers.'

'I'm sorry, sir,' Aitken said miserably, 'but it was an unexpected – er, evolution.'

'Quite, but it's the unexpected that sinks ships,' Ramage said, his voice neutral. 'Very well, carry on: unbend the cable and ship the buckler – and you'd better get the decks cleared. The ship looks as though the men from the Westminster Fire Office have been fighting a burning street.'

Aitken went back to the quarterdeck with mixed emotions: resentment, annoyance at his own shortcomings, anxiety over what was to come . . . It was still only half past six and on a normal morning the ship's company would by now have washed the decks, polished the brightwork, spread the awnings, and be waiting for the order to lash up and stow hammocks. Instead they had gone through a complete fire drill in the darkness, rigged emergency steering, and prepared to anchor. And all the Captain said was: 'You'd better get the deck cleared,' and made a sarcastic remark about one of the fire insurance companies. Of course the hoses were still all over the deck and the tackles were still rove in the tiller flat, although unhooked now and snaking all over the ward room. How the new rope in those damned blocks had twisted and kinked. That was one lesson he had learned – never use new rope in purchases for emergency steering: the men had to use handspikes to untwist them.

As he stopped by the binnacle he thought again of the Captain's words: 'It's the unexpected that sinks ships.' He had to admit there was some truth in it: those twisted purchases had wasted valuable minutes; in fact in heavy weather the ship would have been broached half a dozen times before they'd cleared them, and one bad broach could have left the *Juno* dismasted. And the mistake he'd made with the head pump hoses, and the delay in filling the cistern: by the time the engine was ready, flames would have reached the magazine. At least there had been no actual mistakes in preparing to anchor. Yet he had to admit that the risk of fire was present every moment of the day and night; it was the one thing that, with half a ton of powder in the magazine, could in half a minute transform the *Juno* into scraps of floating timber. And tiller ropes parting – that could happen unexpectedly. He could not seriously dispute that there were twenty hundredweights in the ton of truth that the Captain had just spoken: you had to keep a sharp lookout for the unexpected.

He realized that Wagstaffe was standing in front of him. 'Did the Captain say anything?' the Second Lieutenant asked nervously, keeping his voice low.

Aitken nodded warningly towards the skylight over the cabin. 'Clear away the hoses, pumps and engines, get the tackles cleared away in the tiller flat, then carry on as usual.' As he walked aft to the taffrail he wanted to add, beware of the unexpected, there's a whole day of unexpectedness ahead of us yet.

He looked astern, watching the *Juno's* swirling wake and, on the distant eastern horizon, a long low bank of cloud behind which the sun had risen but was not yet visible. The band of cloud looked hard and menacing, as though bringing a gale of wind that would last a week, but Aitken knew from experience that it was a trick of the Tropics; once the sun had some heat in it the cloud would melt away, leaving a clear sky. Then, slowly and steadily, the Trade wind clouds would form up like balls of white wool rolling westward in orderly lines, and the decks would get hotter as the sun rose higher and higher.

Then suddenly he understood completely what the Captain was doing. That last remark was not just a casual comment intended to spur on the ship's First Lieutenant. Everyone on board, except perhaps Southwick, had expected today's exercises to comprise sail handling and gunnery, rounded off with a thorough inspection of the ship's paint and brightwork. Now he realized that the Captain already knew how good (or bad) the men were at reefing and furling – he saw them doing it all the time. He already knew, from his regular Sunday morning inspection, the condition of the paintwork below. The Captain had known all along what Aitken had only just recognized – the real efficiency of a ship's company was not shown by the speed at which sails and guns were handled; it was the way they dealt with a completely unexpected situation that mattered. In fact, whether sailing the ship in a tropical breeze or taking her into action against the enemy, it was *all* that mattered. By the showing so far, Aitken reflected ruefully, the Captain must be bitterly disappointed.

He heard the bos'n's mates piping through the ship, following the shrill notes with dire threats to anyone who did not hurry to lash up his hammock. On a morning like this, woe betide any man who lashed up his hammock so carelessly that the long sausage of canvas was too fat to pass through the special measuring hoop.

The top edge of the clouds to the east were now lined with gold. Muster and stow hammocks . . . clean arms . . . the watch on deck to coil ropes and spread awnings while the watch below cleaned the lower deck . . . then, promptly at eight o'clock, breakfast. And after that, what had the Captain in store for them?

After breakfast, Ramage had given the order to beat to quarters and the boy drummer, excited by the occasion, had handled his drumsticks with all the flourish of the conductor of an orchestra. The gunner collected the bronze key to the magazine and disappeared below, head pumps were rigged and water squirted over the decks ahead of men sprinkling sand. Gun captains collected the locks for their guns, priming wires, trigger lines, boxes of quill tubes and flasks of priming powder. Tackles were overhauled, guns run in, and handspikes, rammers and sponges unlashed. Small tubs were put between the guns, ready to soak the sponges: other tubs with notches cut at intervals round the top were placed nearby and short lengths of slow matches, in effect slow-burning fuses, were tucked in the notches, the glowing ends hanging down safely over the water but ready for instant use should the flint in a lock fail to make a spark.

As soon as the men were standing by the guns ready for the order to load, and with Southwick at the conn and each of the four lieutenants standing by his division, Ramage sent for the gunner.

Johnson came up from the magazine with the big key in his hand as proof that he had left the door locked. He was a tiny man with iron-grey hair and although the skin of his face was wrinkled as an old leather boot he usually wore a cheerful expression. Now, as he reported to the Captain, he looked worried: he had seen what had already happened this morning and dreaded to think what surprises were in store for his little kingdom of guns, powder and shot, ranges and trajectories, flintlocks and slow match.

'We'll inspect the guns, Johnson,' Ramage announced, and led the way. At the first gun he pointed to two of the gun's crew. 'You two stand fast and the rest of you go and stand by on the fo'c'sle.' He did the same at the next gun and repeated it until only two men stood by each of the frigate's twenty-six maindeck guns, the rest of the men now crowded on the fo'c'sle. Then he led the way back to the quarterdeck, passing the word for the First Lieutenant and followed by a puzzled Johnson, who kept looking at the men grouped forward and shaking his head.

As soon as Aitken joined them Ramage said: 'We are in battle, we've suffered heavy casualties, and the men at the maindeck guns are all you have left – forget the 6-pounders. When I give the word, you'll fire two broadsides to larboard and two to starboard.'

'But sir,' the gunner protested, 'two men can't run out a gun, it's much too heavy!'

'Tell that to the French, Mr Johnson,' Ramage said grimly. 'Imagine that we are trapped, running between two enemy ships, and our only chance of surviving is keeping up as rapid a rate of fire as possible.'

'But sir –' Johnson broke off as he saw Ramage rubbing the scar over his brow, and then taking out his watch. The First Lieutenant gestured to the gunner to follow him and hurried down to the maindeck taking Orsini with them.

Southwick walked over to Ramage and grinned, removing his hat and running his fingers through his flowing white hair. 'It's been quite like old times so far today, sir,' he commented.

Ramage nodded. 'Except that we learned all these things the hard way!'

'Aye, and I'm beginning to wonder if that gunner has ever been in action before. He seems a conscientious man, but 'twould seem to me he lacks experience.'

'He's been in action half a dozen times, but only a few casualties,' Ramage said. 'That's – '

He broke off as Orsini hurried up, saluted and reported that they were ready to open fire.

'My compliments to Mr Aitken,' Ramage told him, 'and tell him to open fire when he is ready.'

Ramage was curious to know what Aitken and the gunner had contrived, but he had decided right from the start that today he would be an onlooker; an observer with a watch in his hand. Later this afternoon he would have a word with the ship's company, and then the officers would be invited down to his cabin while Southwick acted as officer of the deck. He would hold an inquest on what did happen and what should have happened, and in front of him would be the sheet of paper with times written on –

There was a shout from forward and several guns on each side fired, the sharp explosions followed a moment later by the heavy rumbling of the trucks rolling across the decks as the guns flung back in recoil. Ramage saw that alternate guns had fired: the remainder were still run out.

The spurts of smoke merged into oily yellow clouds drifting forward in the following wind and some of it, swirling across the group of men on the fo'c'sle, set many of them coughing. Ramage glanced at his watch and waited as men hurriedly sponged them and began to reload. Then the remaining thirteen guns fired and Ramage, stifling a sigh of relief, glanced across at Southwick, who was nodding his approval.

Aitken and Johnson had done the right thing. They had obviously had all the guns loaded – two men at each gun could manage that. Then two men from alternate guns had helped the two at the next to run out and fire – that accounted for half the broadside on each side. Each four men had then run out the remaining guns, which had fired the second half of the broadsides.

So far, so good: the real test was how long it would take two men to reload each gun and then repeat the whole performance. But the important thing, Ramage knew, was that Aitken and Johnson, faced with two choices, had picked the right one. They could have run all the guns out and fired a full broadside, or they could divide them. Either way was effective but Ramage had a particular reason for preferring the divided broadsides. A ship firing full broadsides but at long intervals revealed to the enemy that heavy casualties had slowed her rate of fire. However, dividing the broadsides meant that at least some guns were firing frequently – and making a lot of smoke which would certainly obscure all the gun ports and probably conceal from an excited enemy that the real rate of fire was very slow. In battle it might prove decisive: at a critical moment for the *Juno* the enemy might sheer off, convinced they were doing no good. It will be interesting to hear the explanation of Aitken's choice, Ramage thought; it is easy enough to do the right thing for the wrong reason . . .

Ten minutes later the guns had been sponged out and secured, the magazine locked, rammers and sponges lashed, tubs emptied and stowed and men were busy washing away the sand which had already dried on the deck from the hot sun. Ramage thought of the other orders which he could give to test the ship's effectiveness in battle – rigging out boarding nets, hoisting grapnels to the yardarms ready to run alongside an enemy ship and hook them in the rigging so they could board, making the men shift guns from one position to another – but he was satisfied. The men were working with a will and the officers were wide awake. Later there would be extra questions for the officers, and he already knew what they would be.

Finally the *Juno*'s decks were clean, the brasswork shone, ropes were coiled neatly, leather buckets were back on their hooks. The time had come to begin his inspection, accompanied by Aitken and Southwick, with young Benson following, armed with a pencil and notebook ready to write down any faults that Ramage might find. It took two hours, and by the time he had finished Ramage was hot and weary: below decks the heat was stifling, even though ventilators and wind sails were rigged. The ship was making six knots but the Trade winds were blowing at a little more than fifteen, giving a breeze of only nine knots across the deck: not enough to make a decent cooling draught through the ship.

Ramage had to admit that the general condition of the *Juno* was a credit to Aitken, even if not to the Portsmouth Dockyard. Paint bubbles on beams and planking had set Ramage digging with a knife that revealed patches of rot; many beams and some futtocks should have been doubled before the ship left Spithead for the West Indies. Benson scribbled hastily as Ramage made his comments, and Aitken had been shamefaced at some of them. Most of the axes stowed ready for wreck-clearing or any other emergency were not only blunt but had their blades pitted and scarred where at some time or other they had bitten into metal. More than half the tomahawks and cutlasses which would be wielded by a boarding party would not, as Ramage had commented acidly, have cut into a ripe paw-paw, and while the heads of boarding pikes were neatly black-enamelled most were so blunt they would hardly drive through a rip sail, let alone a thick-skinned Frenchman.

Finally, back on the quarterdeck, Ramage had taken Benson's notebook, glanced at it and given it back to the boy. 'Can you read your own writing?' he asked incredulously, and when the midshipman, his face crimson, said he could, Ramage ordered him to go down to the midshipmen's berth and make a fair copy.

The First Lieutenant waited anxiously, wondering what orders would follow. Ramage looked at his watch. 'Well, carry on, Mr Aitken. It's half-past eleven – clear decks and up spirits, and make sure the men get their dinner promptly at noon: I don't doubt but they have a good appetite.'

'And this afternoon, sir?' Aitken asked timidly.

Ramage laughed drily. 'We'll let Mr Southwick write in his log, "Ship's company employed A.T.S.R.",' he said referring to the time-honoured abbreviation for 'As the service required'. Then he added: 'I want to hear that grindstone at work: axes, tomahawks, pikes and cutlasses. Check them all. And have Mr Johnson check every musket and pistol . . .'

CHAPTER FOUR

Ramage was sitting at his desk, trying to finish all the forms the Rear-Admiral would require when they arrived in Barbados, when Southwick came down with the noon position written on a piece of paper. He pointed to the longitude. 'We're making our westing. If this wind holds, we should make a fast passage.'

Ramage glanced at the figures as he gestured to the Master to sit down. The old man put his hat on the cabin sole and wriggled himself comfortable, a movement that Ramage knew from long experience meant he wanted to have a serious talk about something.

Ramage looked at him quizzically. 'How do you think our

"Monday morning" went?'

'Better than I expected, sir,' Southwick said frankly. 'A lot better than I thought possible when we dropped the Lizard astern.'

'You and Aitken have worked hard,' Ramage said.

Southwick shook his head. ''Twasn't Aitken and 'twasn't me, sir. The credit is yours.'

'Mine?' Ramage was obviously startled.

'Yours and those dozen scalawags of ours. I must admit I never appreciated them fully when we were in the *Triton* but they turned the trick here. What with you wielding the stick and carrot from the quarterdeck and those fellows sermonizing on the lower deck like some of Mr Wesley's preachers, the ship's company – well, they're a deal different from the crowd I first clapped eyes on when I boarded at Spithead!'

Ramage rubbed his jaw reflectively. 'Well, all that's past now. I wonder what the Admiral has in store for us at Barbados.'

'Convoy work,' Southwick said gloomily, 'I can feel it in my bones. Taking a dozen merchantmen from Barbados to Grenada and waiting a week while they drum up business, and then take the mules on to St Vincent and St Lucia, and the same there, and an even more infuriating sail up to Antigua with them dropping astern at night and French privateers scurrying out of Martinique to snap 'em up. Mules,' he repeated crossly, 'there isn't a master of a merchant ship that isn't a mule!'

'It may not be as bad as all that,' Ramage said mildly. There was no harm in confiding in the Master. In many ways theirs was a strange relationship; one which had begun years earlier in the Mediterranean when Ramage took over his first command, the *Kathleen* cutter. He had been given her, he imagined, because Commodore Nelson had taken a liking to him. He had been lucky, as a very green lieutenant with his first command, that Southwick arrived as the *Kathleen*'s master. Southwick was old enough to be his father and was probably one of the finest seamen in the Navy. He could handle the toughest ship's company, treating them like a benevolent father or the Devil's drill sergeant, as the occasion required. Apart from his skill as a Master, though, what had endeared him to Ramage was the way the old man, without ever once overstepping the invisible line separating the captain of the ship from the master (who was only a warrant, not a commission officer), had never let him make a mistake. At times there had been an almost imperceptible shake of the head, at others a cough, occasionally one of the famous sniffs. More important perhaps, was the knowledge that the old Master was on board, a cyclopaedia of knowledge, always at hand, and whom Ramage had never seen ruffled, whether at the prospect of having the tiny cutter rammed by a Spanish line-of-battleship – for that was how the *Kathleen* had been lost – or by a hurricane, which had sent the *Triton* brig's masts by the board.

'I'm carrying orders from the First Lord to Rear-Admiral Davis for some special operation,' he said.

'I guessed as much,' Southwick said. 'But is the *Juno* named in them?'

Ramage shook his head. 'I don't think so. When His Lordship gave me my orders, they were simply "to make the best of my way" ' – he parroted the traditional phrase – 'to Barbados, place myself under Admiral Davis's command, and deliver the usual budget of papers. His Lordship did just mention that there was a special operation forthcoming . . .'

'Aye, but if he didn't name the *Juno* then it won't be for us, sir,' Southwick's voice was even gloomier. 'The Admiral has probably asked for more frigates – admirals never do have enough o' them. His Lordship decided to give you the *Juno*, since you've just been made post, and send her out to Admiral Davis. If there's any special operation you can be sure the Admiral has his favourites; he won't give plums to a stranger – you don't know him, do you, sir?'

Ramage shook his head. Southwick was right and only echoed his own opinion. The *Juno* was just another frigate bringing out orders and mail for the Windward and Leeward Islands station; it would be convoy work through the islands. The favoured few captains would be away patrolling the areas off the Spanish Main where there was a chance of finding enemy ships and taking prizes; those out of favour would be with the convoys. An admiral could make a young frigate captain rich in this way (and himself, too, since he shared in the prize money), and one could not blame him if he favoured the captains who had served with him a long time.

That was one of the advantages of becoming an admiral and commanding a station like Jamaica or the Windwards: in time you could promote the young lieutenants you liked or trusted. The simple reason was that the West Indies was an unhealthy spot. A frigate's first lieutenant died of yellow fever – whereupon the admiral promoted the third lieutenant of his flagship and sent him over. A captain died and the admiral exercised his privilege of making a lieutenant post in the dead man's place – often the first lieutenant of his flagship – knowing that the Admiralty would confirm the appointment.

A favoured young junior officer, a fourth lieutenant, say, coming out to the West Indies in an Admiral's flagship would be very unlucky if he was not the captain of a frigate by the time the admiral was replaced two or three years later. He would need only average luck to make several hundred pounds in prize money, and Ramage could think of half a dozen young captains who had served under Sir Hyde Parker at Jamaica (though Sir Hyde was among the more notorious admirals who played the game of favourites) whose frigates had never escorted a convoy; they had spent their time patrolling, cruising – call it what you will, it meant searching for the enemy, which in turn meant prize money. And each of those captains now had several thousand pounds safely in the Funds, apart from the early promotion which meant that their names were high on the Navy List.

So far as Rear-Admiral Davis was concerned, Captain Ramage and the *Juno* would be another junior captain and another frigate. Perhaps that was what Lord St Vincent had intended in giving him the command. Certainly he had had his share of excitement in the past few years, enough of his dispatches published in the *Gazette*, and he was probably being unreasonable in expecting it to continue. Perhaps, he thought wryly, His Lordship intended Captain Ramage to settle down a bit . . .

'Is all your paperwork ready for the Admiral?' he asked Southwick.

'Nearly, sir. I'll have it ready by tomorrow.'

'You'd better check up on the gunner, carpenter and bos'n.'

Southwick picked up his hat. 'I'll do that now; they can fill in their forms while you are seeing the lieutenants.' He paused and scratched his head. 'I – er, well, I was quite impressed this morning, sir; I don't think we have much to worry about, whether it is convoys or hurricanes.'

Ramage grinned and the Master left the cabin. It was typical of the old man's sense of fairness and concern for the ship that he put in a good word for the four young officers who were, technically, his superiors – though it would be a very unwise junior lieutenant that ran foul of a master, and most first lieutenants trod delicately.

Late that night, as he filled in his Journal, Ramage reviewed the day. He had deliberately made no comment to the lieutenants, so that when he mustered the men aft just before sunset they had no idea of their Captain's verdict on the morning's activities. From the looks on all their faces and the shuffling, they had obviously condemned themselves – that much was very clear. Gathered round the scuttlebutt getting their mugs of water, under the watchful eye of a Marine sentry, sweeping the decks in pairs, stitching an old awning – clearly they had talked among themselves and decided that the morning had been a disaster; that the Captain had mustered them aft simply to tell them that the rest of the voyage to Barbados was going to be a prolonged punishment.

Hard put to it to keep a straight face, Ramage had clasped his hands behind his back, scowled, and walked along the ranks of the men, looking them up and down. Half of them looked as though they were about to jump over the side, preferring to take their chance with Neptune and the sharks. Despite the harrowing morning, the men were neatly turned out: queues had been re-tied, hats were worn square, shirts tugged hard to hide creases.

He had then walked back to stand aft, facing them, and told them quite bluntly they had all done well; far better than he had expected when he had mustered them aft off the Lizard. That had produced smiles, and his comment that he no longer despaired of eventually making seamen of them had put a delighted grin under every hat. And he had everyone's attention when he pointed out that although what they had done this morning had been exercises, the time might come any day or night when they would be doing it to save their lives.

So with the men going off to their supper chattering cheerfully and obviously vastly relieved, he had then had Aitken, Wagstaffe, Baker and Lacey down to the great cabin for the inquest. They had arrived as nervous as poachers hauled before the magistrate, and Ramage called his steward to fetch glasses. He had talked to them about nothing in particular for fifteen or twenty minutes as they sipped their sherry. All four had waited to see what Ramage would drink, and promptly followed suit, the only difference being that they failed to notice that Ramage did not touch his drink. Only Southwick and Bowen knew that Ramage never drank anything at sea.

Finally Aitken had made a weak joke about Monday mornings, and Ramage had laughed more heartily than the quality of the joke warranted, and made a joke himself. Slowly the four youngsters relaxed slightly. Ramage was startled to find himself regarding them as youngsters, although Aitken was his own age, Wagstaffe and Baker a year younger and only Lacey really qualified, being just twenty-one years old.

They were four completely different types of men. Aitken was tall with auburn hair and a thin, almost gaunt face. His skin would never tan; already his face was burned red by the sun and his nose was peeling. He spoke quietly with a calm Highland burr, his grey eyes missing nothing. Wagstaffe, a Londoner, was short and stocky with large brown eyes that gave his face a deceptively innocent expression. He spoke briskly, thought quickly and, like Aitken, was respected by the ship's company. Baker came from Bungay, in Suffolk, and had the East Anglian quietness that could be mistaken for slyness. The smallest of the four lieutenants, he moved with the smoothness of a cat, as though sent on board the *Juno* as a deliberate contrast to Lacey, who was thin and loose-limbed and once provoked the comment from Southwick that he looked as if each of his joints could be tightened up another half turn. He too was quietly spoken, and there was no mistaking that he hailed from Somerset.

Although Ramage sat on the settee with Aitken at the other end and the other three grouped round in comfortable chairs, their eyes kept straying to the desk, where a glass weight held down a piece of paper. Aitken must have told them that on it were written the times of the morning's evolutions.

Although they had relaxed slightly as they sipped their sherries, they were still too tense, as if they knew that the ship's magazine was below them and were afraid the Captain might explode it. Finally Ramage guessed that any further attempt to ease the tension was a waste of time and, as far as the lieutenants were concerned, probably only prolonged the agony.

So he had commented in a conversational tone on the morning's times and then asked Wagstaffe the first question. The Second Lieutenant had carefully put down his glass – Ramage thought for a moment he was trying to gain time, then saw that he wanted to have his hands free to gesture. The question had been totally unexpected and Ramage noticed the other three furrow their brows, obviously trying to think what they might be asked. Wagstaffe had done well, and so had Baker. Lacey knew the answer to the question but was almost too nervous to give it. And Aitken had not been deceived that

Ramage had reached the Fourth Lieutenant without asking the First Lieutenant a question.

When Ramage had asked him to explain what mistakes if any the others made, Aitken had described them with the coolness and fairness of a judge summing up before a jury. On several points Ramage interrupted only to point out that there were often two or three different ways of doing things, and at the end Aitken made a point that Ramage had borne in mind from the start – that actually faced with, for example, a bowsprit and jibboom torn away, it was easier to remember everything that had to be done because you could see it, whereas sitting in the great cabin you could only imagine it. Ramage had agreed – and then pointed out that each and every one of the operations they had been discussing might have to be carried out on a pitch-dark night, probably with a gale blowing off a lee shore, since only bad weather or battle damage were likely to cause the mishaps . . .

But he was satisfied with their answers and told them so, and as he bade them goodnight he had repeated the phrase he had used to Aitken earlier: 'It's the unexpected that sinks ships.' From the look on their faces he guessed that the First Lieutenant had already quoted it, probably with some embellishments of his own.

So now, Ramage told himself as he shut the Journal and put it away in a drawer, the *Juno* was as prepared as he could make her for anything that Admiral Davis or the French had in store. It would probably be convoy work, but despite Southwick's gloomy attitude, it could provide some excitement. The Windward Islands at the southern end of the chain were effectively split from the Leeward Islands to the north by the French in Martinique and Guadeloupe. At Martinique the harbour of Fort Royal – anchorage rather, since Fort Royal itself was on one side of an enormous, wedge-shaped bay – was large enough for a whole fleet, with plenty of room for them to swing. Guadeloupe, shaped like a ragged butterfly pinned to a board, was one of those islands with dozens of small bays protected by reefs, and designed by a spiteful Nature as a perfect haven for privateers.

For a minute or two he listened to the seas hissing past the *Juno*'s hull as the rudder pintles grumbled in the gudgeons. Although he had been up long before dawn he did not feel sleepy. With the *Juno* making some two hundred miles a day, they would soon be in Barbados, anchoring under the watchful eye of the Admiral. There was little at the moment to raise his wrath: not one man on the sick list, thanks to Bowen, who must be one of the finest surgeons in the Service; not one man killed or injured in an accident; not one sail blown out, though that was due more to the eagle eye of Southwick, who saw to it that sails were sent down for repairs in good time: most of the sails in the *Juno*'s outfit were as ripe as pears, the canvas so old that the sailmaker swore incessantly as he tried to make stitches hold when sewing in new cloths or cringles.

If the Admiral wanted to time the ship's company he would find they could make sail, reef and furl as fast and as well as any frigate Ramage could remember. The only thing that could spoil it all would be for him to make a mistake while bringing the *Juno* into Carlisle Bay at Barbados or have a gun misfire when firing the salute, throwing out the timing. Or for the cable to kink while running through the hawse so the anchor touched the bottom a couple of minutes late, putting the ship a hundred yards or so away from where she should have anchored and perhaps letting her drift into another ship – the flagship, for instance.

Ramage tugged his ear thoughtfully. Many a new ship joining an admiral had through some small mistake given her captain a poor reputation with the admiral that he never lived down. An anchor buoy rope too short for the depth of water, so that with the anchor down the buoy was submerged; some delay in hoisting out a boat: some trifling form not filled in and delivered to the admiral . . . There was also, Ramage remembered with a grin, the case of the captain who brought his ship in with a great flourish and began firing the salute without the gunner having made sure the guns were un-shotted: the first gun of the salute had put a roundshot through the governor's stables, though fortunately without killing grooms or horses.

He picked up his hat and went up the companionway, acknowledging the Marine sentry's salute. It was a glorious tropical night with more stars than seemed believable. Orion's Belt, Sirius like a glinting diamond, the Milky Way wider, longer and much more distinct than in northern latitudes, and the Pole Star very low on the starboard beam, a bare twelve degrees above the horizon and the navigator's friend. In the northern hemisphere the number of degrees the Pole Star was above the horizon throughout the night was your latitude: they would soon be in twelve degrees of latitude, running their westing down to arrive at Barbados, which was also in twelve degrees, and the Pole Star would be a dozen degrees above the horizon, having dipped a little every night from the fifty degrees of the English Channel. Being sure of your longitude, though, was a different matter . . .

These nights before reaching Barbados were always the best part of a voyage to the West Indies: you remembered all the good things of the Caribbean, and forgot the bad – the whining mosquitoes that destroyed sleep, the wretched and almost invisible sand flies at dawn and sunset which attacked you as though armed with red-hot needles, the sweltering heat and humidity, the appalling sickness . . .

The West Indies: from the time he was a young midshipman who would not need a razor for another year or so, the words had fascinated him. In later years he had come to know them well, from the cliffs and mountains and thick green rain forests of the southern islands of the Windwards like Grenada, St Vincent and St Lucia, to the flatter Antigua of the Leewards, drier and almost arid in parts, from the smoothly rounded high hills – one could hardly call them mountains, and they always reminded him of Tuscany – of the Virgin Islands to the green lushness and mountains of Hispaniola and Jamaica.

The clear blue waters where you could often see the bottom at fifty feet, watching barracuda dart like silver daggers into a shoal of small fish, and the slower, grey shapes of sharks swimming smoothly, looking and waiting. And seeing the Spanish mackerel suddenly leap out of the water like a silver arrow in an arc a dozen feet high to land ten yards away in the midst of a swarm of silversides. The pelicans, outrageous looking birds and gawky when you watched them perched on a broken mangrove stump, holding out their wings like scarecrows, drying their feathers, but masters of the air when you saw them gliding along with wingtips an inch or two above the water, or searching higher in a strong wind, and suddenly diving vertically into the water, to fill the sack of skin under their long beak with fish. And the tiny laughing gulls harrying the good-natured pelicans, following them as they dived and as soon as they surfaced perching on their heads or backs, waiting eagerly to snatch any small fish that might escape from the pelican's beak. The black frigate birds, true scavengers of the sea, long forked tails and thin wings like enormously overgrown swallows, but without the swallow's beauty – indeed, they were menacing-looking birds, all black except for some with white breasts. The frigate bird would often hover high over some headland for an hour at a time, a black speck seemingly motionless, and then swoop and pick up some piece of garbage, never getting its feathers wet, rarely trying for a live fish. He was looking for a piece of rotten fruit, or a dead fish, stinking and bloated.

And the land: always the palm trees, their fronds rustling with the evening breeze, and the flamboyant – now, at the beginning of the hurricane season, they would be flowering, the whole tree a great mass of scarlet as though it was on fire. The frangipani, a spindly tree with flowers like stars with a most delicate perfume. And the belle of the night, which he had been lucky enough to see a few times: a great flower that spent weeks preparing, and then bloomed in one night, becoming a mass of golden strands in a white cup. By next morning, as soon as there was any heat in the sun, it closed up and died, it's brief beauty never seen unless someone came along with a lantern.

Long beaches with dazzling white sand, fringed by palms and often backed by mountains covered with thick rain forests; miles of steep cliffs and fallen rocks; low-lying coasts deeply indented with bays as though rats had gnawed them and with thick mangroves lining the banks, the leaves dark green and dense, the roots growing in and out of the water like thousands of gnarled, tortured fingers grasping down to the bottom or reaching up towards the sky.

Termites, white ants, teredos . . . a fallen tree was soon attacked by termites which left the outside bark apparently sound but when you touched it the trunk began to crumble; wooden houses could look well-painted but a jab with your finger might show the inside of the wood riddled by white ants. A proud ship floating at anchor in a bay whose blueness was so bright as to seem artificial, and its bottom a honeycomb where teredo had eaten up and down the grain of the wood, never breaking through the sides of the plank.

The heat . . . for much of the year bearable because the Trade winds were cooling, but at other times, during the hurricane season, so humid that every movement was an effort that soaked you in perspiration. When iron rusted at a tremendous rate and cloth mildewed; when a wise captain spending any time at anchor aired sails at least every two days, and always after rain. A morning rainstorm without the sails being aired in the afternoon was asking for the black spots of mildew to speckle the sail after a warm night.

Much beauty – indeed, a man who had never seen the

Caribbean could never fully understand beauty – but always it went hand in hand with violence, the violence of Nature: whether the sudden hurricane that tore down half a town, ripped up plantations like a great scythe, washed away tons of soil with torrential rain, and sank ships as though they were children's toy boats, or the sudden violence of sickness that struck a man or woman so that twelve hours after they walked into their homes, laughing and well, they were dying of yellow fever, shuddering in the grip of malaria or dying in agonizing spasms from the bloody flux. Violence, always violence, and never more so than among the planters, many of whom had lived in the islands for several generations. Sugar was the main produce and with it came rum, the cheapest of the 'hot waters', and they drank heavily, and were short-tempered, quarrelsome and often petty as those living in small communities tended to be, clannish and petulant – and hospitable, too; quick to take offence if their hospitality was not accepted.

So the West Indies were, for him, a violent contradiction: the mysterious beauty of the belle of the night alongside the ugliness of a man dying from the black vomit; the glory of a flamboyant tree contrasting with the termite-ridden log lying beside it. And over it, war, always war. That secluded bay with the sparkling beach and waving palms could be an anchorage for enemy privateers; that sail on the horizon could be a French ship of the line. Like an animal in the jungle or a fish in the sea, one always had to be on guard: against the unknown sail and the unknown cloud – for an innocent grey cloud could in five minutes become a vicious line squall which, catching a ship all aback, might send her masts crashing by the board or shred the sails from the yards. And coral reefs and shoals – one watched the colour of the sea for the hint of pale green or brown that warned of shallows, reefs or rocks, for the waters of the islands were only roughly charted, and one's own eyes were the best charts unless you wanted to rip out the ship's bottom. Many a captain's first warning of a reef was the sight of a row of pelicans apparently standing on the water – whereas in fact they had their feet firmly on rocks a few inches below the surface.

Ramage walked aft to the taffrail and looked astern, where the ship's bubbling wake was a stream of pale green fire, like a meteor's tail, phosphorescence that no one understood but which was often bright enough to read by. In a few days he would be back in the West Indies, where promotion was often fast for those that survived, and he wondered how he would find Rear-Admiral Davis. One thing was certain: he would do his best to bring the *Juno* into Carlisle Bay so that no one could fault her.

CHAPTER FIVE

The cry of 'Land-ho!' from one of the lookouts aloft came just after nine in the morning, and the call from the quarter-deck 'Where away?' brought the answer that it stretched from two points on the starboard bow to three on the larboard.

Ramage sent Jackson aloft with a telescope to identify the land – none of the lieutenants had ever been to the West Indies before – and three minutes later Jackson hailed that Ragged Point bore one point on the starboard bow. Southwick nodded knowingly when Ramage glanced at him: it was the eastern point of the diamond-shaped island, and a perfect landfall. They would be in Carlisle Bay by afternoon. Barbados, nearly a hundred miles out in the Atlantic to the east of the chain of other islands, was much flatter; Southwick had once commented that it 'looked like the back o' the Wight', and indeed except for the palm trees along the shore it resembled part of the Isle of Wight.

They had in fact sighted the island late; even now Southwick was taking a bearing and horizontal quadrant angle to work out the distance off, but that was one of the problems of finding Barbados: the Atlantic rollers came smashing in on the rocky eastern shore, hurling up fine spray which drifted as a thin mist, borne inshore by the Trade winds and obscuring the land from seaward.

Well, it was there and it was Barbados all right, and in a few minutes Southwick would be giving the quartermaster another course to steer, a little more to the south-west. They would run along the south-east coast until they passed South Point and then bear up to pass Needham Point and turn into Carlisle Bay, where they would be expected because the watchtower would have reported them.

Ramage had a smug feeling as he looked at the land, now beginning to show as a low, grey-blue smear on the western horizon, with a scattering of cloud lying athwart the tiny Trade wind clouds. In the canvas bag on his desk was all the paperwork for the Admiral, duly completed. The various heads of department on board the *Juno* had written out their 'Demands for Stores', ranging from powder for the gunner and flax, reels of thread and plugs of beeswax for the sailmaker to shirts, trousers and shoes for the purser and rope and light cordage for the bos'n, along with detailed lists of provisions. The 'Abstracts of Remains' would tell the Admiral how much was left on board the *Juno*, while the 'Defects of Ship' which he had drawn up with Southwick and the carpenter was fuller than that normally rendered by a captain thanks to that Monday morning inspection.

The ship herself looked smart enough; smarter than would normally be expected after a voyage of nearly four thousand miles. The paintwork was fresh, not just scrubbed. Two days of calm had allowed men to paint over the side from stagings, and the black hull and distinctive pale yellow sheer strake glistened. The figurehead, the head and shoulders of a rather florid *Juno*, was newly painted, and Ramage had agreed that it should be protected by canvas for the last few days. The masts had been scraped and painted; the tips of the studding-sail booms had been painted black. All the serving on the rigging had been repainted, the big quarterdeck awning had been scrubbed. The boats stowed on the booms were newly painted and once again the black was shiny, with the yellow sheer strakes giving them a distinctive touch, matching the *Juno* herself.

Ramage looked at his watch. Three or four hours to go. Well, it was time to start the routine for going into harbour. 'Mr Aitken,' he said quietly, 'I'll have the sea gaskets off the yards and harbour gaskets on, if you please.' It was a small thing; many ships as small as frigates did not bother, but well-scrubbed harbour gaskets looked smarter; they added a flourish to sails given a 'harbour furl'.

The studding sails had been taken in so that the ends of the booms could be blacked, and he had decided not to set them again, but he noticed that the booms on the foretopsail yard had not been run out to their marks, and he pointed it out to Aitken.

He passed the word for the gunner. The sea was comparatively calm and the ship was not rolling, nor would she when she altered course. When the gunner reported, Ramage said: 'Make sure the guns are unshotted, Mr Johnson, get the half-ports off, and make ready for the salute.'

Southwick came up from below, still holding his quadrant, and when he gave the new course to the quartermaster Aitken shouted the orders to trim the yards round.

'What depth are we likely to be anchoring in, Mr Southwick?' Ramage asked.

'Eight fathoms, sir.'

Ramage turned to the First Lieutenant. 'Have the cables ranged, Mr Aitken, if you please and we'll be needing anchor buoy ropes for ten fathoms.'

He looked around for his coxswain. 'Jackson! Bend on our pendant numbers and hoist them. Those fellows in the watchtower will be having their glasses on us soon.'

The three flags would tell the men in the watchtower that the frigate's number was 367, and reference to the List of the Navy would show she was the *Juno* frigate, thirty-two guns. Ramage pictured the word being passed along the coast to Bridgetown, at the western end of Carlisle Bay, and no doubt Rear-Admiral Davis would wonder if the *Juno* was bringing him orders before going on to Jamaica, or whether she was another ship for his command. For sure he would have the name of her captain wrong: his Navy List would still give the old commanding officer, and the name 'Ramage, Nicholas' would be buried among five thousand other lieutenants.

Ramage watched as the yards were trimmed to keep the sails full on the new course. As soon as the *Juno* anchored in Carlisle Bay two boats would be needed – one to take him to the flagship, or wherever Rear-Admiral Davis had his headquarters, if he was living on shore, and another for Southwick to be rowed round the ship to make sure the yards were square. The lifts were marked but ropes stretched. Ramage wanted both boats hoisted out the moment the Juno was at anchor with her sails furled.

'Mr Aitken,' Ramage told the harassed First Lieutenant, 'have both cutters ready for hoisting out, and see that the stay tackles are prepared.'

'Aye, aye, sir,' Aitken said cheerfully, and Ramage was thankful his days as a First Lieutenant were over: it was a thankless job. If everything went well, no one, least of all the Captain, gave you credit for careful planning; if anything went wrong, you received all the blame and the fact that some order you had given had not been carried out was no excuse.

The word would soon get round Bridgetown that a frigate

was coming in from England and people would be expecting to hear the latest gossip from London, see the latest newspapers (Ramage had remembered to buy several copies before he left for Portsmouth), and receive any mail she might be bringing. There would be invitations for the officers to dine on shore, unless Admiral Davis wanted the ship to sail immediately. Soldiers would want to hear news of the war; the ladies would be waiting avidly to hear news of the latest fashions, the latest scandals ...

For the moment Ramage was more concerned with getting the *Juno* into Carlisle Bay in a smart and seamanlike manner. Half the problem was that there were no regulations for many of the manoeuvres. Firing a salute, for instance: it was not laid down whether a ship began firing the salute when the flagship came in sight – in which case there was a good chance that in a high wind it would not be heard, and puffs of smoke through the ports would be all that told the officer of the deck on board the flagship that a salute was being fired. Or did one wait until the salute could be heard on board the flagship – which could mean that it would not be completed until the ship was at anchor. Most admirals had their preferences, but one only discovered them after the salute had been fired.

Ramage, like many captains, liked to begin the salute as he approached the anchorage, timing the approach so that the last few guns were fired as the foretopsail was backed, the anchor splashed down and the rest of the sails were furled. It was difficult because the guns had to be fired at regular intervals. Again, no interval was laid down, although most captains used five seconds, which was timed by the gunner chanting to himself: 'If I wasn't a gunner I shouldn't be here, number one gun fire! If I wasn't a gunner ...'

As the frigate turned away to the south-east, converging slightly on the coast as it trended away, the grey of the land slowly took shape, becoming low, rolling hills covered with sugar cane, which began to have colour the closer they approached. As the rest of the island came over the curvature of the earth they could see first the heads of palm trees along the beach and then the long line of the sand, glaring white with the sun almost overhead, the sea pale green as the water shallowed.

Finally, past South Point and with Needham Point fine on the starboard bow, Carlisle Bay still hidden by trending inland just beyond it, Ramage took one last look over the *Juno*.

The crew of his cutter were rigged out in white trousers and blue shirts, their round sennet hats shiny with new black paint. There was no need to inspect them; Jackson would have checked over every man, and they would be freshly shaven and their queues newly-tied. Pendant numbers were streaming and the new ensign rippled in the brisk wind. Already Ramage felt the heat of the land, although they were still a mile off-shore, and he could smell – was it hay? Hardly. More likely the smell from the sugar cane.

The four lieutenants were wearing their best uniforms; young Orsini was standing aft with Benson waiting for orders, and both the youngsters, wearing their dirks, were trying not to stare at the coastline – Ramage had heard Aitken repri-mand them for climbing up on a gun for their first real sight of Barbados.

Captain Ramage was bringing the *Juno* frigate into Bar-bados. He had dreamed of commanding a frigate and the dream had come true. He had dreamed of taking his own frigate to the West Indies, and the dream had come true. Yet even as he looked around, felt the heat of the deck soaking through the soles of his shoes, looked around again to check for the tenth time that not a rope was out of place, not the tiniest grease spot on the deck, that the anchors were bent on to the cables, that the topmen were waiting for the order to swarm aloft and furl the sails, knowing that the Admiral would probably be watching with a critical eye glued to a telescope, even now it seemed unreal. He caught Southwick's eye and wondered if the old Master could read his thoughts. Southwick glanced round, saw no one watching, and gave Ramage a broad wink, his face remaining impassive. Still holding his quadrant in his right hand, the Master bent over the binnacle and then looked ahead. 'I don't know how many ships there'll be in Carlisle Bay, sir, but it'll be opening in a moment – you can see Charles Fort and Beckwith Battery. Ah, there! One frigate . . . that's a brig just west of her. The flagship must be just – ah! I can just see the ends of her yards!'

Ramage glanced across at Aitken, but the First Lieutenant was already calling Benson and Orsini. 'Have you got a bring-'em-near, Benson?' The midshipman snatched up a tele-scope. 'Orsini, signal book?' The boy waved the slim volume.

Aitken looked at them sternly. 'Benson, you'd better read the signals faster than the flagship makes 'em!'

The boy ran to the starboard side and climbed up on the

aftermost gun, standing there with the telescope to his eye, Orsini standing on the deck beside him, ready to flick open the book at whatever page told him the meaning of the numbers that would be signalled.

Then the flagship was in sight, a long crescent of sandy beach beyond her, and Southwick was looking through his quadrant. He knew the height of her maintruck from her waterline and had already set on the quadrant the angle it would make at the distance off Ramage wanted to be when he began the salute.

'Another hundred yards, sir.'

'Gunner, stand by for the salute!' Ramage called down to the maindeck.

But there was no signal from the flagship telling him where to anchor. Another case of being damned if you waited and damned if you did not. Some admirals would flay a captain who just sailed in and anchored without being told exactly where, usually on a certain bearing and at a particular distance from the flagship. What did Admiral Davis favour? He shrugged his shoulders. The two frigates – no, three, because another one was just showing clear of the point – seemed to be anchored 'where convenient'.

Southwick took the quadrant from his eyes. 'That's the distance, sir,' he said, and he added quietly, 'Either the watch-tower hasn't passed the word or – judging from where the others are – we just anchor . . .'

Ramage nodded; there was no point in waiting. 'Gunner,' he called, 'begin the salute!' He turned to Southwick and added quietly, 'It might wake 'em up!'

The first gun thundered across the small peninsula forming Needham Point and as the smoke drifted away Ramage saw a flock of pelicans wheeling up in alarm. The second gun boomed and then the third. Aitken was watching the flagship with his telescope and said suddenly, 'Three, no four, officers are watching. One's a captain, and – yes, one's an admiral. Definitely an admiral, sir.'

'Her flag halyards!' Ramage snapped. 'Are men bending on flags?'

'No, sir,' Aitken said firmly.

Ramage picked up the speaking trumpet, noting that the fourth gun of the salute had just fired. 'The outermost frigate,' he said to Aitken and Southwick. 'We'll anchor a hundred yards on his larboard quarter. Are there still eight fathoms that far out, Southwick?'

'Aye, eight fathoms, sir,' the Master answered. 'I'll go to the f'o'csle.'

Not having to anchor in a particular spot made it a lot easier. Several more guns to go; with luck the last of the salute should fire just before the anchor hit the water, but it would be close . . .

He took a deep breath, lifted the speaking trumpet to his lips and shouted the orders that sent the topmen swarming aloft. On the deck other men were standing by, ready to haul or let go. The quartermaster leaned forward slightly waiting for the order that would bring the *Juno* up into the wind.

Then he gave a stream of orders. As the *Juno* began to turn, the courses, topsails, and topgallants lost their swelling shapes as clew lines pulled the corners upwards and diagonally inwards towards the masts. Only the foretopsail remained, rippling as the wind came round on the frigate's beam.

Ramage was watching the other frigate, now on the *Juno*'s starboard bow. A quiet order to the quartermaster and the *Juno* turned into the wind, so that the foretopsail was pressed against the mast, slowing the ship down. The other frigate was dead ahead and the backed foretopsail had almost stopped the *Juno*.

From the fo'c'sle Southwick signalled that all was ready; the bower anchor was hanging clear, the stock clear and below the bowsprit shrouds. The last gun of the salute fired and the smoke streamed aft. Jackson, perched by the mainchains, called that the way was off the ship and Ramage gave his prearranged signal to Southwick. A moment later the anchor splashed into the water and the cable thundered out through the hawse, the smell of singeing rope drifting back to the quarterdeck as friction scorched the thick manila cable. Now the back topsail was beginning to push the *Juno* astern, putting a strain on the cable and digging in the anchor. In the meantime the rest of the sails were being neatly furled. Then the foretopsail, its work done, was clewed and furled.

As Aitken went forward to start hoisting out the cutters he reported to Ramage: 'No signals yet from the flagship, sir, but there are five telescopes watching us!'

Ramage looked at the other frigate and then walked to the forward end of the quarterdeck. He could just see the anchor buoy bobbing in the water. The *Juno*, more by luck than judgement, was where he wanted her. Aloft the sails were furled so tightly that the yards looked bare. Five telescopes, eh?

There was an excited squeak from Orsini, who came rushing to Ramage, signal book in hand. 'Signal from the flagship, sir. *The Captain of the ship signified to report on board the flagship.*' He paused, as though making sure that Ramage had grasped it, and then added: 'The ship signified is 637, and that's us, sir.'

Ramage suppressed a grin at the enormous importance Paolo placed on every word. 'Very well, acknowledge – and keep a sharp eye open for more signals.'

Southwick came aft to report the amount of cable veered, and he took some bearings which he noted on the slate kept hooked on the binnacle box: they would show whether or not the anchor was dragging. Leaving the Master as officer of the deck, Ramage went down to his cabin and glanced in the mirror to make sure his stock had not creased in the hour since he had put on a fresh one. He put on his sword, wiped his face with a towel and picked up the canvas bag containing the dispatches for the Admiral, a copy of his own orders, the *Juno*'s log and the rest of the forms he had been busy filling in for the past few days. He took a second canvas bag, even bulkier: that was for Aitken to give to Wagstaffe. After Ramage was on board the flagship and reporting to the Admiral, Wagstaffe could take over the rest of the letters, newspapers and small packets. There were times, he thought crossly, when one of the King's ships seemed to carry more private mail than a Post Office packet ship.

Baker knocked on the door of the cabin. 'Captain, sir, your cutter is ready.'

He went up on deck, gave the larger canvas bag to Aitken, listened to Southwick reporting that the anchor was not dragging, and walked to the gangway. The side-ropes, newly scrubbed, were rigged and the bos'n's mates and side boys were waiting. A minute later he was sitting in the sternsheets of the cutter and clutching the bag, while Jackson was giving orders for the boat to shove off.

Ramage looked up at the *Juno*'s curving sides. Yes, she looked smart enough and he was glad she had that yellow strake: it emphasized her sheer nicely. And the figurehead – the men had made a good job of painting Juno. The flesh tones had seemed rather lurid viewed from the fo'c'sle, but from a distance they seemed natural.

The men bent at the oars, steady strokes that made the cutter leap across the chop kicked up by the wind. Ramage wondered for the hundredth time what Admiral Davis had in store for him. Just as he left the quarterdeck Southwick had muttered: 'It'll be convoys, sir,' and looking round at the other three frigates at anchor Ramage was sure the Master was right. All three frigates were smartly turned out; all were glistening with more paint than the Navy Board allowed, with touches of gold leaf here and there, showing their captains had dipped into their own pockets to buy the extra to make their ships smart. They reeked of prize money, Ramage thought. Glistened with prize money, he corrected himself. These three frigates were obviously the Admiral's favourites. One of them would carry out the sealed orders in the canvas bag he was holding on his knees.

CHAPTER SIX

Henry Davis, Rear-Admiral of the Red and Commander-in-Chief of His Majesty's ships and vessels upon the Windward and Leeward Islands station, was a short, round-faced man in late middle-age, with stiff black eyebrows that stuck out of his forehead like boot brushes, but he had an open, cheerful face and after greeting Ramage on the quarterdeck of the *Invincible* he led the way down to the great cabin. He had eyed the canvas pouch that Ramage was carrying and was obviously anxious to get his hands on the dispatches and orders it held, but he concealed his impatience.

The cabin was enormous by comparison with the *Juno*'s and furnished as became an admiral in a ship of the line: half a dozen leather-covered armchairs, one of the largest wine-coolers Ramage had ever seen – made of mahogany and shaped like a fat Greek urn – and a sideboard with a rack in which half a dozen cut-glass decanters glittered in the sunlight reflecting through the sternlights. One of the two swords hung in racks in the forward bulkhead was an ornate cere-monial scimitar with a beautifully chased and gilded pommel, the other a curved fighting sword: obviously the Admiral favoured the cavalry type of sabre. The curtains drawn back on either side of the sternlights were a deep red damask woven with intricate patterns of silver thread – the same design, Ramage noted, as the ceremonial sword pommel. Probably bought in Persia, or presents from some Turkish potentate. Together they gave the cabin an atmosphere more suited to some bearded pasha.

'A drink?' the Admiral inquired, waving Ramage to one of the chairs. 'The usual, or there is fresh lime or lemon juice. No ice I'm afraid; the damned schooner hasn't arrived from Nova Scotia. The last consignment lasted only a week; the fools didn't pack it properly. They said they were short of straw, so two thirds of it melted before they got here. Said they had to pump most of the way down.' He gave a mirthless laugh. 'Odd to think that a ship laden with ice blocks could sink itself with the ice melting . . .'

It could not, since ice took up more cubic space than the water it produced, but only a callow midshipman would point that out to an Admiral. 'A lime juice, if I may, sir.'

The Admiral stared suspiciously at Ramage from under his jutting eyebrows. 'You *do* take a drink, though?'

Ramage saw the mottled complexion and bulbous nose of a man who obviously enjoyed a good brandy and hurriedly nodded his head. 'Indeed, sir; it's just that I'm very thirsty. It's hot here in the bay, after the Atlantic.'

The Admiral grunted approvingly. 'Hate this damned bay m'self, but at least it's cooler on board than on shore. My wife – she took the coolest house we could find, but at night, when the wind drops . . .' He shook a small silver bell vigorously and when a steward appeared ordered a rum punch for himself and a fresh lime juice for Ramage.

Ramage opened the pouch and took out the papers, handing the top one, his orders, to the Admiral, who read through them quickly. 'Hmm, I'm glad to have another frigate. Never have enough. Their Lordships don't seem to appreciate the problem of running a station like this, covering dozens of islands with so few ships. Ramage, eh? Any relation to the Earl of Blazey?'

'Son, sir.'

'Mmm, then you are the young fellow I've been reading about in the *Gazette* from time to time. Well, you are going to find it a lot quieter out here. No excitement. Convoys up and down the islands, an occasional chase after a privateer . . .'

Ramage pictured Southwick's face and did not notice the Admiral watching him closely. 'You look disappointed.'

'No, sir,' Ramage said hurriedly, careful not to add that it was what he had feared.

'I don't remember seeing your name on the latest List I have. When were you made post?'

'A month ago,' Ramage answered and knew what the

Admiral was going to say next.

'Hmm, most junior on the station – by a couple of years or so.' He gave a dry laugh. 'That'll be a relief for some of my young firebrands: when they saw the *Juno* I expect they thought she was still commanded by your predecessor, who has more seniority than the rest o' them put together. Now, you have dispatches for me?'

Ramage took five packets and gave them to the Admiral, who looked at the rest of the papers Ramage was holding. 'What are those – Weekly Accounts and that sort of thing – list of defects as long as your arm?' When Ramage nodded, the Admiral rang the bell, which he had put down beside his chair. 'Give 'em to my secretary,' he said, bellowing to the sentry to pass the word for Mr Henshaw. When Henshaw arrived, as thin and nervous a secretary as Ramage had ever seen and obviously also the ship's chaplain, the Admiral did not bother with introductions, merely telling him to take the *Juno*'s Weekly Accounts and start dealing with them.

As Ramage stood, intending to leave the Admiral to read his letters from the Admiralty, he glanced up. 'You haven't finished your drink yet,' he said impatiently. 'Just sit down while I read through this. When were you last at the Admiralty?'

'The beginning of last month, sir, when I was made post.'

'Who did you see?'

'The First Lord, sir.'

Again the Admiral stared at him. 'And how was Lord St Vincent, eh?'

'In good health,' Ramage said lamely, guessing at the questions that must be passing through the Admiral's mind, since it was rare for a young post captain to see the First Lord, and he must have realized that Ramage was still a lieutenant when he entered the First Lord's office.

The Admiral ripped open the first letter – all of them, heavily sealed, were numbered, Ramage had noticed; presumably they were marked in order of importance. As the Admiral read, Ramage twisted slightly in his chair and looked round the cabin again. The Admiral was certainly a man who liked comfort – and who could blame him? The two gimballed lanterns were silver; four other lanthorns clipped to the bulkheads were inlaid with silver wire which was worked in the horn in the same pattern as the sword hilt.

The Admiral grunted and Ramage heard him ripping open a second packet. The canvas covering the cabin sole was new, and it would take several more coats of the pale green paint before the material was smooth. Ramage shifted his position: the armchairs were comfortable enough but leather was hardly a suitable covering for the heat of the Tropics: he could feel perspiration making his breeches stick to the material.

Again the Admiral grunted. 'His Lordship mention any forthcoming operations to you?'

'No, sir.'

'Hmm.' Again the eyebrows lifted and then lowered, and the Admiral opened the next letter, glanced through it quickly and went on to the fourth, which produced a snort of disgust. The fifth hardly appeared to interest him and he gathered them all up again and looked at Ramage.

'Know Martinique at all?'

'A little, sir. I know most of the other islands.'

The Admiral stood up, putting the papers down on his chair and walking over to his desk. There were a dozen or more charts rolled up and stowed in a rack to one side and he looked through them, finally pulling one out. He spread it out and put paperweights on the sides to prevent it rolling up again. Then he beckoned to Ramage, who saw it was a chart of Martinique and realized for the first time how similar it was to the foot of Italy.

The Admiral jabbed a blunt forefinger on Fort Royal, and then moved it to include the great Fort Royal Bay. 'Bane of my existence, that damned place,' he said sourly. 'I have to watch the French there like a terrier at a rabbit hole. That's going to be your job for the next few weeks – months, probably. Sorry for it, my boy, because you are going to get heartily sick of the sight of the Pointe des Salines,' he jabbed a finger on the southernmost tip of the island, 'and Diamond Rock – that's this one here, sticks up a mile off shore like a great tooth – and Cap Salomon.' He pointed to the headland on the south side of Fort Royal Bay. 'Aye, and as far up as Pointe des Nègres.' He gestured at the headland on the north side of the Bay.

With his finger he traced a line from Pointe des Nègres to the southern end of the island. 'Up and down, my lad, twenty-five miles. You'll be the terrier at the rabbit hole, and I don't want a French rabbit to get in or out without you taking him and sending him here with a prize crew on board.'

Ramage said nothing, puzzled at the shortness of the line the Admiral's finger had traced. The Admiral mistook his silence and said crossly: 'If it doesn't appeal to you, there's always convoy work.'

'Oh no, sir,' Ramage said hastily, rubbing one of the two scars on his right brow, 'it is just that – ' he paused, wondering whether he was being indiscreet, and the Admiral said impatiently: 'Come on, out with it!'

Ramage pointed from Pointe des Nègres to Pointe des Salines. 'You made a point, sir, that I should be patrolling only between those two headlands, and I was – '

'You're wondering why I don't want you to patrol round the whole island? A good point, m'boy, since you don't know Martinique well. Luckily for us there's a deuce of a strong north-going current along the Caribbean side of the island, and when it's not going north it's going west.'

He ran his finger down the middle of the island. 'You can see it's mountainous: damned big peaks they are, too, and it means there's usually precious little wind on the west side. The island makes an enormous lee that often stretches twenty miles to the west. What does that tell you?'

'That with a light wind and a strong north-going current,' Ramage said, 'it must be almost impossible for merchant ships to come in from the Atlantic round the north end of the island and beat their way down to Fort Royal, sir.'

'Exactly. They never risk it, so it shuts one door. It forces 'em to come round the south end of the island, using the current to get 'em up to Fort Royal. But even then they're sometimes between the devil and the deep blue sea: if they stay offshore and there's any west in the current they get swept out into the Caribbean, and even when they get out to the lee they're too far to the west for merchantmen to stand a chance of beating back to Fort Royal. So they stay very close inshore, working the current and the offshore and on-shore breezes, anchoring when necessary.'

He pointed to the Diamond Rock. 'They keep close to the coast and pass between the Rock and Diamond Hill, here on the mainland, through the Fours Channel. It acts as a funnel. That's where you catch 'em. Now' – he jabbed a finger on the coast north to Fort Royal – 'the only reason for patrolling as far north as Pointe des Nègres is to snap up anyone trying to use the current to give himself a lift to the north or west. You can go right into Fort Royal Bay often enough to see any ship preparing to sail.'

He took the weight off so the chart rolled up. 'Stop anything sailing by all means, but – and this will be in your orders – your main concern is to stop any ship *arriving*.

Those Frenchmen are desperate for supplies: the Army is yelling out for powder and shot, tents and provisions; the Navy's desperate for masts, spars, canvas and cordage.'

He waved Ramage back to the chair and sat down again himself, picking up his drink. 'Watch out you don't get caught in that damned current yourself, though a frigate can beat back the minute she gets some wind.' He raised his glass as though in a toast. 'Diamond Rock and Diamond Hill – you may not find diamonds, but let's hope you find plenty of gold in the shape of prize money, eh? You can have a word with Captain Eames of the *Alcmene*: he's been patrolling the area for the past three months and has probably picked up a trick or two. I need the *Alcmene* for this special operation,' he added crossly, 'although I can ill spare him for such a long time.'

The Admiral stared at the rum in his glass, his brow furrowed and then glared at Ramage from under his bushy eyebrows. 'Your ship's company,' he said abruptly. 'Any trouble with them?'

'Why, no sir!' said a startled Ramage.

'No sign of disaffection, no troublemakers on board?'

'No sir, a happy ship's company.'

The Admiral nodded. 'Well, watch them. You know what happened to the *Jocasta*?'

'Yes, sir,' Ramage said. 'A year or two ago, wasn't it?'

'Twenty months. Well, the mutineers took her into La Guaira and handed her over to the Spaniards. There's no work for 'em down there, and they're signing on in neutral merchantmen. We've caught a few of them, and some of the men who didn't mutiny have managed to escape. Anyway, there's a lot of loose talk going round, and we've got to be on our guard: mutiny can spread like wildfire – you remember the Nore and Spithead . . . So, be on your guard, and keep a sharp lookout for any former Jocastas in neutral ships.'

'Aye, aye, sir.'

'Very well. Provision and water for three months. Any defects that stop you sailing? No? Good, I'll send your orders over in the morning.'

Back on board the *Juno*, Ramage waited in his cabin for Aitken and Southwick to join him. The steward came in, asking for instructions about supper, but was waved away: Ramage was too disappointed to have an appetite. Captain Eames and the *Alcmene* were to carry out the special operation, whatever it was, and the *Juno* was to be a terrier at a rabbit hole, according to the Admiral. Snapping at an island schooner here, chasing a lumbering little drogher there, tacking back and forth between Pointe des Salines and Pointe des Nègres, watching the current, wary of a calm . . . Capturing prizes – a few tons of sugar, some hogsheads of molasses, an occasional hundredweight of spices: so little that British privateers never bothered themselves.

When the First Lieutenant and Master came into the cabin Ramage gestured irritably towards the chairs and asked Southwick: 'Do you know Fort Royal at all well?'

The Master nodded. 'Aye, sir, I was in and out o' there dozens of times before the war.'

'Well, the pair of you will know it like the backs of your hands by Michaelmas,' Ramage said grimly, and went on to tell them of the news given him by Admiral Davis. 'I'll get my written orders tomorrow, but we provision for three months. That'll keep the ship's company busy with the boats for a day or two.'

'What about water, sir?'

'Three months, but if we need more we can run down to St Lucia for it; Captain Eames says they have plenty at Castries. Some powder, too, but no provisions to spare.'

'We need a tender,' Southwick commented.

'The Admiral's already agreed to that, if we capture something suitable. Captain Eames took a small sloop and used it, but apparently he brought it back here and it's been sold as a prize.'

'Who is watching Fort Royal now, sir?' Aitken asked.

'The *Welcome* brig, but she's waiting to leave for Antigua the minute we relieve her.'

Southwick unrolled the chart and looked at it. 'One thing about it, there are plenty of sheltered anchorages if it comes on to blow hard. Grande Anse d'Arlet and Petite Anse d'Arlet by Cap Salomon; Diamond bay itself, off the village . . .'

'And if it blows a hurricane,' Ramage said with a grin, 'we can either put to sea or join the French up in Fort Royal: they'll be in such a state they won't notice us sneaking in and anchoring in the Salée River!'

Aitken gave a shiver. 'Let's hope we don't get any this year . . .'

Southwick rolled up the chart. 'Always a hurricane somewhere during the season. The last one the Captain and I experienced,' he said nonchalantly, 'started near here. About a hundred miles to the west, wasn't it, sir? Masts went by the board,' he told Aitken.

Ramage nodded and said cheerfully: 'Let's hope hurricanes are like lightning, never strike in the same place twice. Anyway, let's go over the requirements for this "terrier at the rabbit hole" business. There'll be a deal of detached boat work – Aitken, I want you to check with the gunner that we have enough boat guns, and at least two spare ones, in case of accidents. Boarding from boats is something we haven't practised, but we'll make up for that as soon as we are off Martinique. Musketry – I'm sure the Marines need little practice, but the seamen?'

Aitken shook his head ruefully. 'At the moment I'm afraid they're more of a danger to themselves than an enemy, sir.'

'Very well, give 'em plenty of exercise with small arms, and remember they'll be using both muskets and pistols at night, and one gun going off accidentally can raise the alarm. Exercise them at rowing with muffled oars – oh yes, you look surprised, but believe me, Aitken, it's harder than it sounds. It isn't just frapping oars with bits of canvas, it's the whole attitude of the men in the boat – not to bellow an oath if they stub their toes, not to smuggle drink into the boat on the pretext of drinking it to keep warm . . . ' he glanced at Southwick as the Master nodded vigorously.

'More boat operations have been wrecked by drink than anything else, sir,' Southwick said. 'The men hoard their tot and take it with them. They don't realize when they've drunk too much and the officer doesn't see it going on, and then they get stupid or quarrelsome . . . Search every man a'fore they get into the boat, sir, 'tis the only way.'

'The boat guns,' Ramage said. 'Loading, aiming and firing those little brutes is difficult work in anything of a sea. Spray all over the place, shot roll into the bilge, the lock gets wet, and the slow match goes out. Something else to exercise the men at, Aitken.'

'Hoisting out and recovering, sir,' Southwick prompted.

'Oh yes,' Ramage said. 'Easy enough to hoist out a boat with the stay tackle in harbour, and sometimes more difficult at Spithead. But with a sea running . . .'

'I'll see the lieutenants are warned, and with your permission I'll exercise them at it as soon as we can,' said Aitken, his face getting longer and longer.

'Night work with boats means using a compass and knowing where the devil you are,' Ramage went on relentlessly, anxious to make sure that Aitken realized that the *Juno* would soon be engaged on a type of operation of which the First Lieutenant had no experience. 'It means developing a sense of – well, of *position*, more than navigation. On a night when cloud hides the stars, most men completely lose their sense of position after a boat has rowed round in a circle a couple of times. I don't mean simply knowing you are still off a certain headland, that's obvious even to a blockhead. I'll give you an example: supposing you are leading three boats in a cutting out expedition against a ship of war at anchor in Fort Royal Bay, and you run into some guard boats and have to dodge. It's being able to keep in your mind the relative positions of the rest of the boats that matters. Like playing chess when you are blindfolded after the first four moves.'

Southwick looked startled. 'Please don't say anything like that in front of Bowen, sir,' he said pleadingly. 'That is just the sort of thing that would appeal to him, an' I'm glad to say he hasn't thought of it yet.'

'You must get Aitken interested in chess,' Ramage joked, knowing that the Surgeon was always after the Master for a game, but one look at the First Lieutenant told him that Bowen already had another victim.

'I said I knew the game before I knew what a good player he was,' Aitken admitted ruefully. 'He caught Wagstaffe, too, and now he's busy teaching Baker and Lacey.'

'It's a good exercise for the brain,' Ramage said airily – he himself was now safe from being dragooned into games. 'I'm sure you all benefit from playing with Bowen.'

Southwick caught his eye. 'Oh, we do indeed, sir,' he said gravely. 'I'll soon be walking the deck making the knight's move – two steps forward and one to the side.'

CHAPTER SEVEN

A brisk easterly wind that probably started life off the African coast, three thousand miles away across the Atlantic, brought the *Juno* surging through the channel between the south end of Martinique and the north end of St Lucia, her bow wave creaming away and soon losing itself among the white caps. Flying spray sparkling in the bright sun left salt drying like white dust over the decks and guns. The men were thankful for their sennet hats to keep the sun's direct glare out of their eyes.

From several miles out Ramage had identified Martinique with the three high peaks jutting up from the mountain chain running from one end of the island to the other. At the northern end and four thousand feet high, the volcano of Mont Pelée had its peak hidden in cloud, as though cooling off; Les Pitons du Carbet, a series of peaks, the highest of which was only five hundred feet lower than Pelée, had thin cloud streaming away to leeward like lancers' pennons. Only Vauclin, nine miles short of Pointe des Salines at the southern end of the island and 1650 feet high, was clear of cloud.

Southwick lowered his telescope. 'That's Cabrit Island, the big rock off Pointe des Salines. The big hill in the distance almost in line with it, sir: that's Diamond Hill, and you'll see Diamond Rock in a moment.'

Ramage looked through his telescope to the north-west. 'There!' Southwick said. 'Like a big tooth sticking up out of the sea. More than five hundred feet high, and deep water nearly all round it!'

For a few minutes, before its outline was lost against the high land beyond it, Ramage stared at the magnified picture in the lens. A tooth, yes; the tooth of an old horse, vertical sided and slightly rounded on top, sticking up out of the sea as though Nature had accidentally dropped it, for there were no other islands anywhere near. It was going to be very useful as a navigational mark: as useful for the *Juno* as Mr Eddystone's remarkable lighthouse was for ships approaching Plymouth. Southwick's chart, admittedly copied from some other master, showed a five fathom patch on the north side where it might be possible to anchor. Otherwise the rock was surrounded by depths of fifty fathoms or more.

He put down the telescope. His immediate task was to find the *Welcome* brig, hand over her orders from the Admiral and send her on her way. He squared his shoulders and began striding up and down the starboard side of the quarterdeck, hardly noticing that everyone else moved away, for traditionally that was where the Captain of a ship could walk alone with his thoughts, be they of battle or nagging wives, duty or doxies.

Yes, there were many advantages in being a post captain, even though at the bottom of a list, and a frigate was a nice command. He ran a hand along his jaw and felt the skin smooth. The Captain's steward provided hot shaving water, while poor lieutenants had only cold in which to work up a lather. A clean shirt every day and he could change his stock as often as he wanted, knowing that the steward had several more ready, laundered and ironed. If the whim took him he could call for his steward, even though it wanted a couple of hours to noon, and demand his supper. He could insist that the officers wore their hats back to front. At a snap of his fingers he could have every alternate man flogged – or allow them to laze in their hammocks for the rest of the day.

He was king of all he surveyed, as far as the *Juno* was concerned, and he enjoyed it. Not because of the power he wielded, for that was only comparative (Rear-Admiral Davis had taken only seconds to decide that Captain Ramage should spend the next few weeks watching for rabbits off Martinique), but because it gave him the chance of handling a much larger ship and moulding the men. The *Jocasta* business seemed to have worried the Admiral, and if he had asked the question about the loyalty of the ship's company off the Lizard, Ramage would have had to give a different answer. Now the Junos were cheerful; many an evening the fiddler was in demand on the foredeck so the men could dance and skylark.

Being made post mattered in small things and in large. The large of running your own ship in your own way, the small of having hot shaving water. When they met the *Welcome*, the brig would have to heave-to and the lieutenant commanding her would have to report to Captain Ramage on board the *Juno*. A small thing, but he was damned glad that for once it was someone else who had to scramble down into a boat and get soaked with spray . . . The *Welcome* brig's lieutenant would not know he was the first commanding officer that Captain Ramage had ordered to report on board. And he was going to be lucky in one respect: Ramage had suffered from overbearing, condescending or pompous captains when he had been a lieutenant and had vowed he would never be guilty of those particular attitudes, unless provoked . . . He found himself humming as he reached the taffrail and turned to begin his walk forward again. The deck was confoundedly hot; the warmth seeped through his shoes and both his brow and cheek muscles ached from squinting against the glare off the sea. With luck all the mosquitoes that had swarmed on board in Carlisle Bay had been blown away now they were at sea again.

One thing to be said for the Admiral packing them off after the rabbits was that they had escaped the perils of Bridgetown's social life. A sheaf of invitations had arrived on board from hostesses who obviously relished the idea of hearing London's latest gossip retailed by an earl's son, but he had been spared the worst of it. He had accepted dinner with the Admiral and his wife (it had been surprisingly enjoyable: the Admiral had a lively sense of humour) and pleaded urgent work to avoid the rest. Still, the lieutenants had enjoyed themselves, finding Southwick only too willing to stand an anchor watch. They would have been startled if they knew that on one of the two evenings, while they were wined and dined on shore, the Captain had relieved the Master for a couple of hours so that Bowen could have his game of chess.

All the weeks of training the ship's company, the days of having the ship reek of fresh paint, the days of thrashing to windward out of the Channel and across Biscay, were worth it for a morning like this. Tomorrow, when they went after the rabbits, it might be a different story, but now he was happy and satisfied.

'Two miles off Cabrit Island, sir,' Southwick reported.

'Can we bear up for the Diamond?'

'Yes, sir, and I'd like to stream the log and then get some idea of the current at the moment. At a guess we have a couple of knots o' west-going current under us.'

'It'll begin to trend north-west and follow the coast now we're rounding the Point,' Ramage said, for Aitken's benefit.

As Southwick gave orders for the log to be streamed and men fetched out the reel and half-minute glass, Ramage pictured the chart of the southern end of Martinique, still fascinated by its similarity to the foot of Italy. They were just rounding the heel and were going to bear away to sail across the inward-curving instep, heading for Diamond Rock, which showed on the chart like a tiny pebble on which the ball of the foot was about to tread.

Suddenly there was a hail from the foremast-head: 'Sail ho!'

'Where away?' Aitken bellowed through the speaking trumpet.

'On the starboard beam close under the land, just coming clear of the headland, sir.'

Ramage snatched up his telescope. The heel of the island, where a stirrup would fit, formed a deep, narrow bay; the headland was Pointe Dunkerque and the bay went inland for a couple of miles. He could see a sail – no, two sails, squaresails, but the rest of the ship was hidden below the curvature of the earth.

'What do you make of her?' Aitken shouted.

'Too far off, sir. Two masts, steering south-east, but that's all.'

Ramage looked round for Jackson, handed him the telescope and gestured aloft. The American ran to the main-chains and a moment later was going up the ratlines like a monkey.

The First Lieutenant looked questioningly and Ramage nodded. 'Beat to quarters, Mr Aitken. Pendant numbers ready, and I'll let you know the challenge and reply in a moment. And bear up for the Point; don't lose anything to leeward.'

With that he went down to his cabin and unlocked a drawer in the desk, taking out a heavy canvas bag. It contained the ship's secret papers, and he pulled the lines that kept it closed through the brass grommets. He took out the lead weight that would make sure the bag sank quickly if it had to be thrown over the side to avoid capture, and removed the papers. On top was a white card on which three tables were drawn. These were the challenge and reply, which changed daily for the next three months. He ran his finger down one column, noted the challenge for the day of the month, then moved his finger sideways and read off the reply. Two three-figure numbers. He never trusted his own memory and scribbled them down on a sheet of paper before restowing the documents and the weight and returning the bag to the drawer.

As he went up the companionway he heard the bustle of men going to general quarters: the gunner would be down in the magazine, gun captains would be collecting the locks and prickers for each gun, already the decks would be wetted and men sprinkling sand. The boys would be waiting at the magazine scuttle with their wooden cartridge boxes, and the Marine Lieutenant would be stationing his men round the bulwarks.

He reached the top of the companionway and glanced aloft. The *Juno* was now stretching northwards, rolling with the beam sea. He looked forward to see a strong west-going current setting the *Juno* crabwise away from the headland. Why didn't Aitken brace the yards sharp up? They would end up well to leeward of the brig at this rate.

Southwick hurried up and, guessing what Ramage was about to say, explained apologetically: 'There are reefs up to a mile off the Point, sir, and Jackson says she's a brig, and from the cut of her topsails she's British.'

'He should know,' Ramage said, and the Master grinned. The *Triton*, in which all three of them had served for nearly two years, had been a brig, built at the same yard as the *Welcome*.

Ramage watched the brig for a couple of minutes and then ordered: 'Rig side-ropes and have a boat-rope ready in the forechains. We'll be heaving-to on the starboard tack and her captain will come on board, Mr Aitken.'

He looked round for the midshipmen. 'Mr Benson, prepare the signal for the Captain of the *Welcome* to come on board. Make sure you look in the right section of the signal book.'

The boy thumbed through the pages as he was joined by Orsini. 'Signals from private ships,' he muttered, half to himself. 'Ah – here we are, *For the captain of a particular ship to come on board*. Union Flag at the mizen topmasthead.'

Ramage remembered that entry in the signal book. 'Benson!' he growled, 'what *particular ship* are you signalling to?'

The boy hurriedly looked back at the page and Ramage could visualize his grubby finger running across to the columns. 'Sorry, sir, Union at the mizen topmasthead, *and ship's signal.*'

'Well,' Ramage said sternly, 'make sure you get her numbers right. Now, get the signal bent on, and I'll masthead the pair of you if the halyards are twisted!'

As the two midshipmen scurried aft to the flag locker Ramage handed the piece of paper he was holding to the First Lieutenant. 'The challenge and reply. Hoist the challenge as soon as she's close enough to read it, and the moment she replies I want to see that signal' – he gestured to the boys – 'run up like a rocket!'

There was a hail from aloft, and Jackson reported that the strange sail was definitely a British brig.

'I wonder if she's gone to general quarters,' Southwick muttered to himself.

'I doubt it,' Ramage said. 'She's expecting a frigate to relieve her and she sees one . . .'

'No ship's a friend until she's made or answered the challenge correctly,' Southwick said stubbornly. 'There was none o' that slackness in the *Triton*!'

'Steady on,' Ramage said mildly, 'we don't know she hasn't gone to quarters yet!'

'Ah, but I know how slack these youngsters get in the West Indies.'

'The only brig in which you served in the West Indies was the *Triton*,' Ramage said sarcastically.

'Sorry, sir,' Southwick said apologetically, ''fraid my liver hasn't recovered from Bridgetown. Those planters do spice their food so. And all those foreign kickshaws they serve.'

By now Pointe des Salines was drawing abaft the beam, with Pointe Dunkerque broad on the starboard bow and two miles off. The brig was still partly in the lee of the hills and Ramage said to the First Lieutenant: 'Mr Aitken, we'll let her come down to us; there's no point in us getting in on the lee over there. Back the foretopsail.'

There are distinct advantages in being the senior officer, Ramage thought to himself, and resumed walking up and down the starboard side of the quarterdeck as orders were shouted and bos'n's pipes twittered, and men ran up to brace round the yard as the helm was put up. The *Juno* came up into the wind a few degrees until the wind was blowing on the forward side of the topsail, pressing it back against the mast and trying to push the frigate's bow round to leeward, a push which was counter-acted by the rudder and the after sails, which were trying to push her bow up into the wind. Careful sail trimming balanced both forces until the *Juno* was lying almost stopped in the water.

Ramage watched the *Welcome* approaching, slowly at first, almost wallowing in the wind shadow thrown by the high ridge of land running down to Pointe Dunkerque but then heeling slightly as the first few puffs caught her coming out of the lee. Through the glass Ramage saw her yards being trimmed, then she heeled more and the sails billowed and the canvas tautened as she caught a fresh breeze and came alive.

'Make the challenge, Mr Aitken,' he said. 'Stand by with your glass, Mr Benson!'

The three flags soared upwards. Ramage counted to himself – ten seconds, twenty, forty, a minute, two minutes . . . Then three flags were hoisted aboard the brig, and even before an excited Benson called them out Ramage read the numbers: the correct reply. And the *Welcome*'s pendant numbers.

Hearing a hurried curse from the First Lieutenant, Ramage turned to see Orsini standing helpless, flags flapping round his legs.

'Jump, boy!' Aitken shouted angrily, 'but don't let go of

that halyard! Here, quartermaster, give him a hand. Benson, put that telescope down and bear a hand. It's a mastheading for the pair of you!'

Orsini, near to tears with embarrassment, jumped up but caught a foot in the cloth of the Union Flag and fell flat on his face. The burly coxswain lifted him up, shook him until his foot was clear and pushed him unceremoniously to one side, taking the halyard from his hands. He hauled as Benson cleared the flags and they rose upwards.

'The first time, too,' Ramage heard Southwick mutter at Ramage's elbow, and he knew the same thought was in the Master's mind: Ramage's first signal, his first order as a captain to the commanding officer of another ship.

'Don't tell the Marchesa,' Ramage murmured, 'she'd kill the poor lad!'

'I'd gladly do it for her at the moment,' Southwick said sourly. 'All wrapped up with coloured bunting like a bumboat laundry woman.'

Ramage turned forward so that Aitken and the midshipmen should not see him laughing. The best-laid plans of mice and post captains brought to nought by Gianna's nervous nephew. He wondered how many times in the past when, as a lieutenant, he had been ordered on board a ship and had had an ill-tempered reception from her captain, some similar episode had taken place a few minutes earlier. For that matter, he remembered, the *Invincible*'s captain had been unduly taciturn when he went on board to report to Admiral Davis. Had the Admiral just squared his yard for not reporting the *Juno*'s arrival earlier? Had the watchtower along the coast not spotted them, or not passed the word, or had the word been passed but not reached the flagship? He suddenly realized that he was getting a new insight into command, or rather command where you were the senior officer.

The commanding officer of the *Welcome* was handling her well: Ramage watched with a critical eye and guessed that the lieutenant was hurriedly deciding whether he should heave-to the brig to windward or leeward of the frigate, and the bos'n would be preparing to hoist out a boat.

An hour later Ramage watched the *Welcome*'s boat being hoisted in and stowed on the booms; then the foretopsail yard was braced round and as the sails began to draw the brig slowly gathered way, headed round towards the Diamond. Two hours later her hull was hidden by the curve of the earth. The young lieutenant commanding her had been jubilant when Ramage had handed him the various packets from Admiral Davis: after a brief call at Antigua he would be bound for England.

Ramage also guessed that the lieutenant was thankful to be going to Antigua direct, and not by way of Barbados because his three-week patrol off Fort Royal had met with little success. He had sighted a small island schooner leaving Fort Royal at dusk and chased her northwards, losing her in the darkness. In daylight a week later he had sighted a drogher in the Passe du Fours between the Diamond and the mainland but before he could reach her she had run up on the beach and the crew had fled ashore, leaving the drogher in flames. From the way she burned the lieutenant thought she had been carrying spirits, and was probably a smuggler bringing in rum from one of the southern islands.

He had looked blank when Ramage asked about boat operations at night in Fort Royal Bay. Captain Eames had responded in the same way to the same question. Most of the time the *Welcome* had found the current north-going, except at the southern end of the island, where it was usually west-going. Only once, after three days of light breezes and with the moon in the first quarter had he failed to find any current. No, he had never tried to anchor off the Diamond; yes, there were several French batteries along the coast between Pointe des Salines and Cap Salomon, but he had not landed seamen and marines at night to attack them and did not have their exact positions. The guns had never bothered him, he said, and as far as he knew Captain Eames had left them alone for the same reason.

He had been down to St Lucia once for water: half the casks filled in Barbados had been undrinkable. To Ramage's most important question his answer had been vague: as far as he knew there were two French frigates in Fort Royal, both stripped of their yards, and five merchantmen, none of them ready for sea. Half a dozen local schooners, perhaps more, were reported to be anchored inside the Bay, in the mouth of the Salée River, but he had not been far enough into the Bay to see them for himself. They could be privateers but he did not know for sure. A dozen droghers were also reported to be in the Salée River, but none of them ever went to sea, or if they did he had seen none, apart from the one that beached herself, and she was heading for Fort Royal. Captain Eames had only caught one vessel, which he had used as a tender.

Obviously the lieutenant lacked 'interest' with Admiral Davis and was anxious to get back to England with a whole skin and an undamaged ship after a year in the Caribbean. His heart had not been in his terrier-at-the-rabbit-hole task and Ramage found it hard to blame him. Captain Eames' inactivity was another kettle of fish: it was up to Eames to interpret the Admiral's orders, but it was galling that a man who had spent three months off Martinique tacking back and forth without doing anything to discomfort the French had been chosen by the Admiral to carry out the special operation ordered by the First Lord . . . Eames must be one of the Admiral's favourites.

Ramage walked aft, hands clasped behind his back, and stared over the taffrail at the *Juno*'s wake. What the devil was that special operation? The only enemy-held islands within Admiral Davis's command were Martinique and Guadeloupe. Obviously it did not concern Martinique, and the other island was of little importance: the First Lord would not concern himself with French privateers based there. That left the coast of South America. The eastern end of the north coast was Admiral Davis's responsibility – the Spanish Main was divided, so that the western part came under the Commander-in-Chief at Jamaica. Trinidad and Tobago and the Spanish province of Caracas . . . what was happening along there – apart from cruising to intercept Spanish ships, which was routine anyway – what could suddenly have aroused the interest of the First Lord? Some operation that could be carried out by a frigate? Ramage turned away, admitting that he was jealous of Eames and angry with himself for being childish enough to think that just because he brought out the orders he ought to be allowed to carry them out.

By now the *Juno*, jogging along under topsails, was approaching the Diamond Rock, and Ramage searched the coast from the headland at the foot of Diamond Hill round to the eastward, to half-way along the instep. He was irritated that the *Welcome*'s commanding officer had not been able to tell him the precise position of the shore batteries, and he knew that at this very moment Frenchmen would be watching the *Juno* with telescopes, noting and reporting to Fort Royal that the brig had gone off to the north and a frigate had taken her place.

Having criticized Captain Eames and the poor fellow commanding the *Welcome*, who had obviously been thankful to have lasted a year in the West Indies without dying of yellow fever or running the *Welcome* on a coral reef, Ramage had to decide what they should have done, and do it himself. The Admiral's orders were simple enough: blockade Fort Royal. The French Army is desperate for supplies, and so is the Navy. Paris probably knows about it and various ministers may be trying to do something to help.

He put his telescope away in the binnacle box drawer and resumed walking the deck oblivious to the fact that the officers had noted his furrowed brow and were alarmed at the way he was glaring at a spot a few feet ahead. Paris must be well aware of the position, but what would the ministers do? They could dispatch a single merchantman, hoping that they could sneak past the British blockade. In that way supplies could be sent out as soon as they became available. He knew well enough that the dockyards and arsenals of France were short of almost every item needed to keep a ship at sea and an army on its feet. The alternative was to send out a convoy escorted by two or three frigates or even a ship of the line. A convoy with three frigates might well be able to find its way through the blockade – especially if Paris knew that there was usually only a single British frigate on patrol. That was the one thing about which Paris could never be sure: Admiral Davis had said that he appeared occasionally with the *Invincible* and two or three frigates off Fort Royal Bay . . .

A convoy seemed more likely than single ships. If the convoy had an escort of two frigates, then the *Juno* had a chance of picking off a merchantman or two and of surviving. If there was a ship of the line he had the choice of making a fight of it or bolting for Barbados to warn the Admiral. Unless the convoy was spotted far out in the Atlantic and a warning passed to Barbados, the first he would know of it would be when he saw it rounding Pointe des Salines and bearing up for Diamond Rock.

That raised another problem: he could not be in two places at once. If he was watching off Fort Royal Bay, then the whole French fleet, let alone a small convoy, could round the Pointe and get half-way up to Cap Salomon without him seeing it until it had only fifteen miles to sail to get right under the guns of Fort Royal itself.

All that was obvious enough, he told himself crossly, and until the convoy appeared it was useless making any plans: what he did depended on the size of the convoy and escort, whether it was sighted by day or night, and its position. And the wind's strength and direction. And – a dozen things.

Very well, that deferred the problem of a convoy until the *Juno*'s lookouts sighted it, which could be tomorrow or in two months' time. What could he do in the meantime to rattle the bars and annoy the French? The only bars worth rattling were those at Fort Royal. What about those two frigates that the *Welcome* reported in the bay? They were stripped of their yards, but that could be of no significance.

Damn, the sun was bright. He pulled his hat down to shield his eyes. What was the possibility of one of those frigates crossing her yards, bending on sails and suddenly appearing off Cap Salomon or the Diamond, loaded with troops and with half a dozen privateers in company? He rubbed the scars over his brow: the more he thought about it, the more the possibility became a probability. It was a good twenty miles from Fort Royal Bay down to Pointe des Salines. From the time she looked into Fort Royal, went south to look round Pointe des Salines and returned to Fort Royal, the *Juno* would have to cover forty miles. In a light breeze that could take eight hours.

Eight hours – yards up, sails bent on, and the ship under way: yes, it would need careful preparation but the French could do it. But in fact unless he looked into Fort Royal at dawn every day the French could have the whole night as well, with special lookouts along the coast warning them as the *Juno* made her way back north again . . .

Those two frigates which had caused both Eames and the *Welcome*'s lieutenant so little concern could break the blockade. If they knew when a convoy was due they could sail out and either capture the *Juno* or drive her off, and then help escort the convoy in. It was all very well for Admiral Davis to shrug off the little harbours of La Trinité and Robert on the Atlantic coast of Martinique. Certainly they were too small for landing supplies which would then have to be carried right over the mountain ridges to Fort Royal; but either harbour was ideally placed for a small French ship to sail in from the Atlantic and warn of a convoy's approach. Suddenly the blockade of Fort Royal took on a different appearance. Captain Eames and the *Welcome* brig had been lucky . . .

Ramage found himself standing on the fo'c'sle by the belfry with no memory of having left the quarterdeck, but he was at last fairly clear in his mind what the blockade of Fort

Royal entailed. He was startled to see Diamond Rock only a couple of miles ahead, fine on the starboard bow, and it was a fantastic sight: a rocky, stark islet jutting up out of the sea like an enormous tooth, nearly 600 feet high and each side about 400 yards long. Greyish rock mottled with patches of green and brown, like a great cheese attacked by mildew. With an effort he switched his thoughts back to the main problem.

First, he had to find out about the French frigates, and that meant going in close to Fort Royal to have a good look. Then he needed to know exactly what other ships and vessels the French had available in Fort Royal Bay, and that included the schooners and droghers anchored in the Salée River, on the south side. That was going to be more difficult task because almost the entire Salée River anchorage was hidden behind Pointe de la Rose, with a fearsome number of shoals protecting it: even the French did not attempt to pass through them without local knowledge.

How well Fort Royal itself was protected was another question. The city itself did not matter, but the anchorage where the frigates were was vital. The batteries would be somewhere in the lee of Fort St Louis, which was built on a spit of land poking out southwards like a thumb. There would be other batteries, but the guns of Fort St Louis would be the most dangerous. Again Captain Eames and the *Welcome*'s lieutenant were vague . . .

He strode aft and told Wagstaffe, who was the officer of the deck, to pass the word for Mr Southwick to come to his cabin with the chart of Fort Royal Bay. At the top of the companionway he stared once again at the Diamond Rock. It seemed less menacing now because there was a scattering of green over the grey rock, like shreds of baize, and shrubs clung precariously to the almost sheer slopes. Beyond the Rock, across the Fours Channel, he could see a long silvery band of beach on the mainland: that must be the Grande Anse du Diamant, where the *Welcome* ran the drogher ashore, and which ended at the cliffs of Diamond Hill.

He acknowledged the Marine sentry's salute, went through to the great cabin and sprawled on the settee, feeling a sudden weariness which was mental rather than physical. He was asking too many questions and not finding enough answers. Southwick knocked on the door and came through into the cabin, a cheerful smile on his face. His expression did not change when he saw Ramage's furrowed brow.

'That Diamond Rock is quite remarkable, isn't it, sir? I've been sketching it in the log. I estimate it is more than 550 feet high. And so parched I wonder how those goats manage to survive.'

'Goats?' Ramage exclaimed.

'Aye, I saw fifty or more through the glass, and that was only on the south-west side. Must be hundreds altogether. Means we can hunt for fresh meat when things are quiet — nice haunch of goat would make a pleasant change.'

Ramage snorted in disgust. 'You'd need to file your teeth first: the meat of those goats would serve as boot leather. They must live off the bushes; there's almost no grass except perhaps a little on the lower slopes.'

'It'd give the hunters plenty of exercise,' Southwick said happily, obviously not concerned about the toughness of the meat.

'Anyone needing exercise can arrange races up and down the rigging,' Ramage said crossly. 'Now, you have the chart of Fort Royal Bay?'

The Master unrolled it.

'Where would you expect the frigates to be anchored?'

'Carénage Bay,' Southwick said promptly, 'it's the deep cut just on the eastern side of Fort St Louis,' He turned the chart round and held it out for Ramage to see. 'If not there, then in front of the city — where it's marked "Anchorage des Flamands".'

Ramage stared at the chart. 'Hmm, if we went close enough in — up here to the north-eastern corner of the Bay — we'd be able to look into the Salée River anchorage.'

'That's our best chance: I wouldn't feel confident taking the ship closer to the Salée,' Southwick admitted. 'Looks bad enough on the chart, and that doesn't show a tenth of the shoals. Coral grows there like weed in a garden. I'd say it was impossible to get into the anchorage itself without a local pilot. That's why the privateers like to use it. They know they're safe.'

'Safe from a frigate,' Ramage said thoughtfully, 'but sitting ducks for a boat attack.'

Southwick shrugged his shoulders. 'I must admit I'd sooner see those frigates out o' the way first, sir.'

'We've plenty of time,' Ramage said, beginning to cheer up. 'The frigates, the schooners, the droghers, the short batteries and then the goats if there's time to spare.'

'It'd be good exercise for the Marines,' said Southwick

sardonically. 'Turn 'em loose on the Diamond with enough water for a week and tell 'em they have to live off the goats. Plenty of caves for them to sleep in – I saw three or four as we came by, some of them quite large.'

Ramage eyed Southwick with mock suspicion. 'I think you'd like to retire to the Diamond when the war is over.'

'We'll see.' Southwick was noncommittal. 'What are the orders for tonight, sir?'

Having discussed the navigation with the Master, Ramage passed the word for the First Lieutenant to join them. When Aitken arrived he told them briefly of the information passed on by the commanding officer of the *Welcome*. The First Lieutenant and Southwick both gave contemptuous sniffs, which Ramage found encouraging. The Master was always eager to seek out action, but up to this moment Ramage had had no chance to gauge Aitken.

'Do we have to leave those frigates in there, sir?' the First Lieutenant asked plaintively.

'Mr Southwick and I have just been going over the chart of Fort Royal Bay,' Ramage said. 'Have a look at it.' He gave Aitken a couple of minutes to absorb the general situation and then pointed to the two places where the frigates could be at anchor.

Aitken measured off distances from the latitude scale. 'Close enough to the Fort. Point-blank range . . .' he said mournfully.

Ramage felt disappointed: so the First Lieutenant was no fire-eater.

Aitken looked closely at the few soundings shown on the chart, and then dumbfounded Ramage by commenting: 'We'll have to sink one, since we can't tow 'em both out. Not unless they're rigged, in which case we could sail 'em.'

Ramage nodded as he thought the commanding officer of His Majesty's frigate *Juno* should nod when his First Lieutenant reached a conclusion he had himself reached a couple of hours earlier.

Aitken took out his watch and said eagerly. 'You plan to attack tonight, sir?'

Southwick shuddered and Ramage shook his head. 'We need to know a little more precisely where they are, and I don't think Mr Southwick would fancy piloting us into a harbour in the dark when he hasn't seen it for a few years. Not that I would ask him to, either!'

Aitken realized that his enthusiasm had run away with him.

'Of course, sir – but I'll take a boat in tonight, if you wish. That way the French won't know the *Juno* is nearby.'

Ramage caught Southwick's eye and knew there was no need to worry about Aitken's aggressiveness; indeed it might be necessary to curb it. 'Don't worry about that: I'm sure the Governor at Fort Royal or St Pierre already knows we've relieved the brig. He's used to a British frigate tacking up and down the coast – this place has been under blockade for months.'

'That's what I find so puzzling about those frigates, sir,' Aitken said. 'Why haven't the French rigged 'em and used 'em to capture or drive off our ships?'

'The obvious reason may be the right one,' Ramage said quietly. 'Spars rotted or broken, short of cordage or sails . . . Probably waiting for supplies to arrive from France to commission them.'

Aitken looked at him admiringly, and Ramage felt embarrassed: it had been obvious enough to him, but not apparently to the First Lieutenant, nor, he saw from the look on Southwick's face, to the Master either.

'Give us a little more time,' Southwick commented.

'I hope so,' Ramage said, 'but I hope your thoughts aren't dwelling on those goats!'

'I'll let them take their turn,' Southwick said and began explaining the joke to Aitken, who looked excited and said enthusiastically: 'I did a lot of deer hunting when I was a boy in Scotland, if that'd be any help.'

'Frigates,' Ramage said sternly, 'I'd be much obliged if you gentlemen would confine your thoughts to frigates, privateers and droghers.'

'Of course, sir,' said a chastened Aitken. 'Your night orders, sir?'

'Boat exercises,' Ramage said promptly. 'As soon as it is dark, we hoist out the boats and send away boarding parties. Issue them with muskets and pistols. Now's the time for them to make mistakes, out of earshot of the French. They'll row twice round the ship and then exercise at boarding us. We recover boats, hoist them out again, and do it once more. There won't be much sleep for anyone, but we'll have an easy day tomorrow.'

Southwick and Aitken glanced at each other at his last words, but Ramage decided against explaining his plan. The ship's company was in good spirits because it was confident. Now the men had to develop another kind of confidence –

that they could deal with anything unexpected while in the
the boats. Most important of all, how to scramble up a ship's
side while armed with a pistol, musket, cutlass or pike, and
with a determined enemy firing down at them. There would
be no shooting while they exercised boarding the *Juno* in the
darkness, but it would teach them that the side of a prison
wall and the side of a frigate could be just as difficult to
scale.

CHAPTER EIGHT

Next morning the Surgeon reported to Ramage shortly after
dawn, holding a list in one hand and his journal in the other.
Bowen had a long face and said mournfully, 'It's been a long
time since I had to report men on the sick list, sir . . .'

'You'd better start getting used to the idea,' Ramage
said grimly. 'We'll be seeing plenty of action in the next
few weeks, I hope. Now, what sort of harvest did you reap
last night?'

Bowen held out the list. 'The men are so careless,' he
grumbled. 'They don't seem to give a thought to their own
safety.'

'This list certainly bears *that out*,' Ramage said crossly, and
Bowen looked up, startled. 'Four men wounded by the
accidental discharge of pistols, one by a musket ball, one cut
by a cutlass – how the devil can that happen? – and three with
rope burns to the hands and shins.'

'Accidents will happen, sir,' Bowen said lamely.

'Accidents? Five shots fired. Can you imagine that happening as boats row up with muffled oars to make a surprise
night attack on an enemy ship at anchor? Even one shot
would give the alarm. The enemy is alerted and opens fire,
and every man in our boarding party might be killed. Twenty
men die – many more if there are other boats – all because of
the stupid, criminal carelessness of one man.'

He looked down at the list and said wrathfully: 'That can
happen if *one* man is careless, but just look at this.' He waved
the paper. 'Not one man but *five*. And in every case the man
shoots himself or another of his shipmates. Well, I'm warning
the ship's company that the next time I'll have each man
flogged –'

'Fortunately, sir, all the wounds are slight. I have – '

'Bowen,' Ramage snapped, 'frankly I don't give a damn about the wounds. What concerns me is the noise. A pistol shot at night can be heard for a couple of miles, let alone a couple of yards. Can't you understand that one man's carelessness can kill all his shipmates, and wreck a carefully planned attack?'

'Yes, sir, I do understand about the gunshot wounds, but the rope burns – '

'Rope burns!' Ramage exclaimed. 'Damnation take it, Bowen, these men are supposed to be seamen. Do I have to start training them to climb ropes?'

'Excuse me, sir,' Bowen said nervously, not having seen Ramage so angry before, 'I did question those three men because it surprised me too, and it was due to enthusiasm. All three were climbing the same rope to board the *Juno*, and apparently the lower two men were urging on the man above them. In his excitement he missed his grasp with one hand, began to slide and took the rest of the men down with him.'

'Very well,' Ramage said, a little mollified. 'But this fellow with the cutlass wound?'

'Didn't Orsini report that incident to you, sir?' Bowen asked cautiously.

'What incident?'

'Oh dear, sir, I seem to be getting into deep water. I don't want to get Orsini into trouble . . .'

'Out with it,' Ramage ordered, 'otherwise I'll send for Orsini. I'll have to anyway, if it is something he should have reported.'

'Well, sir, apparently the boarders from the cutter came over the starboard side of the fo'c'sle and those from the launch over the larboard side. Both parties began boarding at the same time, and when they met on the fo'c'sle one man from each party began quarrelling about who was first on board. I'm sorry to say they came to blows.'

'With cutlasses?' Ramage asked incredulously.

Bowen nodded. 'One of them was cut and they only stopped slashing at each other when Orsini jumped between them. It was a very brave act on the part of the boy,' he added.

'Very foolish if you ask me. Were the men drunk?'

'No, just excited. You see, sir, they're so proud of the ship now that they're all trying to outdo each other and be first

114

at everything. I'm surprised—'

When the Surgeon broke off, Ramage said, 'Well, go on, man!'

'I was going to say, if you'll excuse the boldness, sir, that I was surprised you had not noticed it. All the lieutenants have been commenting on it for some time, and Southwick is most gratified . . .'

'*Proud*, are they?' Ramage exclaimed. 'Well, after that farce last night they ought to be thoroughly ashamed. I assure you, Bowen, that I am heartily ashamed that I command a ship which is incapable of sending off boarding parties that don't spend their time shooting at each other.'

He gave the list back to Bowen. 'It's your job to treat these men, Bowen, but have you ever thought what a captain feels? I'm trying to train them so they stand the best possible chance of carrying out any orders I give them without unnecessary casualties. If I send out boarding parties made up of untrained men to attack a French ship and the boats return three-quarters full of dead and dying men, you'd be justified in blaming *me*. I'm trying to make sure it never happens; that every man realizes that a mistake, however slight, can get everyone killed.'

Bowen nodded and folded the list. 'I understand, sir,' he said quietly. 'If you'll just sign the entry in my journals . . . I'll have these men back on their feet as soon as possible.'

Ramage went to the desk and took out pen and ink from the rack. He glanced down the names and was thankful to note that none of them was a former *Triton*. Under the 'Disease and symptoms' column he saw that the gunshot wounds were comparatively slight. The cutlass wound was a gash on the forearm. He scribbled his signature and gave the journal back to the Surgeon.

Bowen hesitated for a moment and then said cautiously: 'Orsini's failure to report the episode, sir . . .'

Ramage raised his eyebrows. 'Orsini?'

The Surgeon grinned. 'Thank you, sir. He's a lad with plenty of spirit—I sometimes wish the Marchesa could see him now.'

An hour after sunrise the *Juno* tacked off Pointe des Salines at the south end of Martinique and steered northwards along the coast, keeping as close in to the shore as Southwick's sketchy charts allowed. Jackson was aloft at the foretopmast-head with strict orders to watch for any signs of shoals, and the Master had the chart spread out on the binnacle box, held down by weights and his quadrant.

The *Juno*'s guns were loaded and run out, the lieutenants stood by on the maindeck, watching their own divisions, and Ramage stood aft beside the quartermaster, a speaking trumpet on the deck beside him and a telescope in his hand.

The land here was flat but rising slightly towards Pointe Dunkerque. That was a good place for a battery, to cover one side of the deep but narrow bay forming the anchorage of St Anne, with the village of Bourg du Marin at its head. It was a fine little anchorage for droghers carrying sugar cane from plantations at the south end of the island up to Fort Royal and St Pierre – and an equally good place for privateers to lurk, ready to snatch up a British merchantman making its way up or down the coast, while safe from any British frigate which would not risk the shoals almost closing the entrance. Yet, Ramage remembered, the *Welcome* brig had been close in under Pointe Dunkerque, and had not been fired on. Perhaps the French were short of guns, too, using those they had for the defence of Fort Royal and perhaps St Pierre, which had no harbour.

The Pointe soon drew round on to the *Juno*'s quarter as Ramage took her over towards the headland on the northern side of the entrance. He now saw it would make more sense to place a battery on that side because any vessel beating into the bay, which ran north-east, would have to pass within a hundred yards of it to avoid shoals on the other side.

He lifted the speaking trumpet and shouted the order that would brace the yards and trim the sheets as he gave the quartermaster instructions to steer a point more to starboard. Through the telescope he examined the headland, nearly a mile distant. There was a hint of a pathway leading up to an old stone wall partly overgrown with bushes. Then he noticed that the bushes round the wall were withered; the leaves were brown while those shrubs nearby were a living green. Was that some movement beyond the wall? It was hard to tell at this range.

Suddenly two red eyes seemed to wink in the wall and a moment later two spurts of smoke changed into a billowing puff drifting away in the wind. 'Just west of the top of the point,' he shouted at Aitken and glanced round to look for the fall of shot. Two thin columns of water leapt up into the air a hundred yards short of the *Juno* and well ahead.

There was little chance of doing the battery much damage,

and opening ineffective fire would show the French gunners that they were safe from a frigate's guns. It might be a better idea to let them continue to think so, but it was an equally good idea to let the *Juno*'s men fire their first shots in anger.

'Mr Aitken – a single round to try the range!'

The *Juno*'s 12-pounders could reach the battery, but the frigate was rolling just enough to make aiming difficult for the gun captains.

The aftermost 12-pounder – the one in his cabin – grunted and rumbled back in recoil. More marks on the painted canvas from those damned trucks. A moment before smoke swirled up from the port Ramage saw several spurts of dust just below the battery as the shot hit twenty yards below the wall and ricocheted up the slope. He managed to stop himself calling down to Aitken: the First Lieutenant knew what to do, and even now men with handspikes would be lifting the breech of the next gun and sliding out the wedge-shaped quoin a fraction to increase the gun's elevation.

'One more round to be sure,' Ramage shouted and the gun fired almost immediately. Through his telescope Ramage saw stones thrown outwards at the same level as the battery but apparently just to the right of it. Then he saw that it had in fact hit the wall.

'That's better,' he shouted, making sure all the men at the starboard side guns heard him. 'Now, every gun to fire as it bears – gun captains take their time and don't waste shot!'

Southwick, completely unconcerned with the thunder and smoke of the *Juno*'s guns, was crouched over the compass, taking bearings of the tip of the Point and the battery. He straightened up and went to the chart on the binnacle box as the next gun fired. Within half a minute each of the *Juno*'s starboard side guns had fired and was being reloaded. Smoke, acrid and biting the throat and nose, drifted back over the quarterdeck before being swept away to leeward.

Much of the wall had been demolished; through the glass Ramage caught sight of men in blue jackets scurrying about. Again a red eye winked and there was a spurt of smoke. He did not bother to look for the fall of shot – gunners who had just heard or felt thirteen 12-pounder round shot crashing about them would not be aiming with much skill. Only one shot. The other gun had not fired. Had a lucky shot dismounted it?

Even as he tried to catch sight of the actual guns, those on board the *Juno* began firing again; firing carefully, every gun

117

captain sure of his aim before tugging the lanyard, as far as the *Juno*'s captain was concerned. Another section of the stone wall collapsed, leaving only a pyramid standing in the middle; then more rocks began rolling from that, and he glimpsed a large black tube pointing up in the air, and beside it another such tube lying at an angle, like a log that had fallen from a cart.

'Secure the guns!' he called down to Aitken. 'Good shooting – you've dismounted both of them.'

Immediately the gun crews began cheering and the lieutenants bellowed for silence. Ramage's eyes narrowed. The men were children to be cheering at what was little more than an exercise. He turned to the quartermaster, ordered him to bear away, and gestured to Southwick to give the order for trimming the yards.

Then he went to the quarterdeck rail and looked down at the men at the guns. Some were stripped to the waist, all had narrow bands of cloth tied round their foreheads to stop perspiration running into their eyes. They were grinning and gesturing to each other.

'Listen you men,' Ramage roared. 'With twenty-six rounds of shot, two full broadsides, you've managed to knock down a dry stone wall and dismount two small guns behind it, and you cheer! The battery is low down and easy to see, thanks to those Frenchmen forgetting to cut fresh shrubs to hide the front of the wall. But you'll all learn about firing at batteries when you have to tackle one on top of a cliff and firing down at you. One where every gun is aimed coolly because they know there's precious little chance of your shot reaching them. Now, get those guns sponged out, and let's have no more of this childishness!'

He marched back aft to join Southwick, his anger already evaporating. He was glad in a way that the men were pleased with their shooting, but he wanted them to be under no illusion about what the plunging fire of a well-placed and well-manned battery on the top of a cliff could do to a ship of war. The two guns they had just dismounted were probably firing at a ship for the first time.

Southwick was carefully pencilling in the battery's position on the chart and as Ramage bent over to see that a road below the battery went round the back of the hill, to the village of Bourg du Marin, the Master whispered: 'Nevertheless, it was good shooting, sir!'

'I'm not denying that,' Ramage muttered. 'I just don't

want them to think that the fire from Fort St Louis will be like that.'

'Ah,' Southwick said and then, with a sideways glance, added: 'It mightn't be so bad in the dark.'

'Quite,' Ramage said coldly. The Master might feel he ought not to have been so harsh with the men, but too much praise was as bad as too little; over-confidence could kill them just as easily as a lack of it. Striking the right balance, that was the Captain's job, and he was finding it hard. A naval officer in wartime had to order men into battle, but it did not follow that he had to shrug his shoulders when they were killed. It was deuced hard work trying to train them so that they had the best chance of surviving, and that was what he had been trying to tell Bowen earlier. A childhood memory came back to him – his father about to give him a beating for some escapade which had ended up with his horse bolting, and saying with genuine sadness: 'It's for your own good, boy.'

Southwick was saying something and gesturing at the chart, indicating another headland five miles along the coast to the westward and a mile short of the long stretch of Diamond beach. Realizing that Ramage had been preoccupied, he repeated: 'I think that's where we'll find the next one, sir: Grosse Pointe. There'll be nothing along the beach here, the land's too low. Then another one somewhere here, on the headland in front of Diamond Hill. I see they call it "Morne du Diamant".' He peered closely at the chart. 'Sixteen hundred feet high. This ridge here must be about five hundred feet. That's where I'd put one if it was up to me.'

'The gunners wouldn't thank you,' Ramage said, pointing to the nearest road, which ran along the back of the Diamond beach and stopped at the bottom of Morne du Diamant, a mile or more short of the peak. 'Imagine carrying powder and shot all that way.'

'They'd use donkeys and slaves,' Southwick said. 'I can't see French artillerymen exerting themselves.'

'Those fellows back there stood their ground well enough,' Ramage reminded him.

'They didn't know what was coming,' Southwick said contemptuously. 'Otherwise they'd have bolted when that second shot caught the wall and ricocheted past their ears.'

By noon the *Juno* had passed Cap Salomon and sheets and braces were being hauled as the helm was put up for the frigate to begin beating into Fort Royal Bay. Southwick had been right, there had been a battery at Grosse Pointe and two guns had fired, but Ramage had not fired back. Dismounted guns could be remounted on new carriages; the Grosse Pointe battery and the one that had fired a single gun from a third of the way up Diamond Hill would have to be destroyed completely. As a result they had been left alone, and Southwick had marked their precise positions on the chart and made neat sketches in the log. The fourth battery had predictably been sited at Cap Salomon: four guns which had fired a dozen shots each as the *Juno* sailed slowly by a mile off, well within range. Not one of the shots landed within two or three cables of the frigate, and the battery was so high there was little danger from ricochets skimming low over the sea.

The frigate had no sooner rounded Cap Salomon than the city of Fort Royal came in sight as the great bay opened up. Built on the northern side, it was only just inside it. The higher buildings showed up white and red in the telescope but with the mouth of the bay nearly four miles wide it was still impossible to make out much detail.

The ship's company had had dinner and were in good spirits; Aitken reported wryly that he had heard much among the men about how they could have knocked out the other batteries, and that the Captain was probably leaving them for the time being, intending to tackle one a week to keep the guns' crews in practice.

Ramage smiled and glanced at the dogvanes from time to time. The wind was light and from the east, but they were still in the lee of the mountains behind Cap Salomon. Once they came clear of the headland – and the north-going current was giving them a good lift – there should be a good wind all the way up to Fort Royal because the land on the eastern side of the bay was low.

Ramage felt the excitement growing on board the frigate: the men were still at quarters and Jackson, Rossi, Stafford and several other former Tritons were conspicuous for their nonchalance. They had been in action too many times to be impressed by the distant sight of a French port. Young Orsini and Benson were wearing their dirks with all the flourish of fencing masters, eager as ferrets to catch his eye in case there was a message to carry or an errand to perform.

'Mr Aitken, I think we can be sure the Governor of Fort

Royal has a list of the Navy so we might as well introduce ourselves. Have our pendant numbers hoisted.'

The First Lieutenant snapped the order to the two midshipmen, who ran to the flag locker, and the men watched the three flags being hoisted. Hearing a curious murmuring, Ramage walked to the quarterdeck rail to look down on the maindeck. The men were grinning and clapping each other on the back, obviously delighted that the flags streaming in the wind were advertising their presence in an enemy port.

Ramage walked aft again. It was a small thing, but the men obviously wanted Fort Royal to know that the frigate was the *Juno*. Perhaps that was what Bowen had meant, but pride in their ship was still a poor excuse for firing pistols all over the place.

He suddenly realized that the men and, damnation take it, the lieutenants too, were behaving as though they expected the *Juno* to stay on this tack and storm Fort Louis! He gestured to the First Lieutenant and Master to join him by the capstan, where they could talk out of earshot of the quartermaster and the men at the wheel.

'My intention,' he said heavily, 'is to beat into the bay until we get a sight of the Salée River anchorage and can see what vessels are there. After that we will bear away round the south end of the shoal to the east of the city, then bear up again towards the Carénage and Fort St Louis for a sight of the frigates. After that we'll bear away so we can run past the front of the city and out to Pointe des Nègres. By that time I hope to have a complete list of every ship and vessel in the bay that might interest us, with their positions.'

Aitken looked disappointed but the veteran Southwick was obviously puzzled, wondering why the Captain was mentioning anything so obvious.

'I want a good man in the chains with a lead, and another man ready to relieve him,' Ramage added, 'and Jackson aloft with a telescope. He's the best man on board for identifying ships. How much water have we over the southern end of the shoal they call Grande Sèche?'

Southwick shook his head. 'Only three or four fathoms at the most, sir; we can't risk it. But we should see it clearly and it'll be as good as a row of buoys once we bear away from looking into the Salée River.'

'Very well. By the way, Mr Aitken, you can tell the men what we shall be doing; they seem to be expecting me to tow Fort St Louis back to Barbados and then give them shore leave.'

Once clear of the mountains the wind freshened to a strong breeze. As the *Juno* entered the bay it began veering to the south-east so that the frigate, close hauled on the starboard tack, was able to clear all the small headlands and shoals on the south side, heading east-north-east to get far enough in so that Pointe de la Rose did not hide the vessels at anchor in the Salée River, which was a deep indentation at the east end of Fort Royal Bay.

The sun was hot and dazzling as it reflected off the sea and Ramage wished he could have had the awning rigged. The deck was like the top of a stove and his feet throbbed inside his boots. His stock was damp with perspiration, though the fresher breeze was beginning to cool him. The men did not seem to mind – but they did not have to wear uniform.

'That's Pointe de Boute, sir,' Southwick said, 'and you can just see Rose Point beyond. Another mile or so on this tack and we'll be able to see right into the Salée.' He turned and pointed over the larboard bow. 'That lighter patch, that's the Grande Sèche.'

Ramage nodded: that was one advantage of the clear waters of the West Indies. With a little experience you could judge the depth of water by its colour in the sunlight. It was a paler blue where Southwick had pointed, which meant only three fathoms or so, but closer to the land it would turn into a light green, which warned of two fathoms or less. The sun had to be reasonably high, however, otherwise the reflection spoiled the navigator's best insurance.

Ramage thought Fort Royal Bay one of the loveliest in the Caribbean. The ridges of the hills and mountains to the north and south made interesting shadows, so that valleys emphasized peaks, while the low land to the east gave it a scale. The city was well-placed, sheltered from the northers of the winter yet pleasantly open to the cooling Trade winds from the east.

A hail from the mainmasthead interrupted his daydreaming as Jackson reported that one frigate was anchored in front of the city with masts stepped and lower yards crossed, and a second frigate was right in the Carénage with yards and top-masts down. Southwick was jotting down notes when Jackson shouted down that he could just begin to see into the Salée anchorage as it came clear of Rose Point.

Ramage swung round to look over the starboard side. The

Salée anchorage was backed by mangrove swamps with an island in the middle and a small cay beyond, and within a couple of minutes he could see a dozen or more vessels at anchor, most of them heading to the south-east but a few lying more to the east, showing a local wind eddy. He began counting. Five . . . six . . . nine . . . ten . . . eleven schooners, low and rakish, and which obviously could be used as privateers. Only the seven largest had sails bent on. Hard to distinguish, but they seemed to be pierced for four guns a side. Those seven could carry a hundred men for a short voyage. There were nine droghers, slab-sided with apple-cheek bows, unhandy but able to carry a lot of cargo, and that was all. He could now see all of the anchorage where there was enough water for anything larger than a small fishing boat to float. He glanced at Southwick, who nodded and tapped his notebook, repeating the same totals that Ramage had counted. The Master then glanced significantly over the larboard side and Ramage looked across to see that the Grande Sèche shoal was drawing uncomfortably far south.

'We'll bear away if you please, Mr Aitken.' Going to the binnacle and then looking over the bow again he added: 'West by north ought to keep us clear.'

Bos'n's calls twittered, men ran to sheets and braces, and the *Juno* wore round until the wind was on the larboard quarter with Fort Royal itself over on the starboard bow. Ramage swung the telescope slowly along the shore, from west to east, finally reaching the grey bulk of Fort St Louis, which now had a large Tricolour streaming from its flagstaff. There was the Carénage and the frigate Jackson had described, stripped except for her lower masts. Had they used her yards and topmasts to start commissioning the one anchored in front of the town? If so, why anchor her out there? Perhaps they reckoned her guns gave the western end of Fort Royal some protection, relying on Fort St Louis to cover the eastern end.

The *Juno* was sailing fast now in an almost flat sea and Ramage watched as the big shoal drew round on to the quarter, leaving deep water right up to the shoal that extended half a mile from the Fort. He wanted a closer look at the frigate, and then that would be enough for today. He looked down at the compass again. 'Mr Aitken, we'll wear round. North by west, if you please.'

Again the men braced up the yards and sheets as the frigate came round on to the new course, putting the wind three points on her starboard quarter and Fort St Louis almost dead ahead. Soon Ramage could distinguish details of the buildings right along the shore; then through the telescope he could see that the French frigate was crowded with men. Many were in the ratlines, but he was not sure whether they had been working aloft or had climbed up to get a better view of the *Juno*. Her ports were open but her guns were not run out.

Smoke was drifting away from the Fort and a few moments later he heard the rumble of guns. The range was more than a mile. He turned to Aitken: 'Hail Jackson and ask him if he saw the fall of shot.'

The First Lieutenant pointed over the larboard quarter. 'I saw five, sir, half a mile away, right in our wake. There! They're firing again!'

Five more shots landed in the position Aitken had pointed out, five pinnacles of water that leapt up as though whales were spouting and then vanished.

'They just reloaded and fired without correcting their aim: not used to firing at a moving target,' Southwick commented. 'Another week's work to be done on that frigate,' he added. 'They must have three hundred men on board – just look at 'em perched in the rigging, like a lot o' starlings. They could get some of their guns to bear, so as they aren't firing they must be a long way from commissioning.'

'Short of powder, perhaps,' Aitken ventured, but Ramage gestured to the Fort, which had fired yet again.

Jackson hailed from the masthead: 'The *Surcouf* – that's the frigate, sir: I just made out the name on her transom when she swung to that gust.'

Ramage looked at Southwick with raised eyebrows. 'Don't know of her, sir,' the Master said apologetically. 'Thirty-six guns and she looks fairly new.'

Ramage closed his telescope with a snap. 'Bear away again, Mr Aitken: steer west by north. We'll just see if they have any more batteries at this end of the Bay. Once we have Pointe des Nègres on our beam I think we'll have rattled the bars loudly enough for today. You've the *Surcouf*'s exact position on the chart I assume, Mr Southwick.'

CHAPTER NINE

Two nights later Ramage stood on the quarterdeck with Wagstaffe, who was the officer of the deck, as the *Juno* stretched northwards under topsails only. It was a dark night, large banks of cloud frequently covering three-quarters of the sky and blacking out the stars. The glass was steady but by midnight there could be either a clear sky or pouring rain. Ramage grumbled to himself about the unpredictability of tropical weather.

Once again Wagstaffe called to the lookouts on either bow, and again both answered that there was no sign of Diamond Rock. The young lieutenant was nervous and Ramage was trying to decide if he should tell him not to keep hailing the lookouts unnecessarily: they knew well enough what they were looking for and would hail the moment they sighted it. He now wished he had not taken the *Juno* so close to the Rock, but the cloud had thickened only in the last half an hour. Anyway he could bear away out to the westward at any moment and be sure of clearing it, but bearing away was just the sort of thing that allowed the damned droghers and schooners to sneak up the coast, pass through the Fours Channel between Diamond Rock and Diamond Hill and get into Fort Royal. They would be impossible to sight from seaward, hidden against the high land.

He would stay on this course. For the next few weeks they were going to be staying close in to Diamond at night and the sooner everyone got used to the idea the better. The cloud seemed to be getting lower and the wind was freshening: there was a sudden chill which gave warning that it was going to rain in a couple of minutes. He turned to Orsini and said: 'Go below and fetch oilskins – mine is on the hook outside the door. And fetch Mr Wagstaffe's and your own at the same time.'

Damn the rain: it would cut visibility to a hundred yards or less. As the Rock carried deep water right up to its side from the south, there was no point in having a man in the chains with a lead. He was still torn between bearing away and carrying on so that Wagstaffe should gain confidence. Then he decided that Wagstaffe's confidence was less important than the safety of the ship. As he turned towards the lieutenant there was a scurry of feet and a man loomed up out of the darkness: 'Rossi, sir, lookout on the starboard bow. There's a sail close under our starboard bow a cable off: I dare not shout!'

'Very well,' Ramage snapped, 'warn the man at the main-chains not to shout either. Get back forward and tell the other man to keep a sharp lookout to larboard.'

He turned to Wagstaffe: 'Send the men to quarters, but no shouting!'

He strained his eyes over to starboard but could see nothing. Now the rain was coming, and he groped in the binnacle box drawer for the night glass. He swung it from ahead to far round on the quarter, but nothing was visible in the darkness and he moved it slowly forward again, resting his arms on the top of the binnacle box. There was a hint of greyness out there, a patch not quite as black as the rest of the night, but he lost it as a squall of rain swept the deck. The shape was distinctive enough – the sails of a schooner on almost the same course as the *Juno* and perhaps two hundred yards ahead on the starboard bow.

He hurried over to the larboard side, almost knocking over Orsini, who held out oilskin coats. He balanced himself and looked over the bow, hoping the squall would not have reached out that far yet. What he saw was the similar grey shape of another schooner! There was no doubt about it; he had spent too many years allowing for the inverted image shown in a night glass.

He sensed rather than heard men hurrying to quarters. Aitken came up in the darkness, buckling on his sword, followed almost immediately by Southwick. He looked around for the Marine Lieutenant and called him over.

The three officers gathered round him and Wagstaffe edged over to hear as much as he could. There was no time to wait for the Third and Fourth Lieutenants.

'Two French schooners, one on either bow, on the same course,' Ramage said crisply. 'Probably privateers packed full of men. Perhaps even French troops. I think they are waiting for the rain to stop, then the moment the sky starts clearing and they can see they'll try to board us, one on each side.'

Southwick gave one of his famous sniffs. 'They must think we're all asleep.'

'When Rossi spotted the first one, it was more than a cable away. I wonder –'

Ramage broke off: it was not for the Captain of a ship to wonder aloud, but why were these schooners planning an attack on the *Juno* when they had left the *Welcome* brig and Captain Eames's frigate alone? Was a convoy expected or did they fear an attack on the frigate anchored off Fort Royal?

He turned to Orsini. 'Run forward, boy. Warn all lookouts not to shout. Tell the larboard lookout there's a second schooner on the larboard bow and stay there yourself, ready to bring back more reports. The lookouts will have lost sight of them in this squall.'

He left his officers standing by the binnacle and walked aft thinking hard. He pictured the two schooners sailing back into Fort Royal tomorrow morning with half their complement on board the *Juno* and a Tricolour flying above the British ensign. That was what the Governor of Fort Royal intended and what the men in the schooners hoped for. It would, he thought, be a great pity to disappoint any of them.

Yet the risk to the Juno would be enormous if he carried out the plan forming in his mind. If he failed, and was still alive, a court martial would find him guilty of anything Admiral Davis wanted to charge him with. No more risky, he argued, than taking the *Juno* into action against another frigate. And a convoy *must* be due . . . He swung round, rejoined the lieutenants and Southwick, and found that the two remaining lieutenants had arrived.

Orsini scurried up to report that Rossi had sighted the starboard schooner again in the same relative position but they had not managed to sight the one to larboard. 'Tell 'em to keep a sharp lookout,' Ramage snapped, 'the second one is there all right.'

He turned to the officers. 'There's not much time, so listen carefully. I want those two schooners to try to board us. I want them alongside, hooked on with grappling irons, because I want to capture them undamaged. The only way we can do it is by surprise. Let them think they are surprising *us*: they'll range alongside and start boarding on both sides. Then we surprise *them*: the whole ship's company will be crouching down behind the bulwarks, waiting for the word to repel boarders. That means we have a hundred men on each side to fight off perhaps a hundred in each schooner, but their freeboard is low, and they'll have to climb up our sides. We stand a good chance of succeeding. I want to capture those schooners undamaged,' he repeated.

Swiftly Ramage gave each of his lieutenants his orders, starting with the Marine officer. As each received his instructions he glided away into the darkness to gather his men, check their arms and make sure they had their instructions.

Finally there were only a dozen seamen and Southwick on the quarterdeck with Ramage, apart for the quartermaster and four men at the wheel. Ramage had doubled the number of men usually at the wheel in case of casualties. The dozen seamen were the former Tritons.

While Aitken and the other lieutenants made sure the rest of the ship's company (including those in the sick bay, since all of them could handle pistols) were equipped with muskets or pistols, boarding pikes, cutlasses or tomahawks, Ramage gave his orders to the dozen men and Southwick. The old Master was almost chuckling with excitement at the prospect of action. He had an enormous sword slung from a belt over his shoulder – a sword Ramage always called 'The Cleaver' – and a brace of pistols tucked in his belt. The dozen former Tritons carried a variety of weapons – apart from a pair of pistols, Ramage had let them choose what other weapons they wanted. Jackson and Stafford had cutlasses, Rossi a pike with a tomahawk tucked blade uppermost into his belt.

Ramage's instructions were brief: the former Tritons and the master would remain on the quarterdeck and were not to move until Ramage gave the word: they were to act as a reserve and would only join the fight at a point round the bulwarks where it looked as though the French might break through. 'But,' Ramage had warned them grimly, 'remember that as soon as you can you must get back to the quarterdeck: there might be some other place that needs reinforcement. The moment you get back here remember to reload those barkers: if there are soldiers on board these schooners, they'll know how to use swords . . .'

'And yourself, sir?' Jackson said, and Ramage realized he had neither sword nor pistols. 'I'll be back in a moment, sir,' the American said and ran below.

Orsini appeared again to report that the two schooners were in sight now, both in the same relative positions, according to the new lookouts. Ramage looked at the boy. 'Have you a pistol, Paolo?' he asked.

'Under my jacket, sir,' he said. 'To keep the powder dry in case there's another squall.'

128

Ramage thought of the boy's dirk, perhaps Paolo's proudest possession, but little use in the kind of fighting that would soon be sweeping over the *Juno*'s decks. 'Find yourself a cutlass, boy; don't rely on that dirk. Get forward now, and keep me informed.'

He thought of the afternoon in London when Gianna had asked him to take her nephew to sea with him. He had refused at first, picturing the day when the ship would go into action and he would be torn between sending Paolo to some safe position or letting him do whatever task was appropriate to a midshipman even though he stood a good chance of being killed or maimed. Gianna had insisted that he should not be treated differently from any other midshipman and Ramage had allowed himself to be persuaded. Now with the ship about to go into action he had decided to do as Gianna wished. Paolo was going to have his first taste of battle. If he survived he would not only be proud of his role but he would make a better officer.

Jackson was standing there holding the sword and belt in one hand and the pair of pistols in the other. 'With the compliments of the Marchesa, sir,' he said cheerfully. 'I left the case down below. Don't reckon there'll be much time for reloading.'

Rossi helped him out of his coat and he slipped the sword belt over his shoulder, put on the coat again and took the pistols, reflecting that it was a long way from Bond Street and Mr Prater's shop in Charing Cross. In the meantime the two French schooners were sailing along as though the *Juno* was their flagship. In the blackness on either bow scores of eyes were watching at this very moment, looking for any change in the frigate's sails. That would be their first warning that she was altering course. They would be cheerful and confident of surprising the British, however, because the *Juno* had kept on the same course and there had been no drum-roll sending men to quarters and no shrilling of bos'n's calls. As far as the French were concerned she was jogging along under topsails only, with only half a dozen sleepy lookouts, the men at the wheel, a quartermaster and the officer of the deck on their feet and the rest of the watch probably snatching naps.

He looked over to windward, towards the dark mass of Martinique itself, and saw that the cloud was beginning to break up slightly. Since the schooners could now be seen clearly from the *Juno*, he could expect the attack at any moment. They would edge over slowly on converging courses, then slow down and crash alongside as the frigate came up between them, to slaughter the sleeping *rosbifs*. He looked over each bow with the night glass, spotted the schooners and decided there was time for him to walk round the ship, to see the men and give them a word of encouragement and a word of warning. An accidentally-fired pistol or musket now would ruin everything.

It was a quick inspection: every moment he expected a messenger from Southwick, who had the conn temporarily, warning him that the schooners were altering course . . .

The men were excited but they had learned their lesson. Those with pistols were anxious to show him that they had them at half cock; those with cutlasses wanted to assure him that the blades had been sharpened on the grindstone. One or two of them had strips of cloth tied round their foreheads – to stop the rain running into their eyes if there was another squall, he supposed.

Then he cursed himself: the problem facing them if any of the French managed to get on board would be identifying friend from foe. He turned to Aitken, who was walking beside him, and said urgently: 'Send Benson and half a dozen men down to the Surgeon. I want enough white cloth to make every man a headband. Bring up sheets, bandages – anything that's white and will tear into strips and see that every man wears one, the lieutenants as well. And tell the men they're free to kill anyone without a headband.'

Aitken hissed the order to Benson, who whispered to the nearest half dozen seamen and vanished below with them. Ramage said: 'Everything is a credit to you, Mr Aitken. If we can only be sure the men will stay silent until the last moment . . .' With that he went back to the quarterdeck and told Stafford to find Benson and collect enough white cloth to make headbands for everyone on the quarterdeck, the men at the wheel and the quartermaster included.

Five minutes later the cloud began clearing quickly from the eastward. The *Juno*'s quarterdeck was apparently almost deserted; a night glass on one of the schooners would show only the officer of the deck and half a dozen other men, including those at the wheel. But crouched down below the bulwarks on both sides of the *Juno* were nearly two hundred men, each with a white headband tied securely round his forehead.

Southwick, crouching down and peering through the aftermost quarterdeck gunport, the white headband barely visible below his flowing white hair, said quietly: 'The one to starboard is beginning to close in.'

Jackson, also stretching over a gun and peering through a port on the larboard side, hissed: 'The one this side is doing the same, sir; bearing up on to a converging course.'

Ramage walked to the forward end of the quarterdeck with the night glass and looked at both ships. They were acting together, the windward one easing sheets and coming crabwise down to leeward, the one to larboard hardening sheets a trifle and bearing up. It was difficult to judge, since the sails were ill-defined in the darkness, but they would crash alongside in about three minutes.

There was no need for lookouts any more. He tapped Stafford on the shoulder: 'Go round the ship and tell the lookouts to go to their positions for repelling boarders; bring Mr Orsini back here.'

The French were patient and confident: they could have crashed alongside fifteen minutes ago, when it was really dark, but they had waited for the cloud to clear and give them the advantage of intermittent starlight. That needed courage. The two schooner captains must have been fighting their impatience and anxiety to attack before the *rosbifs* spotted them, but they had waited, believing that almost complete darkness would increase their own problems more than the risk of discovery. They needed a little light, even if it doubled the risk of the *Juno*'s lookouts spotting them. These were cool fellows, and Ramage wondered if they were in fact privateersmen. From the way they had waited and were now manoeuvring, they were more likely to be manned by French naval officers and disciplined men from the two frigates, and probably carrying a few score French troops to carry out the actual boarding. He was up against trained men, not the usual cut-and-run privateersmen whose only concern was loot.

As the schooners converged so that they were now only fifty yards apart more banks of cloud came up from the east. They were taking an enormous risk that they would be sighted . . . Not so enormous now, he corrected himself: both those schooner captains think that even if they are sighted at this very moment the *Juno* has only two minutes to send the ship's company to quarters. The French think they have only to deal with the watch on deck, with the watch below scrambling up sleepily, unarmed and bewildered . . .

Through the night glass he saw the big sails begin to broaden: they were easing sheets, slowing down to let the *Juno* sail between them. Southwick was beside him now, crouched down and peering over the quarterdeck rail. 'They know what they're up to, those fellows,' he whispered.

'They certainly do,' Ramage muttered grimly. 'I'm wondering if they'll get suspicious if we don't give some indication soon that we've sighted them.'

'Leave it until the last moment, sir,' Southwick advised. 'There's not much they can do now except get alongside, even if they do get suspicious. If one of our men gives a shout when they're almost alongside it'd be enough.'

Stafford was back with Orsini now, and Ramage told the boy to hurry round and tell the lieutenants that a minute or less before the schooners came alongside there would be a shout from the quarterdeck. 'But,' Ramage emphasized, 'tell them they are to stay out of sight and do nothing until they hear me shout, "Repel boarders!" '

Orsini repeated the instructions and disappeared into the darkness.

The schooners were barely the length of the *Juno* ahead and edging in. It was excellent seamanship, and he pictured the scores of Frenchmen crouching down on the schooners' decks, pistols, pikes and cutlasses ready, waiting to leap up the *Juno*'s sides.

'Steer small, blast it!' he hissed at the men at the wheel as the *Juno* yawed. It would be ironical if she rammed one of the schooners accidentally. Ironical and dangerous because it would probably smash the frigate's jibboom, if not the bowsprit as well.

Now he could see each schooner's transom clearly, and started worrying about whether the schooner to windward had made allowances for her main and foresail booms, which were now protruding several feet over the lee side and likely to hit the *Juno*. More irony, but he was anxious to capture both vessels undamaged. If one of them escaped his whole plan would have failed.

The *Juno*'s jibboom was now level with the transom of both schooners, and because of the frigate's forward movement the two French vessels seemed to be moving astern. He would wait until their transoms were abreast the foremast, then imitate a lookout's warning. They were abreast now!

'Sail close to larboard!' he yelled in an alarmed voice and took a firm grip on the speaking trumpet.

A heavy thump to starboard, another to larboard, the scraping of wood against wood and metal against metal, the slatting of canvas and a rasping hiss as the schooner to windward let her main halyards go at a run, and then uproar: a fantastic medley of French cheers and curses, threats and orders.

Fear hit him like a blast of cold air as he kept glancing from side to side for the first sign of a French head over the bulwarks. Yes, to larboard! He jammed the speaking trumpet to his mouth. 'Repel boarders! Come on, Junos, let every shot count!'

Suddenly the frigate's bulwarks were swarming with men. Some seamen perched on the hammock nettings were firing into the schooners; others hung over the nettings slashing down with cutlasses. More were squeezing through the ports and jabbing with boarding pikes. Pistols and muskets were going off along both sides with the curious popping that never sounded dangerous. There was a rattle and a crash as the schooner to leeward lowered its mainsail and a moment later the foresail came crashing down. From the screams that followed Ramage guessed that the gaff had landed on men below.

'We're holding 'em,' Southwick said excitedly.

'They haven't sorted themselves out yet,' Ramage snapped.

He saw grapnels with ropes attached being thrown up on to the *Juno*'s decks: the French weren't risking the ships drifting apart, and this should help him more than them.

Southwick suddenly pointed with his sword: 'There, sir, by the starboard forechains!'

The Junos were being forced down to the deck and Frenchmen were swarming over the hammock nettings, screaming and yelling. The flash of pistol shots flickered across the deck. Ramage waited: his dozen former Tritons were the only reserve. Let the French get right down on the deck; it was easier for the Junos to get at them there.

The white headbands were effective and showed up well. Now the French were bursting over by the mainchains; a dozen or more had reached the deck and he saw a group of Junos dash into the middle of them. They were being held off along the larboard side, but more were pouring at the same two places on the starboard side.

'More'n a hundred o' them to starboard,' Southwick growled.

Ramage still felt chilled although the fear was going. He

began rubbing at the scar on his brow but found the white band in his way. How many Frenchmen were down there? The two masses of men moved like clumps of seaweed in a swirling current. There were few pistol and musket shots now; just the clang of cutlass against cutlass and the screams of men cut down. Slowly the two groups were melting into one. The Junos were holding their own the rest of the way aft along the starboard side and all along the larboard side, but the group of Frenchmen was growing as more men poured over the bulwark.

There was no chance of the Junos holding them there: the men covering that section must have been killed or wounded. Down in the schooner someone was directing the boarders, sending up more men wherever they would be most effective. They had found the weak spot along the *Juno*'s side and were quick to exploit it. If another twenty Frenchmen got on board the *Juno* she might be overwhelmed.

'Southwick, take the conn,' he yelled. 'You Tritons, follow me!'

Before he could move, wrenching at his sword and holding a pistol in his left hand, there was a shout of protest from Southwick: "Tis not for you to fight off boarders, sir! You handle the ship! Follow me, men!'

Before Ramage could stop him the old man, sword whirling over his head, ran to the quarterdeck ladder, bellowing: 'Junos, come on, m'lads, cut 'em to pieces!'

Jackson and Stafford were close behind him, yelling their heads off, and the rest of the seamen followed. A startled and angry Ramage found himself on the quarterdeck with only the four men at the wheel and the quartermaster. He thrust the pistol back in his belt, thought better of it and sheathed his sword instead. He took out the second pistol, cocked them both and ran to the starboard side. The schooner's taffrail was below and five yards forward, and he could just make out men grouped round the binnacle. In the flash of a musket shot fired from the schooner's deck he saw that two of the men were wearing uniform. They were staring up at the *Juno*'s mainchains.

He aimed carefully at one of the men and fired. Though the flash blinded him momentarily he thought he saw the man fall. Hurriedly switching pistols, he saw the second uniformed man crouching over the first, who had fallen to the deck. Again he aimed carefully, cursing the excitement that made his hand tremble like a leaf in the breeze. He held his breath for a moment and fired again, and saw the second man collapse.

With luck they were the captain and first lieutenant, though whether their loss would make any difference now he did not know. He should have put Marine sharpshooters round the quarterdeck, but he had forgotten. He ran to the quarterdeck rail and looked forward. Along the larboard side there was fighting on the deck but the only Frenchmen who had managed to get on board were being dealt with. To starboard the group of Frenchmen on the *Juno*'s deck was being broken up: men without white headbands were running in all directions, bolting, trying to find somewhere to hide from flashing cutlasses and jabbing pikes.

He saw Southwick's white hair in the midst of the mêlée; even above the din he could hear the old man yelling encouragement as he swept left and right with his great sword. Paolo's small figure was beside him wielding a cutlass and screaming excitedly in high-pitched Italian. Ramage could distinguish a scream of blasphemy that would have made a hardened Neapolitan brigand blench.

He stood helpless at the quarterdeck rail, separated from the fighting and holding two empty pistols. Dare he leave the quartermaster to cover the quarterdeck? He looked back along the larboard side again and was surprised to see that there was now very little movement. Men with white headbands were back on the hammock nettings – damnation, not just on the nettings but going over the ship's side, down into the schooner, with Aitken standing at the break of the gangway waving his sword and leading the men! There were bodies lying all round the guns but he was thankful to see that only a few of them wore the white headbands.

On the starboard side Southwick's men were slowly breaking up the group of Frenchmen. He saw two French turn and bolt back to the bulwarks, obviously trying to jump back on board the schooner. A third man followed, and then three more.

Further aft, only a few yards away from him, Wagstaffe was standing up in the hammock nettings surrounded by Junos and a moment later he vanished from sight and the nettings cleared of men. Ramage ran to the side and looked down, watching Wagstaffe lead his men aft along the schooner's deck. More Junos were dropping down and suddenly a group of French appeared, scrambling over the nettings from the frigate's deck, some falling in their haste, and

135

tumbling down to the schooner. A moment later Southwick was standing on the nettings above them, his sword waving. He leapt down on to the schooner's deck, followed by a dozen or more men with white headbands.

Except for sprawled figures, the *Juno*'s decks were now clear. Ramage ran from one side to the other frantically trying to distinguish what was going on in the darkness. From the deck of the schooner to larboard he could hear Aitken's voice, the Scots accent very strong, shouting orders, not yells of encouragement. The Marine Lieutenant was bellowing at his men to form up aft. Well, he thought grimly, that schooner is secured. He ran back to the starboard side in time to see Southwick leading his men in a rush aft to a knot of Frenchmen who were standing with their backs to the taffrail. There was shouting, though he could not distinguish the words, but Southwick had paused. Now he could see Frenchmen throwing down their swords and pikes in surrender.

His knees were shaky, his hands trembling, his stomach queasy. He wanted to giggle, and he wanted to talk to someone. He only just stopped himself from clapping the quartermaster on the back. Three minutes ago he had been afraid he had failed and that the *Juno* would be taken.

Benson, waving a cutlass, was trying to catch his attention. 'Message from Mr Aitken, sir: he – ' the boy realized he was gabbling and made an effort to keep his voice even. 'Mr Aitken's respects, sir, and the schooner to larboard is secured.'

'Very well, Benson,' Ramage said. 'My compliments to Mr Aitken, and ask him to report to me as soon as he finds it convenient.'

The boy ran off, and Ramage hoped he would remember the exact wording: Aitken would appreciate the 'convenient'. Then Jackson was standing in front of him, white band askew, the blade of his cutlass dark. 'Mr Wagstaffe has the schooner to starboard under command, sir, but he said to tell you it'll be half an hour before he's ready to get under way.'

Ramage laughed, a laugh which nearly got out of control. 'Very well, Jackson, my compliments to Mr Wagstaffe and tell him to let me know how many prisoners he has.'

'The French captain and the first lieutenant are dead, sir; we found 'em lying together by the binnacle. She's called *La Mutine* and was manned by French seamen with soldiers for boarders.'

As the American hurried forward again, Ramage realized he was still clutching his empty pistols and jammed them into

136

the band of his breeches. They had proved accurate enough, although they were only as effective as the man that held them, and he had used them too late. If he had thought of picking off the two officers a few minutes earlier . . . if, if, if . . . Always, after an action, came the ifs, and before dawn he would have thought of plenty more. If he had done this he would have saved a dozen men's lives at the starboard mainchains; if he had done that he would have saved a dozen more to larboard. Mistakes he had made – no Marine sharpshooters for example – and probably some which would become apparent within the next few hours. Mistakes that only he might know about, but which had killed men unnecessarily . . .

The *Juno* was still under way, dragging the schooners along with her, each being held by the grapnels thrown on board the frigate by the confident Frenchmen. Aitken was standing in front of him, his left hand jammed into his jacket, which was buttoned, and a dark stain on his left shoulder. 'Baker and the Marine lieutenant have everything under command down there, sir. About three dozen prisoners, with the Marines guarding them. Twenty or thirty Frenchmen dead and as many more wounded.'

'Our own casualties?' Ramage asked quietly.

'About a dozen dead and wounded to larboard, I should think, sir. I have parties going round attending to the wounded, and Mr Bowen has half a dozen men helping him.'

'Very well,' Ramage said soberly, 'we were very lucky.'

'Lucky?' Aitken was too startled to say 'sir', and added: 'It all worked perfectly!'

Ramage turned back to the quarterdeck rail. Perhaps it had worked out perfectly so far, but none of them realized that up to now they had carried out barely a third of his plan: the hardest part was yet to come.

Two hours before dawn Ramage was weary but still excited. He had questioned the captain of the larboard schooner for half an hour and by playing alternately on the Frenchman's pride and his fear of what was going to happen now he was a prisoner, had managed to discover what the French had intended.

The two schooners, *La Mutine* and *La Créole*, had been taken over by the French Navy the day before the *Juno* sailed into Fort Royal Bay, and the first lieutenants of the two frigates had been put in command. Each had forty men taken from the frigates and embarked seventy soldiers from the 53rd Regiment. Their mission, the French lieutenant had said, was to board the *Juno* simultaneously from each side and take her into Fort Royal. After that the Frenchman would say no more. Ramage guessed that the man had decided it was proper to discuss the operation, but the way he had then refused further information made Ramage suspect him of hiding a great deal more than he revealed.

He had just signalled to the two Marines to take the Frenchman away when Aitken came into the cabin, obviously excited. The moment the Marines and their prisoner had left he said: 'Orsini and Rossi, sir: they've found an Italian among the prisoners who wants to quit the French and serve with us! He's a quartermaster and seems an intelligent fellow.'

'Fetch him in – but I'll talk to Orsini first.'

The midshipman was almost giggling with excitement. He and several seamen, including Rossi, were guarding prisoners, he told Ramage, when Rossi had made some comment in Italian. One of the prisoners immediately spoke – 'In the accent of Genoa,' Orsini said, with all the contempt of one who spoke with the clear accent of Tuscany.

'Go on, boy,' Ramage said impatiently. 'What did he want?'

'We took him away from the other prisoners – in case any more of them spoke Italian – to see what he wanted. It seems he comes from a village twenty miles from Genoa. When Bonaparte invaded Genoa and renamed it the Ligurian Republic, many able-bodied men were forced to serve in the Army and Navy. They had no choice, this man says.'

Ramage nodded: he could not imagine the French giving able-bodied men any choice. Rossi had been fortunate in quitting the Republic before the French arrived (indeed, Ramage suspected the police were after him). So this prisoner might well have been serving the French against his will and, like Rossi, might prefer to serve in the Royal Navy. Well, he thought grimly, that depends on how much he knows and how much he tells.

'Anyway, sir,' the boy continued eagerly, 'this man – his name is Zolesi – told us that the Governor will be very angry that the schooners failed to capture the *Juno*: apparently a convoy is due very soon, and he wants us out of the way.'

Ramage stared at the boy. ' "Very soon" – he said that?'

When Orsini repeated the Italian phrase, mimicking the

Genoese accent, Ramage said impatiently, 'Fetch the man. And bring Rossi.'

Zolesi was a stocky man with fair hair and blue eyes, and Ramage guessed that his forebears were mountain folk. He saluted smartly but Rossi, holding a pistol, watched him warily. He began by speaking to Rossi, expecting he would translate, but the seaman said: 'The captain speaks Italian.'

Ramage, impatient to question Zolesi about the convoy, had first to listen to the man's request to be allowed to serve in the Royal Navy. His story sounded plausible and Ramage noticed Rossi nodding as he described how the French sent naval press-gangs and army squads through the streets, rounding up all able-bodied men.

Finally Ramage interrupted him. There were a few questions, based on what the French lieutenant had said, which would check the man's reliability.

'You were serving in *La Mutine*?'

'For this operation, sir.'

'Before that?'

'In *La Désirée*. Forty of us were sent to the schooner. And seventy soldiers.'

'What regiment?'

The man's brow wrinkled. 'The 53rd Regiment, sir.'

'Who commanded *La Mutine*?'

'The first lieutenant of *La Désirée*. He was killed, sir.'

Ramage nodded. 'Is the *Surcouf* ready for sea?'

'Not yet, sir, but they are working hard.'

'And *La Désirée*?'

'*Accidente*!' Zolesi exclaimed. 'They are short of everything: yards, rope, canvas, wood for repairs, blocks, hammocks – everything!'

'Yet the French expect to commission her?'

'Oh yes, once the convoy arrives.'

'But that has been delayed,' Ramage said, deciding that Zolesi was not likely to lie in this type of conversation, and the Italian's reply was just what he wanted.

'Delayed, sir? But it's expected within a week! A week from today, in fact. Have the British captured it?'

Ramage shrugged his shoulders. 'I don't know, but it's not a large convoy anyway.'

'I don't know how big it is, sir, but the French are terrified of something happening to it. That's why the two schooners were sent out to capture this ship.'

'Will they send out more?'

Zolesi shook his head expressively. 'No! There was a good deal of trouble over these two. They were privateers and the owners refused to let the Navy use them.' Seeing Ramage's puzzled expression, he added: 'The Governor took them over by decree.'

'But why no more attempts?'

'I heard the privateer owners sent a deputation to the Governor, swearing that if he tried to take over any more the owners would sink them first.'

'What did the Governor say?' Ramage asked curiously.

'I heard he was very worried: the owners of the privateers are powerful men in Martinique. Now you have captured these two . . .' Zolesi stood with his arms spread out in front of him, palms upturned.

Ramage nodded to Rossi and said in English, 'Take him away and keep him separated from the others.'

'Can he . . .' He broke off, obviously worried that Ramage would think him impertinent.

'Keep him apart and see what else he knows about the convoy and the French defences in Fort Royal. And anything more about the other frigate. You can hint that he'll be allowed to enlist – and get the bounty, too!'

By now all the unwounded from the two schooners were being guarded by the *Juno*'s Marines. The bos'n and his mates were busy sewing the dead men into hammocks ready for funerals at daybreak, with the gunner cursing that it was going to be a waste of roundshot until Ramage pointed out that there was plenty in the schooners, and it was more appropriate that Frenchmen should be buried at sea with French roundshot sewn into the foot of their hammocks.

Ramage sent for Aitken and Southwick and when they arrived he told them to sit down. The First Lieutenant was holding himself a little stiffly, the result of a bandage Bowen had put on the shoulder to cover a gash from a French pike. Ramage asked if they wanted hot drinks – the galley fire had been lit earlier to give the men a hot breakfast and provide Bowen with the hot water he demanded for the treatment of some of the badly wounded men. When both men refused, Ramage handed Aitken the sick list that Bowen had scribbled out and sent up to him. Nine Junos had been killed, seven seriously wounded and eighteen more had wounds that needed treatment but which allowed them, in an emergency, to go to general quarters.

The First Lieutenant, his face drawn with weariness but his eyes still bright, passed it to Southwick. 'The figures are fantastic, sir. That's 139 French dead and wounded as against thirty-four Junos killed or wounded, and eighteen of ours were little more than scratches.'

'Surprise,' grunted Southwick. 'That's what did it. Johnny Frenchman was too confident. The French were just standing there in both schooners, a solid mass of men waiting to leap on board. The Junos just leaned over the hammock nettings and fired right down into them!'

'We were damn' nearly too confident, too,' Ramage said.

Southwick sniffed. 'Well, sir, I'd better report on the schooners. The *Mutine*'s foresail is badly torn and the gaff's broken. They dropped the sail in a hurry and the gaff crushed a couple of their own men. The sail's being repaired and the carpenter is fishing the gaff. It's a long break, so it isn't too difficult. Decks cut up with pistol and musket shots, a few shrouds parted – they're already knotted – and she'll be ready to get under way in an hour. The French had forty seamen on board; we can manage with ten. *La Créole* suffered no damage to speak of, except for bullet holes in the deck. She can get under way the moment you give the order. I've chosen the two prize crews, as you told me to. It's just a question of . . .'

'Exactly,' Ramage said, 'who is to command them.'

Aitken nodded. 'It'll take a week to sail 'em to Barbados and get our men back – perhaps more.'

'We needn't worry about Barbados for the time being,' Ramage said, and both men looked up quickly, obviously puzzled. Ramage decided to tease them for a little longer.

'That Tricolour, Southwick: have Jackson and Rossi finished it yet?'

'No, sir. It's so big. It's taken all the red cloth we have on board including the red baize. I hope you won't be ordering many floggings . . .'

'You won't regret it,' Ramage said enigmatically. 'I hope the other men have finished the smaller Red Ensigns.'

'I forgot to tell you, sir, we have three or four on board we can use, apart from the ones in the flag locker.'

Ramage nodded. 'Anyway, we have to decide who is to command the ships.' Southwick gave yet another sniff. It was clear that he considered taking a schooner to Barbados with a prize crew was an easy voyage to be left to the master's mate in one and perhaps the Fourth Lieutenant in the other.

Ramage thought the time had come to stop teasing both the Master and Aitken, but could not resist one last dig.

'I was thinking of putting you in command of *La Créole*, Aitken, and I hope Wagstaffe can manage *La Mutine*.'

The First Lieutenant's jaw dropped, and even though the light from the lanthorn was dim, Ramage saw that he had gone white. He realized that Aitken thought he had failed in his duties during the night's attack and was being put in command of the schooner to get him out of the way to allow another of the lieutenants to be promoted in his place.

Ramage reached out and touched his arm reassuringly. 'Cheer up, Aitken. Listen to me for a minute or two and after that you will be perfectly free to refuse the command and stay on board the *Juno*.'

Aitken swallowed and tried to smile, while Southwick looked completely puzzled, as though he feared for his Captain's sanity.

'Some time this morning,' Ramage said quietly, 'the French Governor in Fort Royal, and the naval commander, will be expecting to see *La Créole* and *La Mutine* sailing into Fort Royal Bay, escorting the *Juno* with a Tricolour flying above the Red Ensign . . .'

He paused for a moment to make sure both men pictured the scene.

'On a Sunday morning everyone will be out in the streets cheering and I wouldn't be surprised if the guns of Fort St Louis began firing a *feu de joie*. The schooners will sail up to the anchorage, tack and wear round the *Surcouf* frigate a couple of times to show off. The French prize crew will bring the *Juno* in and prepare to anchor her close to the *Surcouf*. Just imagine the scene with everyone cheering and yelling, the crews of the schooners lining the bulwarks and waving, and the French prize crews on board the *rosbif* frigate *Juno* manning the rigging, singing revolutionary songs, no doubt.'

'But, but sir,' Aitken stammered. 'The French haven't captured the *Juno*!'

'No, indeed they have not,' Ramage said quietly, 'but the Governor of Fort Royal doesn't know that yet.'

CHAPTER TEN

The sky was cloudless, an unbelievable, almost gaudy blue, and the hills and mountains forming a wide bowl round Fort Royal Bay were a fresh green from the night's rain squalls. To the north Ramage could see the truncated top of Mount Pelée, and for once it was clear of its usual cap of cloud. The wind was brisk from the east and the sunlight sparkled from the wavelets. It was, he thought, a good morning to be alive; a piece of good fortune emphasized by the fact that an hour earlier he had attended a funeral service for forty-seven Frenchmen and conducted it for nine Junos.

Each of the fifty-six bodies had been put one by one on the hinged plank at the bulwark just above where the standing part of the foresheet was made fast to the ship's side, and the appropriate flag placed over it. Fifty-six times the plank had been tilted, the flag held, and the body in its shotted hammock slid over the side into the water. He had conducted the service for the Junos and he had asked the lieutenant who had commanded La Créole to carry it out for the Frenchmen; surely one of the few funeral services conducted by a man guarded by armed Marines.

As the Juno stretched close hauled across the mouth of Fort Royal Bay heading for the anchorage off the city, Ramage knew he was really gambling. By comparison last night's capture of the schooners had been a matter of calculation, and he had calculated correctly. Now he needed a gambler's luck, if there was such a thing, because what he was going to attempt was beyond calculation. Like some pallid gambler at Buck's, he could only roll the three dice (in this case the Juno, La Mutine and La Créole) and hope for the best, knowing that the croupier would rake in men's lives if he lost. His life and the Junos' were at stake.

He glanced aloft to where the Tricolour streamed to leeward, a third again as large as the Red Ensign beneath it. Every available telescope in Fort Royal would be watching it. Over to starboard Aitken was keeping La Créole well up to windward, while to larboard Baker was making a good job handling La Mutine. Wagstaffe had been disappointed to find that he was not going to get command after all until Ramage had told him his task.

The Junos were exhausted. First they had to transfer all the French wounded to *La Mutine*, where Bowen was still on board, with his instruments and assistants, attending to them. Once the wounded had been made as comfortable as possible in *La Mutine*, the French prisoners were transferred to her as well and secured in the hold, with Marine guards covering them. There was little likelihood of them trying to escape, for Ramage had explained carefully to the French lieutenant that he intended sending them all into Fort Royal under a flag of truce, providing the lieutenant gave his word that the total number of men would be entered on the exchange list, and none would ever serve against the British until the equivalent number of British prisoners in French hands had been duly exchanged. The Frenchman had readily agreed – it was a common enough practice – and drawn up a list of the names of the wounded and prisoners and signed it.

Whether or not the French at Fort Royal would honour *La Mutine*'s flag of truce when they saw what the *Juno* and *Créole* were doing was a different matter, but Baker had his orders. If necessary he could free the lieutenant on parole and send him on shore in the schooner's boat to explain matters.

One thing that particularly worried Ramage was the thick anchor cable draped along the *Juno*'s starboard side. To a sharp-eyed watcher on the shore it would seem strange, but with luck no one would guess its purpose. That damned cable, a rope ten inches in circumference, was the main reason why the Junos were exhausted: Wagstaffe had worked them hard, fighting the clock. The cable was made fast round the frigate's mizen mast, then 300 feet of it was carefully flaked down across the quarterdeck, leading out through the starboard sternchase port, round the edge of the transom, and then forward along the ship's side to the bow, where the end was made fast with light line that a slash of a cutlass would cut. Thin line secured it every few feet along the ship's side, to prevent it hanging down in a great bight, but that line was merely seizing, and a good tug would break it.

He stood at the quarterdeck rail and looked around the maindeck of a ship which, as the great Tricolour told everyone in Fort Royal, was a French prize captured during the night in the Devil knew what desperate encounter with the two schooners now escorting her back in triumph, their prize crew on board handling her, as Ramage had carefully explained to Wagstaffe and the quartermaster, with somewhat less skill than she had been handled when she had tacked into the bay a few days earlier. It would be too much to expect a short-handed French crew – the schooners had carried only a total of eighty seamen – to be too expert.

He looked at the *Juno*'s guns run out along the maindeck. Every 12-pounder was loaded with case shot so that when fired it would discharge forty-two iron balls, each weighing four ounces. A single broadside of thirteen guns would sweep the enemy with 546 shot, with another 120 weighing two ounces each from the three 6-pounders. Four-ounce and two-ounce shot was too light to inflict much damage on a ship, but sufficiently numerous and heavy to cut down men in swathes.

The guns were ready. The locks were fitted and the spark of the flints had been checked; the trigger lines were neatly coiled on top of the breech and tubs of water for the sponges stood between each pair of guns with match tubs nearby. The ship's boys squatted along the centreline, sitting on their cylindrical wooden cartridge boxes. The gunner was down in the magazine; the guns' crews were hidden against the bulwarks. At each gun port cutlasses were hung ready for all the men, while pikes were in the racks round the masts. Behind each pair of guns, well clear of the recoil, was a stand of muskets, all of them loaded. The decks were wetted and sanded but the planks were so hot that seamen had to keep wetting them afresh, using buckets and taking the water from tubs.

The skylight over Ramage's cabin had been removed and stowed below: it got in the way of the anchor cable as it led to the mizenmast. A pile of canvas stood by the stern chase port, ready for use as keckling, to prevent the cable chafing at the edges of the port when it was run out. Wagstaffe had wanted to measure the distance from the mast to the port and lash on the keckling earlier, but Ramage had watched the eastern sky lightening and had told him to leave it: there had still been much to do and very little time.

By now Aitken would have given detailed instructions to the twenty Junos he had on board *La Créole*; Baker and the Marine Lieutenant would have done the same in *La Mutine*. The poor Lieutenant of Marines was the only man disappointed at the role he and his men were to play. Not surprisingly, he was not pleased to be acting as jailer when there was a prospect of hand-to-hand fighting, but with the *Juno*'s ship's company now extended over the schooners as well, Ramage could not spare trained seamen to guard the prisoners.

Close hauled, the *Juno* could just lay the anchored frigate, but the quartermaster gave the men at the wheel an order from time to time that let her yaw, so the luffs of the topsails fluttered for a few moments.

Southwick walked up to him, the great cleaver of a sword hanging from his waist. 'The Governor over there must be rubbing his hands, sir.'

'I hope he'll be gnashing his teeth in half an hour or so!'

'No doubt about that,' Southwick said confidently. 'Let's just hope this wind holds – it couldn't be better for our purpose. If it suddenly veers to the south-east . . .' The master left the sentence uncompleted because if it went round that far the *Juno* would stand a good chance of ending up on the rocks at the foot of Pointe des Nègres, at the northern entrance to the bay. Luckily such a wind on a clear day like this was unlikely.

Southwick then nodded approvingly towards *La Créole* as she tacked, the big fore-and-aft sails swinging over, the head-sails flapping for a moment before being sheeted home again. 'He's enjoying handling her!'

'Aitken's first command,' Ramage commented. 'Ironic that it's under the Tricolour! A few extra tacks will give him more confidence.'

'He's going to need it,' Southwick said grimly. 'If he arrives five minutes late it might be all up with us!'

'And if we arrive five minutes early it might be all up with him.'

The Master chuckled. 'I think he took the point when you gave him his orders, sir.' He looked aft at the anchor cable, which covered most of the quarterdeck like an enormous thick carpet patterned like a regular maze. 'If that confounded cable kinks when it begins to run out it'll tear the transom off!'

'Oh, come now,' Ramage said mildly. 'We might need some repairs to the taffrail, and Aitken will grumble about chafed paintwork.' He turned and gestured to the quartermaster, who hurriedly signalled to the men to give a slight yaw.

Southwick lifted the quadrant he had been holding and looked towards the anchored frigate. He knew the height of the *Surcouf*'s mainmast and had already set the quadrant at an angle the mast would subtend at the distance of one mile.

'Half a mile to go, sir. I mean, she's a mile and a half away.'

Ramage nodded as he looked at a white dome of a building at the western end of the city. It was dead ahead and made an easy reference point for the quartermaster. He turned and gave the order. For the time being the *Juno* would not be steering by the compass; it was going to be nip and tuck as the frigate stretched up towards that dome until the anchored *Surcouf* was to the seaward of the *Juno*; to seaward and, when the *Juno* tacked as the water shallowed, fine on the starboard bow.

La Créole tacked again and then *La Mutine* tacked and suddenly Southwick pointed at Fort St Louis. Ramage saw a single puff of smoke drifting westward and began counting the seconds. He reached five when there was another puff of smoke. Damnation, he had forgotten the Fort might fire a salute to the victors! The *Juno*'s guns were loaded with case and there was no time to start drawing shot now to return a salute.

The thud of a gun close by startled him and he saw smoke drifting away from *La Créole*. 'Good for Aitken!' he exclaimed. 'He was quick!'

Five seconds later another of *La Créole*'s guns fired as those on the Fort continued a salute. 'Hope he doesn't get carried away,' Southwick muttered. 'It's time all those popguns of his were loaded with shot!'

The *Surcouf* was gradually drawing round on the *Juno*'s starboard bow as the British frigate reached the seaward end of the anchorage. Southwick lowered his quadrant and said: 'One mile exactly, sir.'

Ramage looked at his watch and then over at *La Créole*, which tacked yet again and began to reach across the *Juno*'s stern. Aitken was keeping his head: he had orders to tack under the *Juno*'s stern when he judged the frigate was a mile from the *Surcouf*, and perhaps young Orsini, who was on board with him, was using a quadrant.

The French frigate was now on the *Juno*'s beam and through the telescope Ramage saw fewer men on board than he had expected. They were all crowding the bulwark, no doubt gleefully, but enviously watching their shipmates bringing in the prize, and he estimated that there were fewer than a hundred. He had expected two or three hundred, and thought *La Créole*'s lieutenant had been deliberately misleading him when he said that less than half the ship's usual complement was working on her.

Looking over the *Juno*'s starboard quarter he could see well into the Salée anchorage now and there was no sign of movement on board any of the schooners anchored there, at least none that could be sighted from this distance although he would be able to see if any of them were making sail.

He had been listening for several minutes to the rhythmic chanting of the depth of water from the man standing in the forechains and heaving the lead. The man had orders only to report depths of less than five fathoms, and he was merely calling: 'No bottom at five fathoms . . . No bottom at five fathoms with this line . . .' Suddenly the note of his voice changed. 'Two fathoms! Two fathoms!'

Twelve feet? The frigate drew more than sixteen forward! Ramage snatched up the speaking trumpet to tack the frigate and a moment later there was a hurried 'Belay that, sir!' from the leadsman and then, as if nothing had happened, he continued his chanting: 'No bottom at five fathoms . . .'

By then Southwick was already hurrying down the quarter-deck by ladder and half-way to the forechains. Ramage saw him talking to the leadsman, who was standing on the chain-whale, a line round his waist.

'The damned fool!' he exploded as soon as he returned to the quarterdeck. 'He wasn't watching what he was doing and heaved the lead so that it caught up in the chainwhale. He felt the weight on the line, didn't realize it wasn't in the water, and read off the mark!'

Ramage shrugged his shoulders. 'Thank goodness he said two fathoms and not three: I realized that with two fathoms we'd have been aground already.'

The episode had taken only a minute or two but the shore was now less than half a mile ahead, with the *Juno* making a good six knots. Already Ramage could distinguish people on the beach and the *Surcouf* was half a mile away on the starboard quarter: too far for anyone on board to hear orders shouted in English but close enough for Ramage to make out every detail.

He walked back to the binnacle: the *Juno* was steering north-north-east on this tack; she should make good south-south-east on the other. He glanced astern at the *Surcouf* and took a rough bearing – south by east. The time had come to roll the dice.

Now fear was creeping in again like evening fog forming in a valley: the sun seemed more glaring, the colours brighter. Cold water seemed to be swilling in his stomach, time was slowing down, and the hiss of the *Juno*'s bow wave seemed louder. The excitement was there; this must be how a gambler felt when, having staked everything, he waited for the dice to stop rolling . . .

Southwick had the speaking trumpet and from now on he would relay Ramage's orders. Yes, *La Créole* had tacked yet again and was steering to the south-east; another couple of short tacks and she would be in position.

Southwick was looking at him anxiously and he realized that the leadsman was calling four fathoms, but the men were already standing by at sheets and braces. Ramage signalled and the Master began shouting orders. The quartermaster spoke urgently to the men at the wheel and sprang to the binnacle. The wheel spun and the frigate began turning quickly to starboard, the whole of the Fort Royal shoreline moving swiftly across her bow. The topsail flapped for a few moments as the *Juno* turned through the eye of the wind and continued swinging until the wind could fill the sails again on the other tack.

'Meet her!' Ramage snapped at the quartermaster, anxious that her bow should not pay off too much. He glanced down at the compass. 'Steer south-south-east.'

Jackson was handing him his pistols and he was jamming the clips into his belt after hitching round his sword. Now the American was offering his hat, discarded earlier in case the French spotted it, and he was putting it on top of the binnacle.

'Stand by the halyard of that damned Tricolour,' Ramage told Jackson. 'When I give the word it had better come down at the run!' Having the Tricolour and British ensign on separate halyards saved a lot of time.

It was a legitimate *ruse de guerre* to use the enemy's flag to get into position to attack, but one was honour-bound to hoist one's own flag before opening fire. Thanks to *Juno*'s temporary role as a French prize, dropping the Tricolour and leaving up the Red Ensign would do the trick and, Ramage thought inconsequentially, Southwick can recover his precious red baize.

He glanced over the starboard quarter and saw that *La Créole* had tacked again and was in the right position; a quick look over the bow, and there was the *Surcouf* at anchor, head to wind, her deck and rigging lined with waving men. A couple of dozen Junos were standing on the hammock nettings waving back – just the number of men the *Surcouf* would expect to see. The rest were crouching down along the starboard side.

'A point to larboard,' Ramage called to Southwick and men trimmed the yards as the wheel turned. Now the *Surcouf* was fine on the starboard bow and a hundred yards ahead.

The *Juno* was making five or six knots. In a hundred yards she had to be nearly stopped abreast the *Surcouf* which should be only a few feet away, giving Ramage time to fire a broadside into her and brace the yards round so they did not lock the two ships together.

Ramage gestured to Jackson to haul down the Tricolour and shouted to the Master: 'Mr Southwick – back the foretopsail!'

He grabbed his hat from the binnacle top and jammed it on his head, looked quickly over the quarter and saw *La Créole* approaching rapidly on the *Sourcouf*'s other side. She had three hundred yards to go, the *Juno* seventy-five and the distance was rapidly decreasing.

The big foretopsail yard was being hauled round agonizingly slowly, it seemed to Ramage, so that the *Juno* was likely to overshoot the *Surcouf*. Finally it was far enough round for the wind to fill the sail from the forward side, pinning the yard to the mast and trying to blow the ship's bow to starboard. A quick order to the quartermaster had the wheel spinning to counteract that. The *Juno* was slowing down rapidly now and there was a chance she would not overshoot.

There was nothing more for Ramage to do standing by the binnacle and he ran to join Southwick at the quarterdeck rail. Then he saw why Southwick was staring forward, a man transfixed: the *Surcouf* was swinging slightly at her anchor, caught by a fluky gust of wind. Her stern swung until she was dead ahead and Ramage was sure it was all over; that fluke of wind meant that the *Juno*, rapidly losing way and therefore manoeuvrability, would ram her from astern instead of coming alongside, and there was nothing he could do to prevent it. The *Juno*'s jibboom and bowsprit would be torn away, the foremast would come crashing down . . . Southwick was cursing steadily in a low voice when slowly, agonizingly slowly, the *Surcouf* began to swing back; swing enough for Ramage to see clear along her larboard side, then swing a little more until, in a minute the gap between them would be exactly as he had wanted it.

He leaned over the rail and shouted down to the maindeck: 'Gun captains – forty yards to go! Fire as we get alongside; sweep the decks!'

Now only the gun captains were at the guns: the rest of the men had rushed to the ship's side to grab a cutlass, pistol, or boarding pike. The men who had been waving from the nettings had dropped down to the deck and armed themselves.

The *Juno*'s stern was now level with the *Surcouf*'s transom but she still had a little way on. Slowly, slowly, she crept on; now the stem was abreast the French frigate's mainmast, now the foremast, and the Frenchmen who had been lining the bulwarks were scattering across the deck. Several officers were shouting and gesticulating; one had drawn his sword and was waving it: not at the *Juno* but at his own men. The *Juno*'s yards were braced sharp up at Southwick's command.

Five guns forward fired in quick succession along the *Juno*'s fo'c'sle and maindeck and the rest followed one after the other. Ramage looked over the quarter again for a sight of *La Créole*: Aitken had timed it perfectly. She would be ranging alongside the *Surcouf*'s other side in two minutes' time, when there was no risk of any of the *Juno*'s case shot sweeping clear across the *Surcouf*'s deck and damaging her.

Now the Junos were swarming up into the hammock nettings or waiting at the gun ports poised with pistols, cutlasses and pikes. The *Juno* had stopped; now the backed foretopsail was drifting her slowly alongside the *Surcouf* and Ramage watched the gap narrowing: fifteen feet, ten, five, then the men, led by Wagstaffe, were leaping on board, and the gun captains were heaving grapnels at the *Surcouf* to hold the ships together. Southwick bellowed the order to clew up the foretopsail; in a few moments the *Juno* was lying head to the wind, alongside the *Surcouf*.

Ramage ran down the maindeck, snatching out his pistols as he reached the entry port at the gangway. Southwick was shouting after him but he neither heard nor cared what the

Master said. He paused for a moment at the gangway, saw the water swirling between the two ships, and leapt on board the *Surcouf*.

Thirty or more Frenchmen had snatched up pikes and cutlasses and were aft, fighting desperately as Junos tried to drive them back. Suddenly a group of Frenchmen poured up the main companionway, pistols in their right hands, cutlasses in their left. A burst of fire cut down several Junos and the Frenchmen ran through the gap, making for the fo'c'sle.

Ramage aimed at the leading man and fired, saw him fall and aimed left-handed at the next. He fired and missed, and suddenly the whole group turned and ran towards him and Ramage was alone: most of the Junos had their backs to him, busy driving the rest of the Frenchmen aft. Ramage wrenched at his sword and backed a few feet to the mainmast. The first Frenchman, four or five yards ahead of the rest, and the man he had missed with his second pistol, slashed at him with his cutlass; a downward slice which Ramage parried, deflecting the man's blade so that the impetus behind the blow made the man trip. A quick flick of the wrist and Ramage caught him across the throat with the tip of his blade and turned immediately to face another man who was lunging at him with a pike. Ramage jumped to one side and the man, his face half-crazed with fear, drove on, his pike sticking into the mast. A swift blow disposed of him and Ramage turned to face the third man, but suddenly there was a roaring and a bellowing which made the man turn and bolt. Jackson and a half a dozen former Tritons were running to his rescue, and at that moment the *Surcouf* lurched as *La Créole* crashed alongside, her boarding party swarming up her side, yelling and shouting.

Ramage was thankful the fighting was now centred round the quarterdeck: that was what he had intended, so that the fo'c'sle would be left clear for the men boarding from *La Créole*. Several of them carried heavy axes and they ran forward, followed by others armed with cutlasses. While the axemen went to one side of the fo'c'sle, the cutlass men went to the other and began shouting over to the group of men waiting on the *Juno*'s fo'c'sle.

A heaving line snaked across from the *Juno* and landed on the *Surcouf*'s fo'c'sle. The men began hauling on it and when a heavier line followed they ran to the bow with it, passing it through the large fairlead. Then they began hauling, but it was hard work and finally they began marching across the deck as though dragging a cart. Finally the end of the *Juno*'s anchor cable appeared through the fairlead and the men kept hauling.

By now the axemen were chopping at the *Surcouf*'s own anchor cable, and Ramage hoped they remembered his strict instructions to leave one strand of the rope until they could see that the cable from the *Juno* had been secured to the bitts.

More men arrived on the fo'c'sle from *La Créole* and seized the heavy cable and dragged it to the bitts. One turn round the bitts and then another; a third and then a fourth. The cable was stiff and heavy; it took two or three men to bend each turn.

The fighting aft was dying down now, and Aitken and Wagstaffe were securing the prisoners. Ramage ran to the fo'c'sle, checked that the cable was made fast and gestured to the men with cutlasses to return on board *La Créole*. After shouting to the men on the *Juno*'s fo'c'sle to cut the lashings holding the cable along the ship's side, he ran back to find Southwick standing at the *Juno*'s gangway, anxiously looking across at the *Surcouf*.

'All secure here,' Ramage shouted. 'Only one strand of their cable left to cut.'

'For Heaven's sake come on board, sir,' Southwick bawled. 'The ships will drift apart at any moment. We're just about to cut the grapnels!'

Ramage paused long enough to shout at Wagstaffe, who signalled that the prisoners were under control, and then bellowed at the axemen on the *Surcouf*'s fo'c'sle to cut the last strand of the French frigate's anchor cable. With that he leapt on board the *Juno*.

One danger remained, that the *Surcouf*'s yards would lock with the *Juno*'s rigging, but already Aitken was obeying his orders and hardening in the sheets of *La Créole*'s mainsail and foresail and backing his headsails. This would haul the *Surcouf* to starboard, to leeward and away from the *Juno*.

'Our grapnels, Southwick?' Ramage asked hurriedly.

'Already cut adrift, sir.'

Ramage glanced up and saw that the *Surcouf*'s yards, bare of sail, were gradually drawing clear as *La Créole* pulled her away. He jumped up into the hammock nettings and looked along the *Juno*'s side. The cable was now hanging from the *Surcouf*'s bow in a big bight that went down into the water and reappeared by the *Juno*'s stern, snaking round and up through the sternchase port.

Everything was going as planned. Southwick looked questioningly and when Ramage nodded the Master lifted the speaking trumpet to his lips, bellowed a string of orders, and the *Juno*'s foretopsail yard began to swing round, the sail falling and then flapping wildly before the wind filled it. Slowly the *Juno* began to move, her bow paying off to begin with, until she gathered enough way for the rudder to get a bite on the water.

The *Surcouf* was dropping away to starboard as *La Créole* hauled her bow round and drawing astern as the *Juno* began to forge ahead. Ramage looked across at the French frigate's quarterdeck and saw Wagstaffe standing by the binnacle while Jackson acted as quartermaster. Two Junos were at the wheel and the French seamen, their hands above their heads, were being marched below.

Southwick was now facing aft on the quarterdeck, his eyes glued to the heavy cable. The *Juno*'s transom was abreast the *Surcouf*'s jibboom end and already the cable was beginning to move where it led out through the *Juno*'s sternchase port: several feet slid out, like an enormous snake leaving a hole, and as the frigate's speed increased more followed.

Ramage was torn between watching ahead to make sure the *Juno* cleared the shoal running south-west from the Fort and looking aft over the quarterdeck in case the cable twisted into a large kink that might jam in the port.

The cable was running freely so far, the friction causing a faint blue haze of smoke round the gun port: perhaps a hundred feet had gone but there were still two hundred to go. And the *Juno* must not be moving too fast when the entire weight of the *Surcouf* really came on the cable. That could be enough to pull the *Juno*'s stern round and throw the sails a'back, and with so few men left in the *Juno* he knew that if that happened the frigate could be out of control for long enough for them to be blown ashore or dragged astern by the weight of the cable so that she hit the *Surcouf*.

He dare look aft no longer: the water ahead was showing a light green, marking the beginning of the shoal off the end of Fort St Louis. It was time the *Juno* began to bear away to the westward to get out of the bay. He snatched up the speaking trumpet and began bellowing orders. The wheel was put over as the yards were trimmed and he knew the frigate was still only towing the cable through the water: luckily the *Surcouf*'s weight had not yet come on it. For a moment he pictured getting into water so shallow that the long curving bight of cable sagging down between the two ships snagged on a great rock on the bottom or caught on a shoal of coral, but every passing moment lessened that risk because the *Juno*'s forward movement was slowly straightening it out.

'A hundred and fifty feet o' cable to run, sir,' Southwick called.

Ramage turned to the quartermaster. 'Watch for the last of the cable. The moment the strain comes on there'll be an almighty kick on the wheel.' The quartermaster nodded and Ramage noticed that there were already four men at the spokes and the quartermaster was positioning himself to give a hand if necessary.

'A hundred feet to go, sir, and it's running well,' Southwick reported.

The *Juno* was slowly turning to starboard now and would clear the shoal by a hundred feet, and once the strain came on the cable she would be able to run out to the west.

'Fifty feet, twenty-five, ten . . . there it goes!' Southwick shouted jubilantly.

There was no sudden shock but the *Juno* slowed perceptibly and Ramage looked aft to see the five men fighting the wheel. Astern the *Surcouf* was slowly gathering way as the cable tautened and Ramage saw the hint of a bow wave. Then, in a direct line from the *Juno*'s stern chase port to the French frigate's bow, the cable suddenly straightened and shot out of the water, and then splashed back, like a whip. The *Surcouf* began yawing, her bow swinging to starboard and then back to larboard. Each yaw increased the dead weight on the end of the cable so that the *Juno* was like a dog with a heavy weight tied to its tail. The five men fought the wheel, cursing and grunting, but then managed to keep the ship under control.

'Give Jackson a few minutes to get used to handling the Frenchman,' Ramage called encouragingly.

Gradually the *Surcouf*'s yawing eased, like a dog settling down on a leash, and in the clear water Ramage could see the shallow curve of the cable. Beyond the *Surcouf* Aitken's schooner was tacking back and forth: *La Créole*'s task now was to cover the two frigates against any schooners that might come out of the Salée River.

He looked round for *La Mutine* and saw her just off the town, coming head to wind with sails flapping and an enormous white flag flying from the peak of her main gaff. Suddenly Ramage realized that in the excitement he had forgotten all about Fort St Louis. There were no tell-tale puffs of smoke. Surely the *Juno*'s sudden attack on the Surcouf had not taken them completely by surprise? But he had no idea whether five minutes or an hour had passed since he had waved to Jackson to drop the Tricolour so perhaps they had had too little time to do anything.

Their progress was painfully slow, but at least the men were not having to fight the wheel now. He walked aft to join Southwick and crouched down to look through the stern-chase port. The cable was making a perfect catenary curve and the *Surcouf*'s yawing had almost stopped.

'I think we can carry more canvas now,' he commented.

'I wish those damned Frenchmen had finished fitting out the ship,' Southwick grumbled. 'It'd have been a sight easier to sail her out!'

'We'd have had a couple of hundred Frenchmen to argue with though, instead of just a handful,' Ramage pointed out.

Southwick shrugged his shoulders. 'If you'd be good enough to keep an eye on the cable, sir, I'll try the forecourse.'

The end of the shoal was on the *Juno*'s quarter now, so there was deep water right out of the bay. *La Mutine* was riding at anchor and he saw her boat heading for the shore, looking like a tiny water beetle from this distance. It would probably be nightfall before he knew whether the French had honoured the flag of truce: Baker was due to rejoin them by midnight.

He looked forward and saw the *Juno*'s great forecourse tumbling down from the yard, creased and shapeless like an enormous white curtain until the men began sheeting it home and the wind gave it shape, swelling it into a billowing curve. He watched the cable tauten slightly, saw that the quartermaster was now standing back from the wheel, quite confident the four men could handle it.

Ramage took out the telescope to inspect the *Surcouf*. There were a dozen men on the fo'c'sle. His orders had included a party with axes ready to cut the cable in an emergency. He thought he could make out Wagstaffe on the quarterdeck and he was standing still, not rushing about, so he must be confident.

Southwick came aft and Ramage gestured astern at the *Juno*'s wake. 'We've picked up a knot or more and she seems to like it. We'll try the topsail as well.'

Fifteen minutes later the *Juno*, with the *Surcouf* in tow and *La Créole* tacking across their wake, passed half a mile south of Pointe des Nègres, at last clear of Fort Royal Bay. A large Red Ensign streamed in the wind from the *Surcouf*, and when Ramage saw it being hoisted he grinned to himself: one of the boarders from the *Juno* must have taken it with him.

He was hot, he was tired, he had not slept for some thirty hours but he was cheerful. He only wanted to hear that the French had honoured *La Mutine*'s flag of truce, taken off their wounded and the prisoners, and released the schooner, and he would know that his gamble had succeeded completely.

There had been casualties, but in the confusion on board the *Surcouf* he had not noticed any Junos lying on the deck. There must have been a few, but so far they had paid a small price for the capture of a frigate and two schooners. He looked down at the compass and then across at Cap Salomon, which was just opening up to the south as the two frigates continued westward.

'Mr Southwick, I think we can now alter course for the Diamond,' he said.

CHAPTER ELEVEN

Ramage's steward brought in a pot of hot tea on a tray, put it on the side of the desk and said: 'When will you be ready for your shaving water, sir? I've laid out fresh clothes.'

Ramage looked up weary and unshaven and put down his pen. His eyes felt full of sand and his head ached. 'Another half an hour,' he said. 'Pass the word for Mr Southwick and bring another cup and saucer for him.' He heard the distant bleating of several goats and the mewing of gulls. Occasionally there was the heavy splash of a pelican diving into the water nearby in the endless search for fish, but apart from that and the noise of men working on deck, there was only the sound of water lapping against the *Juno*'s side as she swung to her anchorage early this Monday morning.

The anchorage, two cables north of Diamond Rock in five fathoms of water, was a comfortable one. The *Surcouf* was lying just to the south, riding to the cable that had towed her down from Fort Royal, and *La Mutine* was between the two frigates and the great rock. Out to the west *La Créole* was stretching seaward until she could see up the coast towards Cap Salomon and then back to round the Diamond. One of the *Juno*'s lookouts aloft was watching the coast but so far he had nothing to report. There was no sign of activity along the two miles of sandy beach forming the Grande Anse du Diamant. No doubt the Governor would send cavalry patrols along the coast to see if the *Juno* and her prize were at anchor in one of the many bays or if both ships were on their way to Barbados. The naval commander would probably have told him that it was easy enough for the *Juno* to tow the *Surcouf* the hundred or so miles to windward; he might even speculate that the *Juno*'s captain would leave the two captured schooners to maintain the blockade, so that the expected convoy, which the French had no reason to think Ramage knew about, had nothing to fear. Ramage was reasonably sure (or, more correctly, trying to persuade himself that he could be) that the French would never dream he would try to finish refitting the *Surcouf*. He was quite sure Rear-Admiral Davis would never dream of it.

He stared down at the report that he had been writing: it was the third draft, and young Baker was waiting to leave for Barbados in *La Mutine* to deliver it to the Admiral. Describing the night attack on the *Juno* by the two schooners and their capture was no problem; using *La Mutine* as a flag of truce, and the *Juno* and the *Créole* to cut out the *Surcouf* was covered in four paragraphs. The warning that the French were expecting a convoy in a week took a couple of lines. He included the polite suggestion that the convoy could be a week early, in which case it could arrive any moment, or a week late. What was hard was trying to tell the Admiral he was getting the *Surcouf* ready for the voyage to Barbados without the wily old man guessing that he intended holding on to her until the last moment, so that he had two frigates to tackle the convoy. The Admiral could, and probably would, argue that Ramage should have used the *Juno* to tow her to Barbados, where many more men were available to get her ready, and that the two schooners could maintain a watch on Port Royal while the *Juno* was away, and that by the time the convoy was due the *Juno* would be back . . .

There were other reasons, too, and Ramage hoped that Southwick, who had just returned on board after spending most of the night surveying the *Surcouf*, would confirm them. He picked up the pen and scratched out a sentence. It was always easier to fight an action than to write the dispatch about it.

He poured out a cup of tea and idly picked up the letter which was sealed with the arms of France and addressed to 'The Admiral Commanding the English Forces at Barbados', thought once more about opening it and decided for the fifth or sixth time to send it on to Admiral Davis for whom, Baker had told him, the Governor of Fort Royal had really intended it.

The French had finally honoured the flag of truce, though it had been necessary to send the French lieutenant on shore first. Baker said it had been a close-run affair. As soon as the French wounded had been taken on shore and the prisoners freed, the French authorities had wanted to seize the schooner and take Baker and his men prisoner. At that point the French lieutenant had unexpectedly intervened. He had described how Bowen had worked without sleep tending the French wounded; how Ramage had asked him to conduct the funeral service over the French dead; said that, as a French officer, he had agreed to the exchange and that he had come on shore in the first place on parole. If the authorities held the ship, he had said dramatically (and Baker had given a fair imitation of the gestures that went with it) he would regard himself as still a prisoner of the English. The French naval commander had finally come down to the beach and threatened to arrest the lieutenant for treason and mutiny; the lieutenant had said his honour and the honour of France was at stake, and that he would welcome being arrested because the news would eventually get back to the English. They would know then that he had not broken his word of honour and his parole but been forced into it by his own senior officers who should know better but apparently did not.

That, Baker said, had decided it. The lieutenant was hustled off, but half an hour later another officer came out and handed over the letter from the Governor and, with ill grace, said that if *La Mutine* was not under way within fifteen minutes the guns of Fort St Louis would open fire. Baker had asked for an assurance that the terms of the exchange of prisoners would be observed but the officer had said he knew nothing about it; he was an aide to the Governor and had been told only to deliver the letter. With that Baker had weighed and *La Mutine* had caught up with the two frigates before they had reached the Diamond.

Ramage heard footsteps on the companionway and a moment later Southwick knocked and bustled into the cabin, his eyes red-rimmed, the flesh of his cheeks sagging with weariness, but in good spirits. He sat down in a chair with a groan, massaging his back, then when Ramage looked inquiringly he said hurriedly: 'Don't mention it to Bowen, sir; he'll only want to slap on a mustard plaister, and they don't do a damned bit o' good.'

'Well, how many plaisters does the *Surcouf* need?'

'None at all, sir,' Southwick said with a triumphant grin. 'She's ready to get under way the minute her sails are bent on.'

'Our spare suit – can we alter any of them to make them fit? Cut out some panels or sew on some more? Her yards look shorter than ours.'

'That's just it,' Southwick said gleefully, slapping his knee, 'all her sails are on board! Sails, clewlines, buntlines, blocks – everything! I reckon they were just about to get them up from the sail room when the best of her men and the first lieutenant were taken off and sent to the schooners.'

Ramage gave a sigh of relief. 'What about provisions, powder and water?'

Southwick dug into his pocket and pulled out a grimy sheet of paper, which he carefully smoothed out. 'I don't know what they intended to do with her, sir, but we know they stripped the other frigate to fit her out, and she's provisioned for three months at our establishment. I know the French usually have a ship's company half as large again as us, but . . .'

'Perhaps they were going to send her back to France.'

'Could be, sir. Anyway the water's fresh, and from what the cooper says the casks were well scoured before they were filled. The powder is very good quality – the gunner says its as good as ours. Salt pork and salt beef, a lot o' rice, fresh bread – I swear it didn't leave the bakery more than a week ago. Not a weevil in it.'

'Have you made an official inventory yet?' Ramage inquired cautiously.

'*Me*, sir?' Southwick asked innocently. 'Oh, no, it'd take a week. No, I only had time to have a quick stroll through the ship with the purser, gunner, bos'n, carpenter and cooper. You didn't mention an official inventory. Proper inventories and survey, sir,' he said with an archness that would have done credit to a bishop's wife, 'take time: two or three days at least.'

'In the meantime,' Ramage said, as though talking to himself, 'any rogues could go on board and plunder the ship: they could take off provisions, water, powder . . .'

'And rolls of canvas, firewood, new holystones – she has a score or more unused in the bos'n's store – new leather buckets, a complete set of surgical instruments, a dozen live sheep: oh dear me, sir, there's no telling what they could take if the prize crew weren't keeping a sharp lookout.'

It was a great temptation; the *Juno* could stay at sea for many extra weeks without provisioning; with several tons more fresh water, for instance, she would not have to go down to St Lucia or across to Barbados to fill her casks; the sailmaker would welcome the extra bolts of canvas . . . But it was risky: the problem would be to account for the extra stores in the *Juno*'s books. If she was desperately short of water or powder or provisions, he would be justified in taking what he needed, but Rear-Admiral Davis knew the *Juno* was well-provisioned, so it became a matter of prize money. Everything on board the *Surcouf* would be valued, including the ship herself, and the *Juno* and her Captain would eventually get their share of the prize money, as would Rear-Admiral Davis. It would be a considerable amount, and by a bit of good fortune once the Admiral's eighth was deducted the rest would go to the Junos. Every British ship in sight at the time of the capture had a right to a share, but the only other British ships were the two captured schooners manned by Junos.

He would risk it if he could take all the blame, but it would mean involving too many others who would also be brought to trial if the Admiral wanted to make an issue of it. The Master, the bos'n, purser, gunner, at least two of the lieutenants . . . An idea that had come to him when he saw the Diamond Rock for the first time – and which he had dismissed as absurd almost as soon as it appeared – was gnawing at him again.

'Cheeses, too!' Southwick said as the memory struck him. 'Never seen so much cheese in all my days, sir, and tubs of butter. Seems a pity to let all those provisions go to Barbados when all we have to look forward to for a change of diet is goat's meat from the Diamond . . .'

Ramage jumped up, put a paperweight on the letter he had

been drafting, grabbed his hat and said to Southwick: 'Come on, we're going for a short cruise in the cutter.'

An hour later the cutter had completed a circuit of Diamond Rock and the men were resting at the oars with the boat drifting twenty yards from a flat, rocky ledge behind which was an enormous cave, its entrance yawning black-mouthed and, as Southwick commented, looking as if a great dragon would emerge at any moment, breathing fire and smoke. There was very little swell as it was too early for the Trade wind to have set in.

'This is the only possible landing place,' Ramage said. 'We'll chance it and inspect the big cave – and the others, if we have time.'

Ramage pointed to the ledge. 'Put us on shore there,' he told Jackson. 'Go in stern first and hold the boat there just long enough for Mr Southwick and me to jump on to the rock, then stand off.'

'Aye, aye, sir,' Jackson said. 'Rossi and I can give you a hand and Stafford can take the boat out until – '

'Mr Southwick and I can take care of ourselves,' Ramage snapped. 'You stay in the boat, and while you're standing off make sure you note any odd rocks: you might be coming back here a few times.'

The men bent to the oars while Ramage and Southwick scrambled across to the stern. 'Looks slippery, sir,' Southwick warned. 'That green weed . . .'

A few moments later Ramage jumped, landed safely and turned to give Southwick a hand. 'Welcome to the Diamond,' he said, and stood watching for a moment as the oarsmen rowed steadily to get clear.

The Rock towered above them almost vertically. Apart from the wide ledge on which they stood and a flat section beyond, it was a home for goats and precious little else. But the cave was enormous, with several more smaller ones nearby and ones higher up the rock face. Ramage eyed the ledge, which formed a projecting point and gave a little shelter to the cove. A gun mounted here would protect it very well, and the surface of the rock was flat enough to allow for the recoil.

He turned towards the cave and saw Southwick about to enter it, the sheer size of the gaping hole dwarfing him. A moment later the Master vanished. Ramage heard him shouting and began running, thinking he had fallen in the darkness and hurt himself. As he heard the echoes, he realized that Southwick was using his voice to get some idea how far back the cave ran into the Rock. It was like entering an enormous cathedral and as his eyes became used to the darkness he saw the long stalactites pointing down from the roof. Yet the air was dry and it was dry underfoot: he had been expecting it to be dank, the sides running with water and green with moss.

Southwick loomed up beside him. 'Big enough to stow a complete frigate,' he said, and there was no mistaking his meaning.

'If anyone could sway a couple of 12-pounders up to the top of the Rock, they'd need a magazine, and this cave is dry enough,' Ramage murmured, obviously doing little more than thinking aloud. 'They'd need a place to store provisions and water. The guns' crews would stand a couple of days' watch aloft while the others were down here; then they'd change over. I don't know how they'd get to the top – rig a jackstay, most probably . . . It would be easier to work that out from the *Juno*, using a telescope: you can't see a damned thing just staring up from the ledge.'

'There's another ledge on the north side, two thirds of the way up,' Southwick said. 'It looks as though something took a big bite out of the rock. I think there's a cave at the back of it. It'd make another fine battery to cover the Fours Channel. A 12-pounder could probably reach the Grande Anse du Diamant. No ship could sneak through the channel without a gun there giving it a hot time. With a pair of guns right at the top – goodness me, nearly six hundred feet high: just think of the extra range – and plunging fire!' Even in the darkness Ramage sensed the old man's increasing excitement as he went on: 'That would give us three guns to cover the channel, and two of those, the pair at the top, can probably fire all round – north, west, south and east. And the lookouts could see all the way down to the southern tip of Martinique! Rig up a mast and they could hoist flag signals which the *Juno* would see while she was up to the north-west. Have to keep out to the west so the Diamond is clear of the land, but just think, a frigate off Fort Royal Bay would know what's going on right down at Pointe des Salines, twenty miles away! Why –'

'Easy now,' Ramage said mildly, 'you don't have to convince me: I've had something like this in mind ever since we first sailed past the place. But don't get too carried away; swaying a pair of 12-pounders nearly six hundred feet up to the top of this Rock will be more than a morning's work, if it can be done at all.'

They walked out of the cave and stood blinking in the bright sunlight, and then walked along looking into the smaller caves. Southwick kicked at the broad-bladed grass. 'The men will like this for making sennet hats.' He pointed to the caves. 'The whole place looks like that cheese with holes in it.'

'Gruyère,' Ramage said. 'And the big cave is where a mouse had a feast.'

'More likely a rat,' Southwick said. 'It's the biggest cave I've ever seen, let alone walked into. Those spiky things hanging down from the roof make it look like a portcullis, I hope none of them drop off!'

They looked into the cave and Ramage turned to seaward and waved to the boat. 'Come on, these caves remind me of witches' cauldrons and bats and vampires . . .'

Back on board the *Juno* Ramage silenced all Southwick's attempts to discuss the Diamond Rock; instead he took him down to his cabin, tossed his hat on to the settee and sat down at the desk. Taking out the pen and ink, he added a single paragraph to the draft of his letter to Admiral Davis.

After calling to the sentry to pass the word for his clerk, he began a letter addressed to 'The Agent for Transport and Prisoners of War'. The clerk arrived and was told to take the draft of the letter to Admiral Davis and make a fair copy, and bring it back when it was ready. 'Don't waste time copying it into the Captain's Letter Book,' Ramage told him. 'Make the entry afterwards from my draft.'

Ramage then finished a brief letter to the Agent, describing how he had landed the prisoners because he was unable to guard them, and saying that he was enclosing a list of their names and the signature of the surviving French commanding officer agreeing that the men should not serve against the British again until the exchange had been regularized. Ramage knew there would be a fuss, but he had covered the point in his letter to the Admiral. The letter to the Agent was a formality to cover the list he was sending.

As he wrote at the desk, Southwick sat back in a chair with ill-concealed impatience. The clerk returned with the fair copy of the dispatch and took the draft of the letter to the Agent.

Ramage turned to Southwick. 'You remind me of an impatient bridegroom. Baker is probably in his cabin packing his sea chest. Find him and bring him here. Once he's on his way to Barbados we can start making plans.'

The clerk arrived with the fair copy of the letter to the Agent, waited until Ramage had signed it and the dispatch, and then took away both letters and the list of prisoners to seal. After wiping the pen and screwing the cap on the ink bottle, Ramage sat back and stared down at the polished grain of the desk top. In the past two days he had not had a moment for real thought. He snatched at ideas as they raced through his mind, rejecting some and adopting others; decisions seemed to arrive already made but without proper consideration. He felt like a clucking hen startled to find it had laid an egg. So far his decisions had been the correct ones, but this was due to good luck rather than judgement. It was only a matter of time, he thought gloomily, before one of the eggs turned out to be bad.

Yes, the present difficulty is Admiral Davis, not the French. Should he have mentioned his plan in the dispatch? He sighed and tapped his fingers on the desk top. Should he, shouldn't he, should he . . . and so it went on. Indecision, indecision . . . Well, not exactly indecision because he had already signed the dispatch without mentioning it, so at least he had decided that much. No, his bother was that, having made the decision, he was starting to question himself. It always happened, and he hated it.

Very well, what are you trying to do, Captain Ramage? You are carrying out Admiral Davis's orders which are simple enough: blockade Fort Royal, preventing any ships from entering or leaving. Splendid, my dear fellow; you have a firm grip on the situation. The new development is that by a stroke of good fortune you have discovered from that boastful French lieutenant that a convoy (he implied a large one) is due in Fort Royal within a week. A large convoy means a large escort, and 'a week' after an Atlantic crossing could mean today or two weeks' time; more, if the convoy met bad weather off Biscay followed by Trade winds.

Go on, Captain Ramage, he jeered at himself, so you had to make a decision: should you send the *Surcouf* to Barbados with a prize crew on board, with one of the schooners to bring the prize crew back, leaving yourself with only the *Juno* (minus the men needed to provide three prize crews) and a schooner to fight off the escorts and capture the convoy – or, at the very least, prevent it from entering Fort Royal Bay? That was the question, and it was a simple one.

The difficulty arises because there is more than one answer. You can hurriedly fit out the *Surcouf*, so that you have two frigates to tackle the convoy, keeping one schooner and sending the other to Barbados with the dispatch to raise the alarm, and hope Admiral Davis is still there with the *Invincible* and some frigates, so that he can get under way for Martinique immediately to help tackle the convoy. (Help, he thought to himself: the *Invincible* and a couple of frigates would be more than enough.)

That is one answer but it certainly is not the one that Admiral Davis will expect. It is the right answer, though – with due respect to you, Admiral – because it takes into account the time factor; that the convoy is just as likely to be early as late: one can be damned sure it will not be on time.

Another answer would be for the *Juno* to tow the *Surcouf* to Barbados, leaving the two schooners to maintain the blockade. That is the answer that the Admiral would expect: a bird in the hand (and so a share of the prize money in the pocket) was worth two in the bush. Admiral Davis would argue that only the *Invincible* and more frigates could deal with the convoy, and that the *Juno*'s absence from Martinique for three or four days was an acceptable risk since the two schooners would be patrolling, and one could reach Barbados and raise the alarm.

If you were an admiral, Ramage asked himself, would you accept that the commanding officer of the *Juno* – a young man at the bottom of the post list – could in fact perform magic, doing something which is a compromise between the two answers? Instead of sending the *Surcouf* to Barbados, fit her out so that quite unexpectedly an extra frigate is available for the Martinique blockade, and send a schooner to Barbados with a warning of the convoy. In the meantime, he had a plan for the Diamond that no one had ever tried . . .

He balanced the quill pen on a finger. Captain Ramage was not an admiral nor ever likely to be, so he ought to look at the situation through the protruberant and bloodshot eyes of the man who was, Henry Davis, Rear-Admiral of the Red and Commander-in-Chief of his Majesty's ships and vessels . . .

The Admiral would not believe it possible, with the *Juno* already stripped of men to provide the prize crews for the two schooners, for Ramage to get the *Surcouf* ready for action within a week. He would also say – and that was much more important – that even if the French frigate *could* be got ready, there was still the problem of manning her. Ramage would have to halve the number of men remaining in the *Juno* and send them on board the *Surcouf*. Instead of two fully-manned frigates ready for action he would have two frigates manned with skeleton crews.

Ramage tipped the feather end of the quill so that it dropped to the desk. He had to admit that the Admiral would (by his own standards) have grounds for complaint. The difference was that the two frigates would be manned by Junos, who had already achieved more in less than a week on the station than Captain Eames and his frigate had in several months. That was not an answer he could possibly give the Admiral, though, since Captain Eames was one of his favourites.

To divide one ship's company between two frigates and two schooners might horrify Admiral Davis, but that was not the end of it. Ramage was proposing to take away another twenty men and use them for a hare-brained scheme which could make him the laughing stock of the Navy.

His thoughts were interrupted by the clerk bringing back the letters, having applied the seals. The man had no sooner left the cabin than Southwick arrived with Baker, both apologizing for being so long. Ramage told them to sit down and stared at the sealed packets. The clerk had a flowing style of handwriting and Ramage picked up the letter addressed to Admiral Davis. It would take only fifteen minutes to write another one. Or he could get the *Juno* under way and tow the *Surcouf* to Barbados. Or he could see if one of the schooners could tow her, with the second schooner in company. Or –

He picked up the two packets and handed them to Baker, deliberately ending the conflict in his mind; he then opened a drawer and took out another letter which he had written earlier.

'These are your orders,' he said. 'They tell you to proceed to Barbados and deliver this to the Admiral and –' he pointed to the thinner packet ' – this to the Agent for Prisoners. If you can't find the Agent, leave it with the Admiral's secretary.'

'Aye, aye, sir,' Baker said. 'I'll be under way in a few minutes: we've already shortened in the cable.'

'My written orders tell you to return here immediately you have delivered the dispatch,' Ramage said. 'It might occur to the Admiral, if he thinks about it, to keep you and *La Mutine* with him in Bridgetown. You might find it possible to ...'

'I'll stay on board the flagship for as little time as possible, sir,' Baker said with an understanding grin.

'What about charts?' Ramage inquired, suddenly remembering this was Baker's first voyage as an acting commanding officer, apart from the visit to Fort Royal.

'I've just been making copies of Mr Southwick's, sir.'

'I've given you copies of the challenge and reply for the next week and you have a copy of the signal book. Remember, guard them with your life and keep them in a weighted bag ready to sink if there's a chance of you being captured.'

'I know, sir.'

'I know you know,' Ramage said sternly, 'but for the whole of your time at sea up to now it has been your commanding officer's responsibility. Now you are the commanding officer ...'

'I understand, sir,' said a chastened Baker.

When the lieutenant left the cabin, Southwick nodded. 'He's a good lad, that one. Not many young third lieutenants could take command of a schooner the way he did and handle that flag of truce business so well.'

'We've a lot to thank Lord St Vincent for,' Ramage commented. 'He sent us good officers.'

The Master straightened up in his chair and said in what Ramage immediately recognized as his serious, let's-get-down-to-business voice: 'The Diamond, sir, what are we –'

Ramage held up his hand to silence him and stood up, going to the skylight and calling: 'Deck there.'

'Benson here, sir,' the midshipman answered from the quarterdeck.

'Has Mr Baker left the ship yet?'

'Just gone, sir; boat's about thirty yards away. D'you want me to hail him, sir?'

'No, it's all right,' Ramage said, and sat down again.

Southwick looked puzzled and Ramage smiled. 'My dispatch to the Admiral told him that we had captured the *Surcouf* and were making her ready for sea. The Admiral will assume I meant making her ready to send her to Barbados. Very well, that dispatch is now on its way. Unfortunately the circumstances changed just after the dispatch had been sent and fresh decisions had to be made . . .'

Southwick slapped his knee in a familiar gesture and grinned broadly. 'So that was why you kept shutting me up.'

'I don't know how you dare suggest that your commanding officer might be party to any deception, Mr Southwick,' Ramage said mildly. 'I should have thought that up to now we were all far too busy to do anything more than write reports and see what was needed to get the *Surcouf* under way, after all, it was my duty to inform the Admiral immediately that a French convoy was expected, and using a schooner was the quickest way. I think any group of captains would see the necessity for that.'

'By jove, yes!' Southwick exclaimed, realizing that Ramage's mention of 'any group of captains' was a veiled reference to the officers forming a court martial. 'So now at last we have a few minutes to decide about the *Surcouf*. After you discovered you could commission her, sir, anyone would agree that you dare not send another schooner with a further report: that would weaken the blockade at a critical time.'

'Precisely,' Ramage said, 'since the convoy is likely to arrive any day.'

'When do we start the work?' Southwick asked eagerly.

'The moment *La Mutine* is out of sight. I want Baker to be able to tell the Admiral in all honesty that when he last saw the *Surcouf* her yards were bare of sails and there had been no time for anything more than a quick inspection by the *Juno*'s Master. That is what I say in my dispatch, incidentally.'

'We'll have those sails bent on and the ship ready for action by this time tomorrow, sir,' Southwick promised. 'How many men can I have for the Diamond?'

Ramage raised his eyebrows in mock surprise. 'What do you propose doing over there? Chase goats or let the men cut that broad-bladed grass and plait sennet hats?'

'I want to get the *Surcouf*'s sheep landed there to start with,' Southwick said. 'Can't stand the constant baaa, and there's grazing plenty at the landing place. After that, a 12-pounder to cover the landing place – or a 6-pounder, if you'd prefer it, sir. Then two 12-pounders hoisted up on top of the Rock and another 12-pounder half-way up on the north-west side.'

'How do you propose getting the 12-pounders up to the top?' Ramage inquired mildly.

'I'll find a way,' Southwick said grimly. 'Give me those dozen Tritons and we'll haul 'em up with our teeth if necessary.'

Ramage shook his head. 'First, I want you to get those sails bent on the *Surcouf*'s yards: use every able-bodied man you can find. The Marines can help if necessary. I think we need Aitken; I'm going to call him in and put Wagstaffe in command of the *Créole*. You'd better rouse out one of the *Surcouf*'s own cables; we are going to need the one we used to tow her.'

Southwick looked puzzled. 'The ten-inch cable, sir?'

'The only way you're going to get those guns up to the top of the Diamond is to rig a jackstay, and the other cables we have on board are seventeen inch, almost twice the weight . . .'

'A jackstay, sir?' Southwick exclaimed. 'But where can you secure the lower end? The water's too deep for the men to dive down and find a big rock, and anyway, that'd –'

A dull and distant boom interrupted him.

Ramage leapt up with an oath. 'That damned battery on Diamond Hill!'

There was a shadow at the skylight. 'Captain, sir,' Wagstaffe called. 'The battery on the Hill – a single shot and it's fallen half a mile short.'

Ramage acknowledged the report and followed Southwick up the companionway. He took the telescope Wagstaffe was offering him and trained it on the ridge that ran round the Hill a third of the way up. It was too late, the smoke had drifted away in the wind and there was no sign of the guns. Suddenly he spotted a brief red glow, barely a pinpoint, and then a puff of smoke.

'Watch the fall of shot,' he snapped. 'I don't want to lose sight of the battery. A clump of six small trees permanently leaning to the west from the wind – they're growing at the eastern end of the battery. A triangular bare rock in front. Yes, there's a track running just below – probably goes round to join up with the road that runs short of the north-east side . . .'

'Fell half a mile short, sir,' Wagstaffe said.

'Pass the word for the Marine Lieutenant,' Ramage said and, looking round, nodded. 'Ah, there you are, Rennick. Take the glass and fix the position of that battery in your mind. Mr Southwick has its position marked on the chart, but you'll have to get up it in the dark tonight, unless their shooting improves and we have to leave in a hurry.'

A third and a fourth shot from the battery fell half a mile short, but both were in line with the *Juno*. Southwick gave one of his enormous sniffs of contempt but Ramage said: 'They're only 6-pounders. If they were 12-pounders we'd be slipping our cable in a hurry. These fellows know what they're up to; they just don't have the range.'

'Aye, belike they'll pass the word to the Governor and he'll decide they need bigger guns,' Southwick said gloomily. 'Better we get under way now and bowl 'em over.'

'Have a look through the glass,' Ramage said patiently. 'The battery stands well back on the ridge that spirals up the mountain. Twenty or thirty yards back, as far as I can see. Once we were close enough to open fire – don't forget they have an advantage of being five hundred feet up – that ridge protects them: it's a natural rampart. We'd need mortars to lob shells over the ridge and down on to them. A bomb ketch.'

Southwick glanced at the Marine Lieutenant, who was slowly swinging the telescope down the side of the mountain and across to the long beach running to the eastward, and muttered: 'He'll never find his way up there in the dark.'

Ramage saw Rennick stiffen but continue his careful survey of the coastline. He had obviously heard Southwick's comment. Then he turned, handed the telescope to Ramage and said: 'If you can spare a boat to land me and my men at the western end of that long beach, sir, I'll have those guns. I estimate the emplacement is large enough for three, though they're only firing one for ranging. I'll get them pitched over the edge within two hours.'

Ramage nodded, pleased at the lieutenant's enthusiasm. 'You can have a couple of dozen seamen too, if you need them.'

'Thank you, sir, but my own men will be sufficient. A few extra seamen in the boat, perhaps, in case there's cavalry patrolling along the beach.'

'Very well, get your men ready. Mr Wagstaffe, a cutter if you please, and a dozen extra men with muskets. Make sure they have plenty of powder and shot for the boat gun – cavalry might arrive before Mr Rennick returns from the battery.'

Half an hour later Ramage and Southwick watched the cutter run up on the beach, having stayed out of range of the battery, wait for a few minutes as the Marines scrambled on shore and then come out again, rowing round to a small cove fifty yards west of the beach and in the lee of the mountain. There, Ramage noted, the boat would be out of sight of any cavalry galloping along the beach.

Southwick grunted in the nearest he ever came to expressing satisfaction with Marines. 'They'll be all right. Pity they can't surprise those damned Frenchmen. Well, sir, I see the men are ready to re-anchor the *Surcouf* to get out ten-inch cable in. I'll go over and keep an eye on them.'

Aitken was now bringing the schooner *Créole* in from the westward: he had seen the *Juno*'s signal ordering him on board and Wagstaffe was waiting with a seabag ready containing his clothes and quadrant. The Second Lieutenant was obviously excited and Ramage knew that this command, however brief it might prove to be, would make up for the disappointment of seeing the Third Lieutenant go off to Barbados in *La Mutine*.

Ramage took a pencil and pad from his pocket and went aft with a telescope, sitting down on the breech of the aftermost gun. He spent the next half an hour examining the Diamond Rock with the telescope, occasionally making a sketch on the pad and scribbling notes.

He had already drawn the south side of the great rock while in the cutter. There it was completely vertical from sea level to within a hundred feet or so of the top; then it sloped back gently for fifty feet, and then more sharply again to the peak. His sketch resembled a tooth, the raking pack at the top being the natural shape to bring the tooth to a point.

His inspection in the cutter had confirmed what he had feared from the start: the only way of getting guns up the Diamond, to whatever height, was by jackstay. Only the gun covering the landing place was going to be straight forward – if lowering it to the sea bed from a boat and then dragging it ashore could be described as straightforward.

He turned to a fresh page and copied the sketch he had made from the cutter, drawing the tooth-shaped rock with the vertical cliff face to the left. Then from sea level he drew a diagonal line up to the top of the cliff. That would be the jackstay, secured at the top round the rocky outcrop, and at the bottom to the anchored *Juno*. Running up the jackstay would be a big block, and from that would hang the gun. The block and gun would be hauled up the jackstay by a purchase, one set of blocks attached to the big block, and the other to the top of the cliff. The hauling part of the rope would come down to the *Juno*, where it would go round the capstan.

As he pencilled in the lines showing the ropes it seemed almost alarmingly simple, though he could imagine the difficulty he was going to have describing it all in a letter to Gianna. Imagine, he would tell her, that you have to hoist a heavy weight from the garden up to a high window in a house. You take a clothes line and tie one end to the window ledge and the other to the base of a tree in the garden, so the line is taut and running down a steep angle.

You put a pulley on the line (Gianna would be furious with him for using the word 'pulley' instead of the nautical 'block' which she understood well enough), and hang the weight on it. Then you hook one more pulley on the weight, and another to the window ledge. You pass a rope from the window ledge down to the pulley on the weight, back round the pulley on the window ledge and then down to the garden. *Allora, cara mia*, as you stand by the tree and haul on the rope, the weight will slowly rise up the line. And that, he would add, is what we did with the guns, give or take a few blocks, several hundred feet of rope and a few tons of weight. He could see her tracing with her finger as she read the letter, working it all out . . . She could never imagine just how close the *Juno* would be moored to the cliff, he thought grimly; so close that the ends of the yards would almost touch the rock face. He put the pad and pencil in his pocket and turned to watch the Marines attacking the battery as the *Créole* came in and anchored.

CHAPTER TWELVE

Next morning Ramage returned on board the *Juno* after inspecting the *Surcouf* feeling much more cheerful. Working through the night with Aitken encouraging them, the men now had the maincourse bent on the yard and furled, and the maintopsail and topgallant were both neatly faked down in slings ready for hoisting. The fourcourse was also bent on and men were sorting out the buntlines and clewlines before furling it. The foretopsail and topgallant were being hoisted up from the sail room. How they had sorted out all that running rigging by lantern light Ramage could not imagine, but by sunset the *Surcouf* would be ready to go into action against her erstwhile owners.

Ramage's main worry when he first heard that the *Surcouf*'s sails were all on board and stowed in the sail room was that the rats would have got at them. They were so bulky (a frigate's maincourse comprised more than 3000 square feet of canvas and a whole suit totalled 14000 square feet and weighed four tons) that it was impossible to keep them inspected properly in a sail room, and even a single rat chewing a tunnel through the folds of a stowed sail could do more damage than a dozen roundshot. However, it was clear that the French had only just put the sails on board and many small patches showed they had checked them over before doing so.

It had been a good idea to fetch Aitken back: he was in his element commissioning the *Surcouf* and Ramage had the impression he had been getting bored with tacking back and forth with the *Créole*. The young Scot was fascinated by the differences in the French and British ways of rigging ships. They were slight but often significant, and he pointed them out to Ramage with all the excitement of a collector. It was an enthusiasm Ramage shared; he recognized in the Scot another man like himself, a squirrel who collected odd and often useless items of information and stored them away in his head for mental winters.

It was a habit, Ramage knew from bitter experience, that could make you unpopular in certain company. Too many men had no real interest in anything and for practical purposes were blind to most of the things that went on around them. Ramage now kept a tight rein on his tongue, but in the past had often commented on something he found interesting, only to find the other person thought he was showing off his knowledge. The episode that had made him vow he would never again begin a conversation with anyone he did not know well concerned pelicans.

He had noticed that when these heavy birds dived at a very steep angle into the water after a fish, often from a considerable height, at the very last moment they bent their long necks close up against their bodies and, for reasons which Ramage could not work out, always surfaced facing the opposite direction. It had been a topic of conversation and observation for Ramage and Southwick for weeks the last time they had been in the Caribbean. One day Ramage had mentioned it in front of a group of captains—he had been a mere lieutenant then – and to a man the captains had stared at him as though they had suddenly found in their midst someone who had just escaped from Bedlam. All of them had served in the Caribbean for at least two years and had obviously not noticed it. Aitken, who had just arrived in the West Indies for the first time, had not only noticed it but already had several theories and, he recently told Ramage, had drawn many sketches which he intended sending to an eminent naturalist he knew in Edinburgh. Apparently he had shown the sketches to Southwick, who had been able to add to them. The two of them had settled down to try to calculate the most driving question of all: why did such a heavy bird as a pelican, diving from such great heights, not break its neck?

As Ramage paused on the quarterdeck, trying to switch his thoughts from the pelicans diving round the Diamond to the problems facing him over the Rock itself, he realized that the Surgeon was waiting to speak to him, and with him was Rennick, the Marine Lieutenant.

'How are the new patients, Bowen?'

'Both in good shape, I'm happy to say, sir,' he said, handing Ramage the copy of the sick list. 'The cutlass wound was a clean cut, and I can see the healing has already begun. The other man is badly bruised but I have given him another thorough examination this morning, and there are definitely no bones broken.'

'He must have fallen fifty feet, sir,' Rennick said apologetically.

'Now he knows the perils of standing near a recoiling gun,' Ramage said grimly. 'I hope you've thought about what I was telling you last night . . .'

'I have indeed, sir. The trouble was that I had heard of that method before – turning a gun with its breech towards the edge of a cliff and firing it. I did it because it seemed certain the recoil would run it back over the edge of the cliff.'

'And so it would have, if the platform had been level, but there you had an uneven and rocky surface. No wonder the damned gun ran round in a curve and turned over. It only needed one of the trucks to hit a bump.'

'Well, sir,' said Rennick defensively, 'at least we managed to roll it over the edge of the cliff in the end.'

'Where it now lies undamaged and ready for the French to salvage, if we give them the chance,' Ramage said sharply.

'A brass gun, too. Worth three iron guns, as you well know.'

'We destroyed the other two, though, sir,' Rennick said contritely.

Ramage nodded, accepting Rennick's apology. 'That's the safest way – double or triple charge, three roundshot and everyone behind some shelter when you fire. That's why you're supposed to carry an extra long trigger line when you attack a battery.'

When the lieutenant went red, Ramage asked suspiciously: 'You *did* carry one, didn't you?'

Rennick shook his head and clearly wished the deck would open up and swallow him. 'No, sir, but I joined up the three the French were using . . .'

Ramage knew that the Marine Lieutenant had learned several lessons and he would not repeat the mistakes again. Apart from that, it had been a brave and well executed attack, and he did not want Rennick to lose confidence in himself. 'Very well, you destroyed the battery, which is what matters,' he said. 'I'll have a word with your men later.'

Rennick gave a relieved grin, saluted and left. Ramage looked at Bowen's sick list. 'I see you've discharged three more men.'

'Yes, sir. At least, they asked to be discharged: I'd have kept them another day, but they insisted.'

'Insisted?' Ramage asked curiously. 'I thought every man's ambition is to get on the sick list for a few days' rest!'

'It is in most ships – indeed, it was for the first couple of weeks after we left England. But all that's changed; these three men apparently heard some rumour about the Diamond –' Bowen nodded towards the Rock ' – and they, well, it seemed to me they wanted to join in the fun.'

'Fun! They'll have to work so hard they'll probably end up back on the sick list suffering from heat stroke!'

'We'll see, sir,' Bowen said with a knowing look.

Ramage walked forward to the fo'c'sle, where Southwick was busy with a party of seamen. He was watching while the carpenter and bos'n worked on an enormous block of unusual shape. The big lignum vitae sheave fitted into a thick wooden shell, one side of which was longer than the other, and open at one end. Called a voyol block, it was a spare one and rarely used. Now it would ride up the jackstay with a gun slung underneath it. Like many things in a ship that are seldom used, the block had been stowed without being washed in fresh water, and the salt had made the sheave and pin seize up. Now the carpenter was driving out the pin with his maul. It would be cleaned and driven back after being smeared with tallow, and a liberal amount of tallow would be put on the sheave so that it turned freely.

Large coils of five-inch circumference rope had been hoisted up from the store room and men were busy long-splicing them to make up an eighteen hundred foot length. That would be used (with the two large single-sheave blocks which had already been smeared with tallow) to make up the enormous tackle which would haul both gun and voyol block up the jackstay. More men were making up strops, using old rope that would not stretch. They would sling the gun beneath the voyol block. Mentally he ticked them off the list as he walked aft again to look over the taffrail, where Lacey, the Fourth Lieutenant, was standing and occasionally shouting down instructions. Already the *Juno*'s two cutters were being secured together, ready to take on shore the 6-pounder gun that would cover the landing place. One spar was lashed across the bow of each of them like a narrow bridge, and another near the stern, so that they were kept eight feet apart.

Amidships the crew of the jolly boat were about to cast off, towing the carriage of the 6-pounder and carrying the breeching, train tackle, handspikes, rammer and sponge in the boat. The gun itself was lying on the *Juno*'s deck with slings round it, ready for hoisting out.

Ramage shouted down to the coxswain: 'Are you ready to go?'

'All ready, sir.'

Ramage called to Lacey, who hurried forward to get into the boat. 'I'm afraid the cutters aren't ready yet, sir.'

'I'll keep an eye on them. Now, you're perfectly clear what has to be done?'

'Aye, aye, sir: tow the carriage round to the cove. If we can float it into the cove and haul it ashore, do so; otherwise secure it so that it floats clear and come back for more men.'

Ramage nodded and Lacey scrambled down into the jolly boat.

Today's work towards the Diamond plan was easy; he could only pray that tomorrow – in fact for the next three days – the sea would stay as smooth, with no swell. He'd be quite content for today to get the 6-pounder mounted on that ledge, to cover the landing place.

A lookout aloft hailed that *La Créole* was coming into sight round the end of Diamond Hill, but had no signals flying. Ramage, noting that Wagstaffe had searched as far as Pointe des Salines without sighting anything, acknowledged the hail and moodily began pacing the quarterdeck, occasionally going aft and looking down at the men working in the cutters. They were doing perfectly well – Lacey, like most young officers, was too keen to let men work on their own.

Fifteen paces forward and he was abreast the skylight over his cabin, three more and he was passing the mizenmast. Three more and the wheel was abeam and the binnacle. Six more and he was passing the companionway, its coaming studded with roundshot which fitted like black oranges into cup-shaped holes cut in the wood. Now he was level with the capstan and the water cask with the Marine sentry guarding it. He had doubled the daily ration for the men while they were doing this heavy work: there was plenty to spare with the *Surcouf*'s casks available.

The deck was scorching hot, even though the awning was stretched overhead, and as he turned to walk aft he felt a momentary dizziness. He was tired and bored. Tired because there was so little time for sleep, and bored because he was the Captain, the man whose life comprised weeks of boredom, of just ensuring that the day-to-day ship routine was carried out properly, punctuated every few weeks (months, more likely) by a few hours of action. He reached the taffrail, glanced down at the cutters, and began to walk forward again.

Now was a good example of the boredom: Aitken was working hard on board the *Surcouf* getting the sails hoisted up and bent on; Baker was on his way to Barbados in *La Mutine* with all the excitement of his first command; Wagstaffe was tacking north again with *La Créole* for another look at Fort Royal. Southwick was busy on the foredeck, preparing everything for hoisting the jackstay tomorrow. Captain Ramage had nothing whatever to do and could only pace up and down, occasionally looking at the work in progress. Even the cook's mate was busy – skimming the slush, from the smell of it; boiling the salt beef in the coppers and taking off the fat that floated to the surface and carefully storing it. When it was cool he would sell it to the men, earning himself some illicit pennies or tots and giving the men something to help the hard biscuit slide down their gullets.

He could go down to his cabin and continue his letter to Gianna: he tried to add a few paragraphs every day so that she had a sort of diary to read when it eventually arrived many weeks later. Or he could start a letter to his father, who would be interested to read about the problems he was facing over the Diamond . . . But he felt too fidgety to sit at his desk and anyway the moment he saw the Captain sitting there, the clerk would come trotting in with papers and reports for him to sign. Being a conscientious man, he would also have a list of trivial reports that Ramage should have made, or chased his officers into making.

He had only just come back from the *Surcouf* and if he returned there now Aitken would start worrying. If he went up to the foredeck Southwick, his white hair matted with perspiration and his temper getting short, would think that Ramage considered his men were not working fast enough.

His next look over the taffrail showed that the two cutters were now secured together and he realized thankfully that he had a job to do. It was not a job for the Captain, but one that had to be done, and mercifully Lacey was over at the Diamond with the carriage in tow.

'Haul round to the starboard side,' he called to Jackson, who was acting as coxswain of the two boats. 'Secure your painter and sternfasts so you are directly under the main yard.'

Two luff tackles were already hooked into the yard tackle pendant and secured to the slings round the gun lying on the deck. They had been used earlier to lift the gun off the carriage which was now being towed to the cove.

A hail to Southwick brought twenty men hurrying aft to man the luff tackles while more ran to the braces. Ramage went to the entry port at the gangway and watched until the two boats were secured alongside. As soon as they were ready he turned to the men at the luff tackles.

'Hoist away, now. You four, tail on those steadying lines, we don't want the gun swinging.'

The men heaved steadily, and slowly the gun lifted off the deck, hanging horizontally from the carefully-placed slings. Finally it was higher than the hammock nettings and Ramage signalled them to stop hoisting.

Another signal to the men at the braces and a hurried warning to the men holding the steadying lines brought the main yard swinging round a few degrees, back to its normal position. This swung the gun out over the bulwarks until it was suspended above the boats.

The men with the steadying lines climbed up into the hammock nettings so they could see down into the boats, and Ramage gave the order for the men at the luff tackles to begin lowering. The gun came down foot by foot at first, and then inch by inch. As it neared the boat, Ramage gave the signal for them to stop lowering. Now he had to make sure that the men at the steadying lines kept the gun parallel with the boats while he gave the final order which would swing the yard round a fraction more, so that the gun was precisely over the gap between them.

Jackson gave Ramage a signal that all was well and slowly the gun was lowered again. The men in each boat held up their hands in case it began twisting, obviously not trusting the men at the steadying lines. Then the gun was in the water between the two boats, its muzzle and breech clear of the spars and a moment later disappearing below it.

Ramage shouted to the men at the luff tackles to stop lowering and saw that Jackson was fully prepared. Four men at the bow of the two boats leaned over to the forward sling and then signalled to Ramage, who told the men at the forward tackle to lower gently. Now the top of the forward sling was almost level with the spar joining the two boats and swiftly the four men put on a rolling hitch, using a short piece of heavy rope. Then they secured the other end to the centre of the spar.

While they had been doing that, four men had been securing the after sling to the after spar while Jackson cast off the steadying lines. Now the gun, six feet long, was slung between the two spars and hanging three or four feet below the water, but the weight was still being taken by the luff tackles.

'All secure?' Ramage shouted, and when Jackson answered that it was, he signalled to the men at the tackles to slack away. Slowly, as the weight of the gun was transferred through the slings to the boats, they sank deeper in the water. But it was an even settling; neither was down by bow or stern. The whole twelve hundredweight of gun – which now weighed less in water – was slung under the two boats, and two seamen with boathooks jabbed at the hooks of the tackles to release them from the slings.

The heavy blocks soared up in the air, the yard was braced round again, and Ramage called to Jackson: 'Carry on then, and make for the cove: Mr Lacey will be waiting for you. And make sure the gun tackle is hooked into the cascabel ring and moused before you let go!'

'Aye, aye, sir,' Jackson grinned, 'otherwise we'll have to dive for it!'

The painter and sternfast were cast off and the two boats edged away from the *Juno*, the men rowing from the outboard side of each one. Progress was painfully slow but Jackson was careful to use the wind so that it helped them in their crabwise course towards the Diamond.

Ramage found Southwick beside him, watching the boats. 'You looked as though you were enjoying yourself, sir,' he said cheerfully, first making sure they were out of earshot of the men.

'I was,' Ramage admitted. 'It's deucedly tedious just marching up and down the quarterdeck like a sentry at the Horse Guards.'

Southwick nodded sympathetically. 'The convoy will soon be here. We'll be busy enough then.'

Two hours later Ramage found an excuse for going over to the Diamond: the men with the jolly boat and two cutters had not returned and it would soon be dinner time, so he ordered the cook to prepare food for the men and had himself rowed over in one of the *Surcouf*'s boats. As an afterthought he had ordered the gunner to fetch up a lock and spare flint, carefully wrapped against the spray, a pricker, trigger line, wads, two round shot and two cartridges, the cylindrical wooden boxes being stowed in a canvas bag as a precaution against both spray and powder accidentally spilling. It was unlikely that the gun would be ready, but he warned Southwick not to be alarmed if he heard a shot.

As the boat rounded the Rock and the cove came into view he was pleasantly surprised to see that the carriage was up on the ledge and close to it what looked like a great letter A without the cross bar. The men had made sheers from the spars that had previously lashed the cutters together, and an oar provided the support. A heavy tackle slung from the sheers had hoisted the gun and several men were now manoeuvring the carriage directly under it.

By the time Ramage leapt on shore the gun had been lowered and he heard an excited yell from Lacey: 'Throw over the cap-squares! Now, in with the bolts!'

The lieutenant pulled off the band of cloth he had been wearing round his brow to keep the perspiration from his eyes, snatched up his hat and jammed it on his head before saluting. 'You beat us by a quarter of an hour, sir,' he said ruefully, gesturing at the men hurriedly unlashing the sheers.

'I've brought you all some food, anyway,' Ramage said with a grin. 'And powder and shot for the first round!'

Within fifteen minutes the men had hurried through their meal and were overhauling the train tackles which had kinked and tangled themselves, carrying the heavy breeching from the cove and clearing small rocks away on the ledge to make the gun platform comparatively smooth. Lacey had chosen a site which was in fact a slight depression with a piece of rock protruding like a stump of a tree on each side, ideally placed to secure each end of the breeching which, passing through the cascabel ring at the breech end of the gun, would bring the gun to a stop after it had recoiled a few feet.

Ramage went over to explore the big cave again while Lacey and his men finished preparing the gun and he was several yards inside the cave, examining it as possible accommodation for the men and a store for provisions, when he was startled to hear Lacey calling him from the entrance, obviously uncertain about entering.

Ramage joined him to find the lieutenant looking embarrassed.

'The men – er, well sir, the men have asked me to, er . . .'

'Take a deep breath and spit it out, man,' Ramage said impatiently. 'I assume they aren't telling me they're planning a mutiny.'

'The gun's ready for firing, sir,' Lacey said hurriedly, 'and the men want you to name the battery.'

'Name it? What on earth for?'

'Well, sir, I believe there are going to be three batteries, and I think they had in mind that it would be easier to distinguish them if each had a name. They seem particularly concerned about this first one.'

Ramage was hot, tired, and in no mood for thinking of names. 'Tell them I'll think of a name tomorrow.'

Lacey's face fell. 'They – well, sir,' he said with a rush, 'they've already chosen a name, and they want you to approve it, sir.'

Ramage frowned. With Jackson, Rossi and Stafford out there, he suspected they had thought of some ludicrous name that would be impossible for him to use in official reports: something like the Nipcheese Battery, as a dig at the purser, or the Checkmate, to tease the Surgeon.

'They want to call it the Marchesa Battery, sir,' Lacey said nervously. 'I – er, I understand there's an Italian Marchesa for whom some of them had a very high regard; the aunt of young Orsini, I think.'

Ramage tried to keep a straight face. Obviously Lacey was picturing some ancient Italian dowager. 'Yes, that is correct; Orsini's aunt is the Marchesa di Volterra.' He began walking towards the battery so that Lacey should not see the delighted grin on his face. 'A most appropriate name in the circumstances; yes, most appropriate,' he said with all the seriousness he could muster. Most of the former Tritons were grouped round the gun: Jackson, Stafford, Rossi, Maxton . . . All could see from Ramage's expression that he had agreed to the name. The gun was ready: the trigger line was neatly coiled on top of the breech, the lock was in position, the rammer, sponge and handspikes were ready. Well clear of the gun were the cartridge boxes with two round shot beside them. Jackson had the long metal primer tucked in his belt and a powder horn on a lanyard round his neck.

They seemed to be taking the naming ceremony seriously, and Ramage decided he should, too. 'I think we might fire a round in celebration, Mr Lacey,' he said briskly.

'Aye, aye, sir!' Lacey said happily and barked out an order. Immediately the eight men sprang forward and the rest stood back. Obviously the gun crew had been chosen while he was in the cave, and all of them were former Tritons.

Jackson, as gun captain, had the long pricker – officially known as the priming wire – and the powder flask ready. Stafford as the second captain was checking the lock, snapping it to make sure the flint made a good spark. One man had picked up the rammer while a fourth ran up with the thin flannel cylinder of gunpowder that was the cartridge, lifted it to the muzzle and pressed it in. He then helped the man with the rammer push it home, took the wad that was handed and helped ram that home. A fifth man came up with shot and that was pushed down the bore and rammed home. Both men jumped back clear of the muzzle as the men at the tackles ran the gun forward. If it had been mounted on board the *Juno*, the muzzle and much of the barrel would be poking out through the port, clear of the ship's side. Now it was run out to leave the heavy rope breeching slack, ready to take the strain when the gun recoiled.

The drill was excellent. Lacey, in contrast to the unnecessary orders he had been giving as the men lashed the cutter together, was now standing silent at the rear of the gun, waiting for Jackson to give the signal.

The American held up his hand and Lacey shouted, 'Prime!'

Jackson went to the vent, rammed the priming wire down the hole and made sure it had penetrated the flannel of the cartridge inside the breech, making a small hole and exposing the powder inside. Then he poured a small amount of powder into the pan, checking that it covered the vent.

'Point!' shouted Lacey.

Jackson took the trigger line coiled on top of the breech and walked back until he was standing at its full extent. He bent down on his right knee with his left leg flung out sideways. As he did that men picked up the handspikes and stood ready.

Jackson sighted along the barrel and called 'Muzzle left!' to the handspikemen, gesturing with his left hand. They levered the rear of the carriage to the right, so that the muzzle of the gun came round to the left, and stopped when Jackson called, 'Well!'

Lacey then gave the third order in the sequence of single word commands normally used. 'Elevate!' he shouted.

The men thrust their handspikes under the breech of the gun, levering it up by using the steps cut into the after end of the carriage as a pivot, and lifted. Stafford pulled out the wedge-shaped quoin and the handspikemen slowly lowered the breech again, watching Jackson as he sighted along the barrel.

The moment he called, 'Well!', Stafford rammed in the wooden wedge and as soon as he felt the weight of the breech firmly resting on it he called, 'Down!' The handspikemen jumped clear but Stafford stood by the breech, awaiting the next order.

'Ready!' Lacey called, looking anxiously at Ramage.

Stafford leaned over and cocked the lock, and the click, combined with Jackson looking round expectantly at him, suddenly roused Ramage; with a shock he realized that he was not sure whether he should first have taken formal possession of the Diamond Rock. What on earth did one do? When you captured an enemy ship you hoisted your own ensign above his, but what did you do with an island? He remembered vaguely that he had occasionally read of some formal annexation when a new island was discovered. A flag was hoisted and speeches were made. Did the same rules apply when you captured one?

He racked his brain for a precedent, could think of none, and hastily decided that too much formality would be better than too little. It was wiser to say a few pompous words that subsequently proved to be unnecessary than to fail to say them and provoke Their Lordships' wrath. Apart from that, young post captains at the bottom of the Navy List rarely capture islands. If Ramage, Nicholas, is setting a precedent, then he will do it in style, he told himself.

He removed his hat and Lacey hurriedly did the same. The men stood rigidly to attention and did it so naturally that he realized they were all expecting some sort of ceremony, though probably for their battery rather than for the whole Rock.

What the deuce should he say? He coughed and tucked his hat under his left arm. He ought to be wearing his sword. Lacey's rapt expression would have been more suitable if he was about to be blessed by the Archbishop of Canterbury rather than listen to his Captain make a fool of himself.

'I, Nicholas Ramage, Captain in the Royal Navy and commanding officer of His Majesty's frigate *Juno* . . .' That was a good start, but what now? He thought for a moment and continued '. . . do hereby take possession of this island, known as the *Rocher du Diamant*, or the Diamond Rock . . . for and on behalf of His Majesty King George the Third!'

The men began cheering wildly and an excited Lacey joined in, waving his hat in the air. Ramage, who had been expecting the men to start giggling, was so pleased with their reaction to words which had sounded ponderous and absurd to him, that he began to grin broadly. After a moment he managed to arrange his expression into a stern look, more befitting a conqueror, albeit of a barren rock and, as soon as the cheering stopped he looked around, as though surveying this newest gem in the King's crown, put his hat back on his head and said in a ringing voice: 'And I hereby name this battery the Marchesa Battery. May it play its part in defending the Diamond Rock!'

Again the men burst out in a roar of cheering and one of them began singing the first line of 'Hearts of Oak are our men!' and the rest of them took it up, bellowing lustily.

The moment they finished Ramage gestured to Lacey who took a pace forward and shouted 'Marchesa Battery — fire!'

Jackson tugged the trigger line and the gun gave a prodigious roar which echoed back from the Rock immediately behind it. Smoke spurted from the muzzle, spreading into an oily yellow cloud. The trucks of the carriage clattered as they ran back over the rocky surface and the rope breeching suddenly tautened and stretched as it absorbed the recoil and then thrust the carriage forward again a few inches. A mile to seaward there was a vertical spurt of water, like a whale spouting.

Ramage walked over to examine each end of the breeching to make sure it had not chafed on the rocks round which it was secured. One round remained, but he decided against using it: the next job was to get more powder and shot over from the *Juno*, but that could wait until tomorrow; then the men would only have to row a few yards. There was no point in leaving the gun manned; the risk of the French making a determined attempt during the night to recapture a barren rock they did not yet know they had lost was, to say the least of it, remote.

He let the men chatter happily for a few minutes, laughing and joking, teasing Jackson that he had missed the invisible ship, and then he said to Lacey: 'Secure the gun now, and we'll do those soundings.'

Fifteen minutes later the jolly boat was being rowed slowly up and down the south side of the Rock, close under the sheer cliff, with a man standing in the bow heaving a lead and reporting the depths he found. Ramage used the boat compass to take rough bearings and Lacey busily wrote down the depths and bearings as they were called out.

They started right close in to the cliffs, so close that the men occasionally had to fend off with the blades of their oars as a swell wave pushed the boat against the rock face. Ramage soon stopped glancing upwards because it made him dizzy: the cliff soared up vertically; from the boat it might have been five thousand feet high, rather than five hundred. Just as it soared up vertically into the sky, so it plunged vertically to the sea bed. The depths right up against the foot of the cliff were staggering, and he was glad he had told Lacey to bring the deep sea lead, as well as the hand lead. They were finding forty fathoms close into the cliff, and fifty fathoms only thirty yards out.

As the boat reached the end of the fifteenth run and turned to begin the next, and the leadsman, with water streaming down him, hurriedly coiling up the line, Ramage leaned across the thwart to look at Lacey's rough chart. The picture of the sea bed slowly taking shape on the paper from the depths and the bearing was far from reassuring. Lacey looked up anxiously, knowing how much depended on the result of the survey, and Ramage commented with as much nonchalance as he could muster: 'We won't risk running aground, anyway.'

Bad as it was, it could have been worse. There was a lot of coral down there, staghorn coral as far as could be judged from the pieces that came up with the lead. The trouble was that the scooped-out depression in the bottom of the lead, which was filled with tallow, was only intended to have sand or mud adhere to it; the tiny bits of coral that the lead knocked off as it hit the bottom were hardly enough for a proper identification. Any sort of coral was bad, though: it was jagged and sharp and quickly chafed anchor cables, and the *Juno*, Ramage reflected grimly, would be laying out four anchors . . . Perhaps only three, if the present calm weather held.

As he watched the birds wheeling round the cliff – he saw a white tropic bird with its long forked tail streaming out like two ribbons – he was thankful that there were no back eddies of wind to drive the *Juno* against the cliff. None, he corrected himself, with the wind in this direction. No back eddies and very little swell. He looked up again at the top of the cliff, which was gaunt, grey and cold even in the sunlight, and so sheer that only a few bushes managed to grow in cracks and crevices, and for the hundredth time he wondered whether he could do it.

CHAPTER THIRTEEN

The sky to the eastward was gradually turning pink beyond the mountains of Martinique early next morning as the *Juno*'s capstan slowly revolved with Bevins, the fiddler, standing on top and scratching out a tune to encourage the men straining at the capstan bars.

Ramage stood at the quarterdeck rail, affecting a nonchalant stance to disguise the tension gripping him. The *Juno* was about to set out on her shortest voyage, less than half a mile, and he was as nervous as a kitten hearing its first dog bark. The ten-inch cable used to tow the *Surcouf* was now amidships, the first hundred fathoms of it flaked down and ready to run, only this time it would be running upwards.

The launch was towing astern with an anchor slung ready beneath it; another cable was flaked out on the quarterdeck ready to bend on to it. The two cutters were also astern, ready to tow the frigate to its final position, and the topmen were waiting ready for the order to go aloft. The jolly boat would be at the cove by now, and Aitken and his men should have started their long climb to the top of the Rock. The young Scot had been confident that he had found a route merely by examining the Rock through the telescope. Ramage, although doubtful, had not argued with him and he went off cheerfully before dawn, his men carrying rope ladders, axes, heavy mauls borrowed from the carpenter, sharpened stakes, speaking trumpet, and several coils of rope.

The *Surcouf* was lying head to wind, all her sails neatly furled on her yards, and only a dozen men on board. The First Lieutenant had worked well into the night to have the ship ready, returning to the *Juno* to report to Ramage at midnight, so exhausted that he was swaying as he spoke. Ramage had sent him off to snatch some sleep, telling him that it would take the *Juno* two or three hours to get into position so that he could sleep on, but Aitken had left orders that he was to be called at dawn.

Wagstaffe had tacked in towards the Rock with the *Créole* and was now stretching north again, and Ramage thought for a moment of *La Mutine*. She should have arrived in Barbados yesterday, and with luck she was now on her way back. By tonight or at the latest tomorrow morning he could expect Admiral Davis to arrive in the *Invincible*. There was barely time to get half the job done.

Slowly the frigate weighed as the sequence of reports and orders passed to and fro between the fo'c'sle and quarterdeck. The yards were already braced sharp up and the jibs were being hoisted but left to flap in the wind.

'Short stay!' came a shout from the fo'c'sle, warning Ramage that the anchor cable was making the same angle as the forestay. He put the speaking trumpet to his lips.

'Away aloft!'

The topmen swarmed up the rigging and his orders followed in quick succession. While men sheeted home the headsails he shouted aloft to the topmen: 'Trice up and lay out!' As soon as the men were out on the yards with the studding sail booms triced up out of the way he ordered the men on deck: 'Man the topsail sheets!' A moment later the topmen were being told to 'Let fall!' and as the sails tumbled down he gave a fresh order to the men on deck: 'Sheet home!'

By now the anchor was off the bottom and the *Juno* was gathering way. It would be two or three minutes before the anchor broke surface and only a few minutes more before the frigate would be anchoring again. He glanced up at the wind vane at the maintruck and then to the eastward, where the sun was just lifting over the mountains. So far, so good; at least the French convoy had not chosen this moment to round Pointe des Salines.

Fifteen minutes later the *Juno* had rounded up off the south side of the Rock and dropped anchor again, gathering stern-way under a backed foretopsail, so that the cable thundered out through the starboard hawse, smoking with the friction.

As soon as Southwick signalled from the fo'c'sle how much cable had been veered, Ramage gave another series of orders which braced round the yards so that the *Juno* gathered way again and sailed a short distance before the foretopsail was backed once more and the larboard anchor let go as the *Juno* went astern in yet another sternboard. Within minutes the topmen were furling all the sails and the frigate was riding to her two anchors, the cables making an angle of forty-five degrees.

The *Juno* was now lying not quite parallel with the face of the cliff fifty yards away. The two cutters were going to have to pull her stern round towards the cliff while the launch was rowed astern to lay out the spare anchor that would hold her there in position. It was the lightest anchor in the ship and one which, in an emergency could be slipped and left behind.

Southwick came striding aft to join Ramage on the quarter-deck, and he wore the contented grin that Ramage knew from long experience meant that he approved of the way his Captain had handled the ship. 'Now to get those cutters towing,' he said gleefully, rubbing his hands. He looked up and commented: 'Y'know, sir, that's a damned tall cliff!'

'I wish you'd mentioned that before,' Ramage said sarcastically. 'It had almost escaped my attention.'

'Can't see Aitken up there yet.'

'Remember Pythagoras,' Ramage said. 'You're looking up the perpendicular side of what that poor beggar is scrambling up the hypotenuse!'

'They're used to it, these Scotsmen,' Southwick said,

blithely ignoring Ramage's bad temper. 'All mountains in Scotland – goats and sheep and haggises, climbing all the time, they are. Especially the haggises,' he added before Ramage could correct him, 'very nimble they are, Aitken tells me.'

Ramage shook his head despairingly. 'Neither the Good Lord nor the First Lord has seen fit to spare me from a Master who is so damnably cheerful first thing in the morning. However, Mr Southwick, oblige me by putting those cutters to work: I have to lay *this* ship alongside *that* cliff before I can settle down to a leisurely breakfast.'

As soon as the men in the two cutters began rowing with the oars double-banked, Ramage ordered the quartermaster to put the wheel over; there might be enough current to give the ship a sheer larboard, which would help the oarsmen. Sure enough the frigate slowly swung in towards the cliff face, and the coxswains of both boats hurried their men to take up the slack.

Now it was the turn of the men in the waiting launch. The anchor was slung beneath the boat and the cable on the quarterdeck led down to it through the sternchase port. The oars were double-banked and the coxswain waited ready. Ramage gave the signal and the launch began to move away, heading almost directly astern of the *Juno*. Men on the quarterdeck slowly fed the cable through the port, careful to let out enough to help the launch, but not so much that the heavy rope hung down in too large a curve.

Southwick now had men bracing the yards round so they were as nearly fore and aft as possible. The *Juno* was going to end up so close to the cliff that the larboard ends of the yards – the mainyard overhung the ship's side by twenty-three feet – might otherwise foul the Rock.

Having done that the Master began supervising the rigging out of the lower studding sail booms on the larboard side. There were three of them, one abreast each mast, and they were shipped and then swung out at right angles from the ship's side at deck level, the outer ends held by topping lifts, with guys holding them fore and aft. Normally used to hold out the foot of the lower studding sails, they would now, Ramage hoped, act against the cliff face when they began hoisting the jackstay.

The launch was almost in position astern and Ramage waited with the speaking trumpet in his hand. If only he could see right down into the water he would know whether the anchor fell so that the cable led over a bank of sharp coral. If he waited another two or three minutes the launch might have moved slightly crabwise so that the cable would miss it. He shrugged his shoulders and hailed through the trumpet. He saw men slashing the strop holding the anchor and a few moments later the boat began bobbing about, floating higher as if it was suddenly freed of the weight of the anchor and the pull of cable, more of which snaked out through the port.

Southwick was already shouting to the two cutters to return to the ship, his voice echoing back from the cliff face. With the *Juno* now moored fore and aft parallel with the cliff and forty yards from it, there was little more to do until Aitken arrived at the top of the Rock – the top of the cliff, rather, Ramage corrected himself, remembering the double slope back from the cliff top to the peak of the Rock.

The Master was bustling round amidships, checking the cable that was going to be the jackstay, glaring at the voyol block as though it was an unruly dog, kicking at the five-inch rope that would eventually be rove through the two single blocks to make a gun tackle. Watching him, Ramage knew that he was worried about his next job. It took a lot to ruffle Southwick – many French broadsides, boarding enemy ships, and a full hurricane had so far failed, to Ramage's certain knowledge. No, Southwick was worried now because he was faced with a tricky task that was far beyond the scope of ordinary seamanship: he and his Captain were planning by guess rather than knowledge, and Southwick's only fear was that the whole jackstay system might not work; that they would fail to get the guns to the top of the Rock. Well, Ramage thought, the old man must know that his Captain is keeping him company; in fact they should be holding hands and comforting each other.

For the next half an hour he and Southwick had the men adjusting the three cables, veering a little on the starboard anchor cable and taking in a little on the larboard, so the *Juno* edged over a little more towards the cliff, and then taking up on the stern anchor so that she came away again. When they were ready, veering the stern cable would give the final adjustment.

They had just finished that when they heard a hail from high above and saw Aitken's tiny figure waving a speaking trumpet. A few moments later he was joined by other men, and Southwick shouted for a crew to man the jolly boat, which had returned to the ship an hour earlier.

Ramage watched Aitken and his men through a telescope. They were holding a small object and securing a line to it. A rock, no doubt, to make sure the line they were going to lower as a messenger would not blow in the wind and snag on a bush or a jutting piece of rock.

He saw Aitken suddenly bend back and then jerk forward, and a moment later a black speck began falling through the air, down towards the *Juno*'s deck, trailing behind it what seemed from this distance to be a black thread. It fell into the sea half-way between the ship and the cliff and the jolly boat leapt forward to grab it before it swung back through the water against the foot of the cliff, and brought it back to the *Juno*.

The jackstay was very heavy, so much so that the *Juno*'s capstan would be needed to hoist it up the cliff. The only way to do that, Ramage had calculated, was to use the tackle that would eventually haul the gun up the jackstay. But to begin with, until the tackle was completely rigged, Aitken's men were going to have to pull the first block and rope up to the top of the cliff.

Southwick supervised the men securing the block and rope to the line thrown down from the cliff, and then took the speaking trumpet and gave a stentorian bellow to Aitken. The line tautened and seamen eased the block and the heavier rope over the side and slowly, agonizingly slowly it seemed to Ramage, it began to rise as Aitken's men hauled away. Their task aloft was made harder by the need to keep some tension on the heavier rope to make sure that it did not swing into the cliff, where the block might jam in one of the fissures.

Finally the block and the heavier rope reached the top and Ramage watched through the telescope as men reached out to grab it. Quickly they took off the light line and made the block fast round a protruding rock, the three parts of the rope forming the upper end of the purchase leading back down in a gentle curve to the *Juno*'s deck.

Southwick came up, rubbing his hands. 'Well, so much for the tackle, sir. The block is made up to the cable, and we can start hoisting whenever you give the word.'

Ramage looked forward to see that the hauling part, or fall, of the tackle was now led through a snatch block and then round the capstan and that men were waiting at the bars. The moment he gave the word they would start turning and the tackle would slowly hoist the heavy cable for the jackstay

192

up towards Aitken.

'It's going to be easy getting the cable up,' Ramage said doubtfully, 'but I'm wondering how we are going to get the block at our end down again. They'll secure a heavy rock to it, I know, but if it starts twisting or jams against something on the cliff face –'

He did not complete the sentence because Southwick knew the risk. It was gun tackle pure and simple, and excellent so long as there was a strain on the block at either end. But once the strain was released the parts of the rope tended to twist, and in doing so spun any block that was not secure, in this case the lower one that had to be brought down to the *Juno*'s deck again once the cable had been hoisted to the top.

'Leave it to Aitken, sir,' Southwick said. 'If he can get himself and his men up there, I'm sure he'll get that block down!'

Ramage nodded ruefully: it was not hard to make a decision because there was no choice, and for once he was thankful. 'Very well, let's see those men stepping out round the capstan!'

The capstan combined with the mechanical advantage of the gun tackle made the men's task easier, but before they finished they would have hoisted the best part of a ton up the cliff, since a hundred fathoms of ten-inch cable-laid rope weighed nineteen hundredweight. But a tackle was one of the best examples that Ramage knew of the old adage that 'You never get anything for nothing'. The three parts of the purchase reduced the amount of effort required to lift the cable, but it also meant that the lower block moved upwards much more slowly. The cable crawled and before it was a quarter of the way up the cliff face Ramage would have sworn it was not moving if he had not seen the seamen amidships hauling the rope clear as it came off the capstan and coiling it down.

'You must be hungry, sir,' Southwick said tactfully. 'It'll be an hour before there's much sign of progress here: more than time for you to have some breakfast.'

Ramage's stomach was so knotted from the strain he had been under since dawn that it would be hard to force down any food, but he remembered the contempt he had felt, as a very young lieutenant, when he saw nervous captains fussing round on deck unnecessarily. Well, he had to admit that Nicolas Ramage was giving a very good imitation of a nervous captain, and Southwick's reminder that he had not eaten for many hours gave him a good excuse to go below.

A sharp rapping on the door woke him and Southwick came into the cabin. When he saw Ramage sprawled on the settee and rubbing his eyes he said apologetically: 'Sorry, sir, I didn't know you were asleep.'

'Just dozed off,' Ramage said blearily. 'I sat down for a moment and –' he took out his watch. 'Why, that was an hour ago!'

'You've had less sleep than any of us,' Southwick commented sympathetically. 'Anyway, sir, the jackstay is rigged! Aitken has his end of the cable secure round a rock and our end is led to the capstan ready. We're just waiting for Aitken to send down the block of the gun tackle.'

With that the Master left the cabin and Ramage went through to the bed place to wash his face. The cabin was hot and stuffy since there was little or no wind and the sun was getting high with some strength in it. He paused for a moment as he dried his face. They had taken two hours up to now, and judging by the time needed to get the jackstay up the cliff it would require three or four hours to sway up the first gun. If they finished by nightfall there would be tomorrow morning to get up the second gun and both carriages. After that, with the *Juno* safely back at her original anchorage, they were going to have to get another gun to the ledge half-way up the Rock on the other side. Could it be done before the French convoy arrived? If the French arrived too soon, all this work would be in vain. He shrugged his shoulders and finished drying his face. Admiral Davis might also arrive too soon and, if he disapproved, bring everything to a stop . . .

He arrived on the quarterdeck to find Southwick lying on his back, holding the telescope to his eye.

'Almost broke my neck trying to see what's happening up there, sir,' he explained as Ramage stared down at him. 'Much more comfortable lying down like this. Aitken has trouble. They've tied a heavy rock round the block and lashed both to a strop which should slide down the jackstay clear of the cliff, but I think the block keeps twisting. They shouted to us to haul it back again . . . Hmm, bless my soul!' he exclaimed. 'Why, they're signalling to start it off again.' He jumped up to make sure Lacey was paying out the rope, looked aloft and said: 'Now there's a man sitting in the strop overhauling the rope as he comes down!'

Ramage snatched a telescope from the binnacle drawer and stretched out on the deck. There was indeed someone in the strop, sitting like a child on a swing, and pulling down on one part of the rope to make it run through the sheaves more easily and help the rock work better, like the weight of a grandfather clock. It was a small person, that much was clear, and wearing white trousers and a short jacket. He raised himself on one elbow and asked Southwick as casually as he could: 'Did Orsini go with Aitken?'

'Yes, sir,' the Master said, 'in fact I think that's him sitting up there.'

If the boy slipped out of the strop he would fall 500 feet. Why did Aitken let him do it? There was little doubt that Paolo had volunteered – indeed, he might well have suggested the whole thing in the first place – but why the devil did Aitken let him? A moment later he told himself coldly that someone had to do it; no officer should ask a seamen to do something he would not risk himself, and Paolo was a midshipman. Aitken had acted perfectly correctly. He would have asked for volunteers, and quite properly chosen the midshipman in preference to one of the seamen; it was a good lesson to young potential leaders. He could only hope that Paolo's letters to his aunt were not too explicit – he could imagine Gianna's reaction to Paolo's description of coming down the side of a 500-foot cliff sitting in a strop.

It took half an hour for the boy to get down to the ship's deck, and Ramage was relieved to see that he was in fact lashed into the strop. Eager seamen undid the lashing and as they waited for him to jump down the last couple of feet to the deck the boy lurched and pitched forward.

As the men hurried to pick him up, Ramage saw from the quarterdeck that the boy's body was held rigid, his buttock and thigh muscles cramped by sitting on the thin rope of the strop. Bowen ran forward and began massaging the muscles of his thighs and Ramage decided to wait for Paolo to report to him. He had been scrupulous so far in avoiding favouritism and all that mattered was that the boy was safely on the *Juno*'s deck, even if he had a sore backside.

Five minutes later Paolo reported to him on the quarterdeck. He could still not stand upright but his eyes were sparkling. 'Mr Aitken's compliments, sir, and everything is ready at the top of the cliff.'

'It took you long enough to get down to tell me,' Ramage

said gruffly, recalling Gianna's injunction that he was 'not to spoil the boy'.

'I know, sir,' Paolo said apologetically, 'but the rope made my hands rather sore.'

'Show me,' Ramage said, and the boy held his hands out, palms uppermost. They were raw. 'Yes, they are a little chafed: ask Mr Bowen to put some ointment on them.'

'He's going to, sir, but I wanted to report to you first.'

Ramage nodded gravely, feeling proud of the boy and noticing the approval of Southwick, who was standing nearby. 'Now, has Mr Aitken found a clear way to parbuckle the guns up the last section of the top of the Rock?'

'Yes, sir, it's steep but we've cleared away the small rocks, and there's a flat area at the top for the guns. We've cleared that, too. Mr Aitken says it is a perfect site for the battery. It could take *ten* guns, sir!'

'Very well, now run along and get those hands dressed.'

The jackstay was sagging badly, and hoisting the gun might increase the sag so much that the gun would swing in too close to the cliff for safety. Ramage had anticipated that this would happen, and the time had now come to tighten the cable.

He turned to Southwick, who was obviously still absorbed with the details of Orsini's report. 'The stun'sail booms are ready?'

'Aye, aye, sir, and I've doubled up on the topping lifts and guys, as you suggested.'

'Very well, let's start heaving in the jackstay.'

Southwick called for men as the two of them walked to the capstan. The cable forming the jackstay came down from the clifftop and led through a block shackled to the deck on the larboard side. From there it was led to the mainmast and made fast, but it could be tightened by clapping a purchase on it and leading the fall to the capstan, making it fast to the mast again when it was tight enough.

It took ten minutes to prepare everything and as soon as Southwick passed the order the fiddler began a tune and the men heaved at the capstan bars. Slowly the sagging jackstay tautened, the men slowing down with the effort as the strain came on the anchor cables.

Ramage walked to the bulwark and watched the cliff face, which was gradually getting nearer. Foot by foot the jackstay pulled the *Juno* bodily towards the cliff as it tautened until the outboard end of the stun'sail boom of the mainmast was

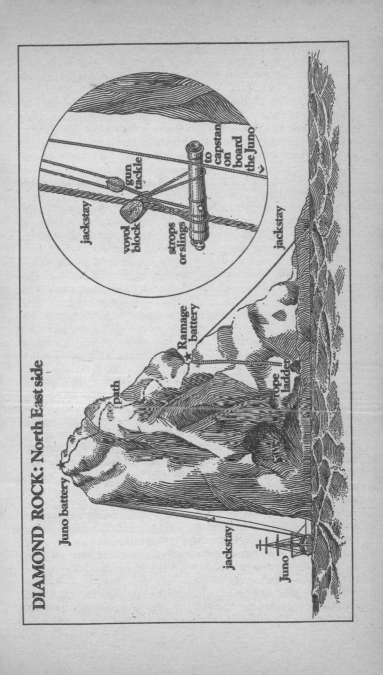

DIAMOND ROCK: North East side

Juno battery

path

Ramage battery

rope ladder

jackstay

jackstay

Juno

jackstay

jackstay

to capstan on board the Juno

gun tackle

voyol block

strops or slings

almost touching the rock. He looked upwards at the jackstay soaring aloft in a gentle curve, with the gun tackle sagging beneath it. He pictured the jackstay with the weight of the gun running up it, suspended from the voyol block. That weight would pull the *Juno* a little closer to the cliff. Just enough to bring the booms against the Rock.

'Vast heaving,' he called, 'and pall the capstan. Mr Lacey, secure to the mast now. Mr Southwick, let's have the voyol block clapped on to the jackstay and secure the slings of the gun!'

He was hard put to keep the excitement out of his voice and Southwick was bustling around the decks like a jovial inn-keeper seating his guests. Three men dragged the heavy voyol block and hung it on the jackstay. More men pulled across the single block of the tackle as others gathered beside its carriage, black, ominous and looking strangely naked.

Quickly the slings and the tackle were secured to the voyol block and the Master looked questioningly at Ramage as the fall of the tackle was led round the capstan again, ready for hoisting.

'Take up the strain with the tackle, Mr Southwick – and get those steadying lines led forward and aft outside the rigging.'

With lines secured to the gun, one leading right aft and the other forward, Ramage hoped to prevent the gun from swinging wildly as it was hoisted up, but the immediate task was to get the gun on the first few feet of its journey without smashing the bulwark or catching in the rigging.

With a sweeping gesture of his arm the Master started the men tramping round, pressing on the capstan bars. The strain came on the fall of the tackle, travelling all the way up the cliff and back to the *Juno*. The slings tautened and jerked once or twice, the voyol block settling on the jackstay as the gun, weighing nearly a ton, started on the first few inches of its five-hundred-foot journey to the top.

The gun lifted and seemed reluctant to come clear of the deck. Then it was as high as the bulwark and still rising as the capstan hauled at the fall of the tackle. Ramage saw that the great weight was making the jackstay sag, but not enough to be a disadvantage: if anything the voyol block would sit better.

The gun was ten feet high now, hanging horizontally and seemingly crawling up the jackstay like some strange animal. Ramage saw that the men at the capstan would have to be slowed down: they were full of enthusiasm now, but did not realize they would be hauling for another three or four hours, possibly five or six. Although there were enough men on board to make up three capstan parties, they would have to be changed every half hour or perhaps even sooner, because of the heat.

It took half an hour to get the gun up to the height of the maintruck, but that was because there had been difficulty in handling the steadying lines. The sag of the jackstay was just right at the moment, but Ramage still feared it might prove too much once the gun neared the cliff top. They could heave the jackstay tighter but it would be dangerous work belaying the tackle with the weight of the gun on it so they could use the capstan for the job.

Now was the time to decide if there was going to be too much sag: it would be better to lower the gun to the deck again, take up more on the jackstay, and start hoisting all over again. If he waited until the gun was almost at the top and found the jackstay sag too much he would lose ten hours, instead of two now.

He had just decided to risk it and carry on hoisting when Southwick came up, beaming delightedly. It was an expression that Ramage could never quite place: it would look well on an innkeeper hearing that a royal duke was about to arrive with his suite; it would be appropriate for a parson who had just learned that his church had been left a large endowment by a rich dowager. It would also suit a poacher returning home with three brace of pheasant in his bag.

'I never thought it would work, sir, and I don't mind admitting it,' he said, after making sure he could not be overheard. 'We'll swing in a bit as the gun gets higher, but those booms will hold us off. It's hard work for the men, but they're cheerful enough.'

'I'll take the sentry off the water butt soon,' Ramage said. 'The men can drink as much as they want.'

'Aye, they're sweating like bulls, but hauling with a will. Seems they already have a name for the new battery.' When Ramage raised his eyebrows Southwick waved his hand across the ship. 'The Juno battery, sir; they're hoping you'll think of the name yourself.'

'I seem to be rather slow in naming things,' Ramage grinned. 'I told you how they caught me unawares with the Marchesa battery!'

Southwick nodded, and then said seriously: 'I've been

199

thinking over that business about taking possession of an island, sir, and apart from "by right of discovery" I can't remember hearing of a procedure. There must have been some ceremony when we captured Martinique, for instance, though that was with a fleet and an army. Pity we ever gave it back again,' he added crossly. 'Just look at the trouble it causes us. All those politicians ever think of is getting a cheer in Parliament. Never consider the lives these damned spice islands cost to capture in the first place, let alone the men killed in recapturing them . . .'

The gun was slowly moving upwards, still hanging horizontally in the slings, and the men at the capstan had settled into a steady rhythm. Lacey was watching, changing them occasionally. One man was sent below to the Surgeon, his face white, and obviously a victim of heat stroke.

The *Créole* was coming into sight again and a quick look through the telescope showed that she was not flying any signals. 'Just the time for the French to round Point des Salines,' Southwick said with an irritating cheerfulness.

Ramage, who had been thinking of that for the past few hours, glowered at him. 'That reminds me, I don't see any axes ready in case we have to cut something adrift in a hurry . . .'

'No, sir,' Southwick said hurriedly, 'I'll see to it at once.'

It took four and a half hours for the gun to reach the top of the cliff and, lying on his back, Ramage watched with his telescope. Aitken and his men had hooked tackles into the slings, taking the weight of the gun and holding it at the top of the cliff ready to start parbuckling it the rest of the way to the top.

Now he could see that the voyol block and the gun tackle were swinging clear. There should be no difficulty in getting the gun tackle block down again this time: there was the weight of the voyol block, and the rope of the tackle was well stretched. Indeed, as the men in the *Juno* eased away on the fall so it came down, Ramage stood up to see Southwick supervising men securing slings under the carriage.

With two hours to sunset there was time to get the carriage up since it weighed only three hundredweight, but that would mean Aitken and his men finding their way down again in the darkness.

He called to Lacey and told him to get the cooper to find the largest tub on board. 'I want to fill it with bedding and provisions and send it up with the carriage. Mr Aitken and his men can spend the night up there. They'll prefer that to climbing down tonight and up again tomorrow.'

Noticing Lacey's hesitation Ramage looked questioningly. 'I'm sorry, sir,' the young lieutenant said, 'I was hoping I'd be able to go up tomorrow.'

Ramage tapped him on the shoulder. 'Your turn will come. Now you know how to rig a jackstay, your job for tomorrow will be rigging one from near the Marchesa battery to the ledge half-way up the Rock and mounting a gun there. I propose landing you and twenty men at the battery with cable, tackles, a 12-pounder and carriage, and I'd like to hear you fire a round by sunset.'

'Thank you sir!' Lacey exclaimed with an enthusiasm that startled Ramage, and hurried off to find the cooper. Ramage shrugged his shoulders and began pacing the quarterdeck. He was lucky to have lieutenants who, after watching today's performance, were almost pathetically grateful to be allowed to rig a jackstay on land, without any help from a capstan.

Ramage went below and scribbled a note to Aitken to be sent up in the tub. He told the First Lieutenant that the carriage and tub were being sent up now so that if there was bad weather tomorrow and the *Juno* had to cast off the jackstay, Aitken would have a complete gun aloft. If there was time before darkness, he added, the tub would be sent up again with powder, shot and the rest of the gear. He paused a moment, wondering whether to add a line of congratulation, but decided against it: he preferred thanking a man to his face.

By nightfall the carriage was on top of the cliff and the tub had made a second trip up the jackstay with the powder, shot, rammer, sponge, handspikes, three spars to make sheers, and a cask of water. It came down again with a pencilled report from Aitken written on the back of Ramage's letter. The news it contained was good. The 12-pounder had been parbuckled to the peak and the carriage hauled to the top while the tub was coming up for the second time. At the time of writing the sheers were being rigged and the gun would be hoisted up on to its carriage and ready to open fire by dawn.

Ramage had folded the note, put it in his pocket and forgotten about it by the time he went down to bed. He had taken the first watch and then handed over to Southwick. He slept soundly, even though he knew that there were only half a dozen seamen and the officer of the deck on watch. In an emergency the rest of the men would come swarming up in a matter of moments. In any case he had given permission for them to sleep on deck if they wished, to take advantage of the cool night breeze, so some would probably be there already. Everyone was exhausted and he wanted all of them to get as much rest as possible, so they would be ready to hoist the second gun and its carriage next day. He also wanted to send the tub up as many times as he could, carrying extra powder, shot, provisions and water. He shuddered at the thought of the alternative, men climbing up what must be sheer rock in places, hoisting sacks and casks . . .

He was just climbing up the companionway at dawn the next morning when there was a heavy boom above and a moment later Southwick was bellowing for the men to go to quarters. Then Ramage remembered the pencilled note from Aitken in his pocket: the First Lieutenant had kept his word.

'Belay all that!' he called to the Master, 'that was Aitken firing the first round from the Juno battery!'

'I've just realized that,' the Master said ruefully, pointing to smoke drifting away from the clifftop. 'He might have warned us!'

'He did,' Ramage said, 'he wrote me a note but I forgot to pass the word.'

'Well, sir, we're ready to start hoisting the next gun,' Southwick said stiffly, 'and the purser is attending to the provisions to go up in the tub. A month for fourteen men, you said, sir.'

'Yes, but we'll make it three months if we have the time: it's the quickest way of getting it all on shore. I want to let go of the jackstay and get clear of here by nightfall. If we can get three months' supplies by then, so much the better. Warn the purser, so he can get them on deck ready. Lacey can go on shore now to start on the other battery.'

CHAPTER FOURTEEN

At noon next day a weary but exultant Ramage stood between the two guns of the Juno battery, 570 feet up on top of Diamond Rock. The sun was almost directly overhead, the sea a deep blue and stippled by waves. The headland formed by Diamond Hill, across the Fours Channel, seemed near enough to touch.

Below him the *Juno* rode at anchor with the *Surcouf* near-by. Wagstaffe was rounding the Rock in *La Créole*, obviously anxious to know what progress had been made. From the schooner's deck Wagstaffe should be able to see the Junos standing at the edge of the battery, even if he could not make out the barrels of the guns which were now pointing towards the headland.

Ramage turned to the north-westward where, in the distance beyond many other peaks, he could see the flattened top of Mont Pelée. Then he looked south-eastward towards Pointe des Salines, at the southern end of Martinique. Still no sign of the French convoy nor of Admiral Davis and the *Invincible* but, more worrying, still no sign of *La Mutine* returning. Perhaps the Admiral had held on to Baker, but that seemed unlikely, and anyway it did not explain why the *Invincible* had not arrived. Today was Friday and Baker had left on Monday. He had been trying to avoid the thought for the past twenty-four hours, but there was only one sensible answer: something had happened to Baker. For one reason or another *La Mutine* had not arrived in Barbados, and so the Admiral had not received the warning that the convoy was due.

It was a distinct possibility: *La Mutine* might have been dismasted in a sudden squall, sprung a leak, or been captured by French privateers. There might even be a French frigate lurking out there, sent on ahead of the convoy . . .

Both the guns were loaded and Aitken was waiting patiently. The man was so tired that he looked like a ghost, but he was still alert and active. He had been pleased at Ramage's praise but was apparently envious that Lacey was at work rigging a jackstay from the Marchesa battery.

Ramage was in no hurry: he wanted to imprint the scene in his memory. If the French arrived before the *Invincible* . . . The convoy would round Pointe des Salines with all the ships bunched up. There would be no stragglers for once, because the captain of each merchant ship knew that Fort Royal was being blockaded. The frigates would be on the alert and the convoy would hug the coast . . . He stood for ten minutes fighting imaginary actions that would prevent the convoy reaching Fort Royal, and trying to calculate all the possibilities open to the French. At the end of it his calculations seemed of little value. What the *Juno* and the *Surcouf* could do depended on three things: the size of the convoy, the size of its escort, and whether or not Admiral Davis had arrived.

Trying to work out tactics now was like trying to guess the sequences in a game of chess against Bowen, who always seemed to have dozens of unexpected bishops, knights, castles and queens at his beck and call. He turned to the First Lieutenant. 'Very well, Mr Aitken, are we ready?'

'Aye, aye, sir, the battery's ready,' the young Scot answered reproachfully, and Ramage realized that he must have been standing staring out across the sea for fifteen minutes or more.

The men, deeply tanned from the sun, their clothes torn, were shuffling into line and Aitken was standing in front of them. Ramage's heart sank as they obviously expected a speech and he had to admit they deserved one. They had slaved away at the battery and many of them had asked to be allowed to stay on and man it. There was not a bit of shade from the blazing sun, except whatever they could rig up for themselves, and no protection from rain.

Aitken brought them to attention and Ramage began speaking. He told them that they and their shipmates in the *Juno* had just done something that most people would have thought impossible and no one had ever previously attempted. He was proud, he said, to name their achievement the Juno battery. He wanted to end his little speech on an amusing note, and thanked them for leaving rope ladders for him to climb up the more difficult parts of the Diamond. 'I still think I should have come up in the tub last night,' he added. 'Nearly six hundred feet is too much for someone whose daily climbing is limited to the companionway!'

The men cheered him and Aitken gave the order for them to fall in at the guns, which were loaded and had already been laid. The First Lieutenant asked Ramage if he thought the shot would reach across the Fours Channel to the nearest part of the mainland, the steep cliffs where Diamond Hill met the sea.

Ramage smiled knowingly. 'We'll have to keep a sharp lookout for the fall of shot,' he said, and Aitken grinned confidently, little guessing that Ramage had anticipated the question the moment he decided to set up the battery and had failed to work out a definite answer.

The Captain had to be infallible. He had to be an expert in ballistics, at home with trajectories and the effect of gravity and range on a 12-pound shot. He had to be a mathematical wizard, able to work out the trajectory (and thus the range) of shot fired from a height of 570 feet when all he knew were some vague ranges for shot fired from sea level.

Neither he nor Southwick were even sure of the distance from the Diamond to the shore: Southwick's chart was the best available, yet far from accurate and drawn on a small scale. It gave the distance as about 2100 yards, but it could be a hundred yards more or less.

An error of two hundred yards in the chart could be critical. The range tables he had on board for a 12-pounder gun, such as they were, gave a maximum of 1800 yards using six degrees' elevation, with a four-pound charge of powder. The *Juno*'s gunner had tables giving shorter ranges, but they were scribbled in an old notebook and the man seemed more concerned with the recipe for making up the blacking for painting the guns than firing them.

Using the ranges he had, what happened when you placed the gun on top of a rock 570 feet high? Did a six degree elevation still give you a range of 1800 yards? Or increase it? Both he and Southwick were sure it increased it, but had no idea how to calculate the amount. When Ramage had begun cursing his own lack of mathematical knowledge, Southwick laughed and pointed out that it hardly mattered; for the battery to be effective, its shot did not have to reach the mainland because no French ship would pass within a hundred yards of the cliff for fear of getting caught by wind eddies off the hill and would most probably stay in the middle of the Fours Channel. 'Never bet on a horse once the race has started, sir,' he added. 'Just look wise and watch where the shot lands!'

It was good advice and Ramage had followed it. The two guns of the Juno battery were loaded with four-pound charges and carefully elevated to six degrees and Aitken was waiting patiently for Ramage to give the signal for the final order that would provide the answer.

Ramage nodded and Aitken bellowed: 'Number one gun, fire!'

Ramage barely registered the crash of the gun firing – apart from noting that up here it was free of any echoes – as he trained his telescope on the rocks at the foot of Diamond Hill. He waited anxiously, but there was no plume in the water showing the shot had fallen short. Nor was there any sign that it had ricocheted off the rocks.

He turned to find Aitken almost dancing with excitement.

'You were right, sir!' he said gleefully. 'It reached, just think of that! I don't know how you calculated that it would, sir, but there's the proof! No splash so it must have hit the land.'

Ramage was embarrassed. An evasive answer and a knowing look had been interpreted by Aitken as the confidence of superior knowledge. For a moment he wondered how many times in the past the various captains under whom he had served had got away with the same thing. Still, Aitken was only assuming that the shot had hit the land because it had not splashed in the sea. It might have disintegrated in mid-flight: that sort of thing was rare but not unknown and they would never have seen the tiny splashes made by the pieces. He had to be sure, and luckily there was an easy way of finding out without revealing his doubts.

'Mr Aitken, let us see how accurately we are shooting. I want the gun captain of number two gun to drop a shot a hundred yards short of the rocks and watch for a ricochet.'

The second round landed just in front of the rocks, ricocheted twice and disappeared. 'Fifty yards short at the first grave, sir,' Aitken reported.

'Very well, I think we can get back to the *Juno*.' He looked round for the petty officer who was being left in charge of the batteries. 'Ah, Richardson. Rig a mast out of those spars you used as sheers and watch the *Juno* and the *Surcouf* for signals. You have a copy of the signals?' The man dug into the inside of his plaited sennet hat and showed Ramage the thin volume. 'Good, and you have a set of flags. Fine, so all you need to do is keep a sharp lookout. You'll see any ship rounding Pointe des Salines long before us. Keep in touch with the lower batteries. Any questions?'

The man shook his head and Ramage smiled. 'You have food and water for three months, and muskets to chase the goats. However, I hope someone will be up to see you before then.'

It took Ramage and Aitken twenty minutes to scramble down the steep slopes to reach the site for the third battery, two hundred feet lower down the Rock. It was a perfect place: a cave in which all the provisions had been stored and still large enough to house a dozen men. With a flat platform of rock in front of it, facing to the north, it was large enough for two or three guns, let alone the single 12-pounder which was all that Ramage could spare from the *Juno*. He saw that Lacey and his men had already rigged the jack-stay.

From this point the rock face dropped down to the Marchesa battery so steeply that men were having to use rope ladders. Ramage commented on the steepness and asked Aitken who had managed to climb it in the first place and get a ladder into position. The young Scot admitted that several seamen had tried and found that after fifty feet or so they could get no higher. In the end he had climbed up himself, with a coil of rope slung over his shoulder. Once he reached the platform he had secured an end of the rope and hurled the coil down to the waiting men, who had bent on a rope ladder which he had hauled up.

Both men were standing on the platform and looking across the Fours Channel to Diamond Hill when they noticed that the ropes holding one of the two ladders were shaking. A minute or two later Lacey's perspiring face appeared over the edge of the rock.

'I'm afraid we're behind, sir,' he reported apologetically to Ramage, 'but I'm just bringing up a party to rig this end of the luff tackle; then we can start hoisting the gun immediately.'

'It might be better to hoist the carriage first,' Ramage said, 'just in case . . .'

Lacey's eyes fell. 'Certainly, sir, if you would prefer it.'

Ramage glanced at Aitken and laughed. 'No, carry on, Lacey, you're in charge!'

The Fourth Lieutenant brightened up immediately. 'If you'll excuse me a moment, sir . . .' he said and ran to the edge of the rock, calling down to the men climbing the ladders to hurry.

He returned a moment later and asked Ramage almost shyly: 'If you could wait a minute or two, sir, I think the men would like you to be here when they secure the luff tackle: everything will then be ready for hoisting. And, sir . . .'

Ramage guessed what was coming next: they had thought of a name for this battery too, and wanted his permission. He was pleased with the names they had chosen so far: Gianna would be delighted, and it was a fine thing to honour the *Juno* frigate. What would it be this time?

'Go on, then,' he prompted Lacey.

'Well, sir, they want to call it the Ramage battery.'

Ramage felt embarrassed for the second time in half an

hour. The men meant well, but . . .

'I am flattered, Lacey, but – well, I think the Admiralty might regard it as . . . er, well, a piece of pretentiousness on my part.'

'Ah, but we thought of that, sir,' Lacey exclaimed triumphantly. '*Officially* it could be named Ramage after your father, because he fought his great battle in sight of Diamond Rock. But we, the Junos, sir, would know differently . . .'

Aitken, sensing Ramage's discomfiture, said quietly: 'The Captain's father is the Earl of Blazey, you know.'

'I know he's the Earl of Blazey *now*,' Lacey said doggedly, 'but he was Lord Ramage when he fought the battle 'cos he hadn't succeeded to the earldom. Just as the Captain is Lord Ramage now, but he'll be the Earl of Blazey one day.'

Ramage realized that Lacey and the men must have had a long discussion about it, but Lacey was too young to remember that the battle had been a desperate affair, his father being sent out too late with only a few ships to fight an overwhelming French fleet. The result had been predictable and his father had been made the scapegoat for the stupidity of the government of the day, receiving no recognition for an action which had revealed him as a brilliant tactician. He suddenly decided that this little battery could indeed be named Ramage, and whatever the Junos thought he would be naming it after his father.

Lacey saw Ramage's face softening and he grinned. 'I can tell the men you agree, sir?'

Ramage nodded and then said emphatically: 'I agree to it being named after my father because of the battle.'

'Oh yes, sir,' Lacey said, 'they'll understand that.'

CHAPTER FIFTEEN

Ramage arrived back on board the *Juno* to find Southwick waiting with ill-concealed impatience and asking for permission to leave the ship for two hours and to use the jolly boat. It was such an unusual request that Ramage frowned for a moment.

'You want to go over to the *Surcouf*?'

'No sir, I want to visit the Marchesa battery,' he said gruffly.

Ramage then noticed that the Master had a bulky canvas bag normally used for carrying papers under his arm.

'You can have the boat,' Ramage said grudgingly, 'but I can't really spare you for two hours. What on earth is there to do at the Marchesa battery? Lacey was just about to sway up the gun when I left.'

Southwick gave one of his sniffs. 'I've got my paints and sketching pad here, sir,' he said. Then in answer to the puzzled look on Ramage's face: 'Masters of all the King's ships are required to send sketches of unusual coastlines and harbours to the Navy Board, sir, as you well know, and I've always been very punctilious about that.'

'I know, I know, and your sketches and paintings are excellent, but what is unusual about the Diamond Rock that the Navy Board don't already know?'

Southwick sighed, obviously unwilling to reveal his real motive. 'I wanted to make a water-colour of the side of the Rock showing the Marchesa battery, sir, and frame it, and I was going to ask you to give it to Her Ladyship with the compliments of the Junos.'

For the third time in an hour Ramage was embarrassed. 'She'll be delighted, Southwick, and so will I.'

With that he decided to go down to his cabin and put in an hour or two studying the chart of Martinique and then bring his Journal up to date. He might as well start a draft of a report to Admiral Davis, reporting that the *Surcouf* was ready and three batteries had been established. —

He spread the chart on his desk and with a pair of compasses scribed a circle round the Diamond Rock so that one edge just touched the land at the foot of Diamond Hill. The guns certainly reached that distance, and it was startling how the western section of the circle would affect French ships making for Fort Royal *outside* the Diamond Rock after rounding Pointe des Salines. It did not add much to the actual distance they would sail – sixteen miles from the Pointe up to Cap Salomon staying inside the Diamond Rock, the most direct route, and only seventeen and a half keeping outside the radius of the Juno battery's guns. But it forced them another couple of miles offshore, into the strong current which might sweep them out westward, well to leeward of Fort Royal.

The last few days had shown him why the French ships, men-o'-war as well as merchantmen, liked to hug the coast once they rounded Pointe des Salines. For half the distance to the Diamond they did not risk running out of wind entirely because the land to the east was not so mountainous. If they lost some of the wind as they came up to the Diamond, intending to pass through the Fours Channel, at least they were out of the worst of the current.

If the current was north-going, they could risk going outside the Diamond, but he knew from Captain Eames's experience and Wagstaffe's brief reports from *La Créole* that it was predominantly west-going. He laughed to himself. If he forced too many French merchantmen so far to the west that they ended up across the Caribbean at Port de la Paix at the western end of Hispaniola, there would soon be complaints to the Admiralty from the Commander-in-Chief at Jamaica that the French forces there were being heavily reinforced with supplies. It was an ill-wind . . .

He rolled up the chart and put it aside. Bowen's sick list was under a paperweight, left there by the clerk, and he glanced through it. Only one man on it, and that the Marine wounded by a cutlass in the attack on the Diamond Hill battery. As young Paolo was not mentioned it showed that the boy was carrying out his duties despite his raw hands.

He opened his journal again, made an entry and then read through those he had made for the previous few days. The *Surcouf* prepared for sea, the guns for the Marchesa, Juno and Ramage batteries installed on the Diamond Rock, with three months' provisions landed for the men, plus water and sheep. *La Créole* maintaining a patrol, the Juno battery's range tried . . . The only thing missing was an entry recording the return of *La Mutine*. The distance to Barbados was just over a hundred miles, but it was a beat to windward. *La Mutine* was close-winded, so would probably cover 180 miles because of frequent tacks. She would make at least six knots to windward, probably eight. At a conservative estimate Baker should have arrived in Bridgetown thirty hours after leaving the Diamond some time last Tuesday. He would have reported to the Admiral, who might have kept him until noon on Wednesday before letting him sail. Or the Admiral might have told him to wait until the *Invincible* could get to sea and make for Martinique. A ship of the line like the *Invincible* would cover the distance to Martinique in eighteen hours at the most. Leaving at noon on Wednesday she would arrive off Martinique in the darkness, which the Admiral might have wanted to avoid, so she might have left that evening, to arrive off Pointe des Salines at daylight on Thursday.

That was yesterday and neither *La Mutine* nor the *Invincible* had arrived. But the convoy was due (as far as the French authorities in Fort Royal knew) by tomorrow at the latest.

He checked his figures again, but he had not made a mistake. So now, this afternoon, he had to assume that he was going to have to attack the convoy and its escorts with the *Juno*, the *Surcouf* and *La Créole*. And the Diamond batteries, of course, with all the advantage of surprise that they would have.

Two frigates and a schooner – he had managed to double the number of frigates maintaining the blockade, and had a schooner as well. It was a nice little squadron for the most junior captain in the Navy List to command, however temporarily. But no amount of juggling with figures could change the fact that he did not have enough men to use all the ships effectively.

He began writing again. Fourteen men at the Juno battery, seven at the Ramage and six at the Marchesa. Lacey had been disappointed at not being put in command of the Diamond, but Ramage needed him. That made a total of twenty-seven men on the Diamond. Wagstaffe and twenty men were in *La Créole*, and the Third Lieutenant and twenty men were away in *La Mutine*, wherever the devil she was. With nine Junos killed in the original fight with the two schooners, he was short of seventy-eight officers and seamen. The *Juno*'s original ship's company had totalled 212, so he had only 134 officers and men left, including Marines.

He checked the figures again. Yes, Aitken and Lacey, Southwick, the Marine Lieutenant, a master's mate who had proved completely useless, two midshipmen, the Surgeon and 126 warrant officers, petty officers and men, to share between the *Juno* and the *Surcouf*. He was seventy-eight short if he wanted to man the *Juno* alone . . .

He sighed, feeling his earlier confidence slipping away as he stared at the figures he had scrawled. Then he took another sheet of paper and drew in two columns, heading one '*Juno*' and the other '*Surcouf*'.

He wrote in his own name at the top of the '*Juno*' column, followed by Southwick, Orsini, Bowen and Jackson. He would sort out the remaining sixty-three later. In the '*Surcouf*' column he wrote the names of Aitken, Lacey, Rennick (which meant that all the Marines would have to go as well), Benson, and the master's mate – he could never remember his name and so scribbled 'M.M.'

It seemed a fair division: Aitken had Lacey as his second-in-command and Rennick was a useful man whose Marines could be relied upon. He could have the gunner and the bos'n, too, and the *Juno* would make do with the mates. The carpenter might as well stay in the *Juno*: in battle he spent his time below, standing by with shot plugs and mauls.

He was hot, sticky, tired and depressed. His head ached from the heat of the cabin and his eyes ached from spending all the morning and much of the afternoon in the glaring sun, climbing up and down that damned Diamond Rock like an outcast goat. Suddenly he sat up as a thought struck him: if the *Juno* was in battle and had sixty-three men and her Captain and Master still alive and unwounded, he would never dream of breaking off the action.

Then he remembered his famous Monday morning lecture to the *Juno*'s officers about preparing against the unexpected. This was a perfect example of what he meant. Put yourself in the place of the senior officers of the French escort, he told himself. If there were three or four frigates, the Frenchman would be the most senior of the captains. If there was a ship of the line, then it would be a very senior captain, if not a rear-admiral.

As the French rounded Pointe des Salines they would be looking for the British ships known to be blockading Fort Royal. They would have been worrying about them for some time; probably ever since they left France. They would not know whether to expect one frigate or four; a ship of the line and three frigates or a carriage and four greys complete with postillions. However, if they saw two manned British frigates they would assume that they were fully manned and ready for action, and would behave accordingly. They would never for a moment expect that neither ship had a third of her proper complement. That, he realized, put the unexpected on his side. And the batteries on the Diamond represented his most powerful surprise.

Aitken needed written orders putting him in command of the *Surcouf*, but there was no point in giving him additional written orders telling him what to do if the convoy arrived because there were too many possibilities.

He remembered the day some years ago when he was the junior lieutenant of the *Sibella* frigate. She had been trapped by a French ship of the line off the Italian coast and a flying splinter had knocked him unconscious. He had recovered to find that the captain and the rest of the officers were dead and he was in command. The ship was sinking fast and almost by chance he had found out from the papers in the captain's desk that the *Sibella* was acting under special orders. That was how he had come to rescue Gianna using an open boat. He had realized then the danger of a commanding officer assuming he was immortal and failing to keep his officers informed about what the ship was supposed to be doing.

Some orders, of course, were extremely secret, but secrecy was rarely vitally important on board a ship, and certainly not now. As soon as Southwick returned from his water-colour expedition he would have Aitken, Lacey, Wagstaffe, Rennick and the Master down here in the cabin. They would go over the chart, discuss the possibilities and, perhaps more important, the three lieutenants would absorb enough of his ideas and attitude to make it all work.

He went to the skylight and called to Orsini, who was on watch, to hoist the signal for *La Créole*'s captain to report on board. Then he returned to the desk and sat down, reaching for the pen and unscrewing the cap of the ink well. Five minutes later he had written and signed Aitken's orders and told his clerk to copy them into the Order Book. The Navy stayed afloat on a sea of ink; if only they could sink the French by firing broadsides of quill pens . . . The only consolation was that the French Ministry of Marine's appetite for forms, surveys, lists, dispatches, copies of letters, orders, logs and muster tables was probably as voracious as that of the Admiralty and the Navy Board. The capture of the Diamond would eventually result in a pile of papers in those two offices quite as high as the Rock itself . . .

He went up to the quarterdeck for a walk in the fresh air, hoping to get rid of his headache. The sun was low now and he saw *La Créole* approaching. Wagstaffe had obviously seen the signal flying from the *Juno*.

As he walked the deck the words 'so few men' echoed with every step. Was he overestimating the effectiveness of the Juno and Ramage batteries against French ships trying to pass? Three 12-pounders could not keep up a fast rate of fire, however eager and well-trained the men. It would be plunging fire and thus much more effective, but that in turn required more accuracy. Firing from sea level meant that a shot falling short of the target would ricochet onwards and might hit, but a roundshot curving down from the height of those two batteries could ricochet in almost any direction.

He stopped walking and stared across the Fours Channel. It was a mile wide and French ships passing through it would be within range of the two batteries for a distance of perhaps a mile and a half. If they were making six knots they would be within range for about fifteen minutes – not long enough. If there were five merchantmen it gave the Juno and Ramage battery gunners three minutes for each ship in theory but they would not change target like that: they would concentrate on one ship, and continue firing until she was disabled.

They must keep the merchantmen inside the segment of the invisible circle representing the Juno and Ramage batteries' range for longer than five minutes. Ideas came slowly to his weary brain as he began striding the deck again. Knowing himself, he did not try to force them. They would come in their own good time.

The schooner was rounding up now and anchoring, and he saw the jolly boat returning from the Diamond with Southwick's rotund figure in the sternsheets. This was his squadron: a former privateer schooner, a captured French frigate and the *Juno* frigate, with the Diamond batteries watching over them all. Here were all his guns and all his men. He had assembled his entire force. If only he could do – what?

Concentration! Somehow he must lure the French convoy and its escort into the Fours Channel and then use the *Juno* to block one end and the *Surcouf* to close the other, with *La Créole* darting in among the merchantmen, helping to create as much confusion as possible. With them all concentrated and confused, roundshot would start plunging down on them unexpectedly from the Diamond batteries. The masters of the French merchant ships would panic. Some would wear round and try and beat back through the Channel the way they came; others might try to carry on through. The French escorts would attempt to fight off the *Surcouf* and *Juno*, but in the meantime some of the merchantmen might collide with each other, drifting with yards locked, bowsprits and jibbooms caught in shrouds. Slowly drifting merchantmen would be perfect targets for the Diamond batteries.

His elation vanished as quickly as it had arrived. It was a splendid dream and no more because the French would never be lured into such a trap. It was eleven miles from Pointe des Salines to the Diamond and that would take the merchantmen a couple of hours to cover. This, in turn, meant that the

French escorts had two hours in which to drive off the British ships. Drive them off, perhaps try to board and capture them, but certainly divert the convoy from the Fours Channel.

The French would not let themselves get trapped – unless they did not know the trap was there until the moment Ramage decided to spring it. His advantage was that he held the Diamond but the French convoy did not know it. It could act as a signal station as well as a battery.

He tried to control his growing optimism in case he had forgotten some obvious drawback. Again he put himself in the position of the senior officer of the French escort. Rounding Pointe des Salines he would only be able to see to the northward as far as the headland of Diamond Hill. He would not see two frigates waiting just round the corner, in Petite Anse d'Arlet, the second bay beyond the Diamond Hill headland.

Petite Anse d'Arlet would serve the purpose: it was just two and a half miles north of the headland of Diamond Hill and the same distance from the exit of the Fours Channel. But if the *Juno* and the *Surcouf*, waiting in Petite Anse d'Arlet, could not see the Diamond they would be as blind as the French.

He thought for a moment and glimpsed *La Créole* out of the corner of his eye. The French would not be at all surprised to see a French schooner stretching south a couple of miles off the Diamond Hill headland: they would recognize the hull and rig, and naturally assume that she was a French privateer coming down to meet them, or leaving Fort Royal on a cruise. What other explanation could there be, from a French point of view? None that he could think of: sighting a French privateer would seem like a good sign. It would suggest to the convoy that there might be no British frigates around at all and that Fort Royal was not being blockaded.

That would cheer them all up and they would surely be confident enough to follow the usual easy route and hug the coast all the way round to the Fours Channel to avoid the current. They might even notice the French privateer hoisting a signal – perhaps a single flag. They would not understand it but they would not worry. In fact the privateer could hoist a Tricolour. The French naval officers might joke about the casualness of privateer captains not identifying themselves, but they would have no reason to suspect that *La Créole* was no longer a French ship, and was flying the Tricolour up to the time of opening fire as a legitimate *ruse de guerre* . . .

Using *La Créole* as his lookout was a far better idea than relying on the Juno battery. It would allow the battery lookouts to signal round the corner to the *Juno* herself. He was now pacing up and down with his shoulders braced back. It was a splendid plan and it worked perfectly – if the Juno battery comprised ten 24-pounders instead of two 12-pounders and the Ramage battery had five 24-pounders and if he had five fully-manned frigates instead of two partly-manned and, of course, providing the French convoy had a weak escort . . .

But he had to make do with what he had. Anyway all this planning and fretting and fussing would probably prove unnecessary because Admiral Davis would arrive in plenty of time with the *Invincible* and some frigates or because the convoy would be late. On the other hand, a French ship of the line could be escorting the convoy and perhaps *La Mutine* had never arrived with the message.

He watched Southwick board from the jolly boat and saw that Wagstaffe was on his way from *La Créole*. Aitken, Lacey and Rennick were already on board, so he went to his cabin to lay out the chart and measure off some distances and bearings.

By dusk, as he watched Aitken and Wagstaffe being rowed to their ships, he felt a little more confident. Lacey was preparing a cutter to take over the men who would form the rest of the *Surcouf*'s ship's company. At least there were a dozen men who had been on board the former French frigate since she had been captured and, as Southwick had pointed out, by now they should know where everything was stowed.

The jolly boat was on its way to the Marchesa battery with written orders for the Juno and Ramage batteries, telling them that they were not to open fire or in any way reveal their presence until either the *Juno* or the *Surcouf* made the signal. The petty officer was told to place the signal mast on the western slope of the peak, where the signals he made would be seen by *La Créole* to seaward but not by French ships approaching from Pointe des Salines.

The Master offered to work out a new general quarters, watch and station bill for the *Juno*'s reduced complement, and Ramage accepted gratefully. He also accepted Aitken's suggestion that all the former Tritons should stay on board the *Juno*. 'They bring you luck, sir,' the Scotsman had commented. 'You've been through a lot with them and now's not the time to tamper with Lady Fortune.'

As Ramage went down to his cabin he felt guilty about poor Southwick. He had more than an hour's work dividing the men into various groups – fo'c'sle men, foretopmen, maintopmen, mizentopmen, after guard, gunners – then he had to divide them into two watches, starboard and larboard, and finally give each man a number showing his place when the ship went into action, what arms he would carry for boarding or repelling boarders, his station for furling, reefing or loosing sails, anchoring or weighing, tacking the ship or wearing, making or shortening sail. It was a tedious job, but it meant a seaman who knew that his number was, for example, 16 could see from the bill that he was a foretopman in the larboard watch, and when going into action he was second captain of a particular gun, that under arms he would have a cutlass and a tomahawk, and for the rest of the evolutions the bill showed him precisely what he did on the foretopsail yard. The *Juno*'s original bill was for a full complement of 212 officers and men. Now Southwick had to make sure that every important task was performed using only sixty-three.

He could hear the clop-clop-clop of the pawls on *La Créole*'s windlass as the schooner weighed to resume her patrol and make sure that by daybreak she would be off Diamond Hill. By then the *Juno* and the *Surcouf* would be under way and heading for Petite Anse d'Arlet, where they would anchor and wait, watching *La Créole* for signals with even more concentration than a fisherman waited for the float on his line to twitch.

He wondered what the Governor of Fort Royal made of the various pieces of information he was receiving. By now cavalry patrols along the coast must be reporting a great deal of activity off the Diamond, and he might be speculating what the *Juno* had been doing while hidden behind the island. The patrols might have heard the ranging shots of the Juno battery, though it was very unlikely they would have guessed where they came from.

He was taking a risk that the Governor might find a way of warning the convoy, but it was a slight one. There were only two ways of passing such a warning – sending out a vessel in the hope that it would find the convoy, or making a signal once it was in sight of the coast. Well, *La Créole*'s frequent looks at Fort Royal and the patrol off the coast made sure that no privateers escaped to raise the alarm, and there were no signal masts anywhere along the coast. If the French hurriedly erected one at Pointe des Salines – the obvious place – it would be spotted by *La Créole* and he could land Marines to demolish it. But in any case the commander of the convoy escort would not be looking for signals: he would know there were no regular signal stations and, not expecting to receive signals, he would be unlikely to spot any made from the shore. There was just a possibility that a small fishing vessel was available in one of the two little harbours on the Atlantic side of the island, but the chance of such a craft being able to beat out against the Trade winds to get to the convoy in time – for its position was not known – was slight enough for him to ignore.

No, as long as he could keep the door shut on the privateers in Fort Royal and keep a sharp eye open for any sign of a signal mast being erected along the coast, especially at Pointe des Salines, he had little to fear. Meanwhile the Governor must be a very frustrated man.

CHAPTER SIXTEEN

By eight o'clock next morning the *Juno* and *Surcouf* were anchored in the Petite Anse d'Arlet three and a half miles north-west of Diamond Rock. They were a few hundred yards off a beach on which a few tiny but gaily-painted rowing boats were hauled up on the sand, their nets draped over rocks to dry. Ramage saw a few huts beyond the fringe of palm trees but apart from the occasional whiff of a cooking fire there was no sign of life: the people in the tiny village had obviously decided to keep out of sight of the ships that had suddenly arrived in their bay.

To the north-east the high peak of Morne la Plaine separated them from Fort Royal Bay while more peaks trended south to end in Diamond Hill, overlooking the Fours Channel with Diamond Rock beyond.

In the bay the water was so clear that he could see the bottom at fifty feet: from the *Juno*'s bow the cable was visible all the way down to the anchor. There was still a slight offshore breeze but that did nothing to shake Ramage's conviction that it was going to be a scorching hot day with very little wind. These were just the conditions he wanted once the French convoy rounded Pointe des Salines because the merchant ships would have little more than steerage way. On the other hand light airs out in the Atlantic might delay the convoy's arrival for days.

As he walked the starboard side of the quarterdeck he reflected that the Master's log would record that the ship's company was employed 'as the Service required' and Southwick would have nothing to worry about if the Admiral suddenly arrived alongside for an inspection. The decks were scrubbed and the hammocks stowed in the nettings round the top of the bulwarks with the long canvas covers well tucked in. The brasswork had been polished with brickdust and reflected the early sun; the capstan was newly painted after being used to hoist the guns. Men were carrying the grindstone below after putting a fresh edge on cutlasses, tomahawks and pikes.

Two 12-pounders had been shifted over to larboard because the three now on the Diamond had all come from that side. He was still not used to the empty port on the quarterdeck where the 6-pounder that was now the Marchesa battery had once stood.

Short of men and short of guns, Ramage thought gloomily that on paper the *Juno* was more like a ship about to be paid off after a long commission than a frigate maintaining a close blockade of the most important French port in the West Indies. At least the paintwork gleamed, the rigging was ataunto and the sails in good repair.

He stopped his pacing and once again trained his telescope on *La Créole*. Not a flag was flying and none of the men's washing was strung on a line. From where she was now, Wagstaffe could see all the way down to Pointe des Salines.

A pelican splashed into the water so close by that it made him jump. He watched it through the port as it raised its great bill, gulping at the fish it caught and then resting. It reminded him of a portly bishop eyeing the port decanter circling the table towards him after a fine dinner.

Southwick came up, mopping his brow with a large and grubby cloth. 'D'you think we might spread the awning, sir? It's so damned hot and we could have it down in five minutes if . . .'

Ramage closed the telescope with an exasperated snap. 'Yes, by all means. The way things are going, we could give the men a week's shore leave.'

'You mustn't take on so, sir,' Southwick chided. 'You can't expect the French to be on time and anyway the calm may also serve to stop us having to share 'em with the Admiral.'

Ramage stared at him, hardly able to believe his ears.

Southwick grinned almost defiantly and murmured: 'I'm certain *I* don't want to, and I'm sure you don't *really*, not if you think about it. Why sir, I can just see the *Juno* and the *Surcouf* escorting two brace o' French merchantmen into Bridgetown.'

'I've thought of it,' Ramage admitted, 'but I've tried and failed to think of where we'd find the guards and prize crews.'

Now it was Southwick's turn to stare. 'Why sir, we won't need guards. We can just turn the French prisoners loose on the beach opposite the Diamond and let 'em walk over the mountains to Fort Royal to give the Governor the glad news. Ten of our men can get one of those merchantmen to Barbados, even if it blows a gale of wind.'

Ramage took off his hat and wiped the inside of the brim. 'Let's get the awning up before the pitch melts out of the deck seams.'

Petite Anse d'Arlet was probably one of the loveliest bays in Martinique. At any other time Ramage would have enjoyed spending a few hours anchored there and would have let the men fish or swim over the side. With a few Marines acting as sentries, the bos'n could have taken a party on shore for a wooding expedition: the cook's eternal complaint was that he was short of firewood for the coppers and soon would not be able to produce hot food. It was the regular complaint of every cook in the Navy and not to be taken very seriously, but wooding and watering, even though it meant finding a freshwater stream and rolling the heavy casks along the beach, was always a welcome task for the men and often, for a year at a time, the only chance they had of setting foot on land.

The day wore on slowly. At half past eleven the order 'Clear decks and up spirits' was given and the rum was served out. At noon the men went to dinner. Ramage and Southwick were doing watch and watch about, and both of them were hard pressed not to hail the lookouts from time to time to see if *La Créole* had hoisted any signals.

The men were still below when an excited hail came: 'Deck there, the schooner has hoisted a French flag!'

Ramage shouted to Jackson to fire a musket shot to alert the *Surcouf* and ordered a bos'n's mate to pipe 'Man the capstan'. For the moment there was no rush: Wagstaffe's signal meant that he had sighted the French convoy rounding Pointe des Salines and definitely identified it. The French had a good ten miles to sail before they reached the Fours Channel, and Ramage did not want to risk his two frigates being seen by a French frigate which might stay out farther to the west. From now on *La Créole*'s signals would be hoisted for one minute only, single flags whose meanings could be known only to those with copies of the list that Ramage had issued to Aitken, Wagstaffe and the petty officer in command of the Diamond batteries.

Southwick had heard the musket shot but not the lookout's hail. Hurrying up the companionway he inquired anxiously: 'The French or the Admiral, sir?'

'The French,' Ramage said crisply, 'and they're on time, you notice. But we can't be sure yet that the Admiral isn't chasing them round the Pointe. Man the capstan and heave round until we're at long stay. We'll be seeing some more signals from Wagstaffe soon and know what is happening.'

Although Ramage had not ordered the men to quarters—time enough for that on the way down to the Diamond—Jackson had already come up to the quarterdeck, where he would act as quartermaster, responsible for seeing that the men at the wheel carried out Ramage's orders. Now Orsini hurried up the companionway, his dirk round his waist and holding the signal book and a list of the special signals for *La Créole*. He had his own telescope under his arm and began strutting along the quarterdeck. For a moment Ramage was reminded of grackles at Barbados, the large friendly blackbirds with long, stiff tails. They too strutted and whenever he saw one he always pictured it with a telescope under its wing. The boy has a right to strut, he thought affectionately. Although at sea for only a few weeks, he has already soaked up more seamanship than most youngsters get drummed into them in a year. Orsini had an all-consuming curiosity about ships and the sea and was eager to learn. He was here on board the *Juno* because he had badgered Gianna into persuading Ramage to take him. Far too many 'younkers' went to sea as captain's servants (an inaccurate description since they were apprentices rather than servants) or midshipmen because their parents decided on it. In many families the eldest son inherited, the second went into the Navy, the third the Army, the fourth the Church, and a fifth was indentured to the East India Company, with high hopes that he would become a nabob and fears he would be hard put to remain a clerk and not fall off his counting house stool. Orsini was there from choice and all the more useful for it.

By now the men were heaving round on the capstan and he glanced across at the *Surcouf*. She too was heaving in, with Bevins the fiddler perched on the capstan. He was thankful he had spent the previous evening with Aitken and Wagstaffe going over everything he and they could think of. It should save a great deal of signalling. *La Créole* reports the French in sight by hoisting a Tricolour and whichever of the two frigates spots the signal first fires a musket shot and both frigates heave in to long stay. After that, the *Surcouf* follows the *Juno*'s movements until they are approaching the Diamond. Then it would be time for the signal book, but both Aitken and Wagstaffe now understood so well what he anticipated would be his tactics that few signals should be needed.

There was another hail from aloft. 'Schooner, sir. She's hoisted a single flag.'

Ramage had barely acknowledged the hail before Paolo, telescope to his eye, was calling, 'Number seven, sir. That's *Enemy convoy comprises seven merchant ships or transports.*'

A big convoy whose ships would carry enough to keep Martinique going for several months. Ramage took off his hat and wiped his brow, although now the perspiration suddenly felt cold. A big convoy meant a big escort and Wagstaffe's next signal would tell him how many frigates there were. The signal after that, if there was one, would tell him how many ships of the line were down there off Pointe des Salines.

'Deck there! She's lowered that flag and hoisted another!'

'Number four, sir!' Paolo shouted excitedly. '*The escort includes four frigates.*'

'Watch for the next one,' Ramage growled, and felt time slowing down as tension knotted his muscles.

'They're hauling the second one down, sir!' the masthead lookout reported.

Were they bending on another flag or simply taking the last one off and making up the halyard on its cleat? A minute passed, and then two. The capstan was groaning, and Jackson was watching him rubbing the scar on his brow, while Paolo kept his telescope trained on *La Créole*.

Aitken had seen the two signals and, like Ramage, was waiting anxiously to see if there was a third. Like Ramage he knew that it would be a death sentence for them all, whether it reported one ship of the line or ten.

He had often wondered how he would feel if he received orders that would probably cost him his life if he carried them out. Now he thought he knew. Many times in the past few years he had been given orders that had sent him into action where there was a chance of being killed or maimed. Although that was always frightening, death was far from certain. The thought in most minds was that death took the next man and left you, so there was a good chance of getting through alive. It was vastly different when the orders told you in effect that the odds were so enormous you were most unlikely to survive.

Such orders were like a long-faced and mournful-voiced judge sitting bewigged in his high chair and passing a death sentence on you. A flag signal from *La Créole* saying there was a ship of the line as well as four frigates with the French convoy would mean that by sunset there would not be a dozen men left alive in the *Juno* or the *Surcouf*. If Wagstaffe carried out his instructions he would survive because he had been given strict orders that if things became desperate he was to escape and get to Barbados to warn the Admiral.

So here he was, a damnable long way from Dunkeld, waiting to see if the judge was going to sentence him and the Surcoufs. Surprisingly, he felt no fear, or at least not the kind of fear he had known before, when his stomach seemed filled with cold water, his knees lost their strength and he wanted to run into a dark corner and hide. Perhaps it was another sort of fear he had never met before. He did not feel it in his body, really, although there was no denying that his stomach muscles were knotting. It was lurking at the back of his mind, like a mist forming in the valley at Dunkeld of an autumn's evening, slowly and gently soaking his jacket and kilt. But it did not make him want to run into a dark corner. In fact it was having the opposite effect, making him a little impatient, perhaps, much as a man sentenced to be hanged might want to get it all over as quickly as possible.

This was not how he had imagined it, and the more he thought the more he knew that although the final effect would be the same as receiving a death sentence from a judge, the way he felt now was not the way he would feel if he was about to be marched off to a condemned cell.

The sunshine and bright colours, the deep blue of the sea, the diving pelicans and slowly wheeling frigate birds made some difference. So did the palm trees along the white sandy

223

beach and the fact that he was commanding his own frigate, however briefly. When he took her into her last battle he would be the captain, and he would be unlikely to revert to being a first lieutenant again because there would be no ship left for anyone to command. Yet it was not really any of those things that accounted for his mood, although admittedly if he had to die it was satisfying to do so commanding his own ship.

He had been watching the *Juno*'s anchor cable through his telescope, noting how it had been hove in until it made the same angle as her mainstay. He glanced back to her quarter-deck and saw a man standing there motionless in white breeches and blue coat, a cocked hat on his head. A man who, with his wealth and social position, could have been standing in a fashionable London drawing-room, with every mother of an unmarried daughter circling him, the girls laughing gaily at his slightest joke, the mothers exclaiming with delight and planning a wedding at Westminster Abbey. Or he could have been in Cornwall, where the Ramage family had big estates, living the life of a wealthy landowner, with nothing worse to bother him than an occasional raid by poachers on the pheasant runs.

There was also this Italian Marchesa. After naming the battery on the Diamond after her the former Tritons had said she was the most beautiful woman most of them had ever seen, with the spirit of an unbroken Highland pony. The men could not understand why Captain Ramage had not married her yet, because there seemed little doubt that they were both in love.

Instead of staying behind in London or on the Cornish estate, Ramage was in the West Indies, two hundred yards away, standing on the quarterdeck of his frigate with deadly danger two or three hours away. But this danger was of his own choosing too, because no one would expect him to take two frigates into action against such odds with not a ship's company shared between them.

Yet he was going to, and it was his own decision. The previous evening Aitken had been appalled and not a little frightened when Captain Ramage had begun by explaining the possibilities open to them, the ways that at least some of the convoy could be destroyed. Gradually he had become interested in the way the Captain outlined the alternatives open to the French and to themselves, then fascinated by the man's words, fascinated by the way he took a sheet of paper, pencilled in a few lines showing ships' tracks and the wind direction, and showed that what had seemed impossible could perhaps be done, using surprise. That was the word he had used frequently, 'Surprise', with the corollary that if you could not find it naturally, you created it.

Looking back on the evening, Aitken realized that the solitary figure on the *Juno*'s quarterdeck was responsible for his present unlooked for but welcome state of mind. It was marvellous that his old fears had vanished in such a way that he felt sheepish ever to have felt them all the times he had previously been in action. Down in the *Juno*'s cabin in the dim lanternlight, listening to the Captain's quiet voice, watching old Southwick nod, hearing the answers to questions from Wagstaffe, fear somehow became remote: something that might be felt by lesser men in other ships and squadrons, but certainly of no interest to any man in the *Juno*, the *Surcouf* or *La Créole*.

The Captain was a sort of mirror, Aitken thought. He held a mirror in front of each man, and the reflection the man saw was of the person he would like to be, fearless, intelligent, resourceful . . . A mirror was not a good simile because it implied having only a glimpse of the ideal that vanished when the mirror was removed. The curious thing about Captain Ramage was that, having made you look at the man you'd like to be, he left you feeling that you *were* that man. He changed you, or your attitudes, so you would never again be fearful or a weakling.

Aitken shrugged his shoulders. He felt the man's influence powerfully but he could not analyse it satisfactorily. Perhaps it was what was called leadership. Until yesterday evening he had assumed that leadership was a question of being the senior officer, the man who gave orders and made decisions. The Captain was his own age, yet he could draw more out of other men than they thought they possessed and leave them determined not to fail him or themselves.

Now he understood the devotion of the dozen former Tritons who had joined the *Juno* just before she left Spithead. Each one of them was just another good seaman, well trained and disciplined, a prime topman and a welcome addition to any ship's company. Yet they were more than that. They seemed to carry a confidence that at times bordered on arrogance. The Captain never showed them any favouritism, rather the reverse and it was something Aitken had never met before. Each and every one of those men would at a word

225

or gesture not only follow Captain Ramage on whatever desperate business he might embark, but had done so many times in the past and only wanted to be allowed to go on.

Jackson carried a Protection declaring him to be an American subject, so that he need only pass the word to an American Consul and he would be released from the Royal Navy. Yet he was the cheerfully willing unofficial leader of the Tritons as well as being the Captain's coxswain. They were a motley group. The seaman Stafford made no secret of the fact that being a locksmith had been a natural stepping stone to becoming a burglar, a calling interrupted only when the pressgang seized him. The Italian Rossi's devotion was such that Aitken had the uncomfortable feeling that at the slightest hint from the Captain, he would slit a man's throat without question . . .

The quartermaster had obviously been trying to attract his attention for some time. 'Mr Lacey hailed from the fo'c'sle, sir: we're at long stay.'

'Very well,' Aitken said, realizing that his thoughts had been miles away from the *Surcouf*.

'An' the schooner, sir, she 'asn't 'oisted another signal.'

Aitken stared at the man. 'How long ago did she hoist the last one?'

'Five minutes or so, sir!' the startled man answered. 'Perhaps more.'

He managed to suppress a sigh of relief. There was no ship of the line with the French convoy, only four frigates against their two. He had been sentencing himself and the Surcoufs to death for the past five minutes, when with only four frigates there was a chance. Not the sort of chance many men would want to take at a gaming table, but certainly not one that would bother the Captain.

Yesterday evening Southwick had asked the Captain what he expected the French to send, and had been told that since it was an important convoy, with mostly naval and military supplies, he would expect six merchant ships or transports, with an escort of at least four or five frigates and perhaps a ship of the line. Not a new 74-gun ship but possibly an old sixty-four. If the convoy comprised a dozen ships he would expect five or six frigates and a 74-gun ship.

Southwick had questioned the size of the escort, pointing out that a British convoy homeward bound from Jamaica would be lucky to have three frigates to escort a hundred ships. The Captain had pointed out that while we could sail large convoys with small escorts, the French could only sail small convoys with large escorts. We had many ships of war at sea, but most of the French fleet was blockaded by British squadrons at Brest and Toulon.

'Sir, the *Juno*'s coming up to short stay,' the quartermaster reported. He seemed to have noticed that his commanding officer was preoccupied, and Aitken cursed under his breath. He must stop daydreaming. He picked up the speaking trumpet and hailed Lacey. It was going to be the very devil of an afternoon, and he was glad that the men had finished dinner before *La Créole*'s first signal had been sighted.

In the *Juno* Ramage waited patiently for the first flag in the next group of signals from the schooner to give him Wagstaffe's estimate of the French convoy's speed. The one after that would tell him something of the formation they were in. Then would come the signal telling him whether the convoy was following the coast to go inside the Diamond or staying outside. Once *La Créole* had told him all that, only the final signal remained. That gave the moment when Wagstaffe judged that the two frigates should leave Petite Anse d'Arlet and sail down to the Diamond to appear in sight of the French and spring the trap. It was putting a lot of responsibility on Wagstaffe's shoulders but there was no choice because the alternative was to risk the French sighting the *Juno* and *Surcouf* too soon.

The capstan had been pawled and the men were resting after their spell at the bars. The pace of events was slow enough at the moment for the men to have time to feel the heat. They were unwilling to stand still in bare feet on the scorching deck and he knew that the fo'c'sle must be like a furnace. Half a dozen men had lowered the quarterdeck awning, in a few minutes it would be lashed up and stowed below out of the way.

The masthead lookout hailed the deck and Paolo trained his telescope. 'Number five, sir.' He consulted the list of signals and added: '*Convoy making five knots*, sir.' There must be much more wind out there if it was making five knots. It was ten miles to the beginning of the Fours Channel, so the French would take two hours to get to the door of the trap. It would take the *Juno* and the *Surcouf* less than an hour, at the same speed, to get into position.

'*La Créole*'s signalling again, sir,' Paolo said, beating the masthead lookout's hail. 'Number nine. *Convoy in loose standard formation*, sir.'

That meant that the convoy was in two or three columns, with a frigate ahead and astern and one on either beam, although they would very soon shift the frigate on the land side out to seaward. That told Ramage much of what he wanted to know: the French were not expecting trouble, otherwise the merchantmen would be bunched up. Fear was the only certain recipe for good station-keeping. The escort must be expecting one British frigate at most, and they would be confident they could drive her off. Most French frigates had thirty-six guns, four more than the majority of the British, and they rarely put to sea with a ship's company of less than 300. They might even have seen *La Créole*, identified her as a French privateer, and concluded that the British had lifted the blockade.

The Master came up to the quarterdeck to report that everything was ready forward and Ramage looked at his watch. 'We won't be weighing for another hour, Mr Southwick. Hoist out the boats, and then beat to quarters. We'll have time to get guns loaded and run out before we leave here. If we have enough grommets, get fifteen extra roundshot on deck for each gun. And make sure the men keep the head pumps busy, wetting the deck every few minutes, in this heat.'

He thought for a moment and remembered that all the Marines were in the *Surcouf*. 'Let's have every musket and pistol on board ready and loaded: stack them along the centre line if necessary, if there aren't enough hooks for them.'

'D'you want grappling irons rigged, sir?'

Ramage shook his head. 'We'll have no need of them. And,' he added, trying to make his voice sound casual, 'make sure the carpenter has a good supply of shot plugs ready . . .'

The stay tackle was hooked on and the launch was hoisted off the booms amidships, swung over the side and lowered. While it was being hauled aft, where it would tow astern, one of the cutters was being hooked on. Fifteen minutes later the *Juno*'s four boats were astern, out of the way. Leaving them stowed on board in their normal position would have meant a grave risk of enemy shot shattering them and hurling lethal showers of splinters over the men at the guns. Splinters caused more casualties than actual shot. Towed astern the boats were out of the way and far less likely to be damaged.

While some men were hauling at the stay tackle, others were hurrying round the deck placing the grommets, thick rope rings, in which shot would rest like grotesque black eggs in a nest. Arms chests were hoisted up from below and muskets taken out and loaded, the first of them being put in the racks on the inside of the bulwarks between the guns. Loaded pistols, cutlasses and tomahawks were hung on hooks beside them, while the long boarding pikes, their ash handles well varnished, were stowed vertically in their racks round the masts, looking from a distance like bundles of steel-tipped fascines.

Now the crews of each gun were going through the loading procedure, working on their own because there were no officers to give them orders. The locks had been brought up from the magazine and secured to the breech of the guns, the flints had been checked and the trigger lines coiled up and placed on the breeches. The tompions protecting the muzzles of the guns had been taken out, the tackles overhauled so the ropes would run freely. Sponge and match tubs were being rolled into position and filled from a head pump rigged amidships which had already wetted the decks.

Down below, heavy blankets soaked with water had been hung up, surrounding the approaches to the magazine, so that no flash from an explosion could get through and detonate the powder stored there. Already the gunner was in the magazine itself, wearing felt slippers (shoes might set off loose powder), passing the cartridges through the blanket fire screens to waiting boys who slid them into the cylindrical wooden cartridge boxes, slipped the lids on and brought them up on deck, where they waited along the centre line behind their particular guns until called by the gun captains.

Black leather fire buckets with 'Juno' painted on them were also being topped up with water at the head pump and put back on their hooks under the quarterdeck rail, where they would swing with the roll of the ship and not spill. The fire engine would be hauled out and its cistern filled with water. In the ward-room Bowen was preparing his instruments and his assistant was winding bandages. The ward-room table had been scrubbed and lines put ready to hold writhing men. Beside it was an empty tub, the receptacle for 'wings and limbs' in case amputations were necessary.

Normally when the *Juno* went into action her Captain and Master were on the quarterdeck, with the four lieutenants at the guns, each commanding a division. Now Ramage was relying entirely on the gun captains, who were trained seamen but nevertheless accustomed to having an officer behind them bellowing orders through the thick smoke and noise of battle.

He had assembled all the gun captains and second captains earlier and told them to use their common sense. The moment they heard Ramage tell them to open fire, they were to continue as long as their guns would bear, but they must fire steadily, with every shot well aimed.

La Créole was still in sight running west for two or three miles from Diamond Hill and then beating back, always in sight of the *Juno* and of the French, her Tricolour flying. Behaving, in fact, just as the French officers in the convoy would expect a privateer to behave. She was fast enough to ignore the current; her great fore and aft sails drove her through the water as though she were a skimming dish.

Less than half an hour after giving the series of orders to Southwick Ramage walked round the ship, listening always for a hail from the masthead or quarterdeck warning of another signal from *La Créole*, talking with the men and inspecting the positions. There had been enough grommets for twenty extra rounds to be stored beside each gun, in addition to those always kept in the shot garlands along the bulwarks and round the coamings.

He peered into the cistern of the fire engine, examined the stands of muskets, sent for the carpenter and listened to his report that shot plugs, boards and tools were ready, heard from a bosun's mate that the tiller tackles were in position, ready to be rigged if the wheel was shot away, and preventer stays prepared in case masts were damaged.

Satisfied that the ship was ready for action, he had an encouraging word with each of the gun captains and went down to his cabin to collect his pistols and sword. Back on the quarterdeck a look through the telescope showed that the *Surcouf*'s guns were run out, her boats in the water astern, and Aitken walking up and down the quarterdeck with enviable nonchalance. Obviously he was satisfied that his ship was ready and, like Ramage, impatient for the final signal from *La Créole*.

The *Surcouf* had fine lines; the French certainly designed handsome ships. The sheer had a graceful sweep and the bow a pleasing flare. Any captain would be pleased with her appearance, and Ramage knew that few admirals would find fault with her. Yet in three hours she might be reduced to a shattered hulk, lying dead in the water with her masts hanging over the side in a tangle of rigging, her hull and decks torn up by roundshot.

He shivered despite the heat. The *Juno* could be close to

her in the same condition with not a dozen men alive in both ships to raise a cheer or cry for quarter. In considering the number of ships, the odds were only two to one in favour of the French, but in numbers of men (and that was what counted in the end) the odds were about nine to one because there would be about 1200 Frenchmen in their four frigates.

Nine to one. It was the first time he had reduced his gamble to actual figures, and it frightened him. Two frigates against four seemed acceptable, but one of his men against nine Frenchmen was monstrous. What right had he to take his handful of men into battle against such odds? They all trusted him, from Southwick and Aitken to the cook's mate and the youngest powder monkey: the sight of the two frigates with their guns run out was proof of that. They trusted him to work out the odds and only ask of them what was reasonable. He had abused their trust. He held out his hands and clenched all but one of his fingers. Nine to one. If you committed suicide, the Church would not allow your body to be buried in consecrated ground. It was just as well that the sea obligingly accepted whatever it was offered. Then he remembered that not five minutes earlier he had pictured the *Juno* and *Surcouf* drifting, shattered shells, manned by corpses, and he cursed his imagination: it killed men and sank ships before their time.

CHAPTER SEVENTEEN

As the *Juno* stretched close-hauled down the coast, making a bare five knots and with the *Surcouf* following in her wake two hundred yards astern, the headland formed by Diamond Hill was fine on the larboard bow. The wind was fluking round the peak and freshening. Ramage guessed that once they were out of the lee of the land it would probably be from the east-north-east.

Diamond Rock had just come in sight clear of the headland and Ramage could see *La Créole* a couple of miles beyond it, well placed to give Wagstaffe a clear view of the convoy approaching the Fours Channel from the east still unaware that two British frigates were coming down from the north-west.

Wagstaffe had made no more signals, apart from reporting

that the convoy was following the coast. He must be confident that it would reach the trap of the Fours Channel just as the *Juno* and *Surcouf* arrived to spring it. Leaving him with the responsibility of timing the operation had put a heavy load on the shoulders of the *Juno*'s former Second Lieutenant. At first it had worried Ramage that so young a man could wreck everything through carelessness or nervousness. But the young Londoner had impressed him at last evening's conference in the cabin: he had asked several questions that revealed a quick and lively mind, not nervousness or indecision.

Ramage looked astern once again. The *Surcouf* was a fine sight in the *Juno*'s wake, topsails and topgallants filled in taut curves, her guns rows of stubby black fingers, pointing menacingly through the ports, her bow wave like a white moustache flowing up from the cutwater. Within half an hour the guns would be belching smoke, but for the moment gulls wheeled round her and flying fish flashed low over the water, silver darts aimed without targets.

The French merchant ships were presumably still in the same formation, probably three columns with three ships forming the middle one and two the outer, but the four frigates would no longer be surrounding them. The land covered the eastern side of the convoy from attack, and would continue to do so all the way up to Fort Royal, so one frigate would probably be ahead, one abreast the leading merchantmen, another abreast the last one, and the fourth astern. This meant that the *Juno*, beating through the Fours Channel to attack the convoy from ahead, would have to dodge two frigates to get at the merchantmen, and the *Surcouf*, going on to round the Diamond itself before tacking up to cut off the convoy's retreat, would have to deal with the other two.

Ramage looked round at Orsini. 'You have signal number thirteen bent on ready?'

'Aye, aye, sir,' he said, and added: '*Prepare for battle, sir.*'

Ramage nodded. 'And the Diamond Rock's pendant and number 123?'

'Aye, aye, sir. To the Juno and Ramage batteries, special signal, *Attack the enemy's convoy of merchant ships or transports.*'

'Don't get them mixed up, then,' Ramage warned, 'so that you hoist the wrong one.'

The boy pointed to two different halyards. 'No chance of that, sir.'

'And don't mislay the signal book, in case I need to make a signal in a hurry.'

'No, sir,' the boy said patiently, and then grinned. 'I doubt if you'll need to use number sixteen, though, *Engage the enemy more closely.*'

Ramage smiled, glad of the boy's confidence. 'No, the lads need no encouraging.'

He watched the steep cliffs, the shadows almost vertical. They were approaching the end of the headland rapidly now. In a few minutes the land would turn away sharply to the eastward and then curve in again like a huge sickle, the point being Diamond Hill headland, the blade the long beach of the Grande Anse du Diamant and the handle the two headlands at the far end. A mile off the tip of the sickle, like a clump of wheat that it was about to reap, was the Diamond Rock.

Southwick came up the quarterdeck ladder, his great sword at his waist, bushy hair poking out from beneath his hat like a half-squeezed mop and his nose bright red from sunburn. 'No sign of the Admiral then, sir?' He rubbed his hands. 'That means we certainly don't share the prize-money – apart from his usual eighth!'

'We might be glad to see him before the day is out,' Ramage said with unintended harshness.

'We'll go through that convoy like a knife through butter!' Southwick declared cheerfully. 'You'll see, sir.'

'They'll be dead to windward of us,' Ramage reminded him.

'And as you mentioned last evening, sir, they'll never expect us to dare to beat up through them. They'll be like a flock of hens waking up to find a fox in the coop!'

As both men talked, they watched the headland of Diamond Hill drawing abeam and Ramage was reminded of watching a theatre stage as a curtain was drawn back, slowly exposing the scenery and the players.

Wagstaffe by now had *La Créole* about two miles south-east of the Diamond Rock; from there he could reach up right into the middle of the convoy. Because *La Créole* was still flying the Tricolour, the moment the French saw the *Juno* and the *Surcouf* they would assume she was fleeing from them and seeking protection.

The men at the *Juno* and Ramage batteries on the Diamond

could see both the British frigates coming down to the headland from the north-west and the French convoy creeping along the coast. 'Like a crossroads,' Ramage said to himself and only realized he had spoken aloud when Southwick swung round questioningly. 'I was thinking of the French coming up to this headland from the east while we're approaching from the north-west. Like two coaches approaching along sunken lanes and not seeing each other until they're almost at the crossroads.'

'Just one coach,' Southwick corrected with a broad grin. 'We're the highwaymen!'

Now they could see clear across the great bight to Pointe des Salines at the southern end of the island that reminded Ramage of a boot. They were rounding the toe cap and could just see the heel with the instep still hidden.

'They must be sticking very close to the coast,' Southwick growled. 'I'd have thought we'd have seen the first of 'em by now.'

Ramage gestured to the end of the headland which was drawing aft at what seemed an alarming speed, but he knew it was only anxiety playing tricks with time.

'Deck there!' came a hail from aloft, 'a frigate on the larboard bow, sir, three miles or more, in line with the headland.'

And there she was, ringed in the telescope lens. He saw a second one beyond her just as the lookout hailed again. The first must be on the convoy's bow, the second on the quarter. Then he saw the third frigate, which was obviously leading the convoy and well ahead of it. The convoy was just at the beginning of the Fours Channel and the timing was perfect.

'Hoist our colours,' Ramage snapped at Orsini. That was the prearranged signal to Aitken that the *Juno* had sighted the French ships and could herself be sighted and identified.

Ramage watched the three frigates closely. At any moment there should be a flurry of flag signals, warning that enemy ships were in sight. With any luck, while the French escort prepared to deal with the enemy *La Créole* would be getting in among them, apparently a welcome reinforcement but actually positioning herself to act as a Trojan horse.

'I can see a merchantman now,' Ramage told Southwick, trying to keep his voice even. 'And another beyond her – the ships in the outer column. And another, and two beyond – the centre column . . .'

With the wind coming free as they passed clear of the headland, Ramage watched the dog vanes. A glance down at the compass showed it trying to make up its mind between north-east and east-north-east.

'Close-hauled, if you please, Mr Southwick; we should be able to lay south-east comfortably!'

Southwick began bellowing into a speaking trumpet and as Jackson gave orders to the men at the wheel, carefully watching the luffs of the sails, seamen hauled at the sheets and braces, flattening in the sails. Astern the *Surcouf* was bearing away slightly on to a direct course for the Diamond Rock and Ramage realized that the French ship was faster than the *Juno*. Aitken would fetch the Diamond with the wind a point free, perhaps more. So much the better; she had farther to sail and the sooner she reached the Rock and rounded it to close off the eastern entrance of the Fours Channel the better.

By the time he looked back over the larboard beam the Fours Channel was in sight and there was the whole French convoy sailing towards him. There were three columns of merchant ships, as he had expected, with one frigate ahead, two out to seaward, and one astern. They were relying on the coast to protect the whole inshore side of the convoy. He must let them go on thinking that the land shielded them.

'If we could only get between them and the beach . . .' Southwick murmured wistfully. 'Still, Wagstaffe timed it well. They're all just about in the Channel.'

'Not yet,' Ramage said. 'Another half a mile to go. They're just outside the range of the Juno and Ramage batteries. Give 'em ten or fifteen minutes.'

'But they might turn and bolt!' Southwick exclaimed anxiously.

'Come now, Mr Southwick,' Ramage chided, 'you don't really expect seven merchantmen to try to beat back to Pointe des Salines, do you?' He glanced astern and saw that the *Surcouf* would now be in sight of the French. 'Why should they be frightened of a couple of frigates when they're so near home and have a schooner coming along to help them!'

'Sorry, sir,' said Southwick with mock contrition. 'I just can't stand the thought of those beggars getting away after all our preparations.' With that he picked up his telescope and looked at the Diamond. 'No sign of the Juno battery – just bushes.' He trained the telescope lower. 'I can just see the cave at the back of the Ramage battery but no sign of guns or men.' He swung the telescope round to the east. 'Wagstaffe's tacked. He'll just be able to lay the tail of the convoy.'

Ramage, still watching the French frigates, saw a string of flags hoisted from the leading one. He cursed his lack of a French signal book: they had searched *La Créole* and *La Mutine* the moment they were captured, but there were no papers on board, not even a muster table. More flags were hoisted and all the frigates repeated them. A few moments later he realized that the second signal must have been to the convoy because the merchantmen were now beginning to bunch up, the outside ships closing in on the centre column. Instead of three columns of ships there was soon just a group, like seven sheep crowding together as a sheepdog circled them. More important, though, they stayed on the same course. They were coming through the Fours Channel . . .

The *Juno*, stretching south-east and sailing fast, was now half-way between the headland and the Diamond itself. The *Surcouf* had almost reached the Diamond and would soon be hauling her wind to round it and then tack north to get at the rear of the convoy. She might need a couple of extra tacks, but it would not matter; it would all serve to confuse the French.

The head of the convoy was at most a mile and a half from the *Juno* and, as best he could judge, just coming into the extreme range of the Diamond batteries. And the wind was strengthening: the *Juno* was beginning to slice up spray over her larboard bow and it was drifting aft in dancing rainbow patterns. The gun captains were putting aprons over the locks, small canvas bonnets that would keep them dry until the last moment.

What the devil were the French escorts going to do? At the moment the convoy and escorts were still sailing the same course, coming down into the Fours Channel and heading straight for the *Juno*. The only sign that they had seen the two British frigates was the two signals and the merchantmen bunching up.

A third signal was hoisted on board the leading frigate and he watched carefully. There were answering signals from the frigates only. Very well, they had received orders – but what were they going to do? He looked back at the merchant ships and stifled an oath of surprise. 'Just look!' he exclaimed unbelievingly to Southwick. 'Some of them are clew-ing up their courses! They're going to jog along under their topsails alone!'

'Just like all merchantmen,' the Master said cheerfully. 'If they were making five knots before, they'll make three now, if they're lucky. Our lads at the Diamond batteries must be rubbing their hands!'

'Are they acting under orders?' Ramage wondered aloud, and at the same moment saw more signals hoisted by the leading frigate. He watched carefully but none of the other frigates answered, so the signal must have been for the merchantmen.

The merchant ship leading the centre column let fall her courses again, as if in response to the signal, and was followed by her next astern, but the other merchant ships were still busy furling, obviously ignoring the order. A minute later the two centre-column ships clewed up their courses again, clearly anxious not to find themselves ahead of the rest.

By now the *Surcouf* had rounded the Diamond and tacked to the northwards and *La Créole* had tacked, too, as though trying to keep well up to windward of her pursuer and reach the safety of the convoy. Ramage pointed them out. 'I think we'll match the *Surcouf* tack for tack for the time being.'

As the Master snatched up his speaking trumpet, Ramage saw that the leading frigate was altering course slightly, as though intending to sail the convoy through the precise centre of the Fours Channel. Obviously the French captain had decided on the change to keep both British frigates on his larboard bow. It was a good move from his point of view because it left the convoy still covered by the coast to the north.

'Belay that!' Ramage called to Southwick, 'we'll stay on this tack!' He wanted to be sure that all the ships in the convoy followed the leading frigate, and the *Juno* tacking might scare them off. Their new course would take them half-way between the headland and the Diamond and would reduce the range for the Diamond batteries to half a mile. It would also leave a wider gap between the convoy and the coast.

Southwick rejoined him and saw what was happening. 'The Rock's a magnet for them,' he said.

Ramage shook his head. 'I think he knows about the current and is afraid the merchantmen under topsails alone will get swept too close to the headland.'

'What's he going to do with those other two frigates, sir?'

'I'm damned if I know. He made them a signal which they answered, but they're still keeping station.'

Southwick gestured towards the *Surcouf*. 'Just look at her, sir, she's eating up to windward. She's at least a knot faster than us.'

'A point which hasn't escaped Aitken,' Ramage said wryly, and began to recast his plans slightly. Two unexpected things had happened. First the French merchantmen had obligingly reduced sail and cut the convoy's speed, and second the *Surcouf* was not only proving faster to windward than he had expected, but she was pointing higher. On this tack, unless the convoy altered course, Aitken could actually intercept the convoy, sailing into the middle of it, instead of arriving astern of it to cut off its retreat.

Ramage began rubbing the scars over his brow and the moment Southwick noticed it he made a mental note not to interrupt the Captain's thoughts. Rubbing the scar meant concentration and perhaps a sudden change of plan. From past experience it resulted in something even more desperate than originally intended but usually more effective. He tried to guess what it would be.

At the moment Southwick thought that the situation was more or less as they had anticipated. The convoy was beginning to come through the Fours Channel towards them; the *Surcouf* was well round the Diamond and heading up towards the convoy to shut the escape door; *La Créole* was almost up to the rear of the convoy. Wagstaffe was making another tack, which was unnecessary unless he was trying to waste time until the *Juno* and the *Surcouf* were in position. The convoy had reduced speed and the leading French frigate was going to bring them through the middle of the Fours Channel.

Southwick shrugged his shoulders. The original plan had been for the *Juno* to try to fight her way through the leading frigates to get at the merchantmen while the *Surcouf* did the same from astern, with *La Créole* doing her best to get into the middle and use her nimbleness to savage the merchantmen like a stoat running amok in a hen run. That seemed good enough to Southwick, particularly when the Diamond batteries joined in.

Ramage looked round for Orsini. 'Give me the signal book and stand by.'

He thumbed through the pages. Making a signal which gave a precise order was frequently difficult for a captain or admiral who wanted to do something out of the ordinary. There were nearly four hundred signals in the book, ranging from *Engage the enemy more closely* to *The ship has sprung a leak*, from *Send boats tomorrow morning for water, for fresh beef, or for any other supplies of which the ship may be in need* to *The physician of the fleet is to come to the Admiral*.

For all that, he was going to have to use two separate signals to give his new order to Aitken. The problem was that the new order was not a complete change. The *Surcouf* was still to attack the convoy, but not from the rear: Aitken was to attack the middle of the convoy from the seaward side. Signal number 33 said *Engage the centre of the enemy*, but might be misunderstood by Aitken as meaning that he was also to attack the frigates which, forming a half circle round the convoy on his side, would immediately close up to drive him off. No, Ramage had to make it clear that the English frigate's target was still the merchant ships. Very well, there would have to be two signals. The first would be number 22, *Attack the enemy's convoy of transports or trading ships*, followed immediately by number 33, *Engage the centre of the enemy*.

He looked across at the convoy. It was also time to make the agreed signal for the Diamond and indicate to them that their orders were unchanged.

'Orsini, hoist number 13.'

'Number 13, *Prepare for battle*, sir,' the boy said, running to the halyard.

Ramage gestured to one of the four men to leave the wheel and give him a hand, and watched the *Surcouf* acknowledge.

He then said carefully to the boy: 'Now the *Surcouf*'s pendant, and then two signals, number 22, and number 33.'

'Aye, aye, sir,' said the boy, repeating the meanings.

Ramage nodded and prayed that the Diamond batteries would not be so excited that they did not notice that the second signal was addressed only to the *Surcouf*.

'We'll tack now, Mr Southwick,' he said and tried to look at the *Surcouf*. The Master had heard him tell Orsini the signals and was obviously puzzled as he walked to the quarter-deck rail with his speaking trumpet. In a few moments more

239

Aitken would not be puzzled: he would know that he had to keep the *Surcouf* on the same tack and heading for a point, at the moment unmarked, where the frigate and the convoy would meet. Then, whatever the French frigates did to try and stop him, he must luff up or bear away, tack, wear, or do anything else that let him dodge the escorts and break through to attack the centre of the convoy.

What would Aitken think? Ramage knew it did not matter, because the battle had to be fought, but the young Scot might think that, at the last minute, his senior officers had left him the desperate part of the fighting, ordering him to make a suicidal attack.

Would Aitken realize that he was now being ordered to attack the centre of the *seaward* side of the convoy so that at his approach two, and possibly three, of the frigates would bear up to fight him off, leaving only the leading frigate to drive off the *Juno* as she beat up through the Channel? Would he see what would happen if the *Juno* managed to avoid the leading frigate and suddenly attacked the convoy from the landward side? It would be a massacre, but by then the *Surcouf* would probably be a shambles. For a moment Ramage sympathized with an admiral with his flagship in the centre squadron who ordered the van or the rear squadron to make some apparently unexpected and dangerous attack and stayed in safety himself. Men would die and never know that they had been part of a larger plan. They might guess it, of course, because an admiral was responsible for the whole fleet, but how about the senior of two commanding officers, like himself and Aitken? How could Aitken be sure that Ramage was not deliberately giving him orders that would take the worst of the fighting off the *Juno* and leave most of it to the *Surcouf*? Aitken might have to fight off two or perhaps three frigates.

The *Juno* was now swinging round on the other tack; the helmsmen were turning the wheel, sheets and braces were being trimmed, and Ramage bent over the compass, shading it from the glare of the sun. He glanced up at Jackson, who nodded: the *Juno* was now sailing as fast and as close to the wind as possible, at right angles to the convoy's course. The lubber line on the compass was steady on north.

He looked across at the convoy, now broad on the *Juno*'s starboard bow. The *Surcouf* had acknowledged his signals and he could see that she would be able to lay at the centre. But what the devil were the French frigates going to do? It looked as though they were going to stay in their present positions in relation to the convoy. Putting himself in the senior French captain's place, he was sure the plan at the moment was for the nearest two frigates to drive off the nearest enemy, without attempting to capture or destroy it.

From the French point of view this made sense: Fort Royal Bay was less than ten miles away round the Diamond headland. Four French frigates had only to keep two British frigates at bay for three hours – less, if they could persuade the merchantmen to set more canvas – and they would all be safe and have carried out their task of getting provisions to Martinique.

The colours, he thought irrelevantly: the almost harsh blue of the tropical sky, the deep blue of the sea which lightened as it closed the shore and, like the edge of a rainbow, merged into pale green along the sand of the beach. The inside of the *Juno*'s bulwarks was a deep blood red; the guns shiny black and the sails aloft not the white of poems and songs but a faint tan, what an artist had once described as raw umber with a touch of burnt sienna.

Looking across at the convoy he was startled at the nearness of the leading frigate. It would be difficult indeed to explain that he had been attacked unawares because he was considering how much raw umber was mixed with burnt sienna . . .

Then he saw two separate signals being hoisted in the French frigate. The *Surcouf* was a mile away from the seaward frigate. Any minute now he expected to see smoke pouring from them as they tried the range. Ramage was just estimating that the leading frigate was perhaps half a mile from the *Juno* when he saw all three frigates answering the signals.

Almost at once the frigates at the rear and on the quarter bore away slightly, obviously intending to drive off the *Surcouf*, while the leading frigate made a bold turn to starboard, to prevent the *Juno* getting between the convoy and the shore. The frigate which had stayed abreast of the leading ships now moved up to take the leading frigate's place at the head of the convoy.

'Most interesting,' Ramage heard a voice comment quietly, and he turned to find Bowen watching.

'It's our move,' Ramage said crisply, 'and perhaps a chessmaster like yourself can see it.' There were two or three minutes to spare and after that the pieces would start moving across the board with startling speed and confusion.

The Surgeon was shaking his head. 'No, sir, this isn't quite my kind of game.'

Ramage gestured to Southwick, to make sure he was ready for the *Juno*'s next move. 'Remember your bishops, Mr Bowen,' he said with what seemed to the Surgeon a devilish grin. 'The unexpected diagonal attack.'

The Master laughed drily and fingered the speaking trumpet. 'Aye, sir, the bishop might do it. Checkmate in three moves!'

The French frigate was turning even more inshore now as the *Juno* crossed ahead of the convoy and Ramage thought she would try to rake the *Juno*, firing her broadside into the British frigate's unprotected bow. Every yard the French frigate sailed took her farther from the convoy; every yard she held on, hoping for that raking broadside, increased Ramage's chances of succeeding with his bishop's move. He glanced at Bowen and nodded towards the companionway. 'I know you'd like to watch, but you must stay alive to tend the casualties.'

CHAPTER EIGHTEEN

Time was slowing down now, and Ramage felt calm; he could understand Bowen's fascination with chess because here were eleven French pieces under attack from three British. And every moment that passed made him certain he could out-manoeuvre the leading French frigate because her captain was at this very moment making a very elementary mistake.

He had started off correctly: the moment the *Juno* tacked across the convoy's course the Frenchman had realized that she might get between the shore and the convoy and had made the proper response, bearing up to cover the gap.

Then he had seen that he might be able to rake the *Juno* in the process. At some point in the last three or four minutes the Frenchman had forgotten that his prime task was to cover the gap, he had become obsessed with the idea of raking the *Juno* and to increase his chances of doing that he was now widening the gap he had been trying to close.

In the meantime the convoy was still lumbering through the Fours Channel. Ramage estimated that all seven merchant ships were just inside the circle he had pencilled on the chart as representing the effective range of the Juno and Ramage batteries but he decided to wait a few more minutes.

The French frigate was fine on the *Juno*'s starboard bow and in a couple of minutes would be in a perfect position to rake her, but a quick glance at the compass showed Ramage that the centre of the convoy was bearing south-east by south. The second frigate was in position leading the convoy and keeping on a steady course through the Channel.

The first frigate was now almost dead ahead; her captain would have to wait another two minutes to be in a perfect position, firing a whole broadside into the bow of a ship which could not fire back. Now for the surprise Ramage thought to himself; it might save a few lives.

'Mr Southwick, we'll tack now, if you please, and tell the men at the starboard guns to get under cover and the larboard side to stand fast! Jackson, steady her on a course of south-east!'

The Master bellowed to the men at the braces and sheets, then shouted to the rest of the men to duck down beside the guns, the safest place when a raking broadside smashed round-shot through the bow and swept the decks.

The French frigate was still not quite dead ahead as the *Juno*'s wheel was put over. Ramage could see every one of her larboard guns and pictured each French gun captain crouching, trigger line in his hand, waiting just one more moment before the *Juno*'s bow came in sight.

Then the *Juno* began to swing fast as she tacked; swinging towards the French frigate's stern as she turned. Instead of an unprotected bow, the French gunners peering through the gunports would see the *Juno*'s broadside guns.

Ramage took up his speaking trumpet. 'Larboard guns, stand by. Fire as your guns bear!'

The gun captains would only have a fleeting glimpse of the French frigate as the *Juno* continued her swing towards the convoy, but if a few shot landed it would help. There was distant thudding over on the larboard bow and he saw the French ship firing wildly, her gunners obviously taken by surprise, but the *Juno* was still swinging round on to the other tack, with ropes squealing through blocks aloft, Jackson cursing the men at the wheel, and Orsini hurling a shrill stream of Italian blasphemy at the French frigate as she passed across the bow. Then a couple of the *Juno*'s forward guns fired and thundered back in recoil, followed in sequence by the rest. Smoke drifted aft and he remembered to breathe shallowly to avoid coughing.

Now the *Juno*'s sails had filled on the other tack and she was sailing fast to the south-east on an opposite course from her erstwhile attacker, heading straight for the head of the convoy.

The captain of the new leading French frigate waited, perhaps in indecision. The *Juno*'s sudden tack directly towards the head of the convoy would show him that he too had made a disastrous mistake – he was much too far ahead of the merchant ships. He could haul round immediately to the north and try to cut off the *Juno* before she reached the merchantmen or he could simply tack and try to get back to the head of the convoy. Give me three minutes, Ramage prayed; please hesitate a little longer! A glance astern showed him that the first frigate had already tacked and was chasing along in the *Juno*'s wake. She hoisted a string of signal flags and almost immediately the second frigate hauled her wind, turning north towards the *Juno*. Ramage watched the Frenchmen bracing the yards sharp up, desperately trying to point higher. The luffs fluttered and she paid off a fraction. That was the best she could do – and he saw it was not going to be enough: the *Juno* would just scrape past ahead, giving her a raking broadside on the way.

He had taken a chance going into action with topgallants set instead of fighting under topsails alone, but so far in this weasel-in-a-hen-run type of action it had paid off. The French were under topsails alone and it was costing them a couple of knots.

More signals came from the first frigate. Suddenly and almost unbelievably the second frigate tacked and came round on the same course as the *Juno*, but nearly half a mile to leeward, leaving the British frigate between her and the convoy.

Southwick, watching open-mouthed, turned to Ramage, and said: 'I must be dreaming. Why the devil has he done that?'

There was only one explanation Ramage could think of. 'They reckon we're going down to join the *Surcouf*!'

He looked over towards her and felt quite sick: Aitken had two frigates bearing down on him. But there was nothing he could do. The time had nearly come for the *Juno* to start the bishop's move.

'Orsini,' he called. 'The Diamond's pendant and number twenty-two!'

'Aye, aye, sir,' the boy yelled, running towards the halyards. *'Engage the convoy!'*

'Mr Southwick, we'll tack again. Jackson, keep her as close to the wind as you can!'

The *Juno* turned north again, heading straight for the shore and leaving the convoy on her starboard side.

'That'll fool them!' Southwick exclaimed gleefully. 'Both the frigates are tacking again. They *did* think we were going down to the *Surcouf*. Not that she couldn't do with a hand,' he added soberly. A moment later he was berating the men at the wheel and glowering at Jackson as a luff fluttered.

With the *Juno* heading for the shore Ramage kept glancing at the convoy over the top of the compass. It looked as though the frigate would run up the beach before the middle of the convoy bore south-east, so he could fetch it on the next tack.

As he watched Orsini arrived in front of him, almost squeaking with excitement and pointing at the far side of the convoy, towards the *Surcouf*. Ramage stared, frowned and then snatched Orsini's telescope, cursing as he had to adjust the focus.

One French frigate had rammed the other! Her jibboom and bowsprit were stuck in the second ship's side and her foremast had come crashing down, locking into the other frigate's mainmast. Even as he watched, her mainmast began to topple, slowly at first and then gathering speed, until it fell over the side, its yards giving it a cartwheeling effect. The *Surcouf*, which he had last seen between the two frigates, wreathed in smoke and obviously trapped, was between the wrecked ships and the convoy, sailing fast. And *La Créole* had hoisted her own flag and was firing into the last ship of the centre column.

Ramage thrust the telescope back to Orsini. 'Watch the *Surcouf* for signals!'

There was no time to tell Southwick: all that mattered now was that the *Juno* stayed close-hauled until she was almost on the beach and then tacked south-east again into the middle of the convoy.

The two frigates the *Juno* had dodged were still tacking, trying to catch up with her. The first one had her topgallants set but Ramage knew there was precious little the Frenchman could do now to save the convoy, unless, of course, the *Juno* ran aground. This was becoming a distinct possibility.

Damn all this tacking! There were seven fat merchantmen almost at his mercy once he got to windward. He glanced up at the luffs, but Jackson and Southwick were watching like hawks. The beach was approaching with alarming speed and already the water had changed to green and close ahead it was an even lighter green. Ramage heard a chanting from the mainchains and saw the leadsman at work, water from the line streaming down his body.

He glanced back at the merchantmen. He needed another fifty yards before he tacked; otherwise he would not lay the middle of the convoy, which was helping him by continuing to steer the same course.

Southwick was watching him anxiously. 'Leadsman reports five fathoms, sir!'

'We'll hold on a little longer, Mr Southwick.'

It was a devilish choice having to risk running ashore or miss getting into the middle of that convoy! He would look a damn fool with the *Juno* hard aground, bows into the beach, while the *Surcouf* and *La Créole* tried to finish off the convoy before the remaining two French frigates beat them off.

'He's reporting four fathoms, sir!'

'I can hear him, Mr Southwick.'

And I can see the sand too, he thought grimly, and almost distinguish the individual palm fronds as well! He looked back over the quarter at the convoy, tried to estimate if there were twelve points between the *Juno*'s jibboom and the merchantmen, and gestured to Southwick: 'You may tack, Mr Southwick. This is the bishop's move!'

He almost giggled at the 'may' and he knew he was getting far too excited.

The wheel spun, the men looking as if they were trying to climb up the spokes; the blocks screeched and the *Juno*'s bow swung along the beach so that palm trees, a few small thatched huts and the mountains in the distance swept across his vision as though he was looking from the window of a runaway coach.

Still no thump under the deck, still no gentle slowing down. The *Juno* had not hit a rock, a coral reef or run on to a sand bar – yet. Then there was a sea horizon ahead – a horizon on which the merchant ships were bunched. He ran forward to the quarterdeck rail. The larboard-side guns had long ago been reloaded and run out again, and all the men on both sides were watching him, rags round their brows and most of them naked to the waist.

He lifted the speaking trumpet to his mouth. 'Stand by, my

lads! This tack will take us right into the convoy. I hope you're more awake than the gunners in that first French frigate!' There was a chorus of shouts and jeers and before giving them a cheery wave he said: 'Pick your targets: every shot must count!' He turned back for a good look at the convoy, knowing he must choose the course through it that gave the gunners the best chance of firing into all seven ships. Orsini was once again jumping up and down, trying to attract his attention. The boy was so excited he was incoherent. Ramage shook him and told him to report in Italian. 'The Diamond batteries, sir! They are firing at the French frigates – not the ones that collided, but the others. The shot are falling all round them!'

'Excellent,' Ramage said calmly. 'Now you continue to watch the *Surcouf* for signals. Look at her!' he exclaimed. The British frigate was within half a mile of the nearest merchant ships and heeling gracefully in the wind as her topgallants were furled. Aitken obviously wanted to make a leisurely job of the merchantmen, but Ramage hoped he would not forget the two remaining frigates.

A glance over the starboard beam reassured him that they were still down to leeward and then he looked back at the convoy. The nearest three ships, which had been on the landward side, were now four hundred yards ahead. As he concentrated on them he saw that their sails were not just badly trimmed, they were flapping, with sheets and braces slack, if not cut. Boats were being lowered round them – the ships were dead in the water and their crews were abandoning them! He looked at the others and saw that they were all being abandoned.

Southwick was also staring at the convoy, disappointment showing on his face like a child whose toys had been snatched away. Ramage, equally dumbfounded, noticed that most of the boats were now fairly leaping through the water as the men in them rowed frantically for the beach. They were obviously scared out of their wits at the sight of the *Juno* beating down on them from the north and the *Surcouf* stretching up from the south.

'Surprise, sir, that's what did it,' Southwick said cryptically.

Ramage grimaced as he said: 'I don't know who was most surprised.'

Seven merchantmen abandoned and drifting out to sea through the Fours Channel and two French frigates neatly tied together in a parcel. He needed the *Surcouf* to help the

Juno capture the two remaining frigates, which were under fire from the Diamond, but first he must secure the merchant ships: they were the main target.

'Bear away towards the frigates, Mr Southwick,' he said. Aitken and Wagstaffe needed orders. He looked round for Orsini and found him proffering the signal book.

He opened the index, looked under 'Prizes' and hurriedly turned to the page listed. Ah, there it was.

'Hoist *La Créole*'s pendant and number 242.' He then read the first part of the signal, for Southwick's benefit. '*Stay by prizes . . .*' He could rely on Wagstaffe knowing that he was to make sure none of the French crews returned to their ships.

Now he was having second thoughts about the two remaining frigates. Dare he leave the one nearest to the Diamond to the batteries while he tackled the other? She seemed to be hove-to, lying with her foretopsail backed. Waiting for her consort to join her perhaps. He looked round for the frigate that had been leading the convoy when it came in sight. She too was lying hove-to.

Ramage took his own telescope from the binnacle box drawer and looked at the frigate nearest the Diamond. Hove-to! Her foretopsail yard was slewed round, the maintopsail in shreds and even as he watched he saw a cloud of dust rising up amidships, the sign of a plunging roundshot hitting her decks. He looked at the ship more closely and there were ominous gaps in the main and foreshrouds. Even as he watched the foretopsail yard canted down as one of the lifts parted, and a moment later the whole yard crashed to the deck. A spurt of water almost beside the mainchains showed a near miss from either the Juno or the Ramage battery. That particular frigate could certainly be left to the gunners on the Diamond. Their first prize was a 36-gun frigate, and they had not a drop of rum on the Rock to celebrate it.

The next decision was not hard to make; one frigate only was left and the *Juno* and *Surcouf* perfectly placed to windward. He examined the frigate carefully through the telescope in case she too had been damaged by the batteries, but she seemed genuinely hove-to, with her captain no doubt wondering how he could report to the Governor at Fort Royal or St Pierre that he had lost the whole convoy and three frigates, and that Diamond Rock was suddenly erupting as Mont Pelée occasionally did, only sprouting roundshot instead of hot rocks and lava. Any moment the frigate captain would wake up, get under way and make a bolt for Fort Royal.

He tucked the telescope under his arm and opened the signal book to check a number. Number twenty-eight would tell Aitken all that he needed to know. *The ships are to take suitable stations for their mutual support, and engage the enemy as soon as they get up with them.* It was not quite the way an admiral would use the signal, but Aitken needed no more than a hint. As he turned to call the boy, he saw the French ship sheet home her topsail and get under way.

'Orsini, hoist the *Surcouf*'s pendant and number twenty-eight.'

Southwick had just bustled back to the binnacle after getting the *Juno*'s sails trimmed to perfection, but he was scowling. 'Did you see that, sir?' he demanded. 'She hasn't the guts to stand and fight, and she has a mile lead of us and a mile and a half on the *Surcouf*!'

'I can't blame him,' Ramage said mildly. 'The world has tumbled round his ears in the last hour!'

The Master gave a monumental sniff. 'It hasn't finished yet,' he announced.

Ramage wagged a warning finger. 'There are three hundred men on board that ship. We have sixty-three, and the *Surcouf* the same. Don't forget that. We haven't captured a frigate ourselves yet: the Diamond knocked out one, and two of them locked themselves together!'

'But they don't know we're short of men,' Southwick said with a broad grin. 'With the *Juno* ranging up on one side of her and the *Surcouf* on the other, 'twouldn't surprise me if she —'

He broke off as Jackson, a look of horror on his face, pointed ahead. A moment later there was a sound like a clap of thunder which rolled and echoed back from the mountains, and where the escaping French frigate had been there was now only a swirling mass of yellow and black smoke spurting and boiling upwards and then curling and billowing. Round the base of the smoke was a mass of ripples surrounded by dozens of splashes as pieces of the ship, flung high into the air by the explosion, finally landed. There was complete silence in the *Juno* apart from the gurgling of the sea as the ship drove on towards the pall of smoke, which was now beginning to drift to leeward. Ramage felt sick but braced himself as he remembered that, dreadful as the sight had been — and still was, for the smoke seemed reluctant to disperse — it had saved the lives of many of his own men, those in the *Juno* and the

Surcouf. Only then did he realize that the French ship must have blown up as a result of plunging fire from the Diamond batteries.

With the remaining frigate disabled there was no need for the Diamond batteries to go on firing at her; she would surrender to the *Surcouf* and the *Juno*.

'Orsini, hoist the Diamond's pendant and number thirty-nine.'

The Master nodded in agreement. '*Discontinue the engagement*. Yes, we might as well tow her back to Bridgetown as a prize. We're assembling a bigger squadron out here than the Admiral has!'

Ramage flicked through the signal book once more and found what he wanted. *Get to leeward of the chase*. That would tell Aitken that he wanted to take possession of the disabled frigate before attempting to sort out the two that were locked together.

He turned to Southwick as the signal was hoisted and pointed to the frigate, which was slowly drifting westward through the Fours Channel, turning slowly like a feather in a stream as the wind caught her torn maintopsail aback and swung her round so far that she tacked and the sail filled. 'Aitken will be getting to leeward of her in a few minutes, and I want the *Juno* tacking back and forth about eight hundred yards to windward.'

'She hasn't hauled down her colours yet,' Southwick commented as he put the speaking trumpet to his lips.

Ramage was less concerned with what was little more than a formality than with the problem of physically taking possession of this frigate and the two that were locked together. There would be nine hundred Frenchmen altogether. One mistake on his part, one hint to any of the three ships that the *Juno* and the *Surcouf* had less than seventy men on board, might result in some enterprising French captain boarding them, capturing both ships, getting the merchantmen manned again, and sailing the convoy into Fort Royal. There he would report the loss of one frigate blown up, two damaged but repairable, and two more captured: a net gain of one frigate for the French.

CHAPTER NINETEEN

Now the *Juno* was running down with a quartering wind towards the disabled frigate, which was beginning to turn again, presenting her transom. Ramage snatched the telescope and read the name, *La Comète*, painted in flowing gold script on a background of red. Like the *Surcouf* she was a well designed ship with the same flowing sheer, but two white strakes along her hull instead of one gave the appearance of lower freeboard – an example Ramage noted, of how a pot of paint can improve the sheer of one ship and spoil that of another.

He looked again, remembering the cloud of dust he had seen rising from one of the Diamond batteries' roundshot, then some of his elation vanished. The two white strakes certainly gave *La Comète* the appearance of a lower freeboard than usual, but the streams of water running through her scuppers told him that there was more to it than appearance: she was settling in the water. She had a bad leak – perhaps more than one – and the Frenchmen were pumping desperately. They had the head pumps rigged, and the steady stream of water pouring over the side amidships was from the chain pump. *That* explained why the French were not rushing about trying to rig preventer stays and get the ship under way. If three hundred Frenchmen could not stop her sinking what hope had a handful of men from the *Juno* and *Surcouf*? He realized that in the past fantastic fifteen minutes he had been counting on having three French frigates as prizes . . .

He waved to Southwick, who came running up to take the proffered telescope. The Master examined *La Comète* for a full minute, then gave the glass back to Ramage. 'Seems a pity to let her slip through our fingers . . .'

Ramage walked forward and leaned his elbows on the quarterdeck rail. He never allowed any men to do that, and he had never previously done it himself, but now his head felt heavy. Scattered round him were ten prizes. If Admiral Davis had caught the convoy with the *Invincible* and three frigates, he would have been delighted with himself for having destroyed one ship and captured the rest. Ramage realized bitterly that that was the difference: ten helpless ships were not ten prizes. Nothing was a prize until she was under his control and now his lack of men was likely to prove disastrous.

One frigate was sinking, two more were locked together, seven merchantmen were slowly drifting out to sea, and the further they got to the west the more the current would catch them. Finally they would come clear of the wind shadow cast by the island of Martinique and probably end up drifting across the Caribbean to Jamaica.

Southwick was still standing beside him, and looking ahead they could both see *La Comète*. She was less than a mile away now, with the *Surcouf* racing down to get to leeward of her.

'It's a good thing we can leave the merchantmen for a while longer, sir,' Southwick said quietly. 'Wagstaffe is tacking back and forth between them and the beach making sure those beggars don't row out again. Leaves us a few hours of daylight to tackle the frigates one at a time . . '

Ramage stared at the two frigates locked together before answering. All their sails had been furled, but the jibboom and bowsprit of one was still locked into the other. Through the glass it seemed as if her bow had ridden up the side and then dropped down in a chopping movement, perhaps smashing a hole in the planking above the waterline. They would not get free for many hours.

'One at a time, Mr Southwick,' Ramage agreed, and the Master's cheery and confident manner helped the plan forming in his mind. 'First we force *La Comète* to surrender . . .'

'Then I'll go over and inspect the damage, sir,' Southwick interrupted eagerly.

'No, you remain on board here. I'll go over and take the carpenter and some of his mates with me.'

'But, sir,' Southwick protested, ''tis not a job for a captain!'

'You don't speak French, and there's more to it than hammering in leak plugs. We need bluff more than planks and nails.'

He cut short Southwick's protests by ordering Jackson to tell a cutter's crew to stand by and hand over to someone else as quartermaster.

La Comète's Tricolour was still streaming in the wind. Would the French go through the ritual, by which they set so much store, firing a broadside before hauling down the Colours? She was still turning slowly and by the time the *Juno* reached her she would be lying with her bow to the south.

'We'll pass along her larboard side about five hundred yards off,' he told Southwick. 'Warn the starboard side guns not to open fire until I give the order. That is most important.'

Now the *Surcouf* was passing a few hundred yards to leeward of *La Comète*, and Ramage watched her bow swing as she began to tack back again.

Southwick brought the *Juno* round so that she was heading south, with *La Comète* broad on her starboard bow. He shouted orders down to the starboard side guns, and then turned to face Ramage, waiting for the next move.

Ramage had the telescope to his eye, watching the French frigate's quarterdeck. A group of officers was standing by the binnacle and men were running to the guns. They had left it very late and there were not many men. A score or more on the other side were still at the head pumps – and the wheel had gone! At that moment there were spurts of flame and smoke as four or five of *La Comète*'s guns fired into the sea: the *Juno* was too far astern of her for the guns to be trained that far aft. Then, suddenly, the Tricolour came down at the run.

Southwick began a bellow of laughter but broke it off to shout through his speaking trumpet that the starboard guns were not to fire. Then he strode over to Ramage, giving another of his contemptuous sniffs. 'You guessed they'd do that, sir,' he said almost accusingly. 'What do they call it?'

'Firing a few guns "*pour l'honneur de pavillon*".'

'Just another way of covering yourself against being accused of surrendering without firing a shot,' Southwick growled, watching closely as the *Juno* passed the frigate.

'It seems to be necessary in the French service,' Ramage murmured, his eyes taking in the damage to *La Comète*'s yards and rigging. 'And they're always careful to fire the shots where they'll do no harm. Now,' he added briskly, 'if you'll heave-to the *Juno* to windward, and pace the quarterdeck like an irascible captain, I'll go over and deal with these Frenchmen.'

'Irascible captain!' Southwick snorted.

'Oh yes,' Ramage said. 'As far as the French are concerned, I'm merely the first lieutenant. You've given me harsh orders which I've no choice but to carry out. You'll listen to no argument . . .'

Southwick grinned as he began bellowing orders to back

the *Juno*'s foretopsail. 'By the way, sir, I'll furl the t'gallants if I may.'

Fifteen minutes later Ramage climbed up the side of *La Comète*, thankful that the French had thoughtfully rigged well-scrubbed manropes. He was followed by half a dozen men armed to the teeth and who, he had noticed as the cutter was being rowed over, were all former Tritons.

As he reached the deck and acknowledged the salutes of the group of French officers he saw out of the corner of his eye that not only was the wheel missing but a gaping hole had been torn in the deck where it had stood. A plunging shot from one of the guns of the Diamond batteries had done terrible damage.

One of the officers stepped forward, proffering his sword, which he was holding horizontally in both hands. Ramage noticed that his uniform was identical with the other officers, but covered in fine dust. The man's face was white and he was gripping the sword like an alcoholic clutching a glass.

'I am Lieutenant Jean-Baptiste Thurot, sir, and to you I surrender the French national frigate *La Comète*.'

Ramage took the sword and then saw that the man's hands were trembling violently. He answered in French: 'I accept the surrender, but your Captain . . .?'

Thurot swallowed and, turning slightly, gestured towards the hole in the quarterdeck. 'He was standing there talking to me . . . There was a terrible crash . . . I was hurled three metres against the taffrail . . . All we found of him was . . .' He pointed at one of the officers, who held out a bent sword and a torn tricorne.

'My sympathies,' Ramage said formally. 'You were the First Lieutenant?'

'Yes, so I succeeded to the command. But before I could warn *La Prudente*, she blew up. Those guns on *le Diamant — mon Dieu!*'

Ramage passed the surrendered sword to Jackson and immediately another French lieutenant stepped forward to proffer his. Ramage took them one after another until Jackson had four tucked under his arm.

Ramage told Thurot to take him on an inspection of the damage. It took ten minutes, and at the end of it Ramage felt more hopeful. *La Comète* had two holes in her. The shot which had killed the Captain and smashed the wheel had come in at a steep angle over the starboard quarter as she tacked back to the convoy. After ploughing through the wheel

254

and deck it had gone on through the half deck and buried itself in the ship's side in the Second Lieutenant's cabin, springing two planks and forcing them outwards but not actually making a hole. A second shot had gone down the main hatch and smashed through the hull planking well below the waterline.

The French carpenter's mates had managed to nail canvas and tallow-smeared boards over the first leak, but little had been done about the second because the carpenter had by then lost both his nerve and his head. Now he was running around in a panic, screaming at his mates, picking up a maul one moment and tossing it down the next. The officers could do nothing with him, nor would he let them set seamen to work. When Ramage approached with Thurot the carpenter caught sight of the British uniform, uttered an enraged bellow and rushed at Ramage, to find himself staring at a hard-eyed Jackson who had dropped the surrendered swords with a clatter and had the point of his cutlass an inch from the man's corpulent stomach.

Ramage wasted no time: he ordered Jackson and Rossi to secure the man while Thurot was sent to get irons and Stafford told to fetch the *Juno*'s carpenter and his mates, who were still waiting in the cutter.

The carpenter took one look and told Ramage what wood he needed and that he and his mates had their tools with them. He would have the leak under control in two hours. Ramage found that one of the French lieutenants spoke English and ordered him to stay with the carpenter to act as translator and make sure he received whatever he needed.

Then he took Thurot to the dead Captain's cabin, intending to give him instructions. As they walked into the cabin Ramage saw that, apart from the battle damage, nothing had been touched. The desk drawers were still closed and presumably locked, and beside the desk was a small wooden box with a roped lid and holes drilled into the sides.

As Ramage stopped and stared, Thurot noticed the box and gasped. He moved towards it but Ramage waved him away and made him sit down. Pulling the lid back, Ramage took out the handful of papers and glanced through them. The French challenges and replies for several more months, a copy of the signal book (there must have been two on board, because presumably one had been on deck) as well as the Captain's orders and letter book.

Ramage sat at the desk with the box between his feet.

Thurot was now verging on collapse. Obviously badly shaken when the shot blasted a hole in the deck, he now realized that he had failed to throw the weighted box containing the ship's secret papers over the side. In the Royal Navy that was, next to cowardice, one of the most serious offences a commanding officer could commit. In the France of Bonaparte Ramage guessed that it might well lead to Thurot's execution if it was ever discovered. He looked at the box and then at Thurot. The man's eyes dropped, his skin seemed to turn green and perspiration beaded his face.

'The Widow?' Ramage asked in a conversational tone.

Thurot nodded. The guillotine, nicknamed The Widow, did indeed await an officer who allowed the enemy to capture such papers. Being 'married to the widow' was the slang expression for an execution.

'My Captain,' Ramage began, as though the affair of the secret papers was of no further consequence to him, 'could send you all to England as prisoners. There you'd rot in the hulks, as well you know.'

Again Thurot nodded, as though fear and misery had made him speechless.

'How many in your ship's company?'

'Two hundred and seventy-three petty officers and men, five warrant officers and four officers, and the Captain.'

'You suffered no casualties?'

'Casualties? Oh yes, I forgot. Eleven dead and seventeen wounded, but only four of them seriously.'

Ramage breathed deeply and noisily, as though considering something. 'My Captain is a stern man. He could send you all to England, even though there is a more – how shall we say it, a more civilized way . . .'

Thurot was obviously trying to pull himself together, and he wiped his face with the back of his hand. 'What way, m'sieur?'

Ramage gestured towards Martinique. 'It would be more civilized to let your men row ashore. A long row, admittedly, but then it is a long voyage to England. The officers would give me their parole, and you would agree that the men do not serve again until formally exchanged . . .'

Thurot glanced down at the box. Ramage kicked it back with his heel, so that it slid under his chair. 'If you agree to those terms, I will take the box away in a kitbag, padded with old clothes, so no one will know . . .'

Thurot gulped, as though his Adam's apple was trying to

leap out of his mouth, nodded his head vigorously and then, to Ramage's horror, burst into tears.

An hour later Ramage stood with Southwick on the *Juno*'s quarterdeck watching as the *Surcouf* tacked up towards the Grande Anse du Diamant beach, towing ten boats astern of her. Southwick commented that she looked like a dog running out of a butcher's shop with a string of sausages.

The boats were packed with men. The first four were the *Surcouf*'s own boats, then came the *Juno*'s launch and jolly boat, and finally *La Comète*'s boats. Only twenty Frenchmen remained on board *La Comète* to handle the chain pump, and by the time the *Surcouf* had cast off the boats as near to the beach as possible and waited for the French to scramble up the beach and the boats to return, the *Juno*'s carpenter would have stopped *La Comète*'s leak, ready for the *Surcouf* to take her in tow.

The heavily-laden merchant ships were the next problem. He had tossed up between them and the two frigates, which were now drifting past the southern end of the Diamond still firmly locked together. Finally he decided that an enterprising French officer, as soon as he landed on the beach, would try to find some native boats (if the merchantmen's own boats had been smashed up by *La Créole*) and, in breach of paroles and exchange agreements, set about getting aboard the merchantmen as soon as night fell.

Fifteen heavily armed Junos led by Rossi were now guarding the twenty Frenchmen working *La Comète*'s pumps. The moment the *Surcouf* returned with the boats, those twenty Frenchmen would be allowed to row to the shore, providing the carpenter and his mates had stopped the leak satisfactorily.

Now, as the *Juno* beat up towards the cluster of drifting merchantmen, *La Créole* finished a sweep close to the shore and bore away towards her.

Orsini, signal book in hand, was standing waiting. 'The *Créole*'s pendant,' Ramage said, 'and the signal to pass within hail. Number eighty-four, I believe.'

He was teasing the boy but Paolo was still taking his work very seriously. 'Number eighty-four, it is, sir!'

The wind eased as the *Juno* closed with the coast and as she approached the wallowing merchantmen the *Surcouf* turned to run back to *La Comète*, her long tail of boats towing astern. Ramage swept his telescope along the beach and could see a long column of men walking towards the western end. He steadied the telescope and saw that a much smaller group of men was waiting there for them, probably the masters and men from the merchantmen. He swung the telescope back along the beach and saw piles of wood gathered every twenty yards or so along the water's edge. Much of the wood was shaped into curves so he realized that they were a dozen or more smashed-up boats from the merchant ships. Wagstaffe must have taken *La Créole* in close and given his men some target practice, or sent a party on shore with axes. Anyway, there was no risk of the French getting back on board again from this beach unless they wanted to swim . . .

Southwick finished grumbling at the quartermaster for letting the maintopsail luff flutter and then came over to Ramage.

'I don't think many of them waited long enough to cut the sheets and braces, sir,' he said, pointing towards the merchantmen. 'I think they just let 'em run. The ropes may have flogged themselves into rare old tangles, but ten men apiece should be enough to get them under way. I'm a bit doubtful about them anchoring in the right places, though . . .'

'As long as they get an anchor down on the five-fathom ledge by the Diamond,' Ramage said, 'I'll be content. They'll have *La Comète* for company, but the rest of us will be under way all night.'

'And the two frigates, sir?'

'I want to go down and look at them as soon as we have these merchantmen safely anchored. I've been watching them, and there's no risk of them cutting themselves adrift. Seems to me the one hit amidships is settling.'

Southwick took the proffered telescope. 'You're right, sir! Well, we'll soon see. I can't wait to hear from Aitken how it all happened.'

The *Juno* now had fewer than forty-five men on board. Apart from the carpenter and his mates, there were fifteen seamen on board *La Comète* guarding the French pumpers. Twenty-five men could keep the *Juno* under way under topsails.

'Pick twenty men,' Ramage said. 'They can handle two merchantmen. Who do I put in charge of each party . . .?' He paused, trying to think of men.

'Jackson and Stafford, sir?' Southwick suggested. 'They're your best men.'

Ramage laughed and agreed. The idea of an American seaman belonging to a British ship of war going off in command of a crew to bring a French prize to anchor had a truly cosmopolitan ring about it. 'That takes care of two ships. Wagstaffe will have to spare ten men, so three ships can come down at the same time,' he said, 'and then he can take the twenty Junos back and with his ten collect three more. His ten men can bring the last one in. That will save time, because the *Créole* gets up to windward better than we do.'

The schooner came down the *Juno*'s larboard side, swept under her stern and, hardening in sheets, came close under the frigate's quarter. Ramage shouted across Wagstaffe's orders and the schooner bore up towards the convoy, men running aft to the falls of the quarter boat, ready to lower it. Southwick already had his twenty men mustered and was giving instructions to Jackson and Stafford. Both told their men to collect arms, and Ramage noticed they all chose pistols and cutlasses.

A quarter of an hour later the *Juno* was lying hove-to to windward of the merchantmen and her two cutters were pulling for the two nearest while *La Créole*'s small boat was already alongside another.

Ramage looked across at *La Comète* and saw that she now had all the *Surcouf*'s boats astern of her. Aitken obviously wanted them out of the way of the cable, and it was a quick way of transferring more men to work on the French frigate's fo'c'sle. Then he saw a single boat leave *La Comète* and pull towards the headland. The *Juno*'s carpenter had been better than his word and the French seamen had already been freed after their long spell at the pump. Ramage did not envy them their long row: their backs would already be aching . . . That would leave one boat on the Grande Anse beach. The French were unlikely to make use of it, but if there was time *La Créole* could go over and destroy it.

'Jackson's done it!' Southwick shouted gleefully. 'Just look at him,' he added, eye glued to his telescope, 'standing there with a cutlass slung over his shoulder and a couple of pistols in his belt! Looks more like a pirate than the Captain's coxswain!'

The ship's yards were being braced round and the sails filled as the men sheeted them home. Slowly she gathered way, slab-sided and bulky, and Ramage saw her Tricolour being hauled down. A minute or two later it was hoisted again, with a Red Ensign above it.

'And there goes Stafford,' Southwick called. Ramage saw another Tricolour come down and the Master commented:

'Jackson's beaten him there—though where he found that ensign I don't know!'

It took nearly two hours to get the seven merchant ships anchored off the Diamond, and by the time the last two arrived the *Surcouf* had towed *La Comète* into position, anchored her, and retrieved the seamen, leaving fifteen Junos on board under Rossi's command.

On an impulse, Ramage had sent word to Aitken to keep two of *La Comète*'s boats in tow, as well as her own, and had taken the third in tow of the *Juno*, giving instructions to Wagstaffe to return to the beach with *La Créole* and destroy *La Comète*'s fourth boat, which the French seamen had tried to haul up.

Then the *Juno* led the way round the south side of the Diamond Rock to the remaining two frigates, which were out of sight behind it. The sun was beginning to dip down now and it would be dark within two hours. The men of the *Juno* and the *Surcouf* were at quarters as they rounded the Rock, Ramage cursing to himself yet again because he was so short of men, but a sudden hail from Southwick on the fo'c'sle warned him that the French ships were in sight. One glance told him that all fighting was over for the day.

The decks of one frigate were almost awash and, as far as he could make out, she was being kept afloat only by the bows of the second, which was now heeled over by her weight and likely to capsize at any moment. The men had cut her masts away, presumably trying to right her, but three boats were rowing round the two ships. As he looked through the telescope he saw black specks in the water round the two ships. There were also white blobs with black specks on them: men holding on to hammocks to keep afloat.

As he watched he felt a chill which had nothing to do with the fact that the heat was going out of the sun and they were getting a stronger breeze as the *Juno* came clear of the land. It was the realization that the three boats circling the two ships probably represented all that could be launched. The rest had presumably been smashed by falling masts and yards.

There must be five or six hundred Frenchmen out there, some swimming, some clinging to hammocks, others to bits of wreckage. Many were still on board one or other of the ships: men who could not swim or who feared the sharks. Five or six hundred Frenchmen to be rescued by the *Juno* and the

Surcouf. Once again there was the risk of rescued becoming captors . . .

Southwick came hurrying up the quarterdeck ladder, a look of alarm on his face. 'It'd be suicide, sir,' he exclaimed, obviously not caring that the men at the wheel and the quartermaster heard him. 'Let those devils on board and they'll seize both ships! Aye, and recapture the merchantmen and *La Comète* too!'

'Quite right,' Ramage murmured, 'and take us into Fort Royal in triumph, and probably put the pair of us in the public pillory for a couple of days to cool our heels while they sharpen the guillotine.'

'Well, sir, I know how . . .' he broke off, but Ramage could guess that the rest of the sentence would have been, 'soft hearted you are.'

'You don't want to leave them to drown though, do you?' Ramage asked in a mild voice.

'They have three boats, sir.'

'Among about six hundred men?'

'I'd sooner leave 'em to drown than hand the two ships over to them,' Southwick said firmly. 'Why, if it was t'other way about, they'd probably sink the boats to make sure *we'd* drown!'

Ramage jerked his head and walked aft to the taffrail, where the Master joined him with a questioning look. Ramage looked astern at the *Juno*'s four boats and one from *La Comète* towing astern. Then he pointed to the *Surcouf*, following two hundred yards in the *Juno*'s wake. 'She has six more. With the three already there, we have fourteen boats in which to tow them to the Grande Anse beach, keeping them at painter's length all the while.'

'I suppose so, sir,' Southwick said grudgingly, 'but no good ever came of trusting Frenchmen, an' you know that better than most.'

The rescue was easier than Ramage had expected. He hove-to the *Juno* fifty yards to the north of the sinking ships, the boats swinging round like a dog curling its tail. Immediately men began swimming to them, and Ramage hailed one of the boats, which approached warily. A lieutenant was in command of it, and Ramage ordered him to row round the survivors and tell them to start by getting into the *Juno*'s boats. As soon as they were full the other frigate would come down and pick up the rest. They would be towed to the beach, Ramage told them, warning the lieutenant not to let the boats get so crowded that they capsized or sank. 'You are fortunate that we are here,' he shouted harshly. 'You will all remain in the boats.'

As Frenchmen scrambled over the gunwales, Ramage took a couple of dozen men from the guns and had them lining the quarterdeck and taffrail with muskets, not so much against the risk of the French swarming on board the *Juno* as to control them if they tried to overcrowd the boats. He soon saw there was little risk of that happening: as soon as one boat was full, the men on board drove off their former shipmates, screaming at them to go to the others.

Once all the *Juno*'s boats were full Ramage hailed the lieutenant, telling him to have his other two boats secured astern of the rest but that he was to stay with his own boat and keep discipline while the second frigate picked up the remaining survivors.

'Three hundred and forty-one men, sir,' Southwick reported.

More than half the survivors were in the *Juno*'s boats, so there should be no problem for Aitken. He was just about to tell Southwick to get the *Juno* under way when there was a sudden violent hissing from the wrecks, followed by the rending and creaking of timber. The frigate that had been almost awash disappeared in a swirling mass of water and the second ship, which had been heeling, began to capsize. It happened slowly, almost effortlessly; there was majesty in the way she turned over into the tangle of masts and yards alongside, the painted black sides vanishing, the bottom emerging green with weed and barnacles, despite the copper sheathing. Air and water spurted and boiled and for a few moments the frigate's keel was horizontal and Ramage saw the rudder was swung hard over. Yards began floating to the surface, leaping up vertically like enormous lances before toppling over to float normally. Then the hull began to shudder as though great fish were nibbling at it and she seemed to float a little higher.

'Her guns just broke adrift,' Ramage commented, breaking the silence that had fallen on board the *Juno*.

Still the hissing continued, and then it increased. Slowly the forward section began to dip and the remaining part sank lower. Great bubbles broke the surface as water forcing its way into enclosed spaces inside the hull drove out the air. Now the bow section was below the water, the line of the keel sloping steeply like the single rail of a slipway. Then, like a dolphin curving down into the water again after taking a breath, the whole forward section of the hull sank as the after section rose. For a full minute the ship seemed to hang almost vertically: the quarterdeck and taffrail reared up, and the watchers saw the name picked out in gilt on the transom. Then it all vanished, enormous bubbles spewing up floating wreckage and concentric rings of small waves spreading, unaffected by the wind and swell waves.

Ramage swallowed and said to the Master: 'We'll get under way, Mr Southwick . . .'

The Master did not move, his eyes still riveted on the pale green circle in the water which for a few moments marked the frigate's grave. Ramage touched his arm gently and the old man gave a start. 'A sad sight, sir,' he muttered. 'Shall I get under way?'

By nightfall the survivors from the two French frigates had been landed at the beach and the *Juno*'s and *Surcouf*'s boats retrieved. The two frigates had then run down to the Diamond, where *La Comète*'s boats were taken over to her. Ramage ordered Aitken on board the *Juno* for a quick conference. After hearing the story of how the two French frigates had collided, he outlined his plans for getting the merchant ships to Barbados and then sent the *Surcouf* off with orders to keep a patrol close in with the entrance of Fort Royal Bay for the rest of the night, watching particularly for any privateers that might try to sneak out to recapture the merchantmen.

The *Juno*'s jolly boat had been sent to the Marchesa battery with written orders for the men on the Rock: they were to rig the signal mast on top of the peak again and be ready to repeat signals they sighted any of Ramage's ships making, while the original instructions concerning the sighting of other ships still stood. Ramage ended his orders by expressing his satisfaction at their accurate fire, and telling them that their victim had been the 36-gun frigate *La Prudente*, while their other target, now anchored below them, was *La Comète* which had been hit by eleven shot, of which two had caused leaks below the waterline. One of the hits, he added, knowing the men were in awe of the peppery little old man, had given the *Juno*'s carpenter a great deal of work before it was plugged satisfactorily.

While the jolly boat was away at the Marchesa battery, the

Juno's remaining boats were hoisted in again and Ramage had Wagstaffe come on board to receive his orders. They were simple enough – *La Créole* was to patrol the Fours Channel, covering the anchored merchant ships. As soon as the jolly boat returned it was hoisted on board and the *Juno* got under way, to spend the rest of the night patrolling between Cap Salomon and the Diamond.

While the frigate was stretching north, making slow progress in a light offshore breeze, Ramage went below to his cabin and began drafting a report to the Admiral. He was so weary that he had difficulty keeping his eyes in focus, and his left cheek was twitching slightly with an irritating monotony. He felt no urgency in sending the report to the Admiral but knew that unless he managed to get the details written down he would forget them; two hours' sleep would leave his memory like a muddy pool.

He described the sighting of the convoy and his plan to attack it, giving credit to Wagstaffe's sense of timing. Aitken's tactics in causing two of the French frigates to collide took up several paragraphs, the problem being to translate Aitken's droll description into the more prosaic phraseology of an official report. The young Scot had been steering the *Surcouf* for the centre of the convoy when the French frigate on its quarter bore away to run down to attack him on the starboard bow. A few moments later the frigate abreast the leading ships of the convoy hauled her wind and came down to attack him on his larboard bow. To begin with, Aitken thought that each would pass down either side, firing a broadside as she went by. This would have been such a bad mistake by the French – it would have left nothing between Aitken and the convoy – that he then decided they were laying a trap for him, and that each at the last moment would cross his bow in succession and rake him. If one then tacked and the other wore, they would stay between Aitken and the convoy. As he held on, waiting to see what was going to happen next, Aitken noted that the wind had veered slightly, but told the quartermaster to steer the same course, realizing that he could steer straight for the frigate on his starboard bow.

That decided him. He told Ramage he remembered the previous night's warning that achieving surprise was half the way to victory, and he bided his time, watching the two frigates racing down towards him. Then he warned his guns' crews to stand by and, with the frigate to starboard a bare quarter of a mile away, hauled his wind and steered straight for her, as though intending to ram her, bow to bow.

The French captain panicked: of that Aitken was sure, because he turned to starboard; bearing up suddenly without firing a shot. Aitken's gunners fired a well-aimed broadside and while the smoke was clearing Aitken saw her continue turning as though intending to wear right round and follow the *Surcouf*, but in the excitement she had forgotten her consort which, still steering a course which would have taken her across the *Surcouf*'s bow if she had not altered course slightly, then rammed her. It had been 'awfu' gude value', Aitken had said, two frigates for the price of one broadside.

Ramage then went on to describe the accurate fire opened by the Juno and Ramage batteries — how *La Comète* had been disabled and the gunners, under the command of a petty officer, had promptly shifted target to *La Prudente* and caused her to blow up.

The rest of the report took up only a few lines. The abandoned merchant ships had been collected and anchored off the Diamond, joining *La Comète*, whose main leak had been plugged by the *Juno*'s carpenter. The remaining two French frigates soon sank after the *Juno* and *Surcouf* reached them and their survivors were taken to the beach and released because there were insufficient men to guard them.

He read it through again and saw that he had not given credit to Southwick and Lacey. He wrote in two sentences and then remembered the name of the petty officer in command on the Diamond and inserted that as well. In the left-hand margin, opposite the description of anchoring the merchant ships, he copied their names from the list given him by Wagstaffe.

Writing the report had cleared his mind a little and he put the draft in a drawer to be read through again at first light before the clerk made a fair copy. As he shut the drawer he sat back in the chair. The fighting is over, he told himself, and you've been lucky. Lucky, and well served by Aitken and Wagstaffe and the men on the Diamond. But there are still a French frigate and seven merchant ships to be disposed of without much more delay. By dawn, as the *Juno* returned to the Diamond after her night's patrol, everyone would be waiting for orders . . .

He wondered for a moment about the fate of Baker and *La Mutine*. When she left for Barbados he remembered thinking that Baker and his men would probably be the only Junos left alive if the convoy arrived before Admiral Davis. *La Mutine* must have sunk. Had she been captured her captor would probably have brought her into Fort Royal. In time he would have to write to Baker's parents. It was the kind of letter he hated writing, but he could praise him without feeling a hypocrite, and tell them that their son died performing a valuable service. He seemed to remember that his father was a deacon.

He was putting off the moment when he had to decide what to do with the prizes. Picking up the pen, he began writing out the alternatives. He could take ten men from each of the two frigates, put them in two merchant ships, and send them off to Barbados with *La Créole* as an escort. The schooner could then bring them back, probably with more provided by Admiral Davis . . .

The thought hit him like a cold shower that the Admiral must have sailed from Barbados, perhaps up to Antigua. He might have left a single frigate behind in Bridgetown which would account for . . . but no, it would not account for Baker, because *La Mutine* would have returned at once, even if for some reason the frigate captain was unable to leave Bridgetown.

Anyway, like that he could start two merchant ships on their way to Barbados. The second choice was to send the *Surcouf* with two merchant ships. It seemed the obvious thing to do, but he knew the Service too well. He would never see the Junos now on board the *Surcouf* again. The Admiral would want to commission the *Surcouf* at once, and taking twenty or so men from each frigate commanded by his favourites would not weaken them. Ramage off Fort Royal was managing with the men he had in the *Juno*, and he had *La Créole* as well. If he found himself undermanned he could always take the men off the Diamond. This would be the Admiral's argument.

It was difficult in a dispatch to persuade the Admiral of the importance of the batteries on the Diamond: unless he saw them in action, or at least firing at targets in the Fours Channel and westward from the Rock, he would never appreciate them. He would read in the dispatch that they sank *La Prudente* and disabled *La Comète*, but he would call it luck.

Ten men from the *Juno* in one merchantman, ten from the *Surcouf* in another: that settled it. The *Juno*'s gunner could command one – he was sufficiently useless for it not to matter if the Admiral held on to him – and the bos'n the other. Wagstaffe would escort them with *La Créole* and would have written orders to bring the prize crews back as soon as the merchant ships were safely anchored and he had reported to the Admiral.

Then he remembered that there were now an extra nine hundred French naval officers and seamen, plus the crews of the seven merchantmen in Fort Royal. He took out his draft dispatch to the Admiral and added a paragraph pointing out that parole and exchange agreements aside, there were a dozen schooners in Fort Royal which could be manned by the former frigate crews. This, he added as the thought struck him, was why he was retaining the *Surcouf* for the present. He read the paragraph again. It sounded convincing; indeed it was the obvious and wisest thing to do.

He put the papers away and picked up his hat to go up on deck to relieve Southwick. It was a warm, starlit night, with the cliffs black to the eastward and the mountains beyond a vague blur. The *Juno* was making three knots, the water gurgling away lazily from her cutwater, the rudder post rumbling occasionally as the wheel was turned a spoke or two. Her wake was a bright phosphorescent path and occasionally a large fish leapt out of the water and landed in a splash of light.

Southwick went below, and his lack of protest at being relieved by the Captain showed that the old man was utterly exhausted. Jackson was the quartermaster, and although he could not see them Ramage knew that the six lookouts posted all round the ship were keeping a careful watch. On almost any other night there might be a chance of one man dozing on his feet for a minute or two, but never the night after a brisk action.

As he began pacing the starboard side of the quarterdeck he noticed a small figure walking up and down on the larboard side. It was Paolo, whose watch ended when Southwick went below. He was about to call to the boy to get some sleep when he realized that he was probably too excited and enjoying every moment of it anyway.

CHAPTER TWENTY

Dawn found the *Juno* two miles off Petite Anse d'Arlet, under way after being becalmed for three hours and with Ramage pacing the quarterdeck in a fury of impatience. The first look-outs aloft reported a frigate a mile to the north, still becalmed, and a few minutes later identified her as the *Surcouf*. Diamond Rock was out of sight behind the headland at the foot of Diamond Hill, and the devil knew what urgent signals might be flying from her signal mast.

Then the wind died again and the gentle curve in the *Juno*'s sails flattened and the canvas hung like drab curtains. 'Bear away!' Ramage snapped at the quartermaster, anxious to turn the ship before she lost way altogether so that she would get the full benefit of any fitful puffs. It was hopeless trying to sail her close-hauled in a wind as light as this; better bear away two or three points and give the sails a chance.

'We could try wetting the sails, sir,' Southwick suggested.

Ramage glared at him. 'That's an old fish-wife's tale,' he snapped. 'It just makes them heavier.'

'The water fills the weave and stops the wind passing through, sir,' the Master said defensively.

'Damnation take it,' Ramage exploded, 'this wind is so weak it can't crawl down the side of a cliff, let alone get through the weave of stiff canvas.'

'Aye, aye, sir,' Southwick said mildly, knowing he had had twice as much sleep as the Captain who, the quartermaster had reported, had his light on for much of the night writing reports.

Ramage looked seaward with his telescope. 'Just look at that wind shadow over there. It's a mile away. It'll be noon before we get another puff here and in the meantime the whole damned French fleet could have arrived off the Diamond.'

'They would be becalmed too,' Southwick offered sympathetically.

'Not a chance! There'll be a nice breeze round Pointe des Salines and right up to the Fours Channel. It's just in the lee of these damned mountains –' he pointed to the half a dozen peaks between Morne la Plaine to the north and Morne du Diamant to the south ' – that we lose the wind.'

At that moment his steward appeared on deck to report that his breakfast was ready and Ramage, who had already put it off twice, decided that his empty stomach was neither improving his temper nor extending his patience. He went below with muttered instructions to Southwick to call him the moment the wind piped up.

He washed and shaved, changed into clean clothes, ate his breakfast, reread the draft of his report to the Admiral and his orders for Wagstaffe, filled in his journal and wrote several more paragraphs of his diary-like letter to Gianna, and still no word came. The sun rose and the sunlight coming through the skylight made circles on the painted canvas covering the deck of his cabin as the *Juno* slowly turned in the current, like a duck feather floating on a village pond.

The clerk brought the dispatch and orders for him to sign and Ramage growled at him to sharpen his quill. Were the order and letter books up to date? he demanded. The clerk said they were. Were any more reports, inventories, surveys and the like outstanding? No, the clerk said, everything was up to date, including the weekly accounts. Ramage dismissed him, irritated that the man had nothing for him to do. At the same time he was amused. The clerk usually had great difficulty in getting him to deal with any paperwork.

The fact was that he was trying to avoid going on deck. The sight of the cliffs and beaches gradually drawing south as the current took the *Juno* north was almost more than he could stand. If only the current had taken the frigate out to the west, where they would get a sight of the Diamond . . .

On deck the ship's company went about the day's work. Hammocks had long ago been lashed up and stowed, decks scrubbed and washed down, awnings spread, brasswork polished and the brickdust carefully swept up afterwards. The gunner's mate had appeared with a request that he be allowed to start the men blacking the guns and shot and complained that much had been chipped off the previous day. Ramage, appalled at the thought of men painting coal tar on to the barrels of guns that might be needed within a few hours, refused and told him that if he was making work for the other gunner's mates they could sew up some more canvas aprons for the gun locks. Usually several were lost when the ship went into action. The gunner's mate had agreed in his doleful voice that indeed it did happen, owing to the carelessness of the men, but all the necessary new ones and a dozen to spare had been completed an hour ago. 'Report to

Mr Southwick,' Ramage said in desperation, but the gunner's mate said he had already done so, and Mr Southwick had sent him to report to the Captain.

'Grommets,' Ramage said firmly. 'We need a lot more grommets.'

The gunner's mate's eyes lit up. 'Ropework is for the bos'n's mates, really sir, but my men will do their best.'

By ten o'clock Ramage and Southwick were pacing the deck together. The *Surcouf* was almost at the southern side of Fort Royal Bay, and the *Juno* less than a mile short of Cap Salomon, but there was not a breath of wind and the sea had flattened into a glassy calm. A dozen times Ramage had thought of hoisting out a cutter and having himself rowed down to the Diamond. It was only the realization that there was nothing he could do when he arrived there that made him finally dismiss it. If enemy ships arrived the only guns that could open fire at them were the Diamond batteries, and they could be relied on to do that anyway.

The very air seemed hot and almost solid and the slightest effort soaked a man in perspiration. Noon came and the men were piped to dinner. With the sun almost overhead, shadows were nearly vertical and the pitch soft in the deck seams. Southwick commented gloomily that they could be in the Doldrums for all the chance they had of getting a wind.

Five minutes later, as the men finished dinner, the wind came. A fitful puff from the north at first which caught every sail aback and started Ramage bellowing orders, and which died a moment later. A longer puff from the east lasted less than five minutes, and then a steady wind set in from the north-east.

Soon the *Juno* was making seven knots with every stitch of canvas set – courses, topsails, topgallants, royals and staysails. Ramage had set every able-bodied man to work: Bowen hauled on a rope next to the Captain's clerk; the cook's mate found himself hauling a halyard and being encouraged by the Captain's steward, who complained that his hands were too soft for that sort of work.

The wind reached the *Surcouf* ten minutes after the *Juno* was under way and Ramage watched as Aitken let fall sail after sail. At last the bays, beaches and headlands were beginning to slide past: Grande Anse d'Arlet and Pointe Bourgos; Petite Anse d'Arlet and then the headland separating it from Petite Anse du Diamant. Jackson was aloft with a telescope, while Orsini waited by the binnacle with the signal book in his hand and a telescope under his arm.

Diamond Rock suddenly came in sight beyond the headland and a moment later Jackson hailed that no flags were flying from the Juno battery mast. Ramage realized he had been standing rigid waiting for that hail, and as he relaxed he turned to Southwick and grinned. 'The nest is safe!'

'Deck there!' Jackson's voice was urgent. 'They're hoisting a signal now . . . three flags . . . three . . . five . . . nine!'

Ramage snatched the signal book from Orsini and read: *The strange ships are of the line; when answered, the signal is to be hauled down once for every ship discovered . . .*

'Acknowledge it,' he snapped at the boy, and shouted up at Jackson: 'The moment we answer they'll haul the signal down, but they may hoist and lower it several times. Count the number of times they lower it!'

He trained his telescope on the top of the Rock. He could just make out the signal, and it was lowered once. There was a long pause. One ship of the line. Then three flags were hoisted again and for a moment Ramage thought it was the signal being hoisted again before being lowered a second time, but Jackson shouted down: 'Deck there! A second hoist . . . three . . . six . . . nought!'

Ramage hurriedly opened the signal book again. Against the figure 360 was printed: *The strange ships are frigates; when answered, the number of frigates to be shewn, as in the preceding signal.*

'Acknowledge,' he told Orsini and again shouted a warning to Jackson. The signal was lowered and hoisted, then again, and then a third time.

A ship of the line and three frigates. A French squadron which had been covering the convoy on its way across the Atlantic? Or Admiral Davis at long last?

He called to Orsini, showed him the two signals in the book and said: 'Make 359 with the *Surcouf*'s pendant and lower it at once when she answers; then her pendant and 360, lowering three times. You understand?'

The boy nodded and ran to the flag locker as Southwick ordered two seamen to help him.

'Mr Southwick, we'll go down to the Rock under topsails!'

'Aye, aye, sir!' Southwick said and began bellowing for topmen.

As the squaresails were furled and the staysails lowered and secured in the tops Ramage cursed the Diamond headland: it was still blocking his view right across the bight down to Pointe des Salines.

The moment the *Juno* was reduced to topsails, Ramage said quietly to the Master: 'Beat to quarters, Mr Southwick . . .'

The Master passed the order that set the calls of the bos'n's mates shrilling, but his face was sombre as he rejoined Ramage at the quarterdeck rail. 'I can't help thinking our luck has run out at last,' he said, 'but the lads will put up a good fight, sir.'

Ramage shook his head and, seeing that no one else could hear them, said quietly but distinctly: 'I don't propose taking either ship into action against a ship of the line and three frigates. It would be the same as locking both ships' companies in a magazine and setting fire to it.'

'We'll be hard put to get past them to make Barbados and raise the alarm,' Southwick said. 'We'd – '

'As soon as we're sure, we'll run round the north end of Martinique. That . . .'

Jackson's hail from aloft cut him short. 'Signal from the Diamond, sir . . .'

Both Ramage and Southwick waited, staring aloft at the American, and listening for him to read out the flags. Orsini was watching through his telescope but said nothing.

'What's happening, blast you?' Southwick roared.

'Sorry, sir,' Jackson called down. 'They began hoisting a three-flag signal but they lowered it again suddenly.'

'More ships of the line coming round Pointe des Salines,' Southwick said sourly. 'I thought just one didn't sound right . . .'

'Hoisting again,' Orsini yelled, followed a moment later by Jackson, who shouted: 'Three flags . . . three . . . two . . . one!'

Orsini had the signal book open in a moment. 'Sir – *The chase is a friend* . . .' He looked puzzled, held the book open between his legs and looked again with his telescope. He consulted the book again, shaking his head. 'Yes, it means that, but I do not understand it, sir. Perhaps they made a mistake.'

Ramage patted the boy on the shoulder. 'No, it's correct. They are having to use the best signal they can to tell us what they mean. The signals were never meant to be used by shore batteries. They are telling us that the Admiral has arrived.'

'Not the French Admiral, then?' The boy sounded disappointed.

'No, Admiral Davis from Barbados.'

The boy made a wry face. 'I suppose that will mean more signals, sir . . .'

The *Juno* was just able to point high enough to pass inside the Diamond and Ramage could see the *Invincible* and her three frigates on the far side of the great bight, running with a quartering wind towards the Rock.

Suddenly Jackson hailed that the Juno battery had hoisted a signal, and a moment later called down the numbers. Orsini looked it up in the book and read it out to Ramage, doubt showing in his voice. 'Number 251 is *Ships' companies will have time for dinner or breakfast, sir* . . .'

Both Ramage and Southwick laughed, and the Master said: 'They know they gave us a scare, and themselves too, I suspect!'

Ramage reached for the signal book, checked a page, and told Orsini: 'The Diamond's pendant and number 112.'

Southwick looked questioningly and Ramage said, '*Keep the maintopsail shivering*. Not much of a joke, but the best I can do for the moment.'

As soon as the signal was hauled down he told Orsini to make number 242 with the *Surcouf*'s pendant. There was no need for both frigates to go down to meet the Admiral, and the sight of the former French frigate tacking back and forth in front of *La Comète* and the seven merchantmen, obeying the order 'Stay by prizes', would help to impress the Admiral, Ramage hoped.

He knew he was going to have to be as sharp as a diamond to make any impression on the Admiral, but he wanted three things. He wanted to get a command for Aitken. Perhaps not the *Surcouf*, she was a tempting plum for one of the Admiral's favourites, but perhaps *La Comète*. After repairs and rerigging she would have to be taken to English Harbour to be careened so that the damaged planks could be replaced, and not many officers wanted to spend a few weeks in such a hot place. She might even have to go to the dockyard in Jamaica. There was also a chance that the Admiral might buy *La Créole* into the service and could be persuaded to put Wagstaffe in command. That would give him a good push up the ladder towards post rank. Lastly he wanted to ensure that the batteries on the Diamond were kept in service. It was a decision that only the Admiral could make, but somehow he felt a proprietary interest in them.

273

Southwick wanted nothing: he had been offered much in the past but asked only that he be allowed to serve with Ramage. There would be prize money for all the Junos. At a guess, the *Surcouf* should fetch about £16,000, so the seamen would share £4000, or about £25 each. *La Comète* would fetch less because she was damaged, say £20 a man. There would be as much again for the seven merchantmen and two schooners. That totalled some £65 a man – the equivalent of six years' pay. Aitken and Wagstaffe would get shares as commanding officers, and only Baker and the men in *La Mutine* would receive nothing because they were not present during the action.

Baker! Did *La Mutine* get to Barbados? Why wasn't she with the Admiral's squadron? Had the Admiral ordered Baker to stay in Bridgetown, with the twenty Junos on board *La Mutine*? Why was the Admiral so late? Plenty of questions, he thought sourly, and no answers . .

'Hoist our pendant numbers,' Ramage told Orsini, 'and then watch the flagship. She'll be making a signal very soon.'

Southwick bustled up. 'We're ready to hoist out a boat, sir.' He looked at Ramage's stock and then down at his stockings. 'There's plenty of time for you to change, sir, if you wish.'

The Master was quite right: within half an hour he would probably be on board the flagship, making his report. Clean stock, best uniform, boots polished, hat squared and mind you do not trip over your sword . . . At least he had recently shaved, and the report to the Admiral was in his cabin, already signed and sealed. The object, he told himself mockingly, is to make everything seem easy: four French frigates and seven merchantmen accounted for yesterday; today no sign of effort . . .

He was still in his cabin, his steward brushing his coat, when he heard through the skylight Orsini reporting a signal from the *Invincible*: the *Juno*'s pendant and number 213. That was one that Ramage knew by heart – *The Captain of the ship pointed out to come to the Admiral* . . . A moment later the boy was at his door, knocking urgently and delivering the message.

Ramage slung the sword belt over his shoulder and finished dressing, crouching as he slid into the coat held up by his steward. He jammed his hat on his head and picked up the canvas bag. It was bulky – not only did it contain his report and the orders he had written for Wagstaffe to take the merchantmen to Barbados, but he decided to take the Master's log and his own journal, as well as his order book. And there were the secret papers from *La Comète*, perhaps the most important of them all.

The *Invincible* was a mile away, steering towards them, with a frigate ahead and one on either beam. Southwick was waiting for orders. There had been no signal from the *Invincible* telling the *Juno* to take up a particular position in the squadron, which told him that either Admiral Davis was in a hurry to hear the news – by now he would have seen the cluster of ships at anchor off the Diamond – or he was not a fussy man who did not trust his captains.

'Heave to ahead of the flagship,' Ramage said, 'and as soon as the cutter is hoisted out get under way again.'

'And after that, sir?'

'Unless you get a signal from the flagship, get into the *Invincible*'s wake, so there'll be less distance to row when I come back on board!'

The *Invincible*'s captain was waiting on the gangway for him. He returned Ramage's salute and his smile was friendly. That was significant: captains of flagships never gave welcoming smiles to junior captains summoned on board to face an admiral's wrath.

Captain Edwards made no conversation as he led the way down to the Admiral's cabin, however, and Ramage wondered whether he might not be regretting that brief smile. It would have cost him nothing to comment on the anchored ships or even to have asked about the *Surcouf*, which was clearly in sight and equally clearly a French ship now under British colours, but Edwards held his tongue.

The Admiral's cabin was large and cool and Ramage remembered it well from his first visit in Bridgetown. Then it had been hot and stuffy, with the ship anchored close in to the land. The cabin was empty and Captain Edwards waved to a chair by the table in front of the stern lights. 'Sit down, the Admiral will see you in a few minutes.'

Ramage could hear the *Invincible*'s yards being trimmed round as she got under way again: she had hove-to just long enough for the *Juno*'s cutter to get alongside and Ramage to scramble on board. The minutes passed and he saw the *Juno* come into sight through the stern lights and take up position two cables astern. Watching her manoeuvring, Ramage felt a glow of pride. Southwick was handling the ship as though he had a full complement on board, instead of less than a third. Once in the flagship's wake, her three masts remained precisely in line. Southwick would be watching the luffs like a hawk, and the men at the wheel and the quartermaster would be meeting each extra puff of wind, every wave that tried to push round the *Juno*'s bow.

The door opened and the Admiral walked in, followed by Captain Edwards and his secretary. Ramage jumped up, watching the expression on the Admiral's face, but it gave nothing away.

'The old fool's arrived too late, eh?' he said by way of a greeting. Ramage fidgeted uneasily, not knowing what to say, but the Admiral waved for him to sit down, walked round to the other side of the table and sat down himself opposite Ramage. Captain Edwards was waved to the seat on his right.

'Tell me what happened,' he demanded, and Ramage reached for the canvas bag.

'I have my report here, sir . . .'

'Written reports tell admirals what captains think they ought to know, and they can't be interrupted with awkward questions.'

The Admiral seemed hostile and Captain Edwards was watching closely. Between the two men he could see the *Juno* following astern, her masts still perfectly in line.

'Well, sir, we sighted the convoy . . .'

'No, begin from the time you arrived here. I know you covered the schooner business in your first report by *La Mutine*, but forget that for the moment.'

The Admiral's face was completely expressionless as Ramage told him of the *Juno*'s look into Fort Royal, followed by the night attack on the *Juno* by the two schooners, and how they cut out the *Surcouf* from Fort Royal. When Ramage referred to sending *La Mutine* to Barbados with a warning about the expected French convoy, the Admiral said: 'Why did you choose her and not the other, what's the name, the *Créole*?'

There was obviously a reason for the question but Ramage could think of none. He shrugged his shoulders. 'It was a matter of chance, sir.'

'She never arrived,' the Admiral said bluntly.

'But my dispatch, sir, you received . . .'

'The dispatch arrived but the schooner didn't; she sprang a plank and sank a third of the way over. Baker and his men rowed. Took them nearly four days. Almost dead when they arrived. Most of 'em still in hospital – sunstroke, sunburn and exhaustion . . .'

'I'm very sorry –'

'Not your fault,' Admiral Davis said gruffly, 'and a very creditable effort by young Baker and his men. But tell me, Ramage,' he continued, his voice cold, 'why didn't you send the *Surcouf* with the warning, instead of a little schooner?'

'I was afraid the convoy might arrive early, sir,' Ramage said frankly.

'So you halved the men you had remaining in the *Juno* and put them on board the *Surcouf*. That hardly doubled your strength, surely?'

'No sir,' Ramage admitted, 'but I was hoping that setting up batteries on top of the Diamond Rock to cover the Fours Channel would give us an element of surprise . . .'

'What's that?' the Admiral exclaimed sharply. 'You don't mean to say you even *dreamed* of getting a gun up on to the top of that Rock? D'you hear that, Edwards? Why, you . . .'

Captain Edwards had been watching Ramage closely and he deliberately interrupted the Admiral: 'Perhaps we might hear what Ramage had in mind, sir?'

The Admiral had now put himself in such a difficult position that Ramage hardly knew how to begin. Davis glanced at Edwards and Ramage, his bloodshot eyes missing little. Although Ramage did not know it, Admiral Davis was a man who knew when to cut his losses.

'*Did* you get a gun up to the top?'

'Yes, sir,' Ramage said, and decided to get it over with at the rush. 'We swayed two up to the top, a third to a ledge half-way up, and a fourth covers the only cove where a boat can land.'

'Bless my soul,' the Admiral said. 'You must have been mad even to try it. Carronades, eh? Men parbuckled 'em up the hill?'

'Ramage said they swayed them up, sir,' Captain Edwards interposed.

'Carronades, though. Didn't do much good, eh? No range, those things. Don't believe in 'em myself.'

Edwards glanced at Ramage and said quietly: 'I noticed the *Juno* is missing some 12-pounders. Three, I believe, and a 6-pounder, too . . .'

Ramage nodded gratefully. 'Yes, sir. You see, I found that we . . .'

'Twelve-pounders?' the Admiral almost shouted. 'Do you mean to tell me you swayed a couple of 12-pounders up to the top of the Diamond?'

'Well, yes sir, you see . . .'

The Admiral slapped the table with a thump that made Ramage blink and miss the old man's expression. 'Splendid! Splendid, m'boy! Dammit, Edwards, I knew I should never have let Eames . . .' he broke off. 'Well, go on, now you have the batteries on top of the Diamond and two half-manned frigates. Then you wait and wait for that damned old Admiral, who never comes, eh?'

He was grinning now, and Ramage decided he could be completely frank. Admiral Davis was far shrewder than he seemed and had a sense of humour lurking beneath that almost purple complexion.

'Well, sir, to be truthful, we waited for the convoy . . .'

'Damme, that's an honest enough answer, eh, Edwards? What's your seniority, Ramage?'

'Last name in the List when I left England, sir.'

'Ah yes, I remember. By jove, for the last few days you've been commanding a squadron of – how many ships?'

'Eleven, sir: three frigates, a schooner and seven merchant ships.'

'Ah yes, now let's hear about the convoy.'

Ramage began by describing briefly how he hoped to lure the convoy and escorts into the Fours Channel, where he could make a surprise attack with the two frigates, using *La Créole* as a Trojan horse and, as soon as the French ships were within range, opening fire with the Diamond batteries.

His attempt to keep his story brief failed completely: both the Admiral and Captain Edwards kept interrupting with questions. How did he time the arrival of the *Juno* and *Surcouf* so the French were squarely in the Channel? How did Ramage expect to break through two frigates with the half-manned *Juno* to attack from the unprotected landward side? How could he expect the *Surcouf* to dodge the two remaining frigates?

Ramage hurried on, trying to hold back the questions. He described how Aitken had suddenly worn the *Surcouf* round so that the two frigates about to attack him on either bow collided with each other. Then he had to digress to answer the Admiral's question about what had happened to them. He related how the Diamond battery had disabled *La Comète* and blown up *La Prudente* so that they could take possession

278

of the whole convoy. *La Créole*'s change of role from a French privateer coming to meet the convoy to a British schooner brought the comment from Captain Edwards about a poacher turning gamekeeper.

They were interrupted by a lieutenant reporting to Captain Edwards that the *Invincible* was now in the Fours Channel, with the Diamond Rock bearing south one mile. The Admiral waved him away impatiently. 'We'll go up and look into Fort Royal Bay. Scare those privateers, in case they're thinking of sneaking out.'

As the lieutenant left the cabin the Admiral's brow creased. 'Who is in command of all these ships of yours?'

'The Master is on board the *Juno*, sir; my former First Lieutenant, Aitken, the man I was telling you about, is commanding the *Surcouf*. My former Second, Wagstaffe, has *La Créole*. Baker was the Third, and Lacey, the Fourth, is with Aitken. I had to leave a petty officer in command of the Diamond, sir, and he did very well. Altogether I – '

'One frigate goes into action with her commanding officer, the Master and less than a third of her complement; another has a first lieutenant and a fourth . . . Ramage, you are completely mad. If you stay alive long enough to give Their Lordships a chance to appreciate you, you'll go a long way in the Service. Your problem will be staying alive. Now we have to find enough men to get those prizes up to Antigua. The merchant ships, I mean. And I have two more frigates.'

He stood up and walked round the cabin for two or three minutes, obviously trying to reach some sort of decision, and then came and sat down again opposite Ramage.

'I need the *Surcouf* for a special service. You say she's fast. Her bottom clean? Good condition? Fine, fine. I'm transferring you to her. Wait a moment,' he said when Ramage's face fell, 'you'll have your own ship's company. For what I have in mind you'll need the extra guns and speed, since she's a thirty-six and the *Juno* is only a thirty-two – a twenty-eight at the moment, rather.'

Ramage knew that if he did not put in a word for Aitken now the Admiral's plans would be completed beyond hope of change. 'Sir, I was hoping that perhaps you could find a place for Aitken . . .'

'Hold your tongue a moment, boy, I'm trying to arrange two things at once. You to the *Surcouf*, so that's settled. This fellow Aitken made post – the Admiralty will confirm it later, no question of that – and given the *Juno*. We have to find a ship's company for the *Juno*, but we'll manage that somehow. *La Comète* needs careening, which means English Harbour, Antigua . . .'

'I was hoping, sir, that Wagstaffe –'

The Admiral glared at him. 'Do you want him as your First in the *Surcouf*, or let him go off as First in *La Comète* and eat his heart out in the dockyard for a few weeks?'

'I'd sooner have him with me, sir.'

'Very well; so far you've only interrupted with suggestions that I've already dealt with in my mind. Be patient!'

He tapped the table with the fingers of his right hand. 'There's *La Créole*. Who deserves her, Baker or your Fourth, Lacey?'

'Baker, sir. Lacey behaved very well, but Baker's row to Barbados . . .'

'I'm glad to hear you say that. Lacey can go as Second in the *Juno*. Good training for him. So that leaves me *La Comète*, and I have a deserving young lieutenant to be made post into her. Very well, anything else?' he asked briskly.

'No, sir. I will leave my report. Oh yes, sir, there is. We have all *La Comète*'s secret papers. And sir, if you felt that you could make a signal to the Diamond, sir . . . The Juno battery, that's the one at the top, they have a signal mast rigged and a copy of the signal book . . .'

'Damnation!' the Admiral exclaimed, 'I've forgotten all about the Rock. Four guns need thirty men or more, and we'll probably strengthen the place. It'll be a lieutenant's command. But how the devil do we arrange the paperwork, Edwards?'

'They'll have to be attached to a ship for pay, mustering, victualling and so on, sir.' He thought a moment. 'That schooner, sir, *La Créole*. If you buy her into the Service, the garrison of the Rock would be on her books. She could keep them supplied, too, because she's fast enough to get over to Barbados for provisions, and she can slip over to St Lucia for water . . .'

Ramage said: 'Perhaps she could be renamed the *Diamond*, sir.'

'Capital,' the Admiral boomed. 'His Majesty's schooner *Diamond* . . . Sounds well. By the way, Ramage, who named the top battery?'

'The men, sir. They named all three batteries,' he added hurriedly. 'The middle one is named after my father, sir, not me.'

'You both deserve it,' the Admiral said, standing up. 'Now, we'll go up and look into Fort Royal. You stay patrolling off the Diamond, and report on board here at ten o'clock tomorrow morning. Your orders will be ready by then. Have Aitken report to me at half past nine.'

Ramage stood up and as he was leaving the cabin he heard the Admiral saying angrily to Captain Edwards: 'I'm sick of that *Jocasta* business! Damnation take that fellow Eames. If only . . .'

The voices faded as Ramage walked away. If only what? And earlier the Admiral had said something like: 'Dammit, Edwards, I knew I should never have let Eames . . .' Eames had been blockading Fort Royal for many weeks, then he had returned to Barbados. Ramage remembered that he was the man the Admiral seemed to have in mind for the special service that the First Lord had referred to in London; the special service for which the *Juno* had brought out the orders.

Had Eames made a mess of them? He shrugged his shoulders. There was no point in speculating; it did not concern him, although he was unlikely to find Captain Eames becoming a friend. That his young successor, far below him in the List, had established batteries on the Diamond was unlikely to delight him. And what did the Admiral mean about the *Jocasta*? She was still in Spanish hands after her men mutinied.

The officer of the deck came up to him and saluted. 'Are you ready for your boat, sir?'

For a moment Ramage was too startled to answer and then he returned the salute with as much coolness as he could muster. 'Yes, when you are ready.'

It was pleasant being a post captain, he thought to himself as the *Invincible*'s great foretopsail was backed while the *Juno*'s cutter, which had been towing astern, was brought up for him to climb down into it.

When he arrived on board the *Invincible* next morning, with fifteen minutes in hand to make sure he was not late for the Admiral, Captain Edwards met him on deck and commented on the beauty of the anchorage. The *Invincible* and three frigates were anchored close in to the long Grande Anse du Diamant. Directly to seaward was the grey tooth of Diamond Rock; to the north-west Diamond Hill.

The sun was getting hot now, and Captain Edwards nodded towards the awning. 'We'll take a turn or two until the

Admiral is ready for you. Tell me, how the devil did you sway those guns up? I don't mind telling you that you spoiled the Admiral's regular game of chess last night. We had charts out, drew diagrams . . .'

As the two men walked up and down the quarterdeck, cool in the shade and with the offshore breeze just setting in to ripple the water, Ramage described how he had moored the *Juno* close against the sheer cliff on the south side, rigged the jackstay and used the capstan to hoist each gun with a gun tackle.

'But a sudden swell,' Captain Edwards interrupted. 'We get them in Barbados – rollers, ten feet high with no warning . . .'

'But not here, sir,' Ramage said. 'They're peculiar to Barbados, so far as I know. I never heard of any of the other islands experiencing them.'

'True, but it's frightening when it happens in Carlisle Bay. I once saw a frigate put up on the beach. The sea was calm with just the usual waves knocked up by the Trade winds and nothing strange about the weather. Then these rollers came up, one after the other. Lasted about an hour or more, and parted the frigate's cable . . .'

Ramage described how he had moored the *Juno* so that if the wind had backed or veered and knocked up a sea, he could have cut the cable of the stern anchor, cast off the jackstay, and swung clear.

'You still took a frightful risk,' Edwards commented, looking at his watch.

'I did, sir,' Ramage admitted frankly, 'but it seemed worth it.'

Edwards gave a dry laugh. 'You've commanded ships before as a lieutenant, but you are very new to the post list. I'm a dozen or so names from the top, and I've learned one thing, which I pass on for what it's worth. If you succeed in something like that, Their Lordships will consider the risk was negligible. If you fail you can expect a court martial and you'll never be employed again.'

'I've learned that already, sir,' Ramage said soberly.

Edwards glanced at him sideways. 'Yes, the Admiral was telling me last night of some of the things he had heard about you.'

The voice was neutral and told Ramage nothing of what the Admiral had actually said or any opinions he might have expressed. They reached the taffrail and turned inwards together to begin the walk back to the quarterdeck rail.

'The Admiral is in a rather difficult position at the moment, Ramage,' Edwards said quietly. 'When you came out in the *Juno*, you carried orders for the Admiral from Lord St Vincent. You know that, of course.'

'For some special service, yes, sir.'

'Did His Lordship tell you what the special service was?'

'No, sir,' Ramage said, realizing that this encounter with Captain Edwards had been far from accidental.

'Nor did His Lordship hint that you might be entrusted with it?'

'No, sir. You see, I had just completed some particular service for His Lordship – it was of a very secret nature,' he said apologetically. 'There had been other things, too, and His Lordship made me post after I had reported to him. He gave me the *Juno* and said I was to serve under Admiral Davis. He told me I was to get under way as soon as possible because of the urgency of the dispatches I was to carry. He also mentioned that I would be carrying orders to the Admiral concerning some special service, and I'm afraid I immediately showed interest, thinking it concerned me. His Lordship made it quite clear that the choice would be up to the Admiral.'

Edwards nodded. 'Hmm, that was the impression the Admiral had and he entrusted the service to his senior frigate captain . . . Well, there have been, er, well, unexpected difficulties, with the result that the particular service has yet to be carried out.'

Edwards paused, and Ramage said in a neutral voice: 'I understand, sir.'

The Captain looked sideways at him and sighed. Clearly he was not enjoying the role the Admiral had given him. 'Good, I thought you would, and you can probably guess the rest.'

'I hope so,' Ramage said cautiously.

'I'm sure you do,' Edwards said, making no attempt to disguise the relief in his voice. 'One thing is important, though: do you have complete trust in your officers and ship's company?'

It was an unexpected question, and Ramage hesitated as he remembered a similar one from Admiral Davis when he first arrived in Barbados. 'In the Master, petty officers and seamen, complete trust, sir: after all, I couldn't have . . .'

'Of course,' Edwards said hurriedly. 'But the officers?'

'I'll only have the Master and one lieutenant left,' Ramage pointed out. 'The others will be new.'

'Quite so,' Edwards said hurriedly. 'Well, wait here, I'll be back in a few minutes.'

When he returned his face was completely expressionless. 'The Admiral is ready to see you now.'

Admiral Davis was sitting in the same chair at the table, with several papers in front of him, and he waved Ramage to the chair opposite, while Edwards excused himself and was promptly told to sit down. The Admiral looked up to bid Ramage a gruff good morning and then continued reading. The *Invincible* was swinging slightly at anchor as the wind eddied off the land. Ramage saw the headland at the foot of Diamond Hill and a minute or two later, as the ship's stern swung, he saw the Diamond Rock. A sharp eye might detect the tiny signal mast, and Ramage realized that at this very moment French patrols along the coast would be looking at it through telescopes, trying to spot where the batteries were, counting ships, preparing a full report for the Governor. Not, he thought with satisfaction, that there is a damned thing the French can do.

Suddenly the Admiral unfolded a paper and pushed it across to Ramage, who recognized the Admiralty seal. 'Read it,' he said abruptly.

Three paragraphs, after the usual long-winded and stylized beginning, about the *Jocasta*. The reasons for Captain Edwards's questions about the officers and ship's company were now only too clear. Ramage folded the paper, and the Admiral slid a sealed envelope across the table. 'They are your preliminary orders – based on what you've just read. The *Surcouf* will be bought into the King's service, and you will command her. You collect up your former ship's company, unless you want to leave the garrison on the Diamond, in which case Captain Edwards will let you have an equivalent number of men from this ship.'

'And my new officers, sir?'

The Admiral shook his head. 'You get only one lieutenant.'

Ramage looked puzzled and was trying to phrase a mild protest when the Admiral said: 'Aitken and Wagstaffe want to stay with you. I've never heard of a first lieutenant trying to avoid being made post, but that young Scot seems to have a very strong loyalty to you. Not related, are you?'

When Ramage shook his head the Admiral added: 'I tried to persuade him – *persuade* him, if you please! – to allow me to promote him into the *Juno*, even though I have several other very deserving young officers. But he said he needed more experience, and he wants to stay with you. So he'll remain as your First Lieutenant in the *Surcouf*. I gave young Wagstaffe the chance of being *La Comète*'s First Lieutenant, but he preferred to remain your Second rather than have a long stay in a hot dockyard. Lacey will be the only one to gain out of your action; I'm giving him the *Créole* – the *Diamond*, rather – because he seems full of initiative and knows Diamond Rock. Baker will be out of hospital by now and he'll be sent up to join you in Antigua.'

'I'm most grateful, sir, and – '

'I want you ready to get under way for English Harbour at dawn. Shift to the *Surcouf* and I'll send someone over to command the *Juno*. Leave the two ships' companies as they are we can sort that out in Antigua. The *Invincible* will tow *La Comète* and I'll send prize crews over to the merchantmen. You'll stay in company with the *Invincible* – a taste of escorting a convoy will do you no harm. You have your final orders . . . No,' he said grimly, interrupting Ramage, 'if you've given any thought to the First Lord's letter you know you've nothing to thank me for.'

AUTHOR'S POSTSCRIPT

In 1804 Commodore Samuel Hood, who was responsible for blockading the French in Martinique, reported to the Admiralty that he had taken possession of Diamond Rock, writing: 'I think it will completely blockade the coast in the most perfect security . . . Thirty riflemen will keep the hill against ten thousand . . .'

Unfortunately Hood gave the Admiralty very few details of how he put the 74-gun *Centaur* alongside the Rock and swayed up 24-pounder guns to the top, but it was seamanship of epic proportions. The garrison held the Rock for seventeen months, and the episode has become one of the legends of the Royal Navy in the Caribbean.

While sailing past the Rock some years ago, my wife and I became fascinated by Hood's feat. The adventures of Captain Ramage described in this book are the result, and they bear out the adage that truth is stranger than fiction. Although the Fort Royal of Ramage's day is the Fort de France of today, the Rock remains unchanged. Recently some of the cannons swayed up by Hood (using the method adopted by Ramage) were recovered from the sea below the site of one of the batteries.

D.P.
Yacht Ramage
Tortola, B.V.I.
West Indies

Geoffrey Jenkins

Geoffrey Jenkins writes of adventure on land and at sea in some of the most exciting thrillers ever written. 'Geoffrey Jenkins has the touch that creates villains and heroes – and even icy heroines – with a few vivid words.' *Liverpool Post* 'A style which combines the best of Nevil Shute and Ian Fleming.' *Books and Bookmen*

A Cleft of Stars

A Grue of Ice

Hunter-Killer

The River of Diamonds

Scend of the Sea

A Twist of Sand

The Watering Place of Good Peace

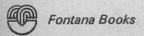 *Fontana Books*

Fontana Paperbacks

Fontana is a leading paperback publisher of fiction and non-fiction, with authors ranging from Alistair MacLean, Agatha Christie and Desmond Bagley to Solzhenitsyn and Pasternak, from Gerald Durrell and Joy Adamson to the famous Modern Masters series.

In addition to a wide-ranging collection of internationally popular writers of fiction, Fontana also has an outstanding reputation for history, natural history, military history, psychology, psychiatry, politics, economics, religion and the social sciences.

All Fontana books are available at your bookshop or newsagent; or can be ordered direct. Just fill in the form and list the titles you want.

FONTANA BOOKS, Cash Sales Department, G.P.O. Box 29, Douglas, Isle of Man, British Isles. Please send purchase price, plus 8p per book. Customers outside the U.K. send purchase price, plus 10p per book. Cheque, postal or money order. No currency.

NAME (Block letters)

ADDRESS

RAMAGE'S DIAMOND

DUDLEY POPE, who comes from an old Cornish family and whose great-great-grandfather was a Plymouth shipowner in Nelson's time, is well known both as the creator of Lord Ramage and as a distinguished and entertaining naval historian, the author of nine scholarly works.

Actively encouraged by the late C. S. Forester, he has now written eight 'Ramage' novels about life at sea in Nelson's day. They are based on his own wartime experiences in the navy and peacetime exploits as a yachtsman as well as immense research into the naval history of the eighteenth century.

The Alison Press published his new novel *Ramage's Mutiny* in 1977.